AF595448

EXILE

EXILE

— PART II —
ROOT AND BRANCH

ANTHONY HODGE

First paperback edition January 2026

Copyright © 2026 Anthony Hodge

This is a work of fiction. Names, characters, places, and incidents either are the product of the author's imagination or are used fictitiously. Any resemblance to actual persons, living or dead, events, or locales is entirely coincidental.

This is a work of human creativity. No large language or diffusion models were used in the process of writing, editing, or designing this book.

All rights reserved. No part of this book may be reproduced or used in any manner without written permission of the copyright owner except for the use of quotations in a book review.

For more information:
Email: ahodgewriter@tuta.com
Web: anthonyhodgeauthor.com
BlueSky: @anthonyhodge.bsky.social
Instagram: @anthonyhodge_writer

ISBN:
Paperback: 978-84-09-82234-8
ebook: 978-84-09-82235-5

For Maite

PRONUNCIATION GUIDE

b, d, f, k, l, m, n, p, q, r, s, t, v, x, z: As in English
c: Always hard as in *c*at
g: Always hard as in *g*irl
h: Always pronounced as in *h*urry
j: As in *j*ump
zj: Like the *g* in camouflage
th: As in tee*th*
rh: Rolled *r*
gh, kh, ch: similar to German/Greek/Scottish *ch*

a: As in f*a*ther.
In Rhenivian, as in *a*pple or b*a*nd
e: As in *e*gg
i: Usually as in mach*i*ne
At the beginning of a word before a vowel, as consonant *y*
o: As in n*o* or h*o*t
u: Similarly to *oo* in l*oo*se
At the beginning of a word before a vowel, as consonant *w*
ae: Rhymes with *eye*
ei: Rhymes with *way*
au: Rhymes with *cow*

Caerian given names usually have the stress on the first syllable, particularly when the name is two or three syllables long (e.g. Válcero, Sáedelas, Jéigo).

Caerian family names have the stress on the final syllable (e.g. Cleontán, Baradón, Corilién).

Otherwise, Caerian place names and other words usually have the accent on the final syllable before the suffix (e.g. cantáris, cantárus, cantáre, Etórium, Nedólian)

CAERIA — 430 N.C.

...And on the pedestal these words appear:
"My name is Ozymandias, King of Kings:
Look on my works, ye Mighty, and despair!"
No thing beside remains. Round the decay
Of that colossal wreck, boundless and bare
The lone and level sands stretch far away.

From *Ozymandias* — Percy Bysshe Shelley

CHAPTER ONE

CAERIA – SPRING'S REIGN – 436

There were days when Razna wanted nothing more than to scream.

'Thane Heirik, welcome back from your visit to Rhenivia,' the Prefect began. 'Last night, a villager of Goretonum awoke and saw flames and smoke on the Etorian side of the River Haepastis. She roused neighbours, who forced the gates open against your men's orders. They crossed the river with buckets and found the East Grove burning. They organised themselves and doused the flames after a time. Apparently, some Etorians and Rhenivian soldiers went to assist. 'At dawn, we sent a squad of palantare to keep order and inspect on my behalf. They say the grove is in a bad state, My Thane. Fully a third of the cypresses are burnt. It is not known who started the fire, though many Goretonians claim to have seen torches amongst the trees on more than a few nights.' Prefect Suletonius coughed and sat down on the other side of the table.

Razna was with Heirik, some of his marshals, and the Prefect in the palace's council chamber. It made a change from the usual long mornings and afternoons in the throne room. Razna had suggested using this room while Heirik had been away, and the Prefect had agreed.

Today, Heirik had refused to hear any petitions or legal cases. He said he was still worn out from his journey. He sat beside her, in the grandest chair at the table.

Heirik sighed. 'Well, I'm sure the fire was an accident, no matter who caused it.'

Suletonius fidgeted with his silver mace. 'It may well be, sir, but the citizens are... not happy.'

A faint clamour reached Razna's ears from the window. The guards had reports that Caerians filled the square outside. They were banging pots and shouting curses at the palace.

She leaned forward. 'Perhaps...'

'I'm well aware they aren't happy,' Heirik said. 'Well aware. But it was an accident, or it must have been accidental, yes?'

'Thane Heirik,' the Prefect replied, 'those trees were memorials to many people. Our ancestors. No Caerian would set them alight. It is a *terrible* crime.'

'Are you accusing us, the Rhenivians, of starting the fire?' Heirik asked softly.

The Prefect's eyes went wide. 'Oh no, no, sir. Of course not!'

Heirik held up his hands. 'Have I not respected your customs? I let you hold your festivals. I apply your Caerian laws, even though you are now part of *our* kingdom. Have I not respected the Caerian people enough?'

Prefect Suletonius cringed. 'Absolutely, My Thane. I did not mean to imply anything inappropriate.'

'Perhaps someone wanted to pay their respects late at night,' Razna said, 'and their torch accidentally touched a tree? Cypresses burn easily, especially in dry weather.'

The Prefect blinked. 'After curfew, My Lady?'

Heirik put a hand on her arm. 'We can't know the cause of the fire. And we can't undo the damage, Prefect. What we must do now is restore peace and order in the city.'

The Prefect nodded. 'Of course, sir, but—'

'I won't have cityfolk cursing *my* name in front of *my* palace.' Heirik rapped his knuckles on the table. 'I will set my best warriors on them if need be.'

'Thane Heirik,' the Prefect said, 'let me send out the palantari first. Let me try to calm the citizens and usher them home.'

Thane Heirik folded his arms and leaned back in his chair. 'You have until the ringing of the next bell. Then we will run them down without mercy. You can tell them that. Go, now.' He waved his hand to dismiss the Prefect.

The Caerian stood and took up his silver mace. He bowed and hurried from the council room.

Razna leaned over to Heirik. 'Actually, My Thane, I have an idea.'

He shook his head. 'Not now, please.'

Razna frowned.

Heirik sighed. 'I know you're trying to help,' he muttered in her ear, 'but right now, I must show authority. You understand?'

Razna shrugged. 'Of course.' She settled back in her chair and glowered at the tabletop.

Heirik nodded and addressed his marshals. 'Alright, what else do you have for me today? Make it quick.'

'A report from the west,' said Daga.

'And a report from the east,' said another marshal.

Grindulf, if Razna remembered correctly.

The chanting from the square grew even louder, barely muffled by the palace wall. Her Caerian was not quite good enough to catch the words.

Heirik got up and slammed the shutters closed, then sat again. 'Let's start with the west. How goes it in the forests?'

'Mostly well, My Thane,' Daga replied. We've cut down plenty of trees. The timber is suitable for many uses—building, barrels and arrows, fires, charcoal for the forges...'

'Yes, yes.' Heirik waved his hand. 'But what about these forest dwellers? Have they surrendered yet?'

Daga squirmed in his seat. 'We haven't seen much of them, sir. But they attack whenever we pass beyond the marked trees—especially at night. We've lost... soldiers and woodcutters at our deepest camps.'

Heirik frowned. 'You can't kill the savages?'

'They don't stand and fight, Thane Heirik. They shoot their arrows and toss their spears, then melt into the woods before we reply. They fight without honour. And now, the Caerians refuse to work in the camps, and our Rhenivian woodcutters are terrified.'

Heirik shrugged. 'So, burn it.'

'Sir?'

'Burn down the forest,' Heirik said. 'All of it, if necessary. I don't care how the fire spreads. Just burn it until these forestfolk have no refuge left.'

Razna turned to him. 'My Thane.'

Heirik raised a hand to silence her. Razna glared at him and gripped the table edge until her knuckles turned white.

Daga bowed his head. 'As you command, Thane Heirik.'

The Thane turned to Grindulf. 'Alright, so what of the east?'

Grindulf cleared his throat. 'Nothing much to report, sir. The towns and cities are quiet for the most part. Your new hall is progressing well...'

'It needs to be progressing much faster. I've been waiting too long.'

'As you wish, sir. The estates are planting grain, and the farmers promise a good crop this year.'

'Finally,' Heirik said. 'But where is Lord Sanadin? He was supposed to be here already.'

'I believe he is still in Sanadium, at his home.' Grindulf replied. 'Or at least that's what I heard last.'

'Well, get him to Etorium, will you?'

Grindulf nodded. 'There is one other thing, sir. A strange tale.'

'Go on.'

'There's a small village on the outer eastern coast, south of Lastria, facing Galatan. Tefos, it's called. The villagers were due to send tribute by the end of last year. Some fruit, olives, wool, that sort of thing. But the tribute never came.'

'Then punish them. Why bother me with this?'

The marshal swallowed. 'Of course, sir. We sent soldiers to the village, but no one was there.'

Heirik raised his eyebrows. 'What do you mean?'

'It's a small village, My Thane. A poor place, clinging to the sea cliffs. It took us a few days riding along a rough track, but when we arrived, we found Tefos deserted, the houses abandoned, no animals in the pens. All quiet, sir.'

'How is this possible?'

'I don't know. We searched the houses. It looked like they had carried off most of their things.'

Heirik looked around the table. 'Northmen? A raid?'

'We considered that,' Grindulf replied. 'There's a cove below the village where they could have beached their ships. But there have been no reports, no sightings of raiders along the coast. Nothing for a few years, sir. Also, there was no sign of looting in the houses. Nothing broken, nor set on fire. No bodies.'

'So, you're telling me the villagers packed up their goods one day and simply...left?' Heirik stared at the marshal.

Grindulf shrugged. 'We went to nearby villages to look for them, but found no trace. And *those* peasants were no help. They told us they had no idea what happened to their neighbours.'

'This has happened before,' Daga said.

'What?' Heirik turned to the other marshal.

Daga nodded. 'A couple years ago, sir, in the hills north of Algados, we found a village abandoned. The story was almost the same, except it seemed they burned four or five people in the village square before they left.'

Heirik scowled. 'Why are you only telling me now?'

'I'm sorry, My—My Thane,' Daga replied. 'We never worked out what happened. But it was only one small village...'

The Thane shook his head. 'I'm in no mood for mysteries.' He tapped his fingers on the table.

They all watched him for a while. But then the fifth bell rang, and Heirik brightened.

'Now, this is something we can solve.' Heirik stood up. 'Daga, Grindulf, with me, to the stables. We have peasants to discipline.'

They left Razna alone in the council chamber. She looked around and sighed. After a while, she got up and left the room. Along the corridor, she met a servant.

The woman bowed to her. 'Lady Razna.'

'I'll have dinner in the royal apartments this evening,' Razna told her. 'I'm not to be summoned or otherwise disturbed—by *anyone*. Understood?'

The serving lady bowed again. 'Of course, My Lady.'

Razna nodded and marched through the palace and up to their bedchamber. She glanced around. It still looked like a Caerian king had only just left. Razna scowled and flopped onto the bed. She stared at the ceiling for a while.

'Where were you?' Heirik stood at the doorway. 'I asked for you.'

Razna pushed away her plate at the bedroom table. 'I was…*in no mood* for dinner.'

Heirik wandered into the room. 'The cowards fled into the alleys as soon as we opened the gates. What a waste of time. This whole business is stupid, anyway. If those *idiots* hadn't handed me the torch while I was tired and distracted…you saw how it was. Honestly, it's all their fault. I'd have them whipped, but it would look suspicious.'

Razna shrugged. 'I don't care.'

He stopped. 'Now, Razna, listen…'

She shook her head. 'What am I to you, Heirik?'

He walked up to her. 'Why, you're…you're my…'

Razna stood up and jabbed him in the chest. 'I am *more* than your concubine. You know that.'

He reached to take her by the shoulders, but she stepped back.

'Who do you think ran this place while you were away?' she asked.

'I trust my marshals to do their duties,' Heirik said.

'And *who* do your marshals listen to when you're not here?' Razna said. She slapped her chest. 'Me. They listen to *me*.'

Heirik frowned.

'They listen to me, because I represent *you*, Heirik, when you are not here. I tell them what you would tell them, and they respect me for it. But they will lose respect for me if you keep treating me like a fool in front of them.'

Heirik watched her, breathing heavily.

'I can do so much more, Heirik. You know it. That's why you chose me. So, trust me. This is a big island. Let me help you rule it.'

Heirik let out a long sigh. His shoulders slumped, and he went to sit on the bed. 'I know, my she-cat. You're right. I'm sorry. They say you did great work while I was away. The people were pleased with your judgments. "Most fair and merciful", they told me.' He looked up at her and smiled.

Razna sat next to Heirik and leaned against him. 'How was your visit, anyway?'

He put an arm around her shoulder. It was warm.

'Pleasant enough. I have missed my uncle and aunt, my young cousins. They're healthy and strong. I thought I would have missed Elborn, my old home, too, but now I see it differently.'

'What do you mean?'

'I always saw it as a grand place when I lived there as a child,' Heirik replied. 'Now its seems quite small. But when our new home is *eventually* complete, I vow it will be grander than both this draughty stone palace and my uncle's old wooden hall.'

'And Galatan?'

Heirik squeezed her. 'Much the same. Sunny and hot already. Lots of lambs on the hills. Do you miss it?'

Razna pursed her lips. 'Sometimes. And you saw the High King, yes?'

Heirik nodded. 'I did. High King Randegar—and his daughter.'

Razna turned to face him. 'His daughter?'

Heirik's lip twitched. 'Ranwen. The King was very keen for me to meet her.'

'Why?'

Heirik looked down at her and smiled.

'And what did you think of this *Ranwen*?'

'Well, she's very beautiful. Hair like gold. Quite tall.' He noticed Razna's scowl. 'But we had nothing to talk about, of course. She is so young—barely more than a child. Nothing on her chest, unlike you.'

Heirik reached over to cup Razna's breast, but she twisted away.

'Razna, please. There's nothing to worry about. As you said, I chose *you*.'

She faced him again. 'Why did you choose me?'

He brushed her cheek. 'You know what? As beautiful as you are, it wasn't for your beauty.'

She raised an eyebrow. 'Oh?'

He leaned closer. 'My she-cat, you are full of fire and iron. Like me. I saw it the day we met.' He leaned all the way, close enough to kiss her.

Razna slipped off the bed and stood before him. 'I'm tired.'

'You know what would help?' Heirik said. 'What would make it easier to take my side before the world?'

'What?'

He bit his lip. 'If you, after all these years...' He swallowed. 'If you could bear me an heir. A son, maybe?'

Razna looked down at him. 'It would be better if you married me first. So our child would be safe—and respected.'

He reached out and took her hand. 'I know. I want to. But it's...difficult. My uncle...' He hunched over and rubbed his temples.

Razna stroked his hair. 'You are a thane, lord of this land. You have the *power*, Heirik.'

He gazed up at her.

'Come,' Razna said, 'let's sleep.'

It was sometime in the night when the bells awoke them. Razna sat up in the dark and reached out for Heirik.

'I'm here,' he mumbled.

She heard Heirik climb out of the bed and pad over to the balcony door. He pushed the doors open and stepped outside, his bare silhouette visible in the moonlight. 'What's this noise?' he called out.

'A fire, My Thane!' someone shouted in reply.

Heirik leaned over the balcony. 'A fire? Where?'

Razna wrapped a blanket around herself and joined him outside. The bells kept ringing.

'I'm not sure, sir,' a soldier called from the courtyard below. 'Somewhere outside the city, to the east.'

'To the east?' the Thane muttered to himself. 'Is the grove burning again?'

'Or Goretonum?' Razna asked.

'Come.' Heirik strode back inside and draped his cloak over himself.

Razna followed him through the passage to an empty room facing east. She clutched his shoulder as he stumbled through the dark, dusty room to the shutters and threw them open.

'There!' Razna pointed at a ball of flame in the distance. It was hard to judge how far, but certainly beyond the city wall and the river twinkling in the moonlight. 'Is it the village?'

Heirik leaned out and squinted. 'No. Wrong direction.' He swore in Rhenivian and punched the window frame. 'I know what it is.'

As the sun rose, they rode out with Heirik's marshals, including Daga, Sederial, and a complement of soldiers. Their horses galloped over the bridge and onto the Field of Bees. They found more Rhenivians gathered at what remained of the Corn Mother's temple. The temple roof had collapsed, and only wooden poles remained jutting out of the blackened earth like a ribcage. The grass and flowers surrounding the temple were singed and dead. Amongst the ruin, the statue of the Corn Mother lay facedown in the ashes, toppled from its plinth. Two unburnt cloaks also lay on the ash—covering bodies, Razna realised.

Brother Frethi stood before his ruined temple, surrounded by soldiers who patted him on the back. The priest's eyes were red and his face was streaked with soot. His hands and forearms were blackened. He wiped his face and tried to smile as Heirik and Razna dismounted.

Frethi sniffed. 'Good morning, Thane Heirik. Lady Razna.'

Heirik waved at the ruin. 'What happened?'

The priest sighed. 'They came with torches in the night, while we slept. They invaded the temple, threatened us, and pushed over the Corn Mother. I'm sorry to say they... despoiled Her. Then they threw the torches against the walls and barred the door from the outside.'

'Who?' Heirik asked.

'I am not certain, Thane Heirik,' Frethi replied. 'It was dark, but I am sure I heard Caerian words. We priests were trapped in the temple. My brothers succumbed to the smoke and flames. I was ready to serve Our Mother to the end, but then She spoke to me. She told me to survive, to rebuild Her temple, as the green shoots rise from the dark earth in spring.'

'Mmhmm,' Heirik said.

'I found a place at the back where the wall was weak, and broke out.' Brother Frethi continued. 'I heard their voices, so I ran into the darkness and crouched in the grass until they left.'

'Where did they go?' Heirik asked. 'Goretonum? Etorium? Or somewhere else?'

'I cannot say, Thane Heirik,' the priest said. 'My heart says they ran off toward Goretonum when the bells began, but I cannot be certain.'

Heirik looked at the gathered soldiers. 'Were any of you on duty at the gates or walls? What did you see?'

'Only the fire burning, My Thane,' a man replied.

'I saw no Caerians leave or return near my gate,' another said.

'Nor ours,' added another.

Heirik gazed at the sky and cursed. 'But you believe they returned to Goretonum?' he asked Brother Frethi again.

The priest smiled and shrugged. 'It seemed that way in the dark. But I cannot be sure.'

Heirik clenched his fists and glared at no one in particular.

Razna surveyed the field. Off in the distance, some locals had wandered out of the village and city to gawp. She took her Thane by the arm and pulled him aside.

'What is it?' he asked her.

'Listen to me, Heirik. You must take action, or the Caerians will lose all fear of you.'

'What sort of action?' he muttered.

'Harsh action,' Razna said. 'Vengeance. You must be swift.'

He put a hand on hers. 'I'm a Thane, a lawgiver. I must punish correctly, or else risk chaos.'

Razna pulled him closer. 'They don't respect you,' she hissed. 'They have pissed on your justice. They piss on your gods. If you do not act, they will laugh at you behind your back. And you—we—will lose *everything*.'

'But, my love, who would I punish?' Heirik whispered. 'They run without honour and hide.'

Razna put her hand on his cheek. 'It doesn't matter. Just make an example so that the rest will fear you. Punish the village. The city is too big, too valuable. The village is easier—and it probably was them anyway.'

'It probably was, yes?' Heirik swallowed.

She smiled and inclined her head.

Heirik drew himself up straight. 'So tired of this city,' he muttered. 'Very well.' He turned to his soldiers. 'Daga? Sederial?'

The two men stepped forward. 'Thane Heirik?' Sederial said.

'Gather a hundred or so of our men. At least a hundred, in case of resistance. You are to go to Goretonum and burn the village to the ground.'

'Burn it, My Thane?' Daga shifted from one foot to another. 'Are you sure?'

Heirik nodded. 'You heard me. Do to them what they did to us.'

CHAPTER TWO

SASIION — SPRING'S FALL — 436

'Well, I think this is as ready as it's ever going to be.' Colus Meretan sniffed and handed the scroll to Valcero. 'Hopefully, the admiral and his captains won't complain how heavy it is this time.'

They were busy in Master Meretan's workshop, surrounded by bits of wood and half-built models of siege engines. Valcero peeked into the papyrus tube.

'That's not for looking at!' Colus barked. 'Off you go. They are waiting.'

Valcero Baradon smiled and nodded to the Royal Engineer. He left the workshop in the corner of the palace complex. He still wasn't allowed to visit the *other* workshop at the edge of Elisdrium. He knew they were making *tecnaris* fire there, but Colus had threatened to whip his back to ribbons if Valcero ever mentioned that to anyone. The boy sighed and trudged across the courtyard.

'Valcero!' Terzjin was waving him over. He leaned against the wall in the shade with a group of lenotare. They chatted while polishing their swords with stones.

Valcero went over to join them.

Master Maltorus grinned. 'Valcero, how are you?'

'Well.'

The soldiers glanced at Valcero and continued with their conversation.

'We're practising sword drills.' Terzjin flicked his blade with his fingernail so that it chimed. 'Would you like to join us?'

'To learn how to fight?' Valcero stared at the bronze sword.

Master Maltorus nodded. 'It's about time, don't you think?'

The boy held up the scroll. 'I have to take this to the admiral.'

Terzjin nodded. 'Ah, of course.'

'But, I'd really like to learn!'

'Well, why don't you deliver the scroll as quickly, then come here before Master Meretan needs you back?' Terzjin smiled. 'He doesn't have to know how long it takes.'

Valcero grinned. 'All right.'

He hurried off, hopefully without looking silly, and entered another doorway in the palace wall. He went up the stairs and knocked on the door to the admiral's quarters.

'If we can split the fleet to surround Khemeto from these—enter!'

Valcero poked his head around the door. Admiral Getaelon and some of his captains leaned over a map on his table.

Getaelon nodded and winked at him. 'What does Master Meretan have for us today?'

Valcero handed him the scroll. 'He says it's a good one.'

Getaelon snorted. 'He always does.' The Admiral unfurled the scroll and examined the drawing with narrowed eyes. His captains crowded around to peer over his shoulders. 'It still looks too big,' Getaelon said after a while.

'Master Meretan says it will balance well.'

'The Khemetese won't need to sink our ships,' a captain muttered. 'This will do the job for them.'

'You can store the ammunition at the rear—the stern—of the ship to balance it out,' Valcero said.

They all stared at him.

Valcero stood up straight. 'It will balance.'

'Aiming the damn thing will be difficult,' Getaelon ran his eyes over the papyrus. 'Especially on choppy water.'

'Master Meretan has some tricks for that.'

The Admiral snorted again. 'Of course he does.' He sighed. 'Very well. Let's try it on a couple of ships and see how it goes.' He looked at Valcero. 'You can tell the Royal Engineer that.'

Valcero smiled and bobbed his head. 'Yes, sir.'

Valcero returned to the palace via a back door. He descended the stone steps into the stores and through to the kitchens. Everyone there seemed to be shouting, running, or banging pots.

'Excuse me, where is Saedelas?' he asked a cook furiously chopping carrots at the nearest countertop.

She glanced about the kitchen. 'Skiving off in the wine cellar with that boy again, most likely.' She jerked her thumb at another door.

Valcero felt hot as he approached the cellar. In the glow of a lamp, he found Saedelas leaning against the wall with that boy Enlet standing before her. Enlet leaned forward, his hand pressed against the wall by her head while he spoke. She smiled back at him. It looked like a smile.

The boy's heart thudded as he stepped forward. 'Uh...'

They both turned as he approached. Saedelas ducked away from the boy and smiled brightly at Valcero. 'Master Baradon! Good to see you. What is it?'

Enlet scowled at the boy and put his hands behind his back.

'I came to ask you something, but...' Valcero looked back and forth between the pair. '...but maybe you are busy.'

'Not at all.' Saedelas grabbed an amphora from the floor and led him out of the cellar. 'What is it?'

'Um, well, Master Maltorus is doing sword practice in the courtyard and I wondered... I wondered if you wanted to watch? He said I could practise too.'

'Oh.' Saedelas grinned. 'Well, I suppose that could be fun.' She put the amphora on a table and prodded Valcero towards the exit. 'Quick, before I have to stuff another goose.'

As they ascended the stairs, Valcero looked back at her. 'That boy...'

'Oh, *him*.' She sighed. 'Enlet's an absolute pest. Chases after all the girls in the kitchen, and it seems this week is my turn.'

'Oh. Do you... *like* Enlet?'

Saedelas shook her head and laughed. 'No, but he knows how to please the kitchen master. So we just have to put up with him.'

They stepped out into the bright sunshine.

Saedelas pointed at the sparring soldiers.'So that's the fighting over there?'

The clanging metal and dull thumps echoed across the courtyard. Terzjin walked around the guards and muttered instructions.

'Sword practice, actually,' Valcero said as they approached. 'They have to keep training to be the best soldiers, you know.'

'And you're going to practise with them?' Saedelas asked.

He nodded.

The girl frowned. 'Have you done it before?'

The boy hesitated. 'Of course! We practised... lots of times.'

'In the desert?'

'Ah, there he is!' Terzjin grinned as they arrived. 'And I see you brought a friend.'

Valcero blushed. Saedelas drew herself to her full height as the men stared at her.

Master Maltorus waved at the lenotare. 'Take a breath, lads.'

The guards backed away to form a circle around Terzjin and the children.

Terzjin inspected the armament rack against the wall. 'Hmm, let's see... We'll start with these, perhaps.' He pulled a round shield and broadsword from the pile and handed them to Valcero. They were smaller than what the guards were carrying, but the weight almost yanked Valcero to the ground. He caught his balance before anyone noticed.

'Which hand do you favour?' Master Maltorus asked. 'Left or right?'

Valcero looked at what he was holding. 'I... I'm not sure.'

Terzjin grinned. 'Oh, a true Caerian! Alright, let's start in the common fashion—sword in your right and shield in your left.'

The boy nodded and fumbled with the armaments. All eyes were on him.

Terzjin bent to pick up another sword. 'And I'll use this.' He checked the blade and nodded.

'Is it safe?' Valcero asked.

'Oh yes.' Terzjin tapped the edge against his arm. 'See? It probably hasn't been sharpened since you went off your mother's milk.'

A few soldiers chuckled. Valcero tried to smile. Did he ever drink his mother's milk? He examined his own weapon. The bronze was weathered and tarnished. Blunted, yes, but still pointed. He tried not to picture it piercing his belly.

He looked at Terzjin and swallowed. 'You're not using a shield.'

Terzjin smiled. 'Probably no need for it today.'

More soldiers chuckled. Valcero bit his lip.

Master Maltorus walked around the boy. 'Alright, first thing. Let's get your stance correct. Shield up and out, like so. Sword up too—ready for anything.'

The boy tried to still his thin arms.

Terzjin looked him up and down. 'That will do. Ah, Saedelas, you should keep clear for this part.'

Her sandals scraped on the paving. Her eyes bored into his back. This was a mistake.

Terzjin backed away and raised his sword out to the side. 'Now, Valcero, I'm going to try to strike you. Try to knock my weapon aside with your shield, and see if you can poke me in return. Ready?'

The boy nodded.

Terzjin raised his blade to head height, point forward. 'Begin.'

Valcero breathed in. Terzjin skipped forward and jabbed his sword at the boy. Valcero flinched and leaned back, almost toppling over.

Terzjin shifted to the right. 'Use the shield. You can do it.' He jabbed again. Valcero tried to block, but the blade stopped just before his chest.

'Almost, almost.' Master Maltorus withdrew and shifted left. 'Here I come again.' He stepped forward and swung his sword downwards.

Valcero raised his shield in time to catch the blow, but the strike jolted him. His ears rang as he staggered backwards and fell over. The soldiers laughed. His cheeks burned.

'No need for that!' Master Maltorus barked.

The laughter stopped.

Valcero clambered to his feet, careful not to meet anyone's eye.

Terzjin gave him a once-over. 'You alright?'

'Yes, yes. I'm fine,' the boy muttered.

'Drop the shield for now,' Terzjin said, 'and let's concentrate on using the sword.'

Valcero let go of the shield and gripped the sword with two hands.

Terzjin patted his chest. 'Try to hit me. Stab forward, and I'll try to deflect with my sword. Ready?'

Valcero jabbed his blade at Terzjin's chest.

Master Maltorus flicked it aside with the tip of his sword. 'Use your whole body. Twist at the waist.'

The boy stabbed again, harder.

The metal chimed as Terzjin batted him away. 'Come on, give it some strength!'

Valcero bit his lip and swung the sword overhead with all his might. Terzjin parried the blow, and the weapon slipped out of Valcero's hand and clattered on the ground.

The audience burst into laughter.

Valcero wiped his palm on his tunic and glanced around. Even Saedelas was grinning.

The boy frowned at her. 'Do you want a turn?'

Terzjin lowered his sword. 'Oh, no. No, I don't think so, Valcero. This is... not exactly *women's* work.'

Saedelas' grin turned to a scowl. 'I suppose I'll go back to the kitchen then.' She swung about and stormed off.

'Wait!' Valcero called after her, but she did not stop or look back.

The laughter faded.

'Perhaps that's enough for today,' Master Maltorus said. 'We should start you on some exercises to build your strength, alright?'

Valcero shrugged.

'How about we see what *you* can do, Terzjin Maltorus?' a Sasiion guard said. 'I'd like a proper lesson, and I promise to be a better student than this one.'

His Sasiion companions laughed and patted his back.

Terzjin nodded. 'Very well. Let's practice some basic parries and thrusts. Step back, please, Valcero. And *you* can step up.'

He gestured to the guard, who assumed a ready stance, then sprang forward to attack. Their swords struck each other twice, then Terzjin twisted right and held his blade to the guard's throat. The Sasiion man froze.

'Remember, you don't have to move in a straight line. You're not a piece on an *efret* board. Think of all directions.'

The guard nodded carefully.

'Again.' Master Maltorus withdrew to a ready stance.

The soldier did the same, then stepped left and right, while swinging his weapon. Terzjin smiled, nodded, then darted forward to thrust. The soldier raised his shield, but Terzjin side-stepped and slammed his shoulder into the man's exposed chest. The guard gasped and fell backwards. The others laughed and clapped. Even Valcero smiled.

Master Maltorus faced the assembled soldiers. 'Try not to be too heavy on your feet, even when wearing armour. You must be agile when necessary, ready to dodge and seize the moment to strike.' He extended a hand and pulled the soldier to his feet. 'Perhaps there's a better way to demonstrate. You three...' He pointed at two lenotare and a Sasiion guard. 'Come, join your companion.'

The men exchanged looks and entered the ring. 'Two on two?' one asked.

Terzjin picked up a shield and shook his head. 'Sometimes we must fight outnumbered, and use all our wits and skills to survive. Now, all of you... attack.'

The soldiers shrugged and advanced on him. They thrust and swung their swords, but Terzjin dodged and parried. They shoved their shields, but Master Maltorus twisted out of reach. They surrounded him, each trying to land a blow, but he danced between them, slashing and jabbing his blade, smiling calmly.

'Is he good?' Valcero asked the Sasiion guard beside him.

The man folded his arms and watched the sparring with narrowed eyes. 'Yes. Maybe *too* good.'

One by one, Terzjin brought down each opponent. A quick sword flick on an exposed stomach and open neck. A sweeping foot to topple another. A bash of his shield on the back of the final lenotarus.

The three soldiers lay groaning and gasping. The rest looked on wide-eyed and silent. A shield rolled about on the ground. Master Maltorus' breath slowed.

'Not a mark on him,' someone whispered behind Valcero.

Terzjin scratched his head with his sword pommel. 'Uh, perhaps too much beer last night, yes? Maybe Valcero can train you for next time.'

The chuckles broke the silence. Terzjin helped the fallen comrades back to their feet.

'*How*?' a guard asked as Terzjin pulled him up.

Master Maltorus shrugged. 'Practice.'

The soldier frowned and shook his head as he limped away.

Valcero crept up to Terzjin. 'Could you teach me to do that?'

The man stowed his practice sword on the rack and held out his hands to take the sword and shield from Valcero. He gazed into the boy's eyes. 'Perhaps. We'll make some kind of warrior out of you one day, lad.'

A lenotarus chuckled as he stowed his practice weapons. 'A weighty task, even for you, Terzjin Maltorus.'

Valcero glowered and handed over the armaments. He glanced at the guard and thought for a moment. 'Terzjin?'

'Yes?'

'There's something I've been wanting to ask you.'

'Go on.'

'Your name. Terzjin Maltorus. It's not a *normal* name, is it?'

'What do you mean?'

'Well...' Valcero pondered some more. 'Your family name sounds like a first name. And your first name sounds like a family name. Except, it doesn't sound Caerian exactly.'

Terzjin stared at him. 'That's because it's not,' he replied softly.

'Oh?'

' "Terzjin" is... Galatani.'

Valcero blinked. 'Why do you have a Galatani name?'

The man looked around, then smiled at him. 'Maltorus isn't a family. It's a nickname from the lenotare I trained with.'

'Oh yes, I remember that!' The lenotarus turned around. 'Old Captain Anacrius gave it to him.'

Maltorus. Valcero's lips moved. ' "North Wind?" Why?'

The soldier grinned. 'Because of the way he fights—cold and unrelenting.'

'Alright, but why is your *first* name Galatani?' Valcero asked.

Master Maltorus smiled more tightly. He put an arm around the boy's shoulders. 'Come, let's walk you back to Master Meretan. He must be wondering where you are.'

Terzjin stared at the flagstones as they crossed the courtyard. Valcero opened his mouth to speak, but the King's bodyguard interrupted.

'Valcero, my name is Galatani because *I* am Galatani. I came to Caeria many years ago.'

'I didn't know that.'

Terzjin shrugged. 'Not many do. I prefer to keep it that way.'

'So, what's your actual family name?'

The man swallowed. 'That's one of the things I had to leave behind in Galatan.'

Valcero nodded as they walked. 'Why did you come to Caeria?'

'Well... you know about the war?'

'The conquest of Galatan?'

'That's the one.'

The war was more than twenty years ago. He looked up at the man. 'So, you and your family escaped the Rhenivians?'

Terzjin breathed in. 'Not exactly.'

'What happened to your family?'

Terzjin's face clenched, and he stopped abruptly at the doorway. 'You know what, you can make your own way to Master Meretan.'

'Oh.'

'Yes, I have work to do.' Terzjin walked off.

'Will we do another fighting lesson?' Valcero called after him.

Master Maltorus paused and half-turned his head. 'War is for men, not boys.' He strode away.

Valcero stared after him, not sure what else to say or do.

CHAPTER THREE

SASIION – SPRING'S FALL – 436

Terzjin paced his room. He sat, polished his sword with a cloth, then stood to pace some more. That boy, always poking and prying. How dare he? What right did he have to ask that? How dare he? He blew out his breath and paused at the table. He tried to read from an open scroll, one of his translated texts from Nemeket. The passage described a way of striking confusion in an opponent's heart, without uttering a word. He raised a hand and made the described gesture. Nothing happened, of course. He sighed and continued his pacing.

The burning rooms. Hiding in the shadows under his bed. The soldiers holding his little brother aloft by the ankle, laughing. He had a brother. His sisters...

Why would the boy even *ask* such a thing?

Terzjin blinked and grabbed his sword from the table. He sliced through a sunbeam. Light flashed across his face. He blinked again. The old man came to find him later. The old man. What was his name?

They raced across the stony hillsides. The old man told him to walk faster. The old man, carrying his shield and spear. The horsemen caught up. They galloped behind him. The fight. And what came after...

Terzjin threw the sword on the floor.

The fight. The horseman dehorsed, lying on the ground, staring up at him, shouting, maybe swearing. The red boar on his breast. Spit and blood on his mouth, his pale face. And then—

'Sir?'

'*What?*'

The servant flinched at the door. 'I beg your pardon, sir. His Majesty requested you in his chambers.

Terzjin rubbed his face. 'Alright, yes. I'll be there in a moment.'

The servant bowed and withdrew. Master Maltorus lingered in the middle of the room and breathed slowly. He picked up his sword from the floor. The blade shimmered silver, with a hint of green. He flicked the metal with his fingernail and listened to the clear chime. He flexed his wrist and spun the sword around. It was light and comfortable in his hand. He breathed some more.

He slipped the weapon back in its scabbard and tied it to his belt.

'Your Majesty?' Terzjin entered King Zjandius' chambers at the top of the palace.

The King sat at a desk with an open scroll before him. The half-shuttered windows blocked most of the bright morning light. He looked up and nodded before dismissing an attendant with a gesture. 'Please, Master Maltorus, sit,' he said as the servant shut the door.

Terzjin sat in a chair before the table. Gulls squawked outside. The waterfall boomed distantly. His sandal tapped on the blue-tiled floor.

'I finally found a bit of spare time,' Zjandius said, 'so I asked to see all the papers Master Meretan gathered from Nemeket.' The King tapped his fingers on the papyrus. 'I am now reading the final scroll, this account that Colus translated. Do you know the one?'

'The account of the city's last days?'

Zjandius nodded. 'Temlet the Scribe—may history record his name. Have you read it?'

'Only parts,' Terzjin said. 'Colus shared some with me at the time. It is grim reading.'

'And I have only learnt of it now.' Zjandius frowned. 'You should have told me about this—both of you. I needed to know.'

Master Maltorus bowed his head. 'I am sorry, Your Majesty. I think, with the goings-on at the time, perhaps Master Meretan forgot. I assumed you had it.'

Zjandius leaned back and sighed. 'No matter. But do you know it contradicts almost everything I learnt as a boy? What should I believe? The stories from my nurse, tutors, and father? Or the final account of a royal scribe?'

Terzjin said nothing.

'I was taught that my ancestors, the royal house of Vaecerion, tried everything in their power to stop the plague and save the city. That it was the scheming priests who thwarted them. Well, *that* part is at least the same. They told me the aristocratic families left only after everyone else had perished. King Olectus and the Vaecerion, the Eledan, the Corilien, the Sanadin, and the Aventan went west to the sea. They joined the Octerian at the coast and sailed away with whatever vessels they had. To Caeria, where the plague and priests would not find them. Now, I read that the aristocrats poured *fire* on desperate citizens and abandoned them to their doom.'

'As I said, grim reading.'

'Do you know what thought I am left with? What chews at my heart? I wonder what accounts people back in Etorium have written. What have they said about their King? That I did everything I could to protect them from the barbarians? Or that I fled like a coward across the sea to become king of a new land? That I forsook them, and my duty?'

Terzjin leaned forward. 'You had little choice, sir.'

Zjandius leaned forward as well. 'Did I? Perhaps I should have fought harder. Perhaps, I should have died rather than surrender the kingdom.' He gazed out through a gap in the shutters. 'Was it a mistake to free the slaves—at least, at that moment? Perhaps the lords would have supported me better.'

Terzjin shrugged. 'Perhaps. But perhaps it made no difference.'

'What if I am just one of those mediocre Vaecerion kings from the histories? Nothing more than a list of mistakes and trivial accomplishments?'

'I think it is a little early to be sure of that, Your Majesty,' Terzjin said. 'Your story is not over.'

'*Ae*, what bright colours will they paint over the cracks in my statue?' The King rubbed his face. 'This is not even why I summoned you. I am wallowing in self-pity to avoid a more difficult subject.'

'Yes?'

'I have received word that Lord Sanadin is leading a rebellion back in Caeria. They are trying to drive the Rhenivians out.'

'Oh? I didn't know that.'

'It is not yet common knowledge,' Zjandius said, 'but it seems to confirm my fecklessness, does it not?'

'My King...'

'Here we are, sitting in a far-off country getting fat on dates and beer, whilst noble Caerians fight for their land.' Zjandius folded his arms. 'It is not certain they will win, but if they do... well, Lord Sanadin would have a good claim to my abandoned throne.'

'Your Majesty,' Terzjin interrupted, 'you have not been idle. You are assembling a new cantaris, and a new fleet—better than Caeria has ever had.'

The King shook his head. 'It is not enough, and time is running out for us. For me.' He groaned. 'And still I am avoiding the matter at hand. Though perhaps we wander closer.'

'Zjandius, you have my ears.'

Zjandius slammed his hands on the table. He sighed and smiled too brightly. 'Very well!' He took a bronze scroll tube from the table's edge and held it out to Terzjin. It was sealed with wax, stamped by Zjandius' royal ring. 'I need you to deliver this letter to Emzentanis, to the Princess. In secret.'

Master Maltorus nodded and reached for the tube.

Zjandius did not let go. He stared at Terzjin. 'You're allowed to ask what it contains.'

Terzjin blinked. 'As you wish, Your Majesty. Another request for an alliance? Or to submit to your authority?'

The King chuckled and released the tube. 'Oh, you are close, but it's so much more than that.'

Terzjin's eyes widened.

Zjandius Vaecerion grinned and nodded slowly.

'Zjandius...'

The King's grin faded. 'It's the only way. We're not yet strong enough. We need the flood princes. And seeing as the Princess of Emzentanis probably won't submit at spearpoint, or be bought, I must try romance instead.'

Terzjin leaned back in his chair and stroked his chin. 'This is a bold step. Are you sure?'

'I am. Just this week, I've had Lord Corilien visit me twice and drop heavy hints about his eldest daughter.' Zjandius sighed. 'She is most lovely, but... I'm not enthused.'

Terzjin hid a smile behind his hand.

'And my... my family have been pressuring me as well,' Zjandius continued. 'The time is coming when I must name an heir, or they will claim their right to do it for me. Which obviously means *brother* Merius. No, a marriage alliance is the best option. With Emzentanis, we will win over the flood princes, and then we have a chance.'

'And what do you know about this princess?'

'Well, I'm told she's beautiful, and very cunning.' The King shrugged. 'Princess Nanepti rules her city well, by all accounts, and has kept the Rhenivians at bay on her northern border. The flood princes respect Emzentanis, which is the main thing.' Zjandius stood up.

Terzjin got to his feet as well. 'And what about her other qualities?' he asked softly.

Zjandius nodded and walked around the table. He patted the sealed scroll tube in Terzjin's hand. 'I must do my duty.'

'Of course.'

'But...' the King bit his lip. 'When you meet her... if you can see...' He looked at the ground. 'If your heart tells you it would be a *very* poor match...'

Terzjin put his hand on his King's shoulder and smiled gently. 'I'll pay close attention, Zjandius.'

'Thank you,' Zjandius muttered. 'When the time comes, do what you think is best.' He paused. 'She hasn't replied to my most recent letters. Apparently, her ministers have turned away every courier at the gates. I don't know if they're doing it under her instruction. So, I need *you* to go and get the scroll to her—directly—and discover the truth of her position towards us. Use your... tricks if you must.'

Terzjin bowed and left the room. He closed the doors and walked down the corridor. The Dowager Queen Porinia popped around the corner. Terzjin slipped the scroll behind his back, but her eyes caught the movement.

Master Maltorus bowed deeply. 'Your Majesty.'

Porinia sniffed. 'And what errands does the King have you run now, hmm?'

Terzjin straightened and arranged his face in a smile. 'Mundane royal matters, Oh Queen.'

'Well, I *am* part of the royal family, boy. What is he up to?'

Terzjin's smile tightened. 'Merely reviewing his personal guard, Your Highness. I assured him I have trained the lenotare personally and can *guarantee* their loyalty. As I can for your lenotare, Highness.'

Porinia frowned. 'What is that supposed to mean?'

'I must congratulate you, Highness, on the marriage of your son Merius. You must be very proud of your Prince of Paeseum.'

'Well, he was already a prince, so it changes little.'

'Of course, Your Highness.' Terzjin inclined his head.

She folded her arms and glared.

'Would you like a full review of the lenotare assigned to you, Your Highness?' Terzjin asked.

Porinia grunted. 'No, no, I don't have time for that. Away with you.' She waved him off.

Master Maltorus bowed deeply once more and then strode down to the stables.

CHAPTER FOUR

SASIION — SUMMER'S REIGN — 436

Terzjin wiped the sweat from his brow and surveyed the city before him. It lay on an eye-shaped island amidst the wide, muddy Emzen River. Tall walls ringed the citadel, and a bridge on either side connected it to the riverbanks. The Emzen twisted back and forth across the plain and disappeared into the hazy distance to the north and south. Villages and farms filled the banks—mud huts between vivid, green fields. A stream of carts and traders hauling sacks on their backs crawled along the road from Paeseum at the bottom of the hill to Terzjin's side. Master Maltorus clambered down the slope and rejoined the traffic to Emzentanis.

He had sailed on a barge up the Tiana to Paeseum and walked further upstream for days before crossing the shallows at the marshlands below the twin falls. He walked amongst multitudes, dressed as a humble trader on the hunt for fresh business in the cities of the Flood. That was the tale he told at the campfires he shared each night along the marsh's edge.

The nightly smoke chased off the midges and mosquitoes that swarmed the floodlands. The water birds' song lulled him to sleep, and the occasional grunts of hippopotami in the dark startled him awake.

More days passed, and they left the marsh to cross the narrow desert strip to the Emzen.

Now, Terzjin tugged his hood lower for relief from the baking sun and to hide his foreign features. He walked in the crowd at a steady pace. Rumbling wheels, occasional muttered words, and tinkling bells from the asses and oxen filled the otherwise hot silence. The east wind carried sweat, smoke and manure to Terzjin's nose. The travellers passed roadside stalls with merchants flogging beer, sweetened wine, and sizzling chunks of braised lamb. But Master Maltorus was already late.

The crowd slowed at the bridge and shuffled into a queue to enter the outer gate. The guards pulled out travellers at random for questioning. Some they let continue, but others they kicked away with shouts and curses. And a few passed on after whispered negotiations and the clink of coins slipped from palm to palm. Terzjin used his trick—a quiet mind, tongue pressed against the roof of his mouth—and kept his eyes on the dirt. The guards said nothing as he passed between them and through the gate.

His shoulders relaxed as he crossed the stone bridge to the citadel. The brown waters sucked against the pillars. A fish splashed out of the deep. The sunlight sparkled over the Emzen. The crowd shuffled along the bridge to the next gate and guards, who extracted more bribes from travellers and traders. Terzjin readied himself to sneak past.

Terzjin Maltorus, Burglar of Cities. He smiled wryly to himself.

He went under the archway and into another Sasiion city of crowded streets and hot smells, shouting hawkers, chanting priests in their temples. Serene stone deities and rulers stood above the chaos, casting blessings and judgments upon the teeming masses. Money pulsed through the city like blood. Gold and silver gleamed and flashed. Spices tickled his nose. Birds shimmered in cages. Covered palanquins borne by slaves swayed and cut their way through the crowd.

He followed the river of people through cramped streets into the heart of Emzentanis, a market square of covered stalls. The Great Palace loomed across the open space. Similar in style to the palaces of Elisdrium and Paeseum, it emerged from the city in pillared tiers and gently sloping walls clad in gleaming lime.

He weaved his way through the market and side streets to a smaller square, bordered by temples on three edges and the palace gates on the fourth. Blue and yellow tiles lined the interior of the archway, where a line of guards in bronze helms, shields, and barbed spears stood before the tall, closed doors. He would have to find another way.

Terzjin kept his head bowed and stole glances to the left and right. Perhaps he could climb the wall from an alleyway? He let the crowd bear him eastwards.

'Terzjin Maltorus?'

He froze.

The palace guard in the centre of the line waved. 'Terzjin Maltorus?' he called again.

Terzjin's hand slipped under his cloak to his sword. His feet tensed. The citizens stopped around him and stared.

The guard beckoned. 'Please, come here,' he said in Old Sasiion.

The other guards watched, still and expressionless.

Terzjin breathed in. He approached the gate, hand on hilt.

'You are Master Terzjin Maltorus, correct?' the guard asked. The Emzentanian was tall and broad-shouldered with a small, beaked nose and heavy chin. He wore a fancier breastplate than his compatriots. Perhaps a captain, or however they ranked them here.

Master Maltorus halted, then nodded. 'I am.'

'Very good,' the captain said. 'Please, come with me.'

Terzjin's fingers tightened around his weapon. Eight guards.

'Please, Master Maltorus, come with me.'

'I have a message for Princess Nanepti,' Terzjin said. 'I am ordered to deliver it to her—in person—and no one else.'

'Of course,' the captain replied. 'The princess is waiting for you. This way, please.'

Terzjin searched the captain's face. The man seemed quite serious. Master Maltorus glanced about and shrugged. 'Very well.'

The soldiers formed two lines around Terzjin and the captain, who signalled to another guard on the wall. The great bronze doors swung inward.

The courtyard was much the same as back in Elisdrium. Soldiers and scribes strode past. Servants carried baskets and shouted at each other. They all paused to gape at Master Maltorus and his escort. Terzjin looked down and hunched his shoulders under the cloak. The captain walked alongside. His forearms were thick and covered in hairline scars.

He followed Terzjin's eyes. 'A hunting accident, mostly.'

As they entered the palace hall, two older men dressed in gold-hemmed robes scurried over to block their path. 'What's going on here?' one asked.

The captain bowed deeply. 'My Lord Minister, we are on the princess' business. She requests our presence immediately.'

The Lord Minister put his hands on his hips. 'I was not informed. Why wasn't I informed?'

The other minister gestured at Terzjin. 'Who's this?'

'A messenger, sir,' the captain replied.

'A messenger? From where?' The ministers came closer and peered at Master Maltorus.

Terzjin pulled back his hood and opened his mouth.

The captain stepped between them. 'His business is with the princess, My Lords.'

'Well, we can pass it to Her Grace,' the Lord Minister said. 'That would be most proper. Come, is it a scroll or a tablet?' He held out a hand and looked Terzjin up and down.

'As I said, My Lords, the letter is for the princess' eyes.' The captain drew himself up to his full height.

His guards followed suit.

The ministers glowered at them all.

'Of course,' the captain continued, 'you are most welcome to join us in the court, My Lords, while the princess receives the message.'

The ministers exchanged glances.

'Very well,' the second minister said. 'Hurry up then.'

The captain, Terzjin and the soldiers swept past the ministers, who scuttled in pursuit. As they all strode down the long hall, a servant darted from a side door. He whispered something in the captain's ear, and the soldier murmured a reply. The servant nodded and ran off down another corridor.

They reached the end of the hall and stopped before another pair of tall, studded doors. The waiting guards saluted the captain and pulled them open.

Sunlight flooded the hall as the party stepped into a paved courtyard. Two long ponds of dark water festooned with lilypads flanked a stone walkway leading to the throne, shaded by a hempen awning and fanned by two slaves. Nanepti, the Princess of Emzentanis, awaited.

The captain bowed deeply. 'A visitor from King Zjandius of Elisdrium, Your Grace.'

The other guards bowed, and Terzjin followed suit. He heard nothing but water trickling in the ponds, but upon some signal, the others straightened up. He copied their movements.

'Approach!' An attendant at the throne called out.

The captain held out his hands. 'Your weapons.'

Master Maltorus frowned, but undid his sword from his belt and handed it over.

The Captain inspected the scabbard and withdrew a few fingers' worth of blade. As the metal gleamed silvery green, he glanced up at Terzjin and narrowed his eyes.

Master Maltorus stared back.

The captain smiled slyly and nodded before pushing the sword back into its sheath and handing it to the nearest soldier. 'Follow my lead,' he ordered.

Terzjin walked with the Captain to the throne. The princess sat in the high seat, bedecked in an elaborate crown and brocade over a flowing white cotton dress. She settled back in the great chair and rested her chin on a long, slender hand. Her dark eyes, lined with glittering makeup, gazed down at Terzjin as he approached. The captain stopped and bowed low again, as did Terzjin.

'Arise.' The princess finally spoke, in a low voice.

Terzjin glanced up. She smiled faintly and stroked her chin while surveying him from on high. 'You must be tired from your travels, Terzjin Maltorus. It is a long journey from Elisdrium.'

Terzjin blinked and opened his mouth.

'Your Grace,' the Chief Minister called out from the back of the courtyard.

Princess Nanepti's face cooled. She beckoned to the ministers.

More courtiers were sidling into the courtyard from various doors. They hung back in the portico shadows, whispering and pointing. Terzjin's skin crawled. His hand drifted to his hip, bare of sword.

The two ministers came before the throne and gave deep but quick bows.

'Your Grace,' the Chief Minister said, 'this is *most* irregular. I must apologise. My servants failed in their duties. This... courier should *never* have disturbed you without the correct protocols.'

'You are forgiven, Chief Minister,' the princess replied. She smiled down at Terzjin. 'I remain... undisturbed.'

The Chief Minister bobbed his head. 'Nevertheless, Your Grace, allow me to assess the credentials of this messenger, and his message.'

The princess waved her hand. 'That will not be necessary.'

'But it is for your protection,' the minister almost whined. 'He could be an assassin, or a fraud looking to steal from the palace.'

'Wederet will protect me.' Nanepti gestured to the captain and smiled again.

Captain Wederet inclined his head, then held out his hand to Terzjin. 'The letter.'

Terzjin withdrew the scroll tube and passed it to Wederet, who approached the throne and offered it up to the princess with both hands. He bowed as she took it.

Nanepti turned over the bronze tube in her hands, then tore away the wax seal with her fingernail. She pulled out the scroll and unrolled it. The ponds bubbled while Nanepti's iridescent eyes examined the scroll.

'It is authentic,' she announced to the gathering. 'I recognise the seal of Elisdrium.'

A faint sigh blew around the courtyard.

'Hear now the true words of *King* Zjandius of Elisdrium,' she continued, 'and... Caeria.'

'Shouldn't one of your ministers have the duty of reading out this message?' the second minister said.

Nanepti raised an eyebrow. 'No. I think it would be best to read *this* letter myself.' She straightened, held out the open parchment before her, coughed gently, and began.

'Greetings,' her voice rang out, 'Your Grace Princess Nanepti of the Ancient Throne of the River, stewardess of Emzentanis and preeminent amongst flood princes and all Sasiion. Hm!' She nodded slightly. 'Your wise counsel, steady leadership, and *great beauty* have won you renown and honour up and down the rivers of this Old Kingdom...'

The letter continued with more flowery language. The ministers quietly groaned and sighed behind Terzjin as the princess reached the conclusion of Zjandius' proposal.

'... therefore, I humbly beg your hand in marriage, so that our great and illustrious lines may be combined for the benefit and glory of all Sasiion, as two vines entwined grow stronger and more fruitful in the joining.' Her lips twitched.

Gasps and whispers broke out in the courtyard.

'I beg that you do not delay in answering my plea, so that my heart might rest in certainty. Yours in service, Zjandius Vaecerion, King of Caeria and rightful monarch by blood of the Old Kingdom of Sasiion.' She lowered the parchment. 'Well, that is certainly a bold letter from *King* Zjandius, I'm sure you would all agree.'

The gathered courtiers tittered and murmured.

'Bold indeed!' The Chief Minister said. 'And impertinent for even *suggesting* such a thing.'

'I will need some time to consider this proposal,' the princess mused. 'However, this messenger shall be refreshed first. And I shall speak with him—*alone.*' She raised her hand to silence the Chief Minister before another word left his mouth. 'I will question him well before announcing a decision to you all, here.'

The Chief Minister stepped past Terzjin with hands clasped at his chest.'But your *safety*, Your Grace.'

'Wederet, with me,' the princess commanded.

Captain Wederet bowed his head and moved behind the princess as she alighted from the throne. He motioned to Terzjin to follow. The trio strolled to the back of the courtyard, where two attendants flanked another set of double doors. They saluted and opened the doors to admit the princess, with Wederet and Terzjin close behind.

They entered what must have been the Nanepti's personal chambers and some kind of reception room. Four long couches surrounded a low table bedecked with copper flasks, cups, and platters of dates, breads, skewered meats, and other delicacies.

'Your Grace, I must apologise,' said Terzjin. 'I am still dirty from my long journey. I did not expect an audience with you so soon.'

'No apology is necessary,' she replied. 'No doubt you would have refreshed yourself before an *unofficial* audience, yes?' She winked.

'Your Grace?'

'It is said you did not follow protocol when announcing Zjandius' arrival in Elisdrium to his cousin Taeto. You did not exactly ***knock*** at the palace door, correct?'

Terzjin nodded slowly. 'You are well informed, Your Grace. It also seems you expected me today. How, if I may ask?'

Princess Nanepti grinned. 'Many things travel up and down the rivers.'

A horse trader had hung around the travellers' camps. A horse trader with only one horse to trade, who had disappeared a few days ago. Terzjin bowed his head. 'Nonetheless, Your Majesty, I am embarrassed. Please, allow me a moment to wash the dust from my face and hands before we speak.'

Nanepti exchanged a look with her captain.

'My guards are holding the courtyard doors,' Wederet muttered.

'I do not think we have the luxury of time. Please, Master Maltorus, be seated, and we shall begin negotiations.'

'Negotiations, Your Majesty?' Terzjin sat across the table from the princess. 'What terms would you like me to take to King Zjandius?'

Nanepti shook her head. 'You do not understand. Whatever decision I make, I will make here today.'

Captain Wederet poured two cups of sweetened wine.

'I am not sure I could negotiate in my King's name, Princess.'

'Of course you can. He trusts you completely. After all, he chose *you* to deliver this sensitive letter, amongst many other tasks—they say.'

'They say?'

Wederet passed him a cup. 'They also say you fight very well, as if the gods guide your hand. Extremely well—at least in practice fights.' His lips curled.

Terzjin squirmed and tried to keep his face blank. He may as well have walked into Emzentanis naked. Who was the spy? Taeto? Or someone low-ranking, easy to ignore?

'Well,' Master Maltorus said, 'your reputation for wisdom precedes you, Your Grace. I will do my best.' He raised his cup.

Princess Nanepti smiled and raised hers in reply. 'So be it.' She sipped her wine.

Terzjin drank some of the sweet, spiced liquid. 'Do you have any questions for me, Princess?'

'Mmm, yes. Tell me, what will Zjandius do for Emzentanis when the Rhenivians retaliate? After all, Thane Leoren watches us from his hills to the north. It is an easy march to my city.'

'The Rhenivians have tried and failed to conquer your city many times,' Terzjin replied.

'Many times, yes, but an army can do much damage on the road to defeat—as they have done before.' She bit into a date and leaned back on her couch.

'As your husband, King Zjandius would be duty-bound to protect your city by any means.'

'And what would I be duty-bound to provide in return? Apart from an heir?'

Terzjin leaned forward. 'The King will request soldiers for his new army. Not too many. A fair amount for your city.'

The princess nodded. 'Ah, yes. His *cantaris*.' The Caerian word sounded odd with her accent. 'We have heard about these soldiers. They march up and down the field well, but are not tested.'

'They will pass the test. My King will defend every part of Sasiion, as his duty.'

Nanepti frowned. 'He did not defend Caeria. Or was that not part of his duty?'

Terzjin inclined his head. 'I will be honest, Your Majesty, we were unprepared. But now we understand what is required. With all Sasiion at our—'

'*All* Sasiion?'

'Of course, Your Grace. We know that if you ally with us—'

'Submit to you.'

'If you ally with us,' Terzjin continued, 'the flood princes will follow.'

'Khemeto will not follow.' She sighed. 'Those pirates follow no one.'

'We have a plan for Khemeto, Princess. We Caerians know how to deal with pirates.'

'Your new ships. Also untested.'

'Khemeto will be the test.'

Nanepti curled her lip. 'So cold. So *certain*.'

Shouts from the courtyard interrupted them. Nanepti glanced at Wederet—who shifted on his feet—then she returned her gaze to Terzjin and fixed a lazy smile on him. But she held her body stiffly, and Wederet's hands were near clenched. The captain leaned ever so slightly towards the door, as if he would dash out at any moment.

Terzjin licked his lips. 'Your Grace,' he said, 'you mentioned earlier that you did not have the luxury of time. What did you mean?'

Wederet drew a sharp breath. Nanepti's mouth tightened.

Master Maltorus looked from one to the other. 'Perhaps I have come to Emzentanis at an ill-omened hour?'

Nanepti sighed. 'I'm not sure there would be a good hour, Terzjin Maltorus. You brought a provocative message into this house.' She sat up. 'Wederet, you are dismissed. Attend to your duties.'

'Your Grace? Are you sure?'

Nanepti smiled gently at him. 'Go,' she mouthed.

The captain glared at Terzjin, then bowed to the princess. 'As you wish, Your Grace.' He darted outside and shut the door behind him.

The princess and the bodyguard regarded each other for a moment, then she gulped down some wine.

'Your Grace, forgive my boldness, but—'

'There are two factions of great families in this city, Terzjin Maltorus. One faction is loyal to me, as a princess of an ancient, illustrious dynasty. But I am a princess in a land of princes—do you understand? The other faction, well, they regard a ruling woman as an embarrassment, a problem to be resolved sooner or later.' She threw up her hands. 'These factions are finely balanced, such that they would tear Emzentanis apart if they went into open conflict. Do you understand the long game of wits I must play in this city, Caerian? Can you guess which faction owns my chief ministers?'

Terzjin said nothing.

She waved to the door. 'My court waits outside, including members of both groups. Captain Wederet's guards hold the doors so no one can leave whilst we speak. Because if my chief ministers *were* to get out, they would send word to the families that I am surrendering Emzentanis to a beggar king from across the sea. The ultimate humiliation! They would start a riot to capture the palace. I may die before the sun sets on this day. Do you understand, Terzjin Maltorus?'

He nodded.

'So, I must make my decision here and now, then declare it to my loyal ministers, so *they* can go forth and spread *my* word to the people, and not the words of those who wish me ill.'

'My Lady, when I return to my King, I will tell him you are as wise and...as beautiful as they say. I would tell him this would be an excellent match. '

Nanepti arose from the couch. '*More* flattery? Was the letter not enough?'

'It is not flattery, Your Grace. I merely state what my eyes and ears tell me.'

The princess rounded the table and came to sit next to him. 'So, you think me beautiful. What else do your eyes tell you?' She smelled of sandalwood. Her warm breath brushed his cheek.

Terzjin leaned away slightly, but Nanepti shifted closer. Her lips parted.

'Your Grace,' he spoke, 'are your people not waiting...?'

'They can wait a little more. Come, Caerian. You say I am beautiful. *How* beautiful? What would you do to prove your words?' She looked deep into his eyes.

Terzjin blinked. 'Your Grace, I could not...'

She put her hand on his thigh. 'Why not? The Princess of Emzentanis commands you.'

He felt her warmth through the cloth of his tunic. He turned to meet her gaze. 'I could not betray Zjandius like that. And, it would not be...right.'

Nanepti withdrew her hand. 'And now *you* have been tested.' She searched his face. 'Either you have a heart of ice...or you are truly loyal.' She shrugged and stood. 'Or perhaps both.'

Master Maltorus stared up at her.

Nanepti returned to her couch. 'So, this King Zjandius trusts you, then?'

'You could say that I am...*his* Wederet.'

Nanepti smiled. 'And do you trust him?'

'With my life.'

The princess reached for another date. 'Tell me about Zjandius. Why would we be a good match? And don't bore me with talk of armies and trade and suchlike.'

Terzjin sipped his wine. 'He is a good man. Clever. He reads plenty. He tries to be a good king, though...' he looked sideways at Nanepti, '...he is not always certain of how to go about it. '

The princess swallowed her date. 'And how does he try to be a good king?'

'He is kind to the people.'

'Ah, yes. He freed some slaves.' Nanepti examined her table of delicacies. 'Kind to the people, you say. But, does he know how to be kind to a person? Just *one* person?'

'I'm not sure I understand.'

The princess looked up at him. 'It is easy to be kind to "The People" with charity and good works. Kindness to a single flesh-and-blood person, out of sight of the world, is a very different matter. A man can be both kind to his city and cruel to those nearest to him.'

'I see. Well, he has been good to me throughout my life. So, yes, I would say he is kind. And again, I think the very fact you ask such a question shows you would be a good match.'

Nanepti inspected him. 'You're very at ease chatting with princesses, which is... interesting for a servant. What's your story?'

Before Terzjin could answer, there was a rap at the door.

'Come!' Nanepti called out.

Noise from the courtyard flooded the room as the door opened and Wederet poked his head inside. 'Your Grace, the court grows restless.'

Princess Nanepti sighed. 'And now the moment arrives. Come, let us walk to my throne while I decide whether to abandon or keep it.' She sprang up and marched out the door with Wederet.

Terzjin hurried after them. A hush fell over the courtyard as the courtiers noticed their princess and broke from their huddles.

Nanepti gathered her gown about her and settled into her throne. She surveyed the court. 'My Emzentanians,' she called out. 'I have considered *King* Zjandius' proposal. It is generous and flattering. Certainly ardent.'

Master Maltorus allowed himself a smile.

'But I must refuse it,' the princess said.

Terzjn blinked. The smile curdled on his lips. The courtiers gasped and burst into a torrent of chatter.

'Silence!' Captain Wederet shouted. 'Attend!'

The crowd went quiet again.

Nanepti nodded. 'I must refuse this proposal. Emzentanis cannot be surrendered so easily—certainly not by a mere written summons from a foreign king.'

'A very wise decision, Your Grace,' the Lord Minister said.

'Agreed!' added the second minister.

A few attendants clapped. Terzjin scowled.

Nanepti now turned her gaze on him. 'You may take my answer to your king, Terzjin Maltorus.'

Terzjin pressed his lips together and nodded. His skin crawled under the gaze of a hundred watching eyes. He would be the talk of the city by this evening.

'Of course,' the princess continued, 'you have made a long journey. Please, rest and refresh before your return to Elisdrium.'

He breathed and tried to still his thudding heart. 'A kind offer, but I should leave immediately—Your Grace. King Zjandius awaits.'

A frown twitched over her face, then she nodded. 'Of course. I understand. Captain Wederet shall escort you to the city gates and ensure you are provisioned for your journey.' She beckoned to the captain and leaned over to murmur in his ear.

Wederet nodded and bowed, then came to Terzjin's side.

'Farewell, Terzjin Maltorus,' Nanepti said.

Terzjin gave a short, sharp bow and turned away.

As they left the courtyard, Captain Wederet retrieved the sword and returned it to Master Maltorus. 'A fine blade,' he commented as they walked down the corridor. 'Quite rare these days. How did you come by it?'

'I found it,' Terzjin replied.

'Where?'

'Where it was left.'

The captain sighed. 'You must be disappointed with the princess' response—humiliated even.'

'Hmm.'

'Politics and the heart are both complex affairs, wouldn't you agree?'

Terzjin looked down the hallway.

They strode in silence out of the palace, through the city to the gates, where a guard waited with a pack of dried dates, flatbread and waterskins. Terzjin glanced into the sack and slung it over his shoulder without thanks. Captain Wederet took him out onto the now emptier, quieter bridge.

Master Maltorus looked over the water to the long road he must now retread. Perhaps he would buy a mule.

'Terzjin Maltorus...' the captain said.

He turned to Wederet. 'What?'

The captain glanced around and stepped closer. 'The princess bade me give you another message for your king,' he muttered.

'Oh?'

Wederet nodded. 'She said that if Zjandius were to visit Emzentanis and make his proposal *himself*, he may receive a response more to his liking.'

Terzjin frowned. 'What are you saying?'

The captain winked and slapped him on the back. 'Safe travels, Master Maltorus.' He turned away and strolled into his city.

CHAPTER FIVE

CAERIA – SUMMER'S FALL – 436

It was a warm evening in the Baker's Square of Etorium, and Heirik stood on the speakers' platform feeling most pleased. Look what he had done, without any Holy Warriors, or his uncle's help. Look what glories he had accomplished.

Every male member of the house of Sanadin was brought before him. Every son, nephew, grandson, father, and grandfather—nineteen altogether. Lord Sanadin glared up at him from their midst.

'Are you sure this is everyone?' the Thane asked Daga and Grindulf.

'Yes sir,' Daga replied. 'Some perished in the fighting. There were a couple more sons—either bastards or disowned—but apparently they died many years ago.'

The Sanadin men huddled together, hands bound. His Rhenivian soldiers surrounded the prisoners, three ranks deep and spears ready, while cityfolk watched from the edges of the square. The Sanadin hung their heads, crushed as he had crushed their rebellion. Heirik grinned. A good day. A triumph.

'And the woman and children?' he asked Sederial.

The Galatani bowed his head. 'Taken care of...quietly, out of the public eye as you requested, sir. In the courtyard of Goretonum fort this morning.'

Heirik nodded. 'And where is our Prefect?'

'Prefect Suletonius sends his apologies,' Daga replied. 'He says he has taken ill with food poisoning.'

Heirik snorted. 'Well, then there's no need to wait.'

He waved for silence. Grindulf blew his horn, and the crowd beyond the soldiers fell silent.

'People of Etorium,' Heirik called out in Rhenivian. Two marshals on each end of the square echoed his words in Caerian.

'People of Etorium, attend to my words! For months, these men here have waged a rebellion against me, even after Lord Sanadin...' Heirik pointed to the aristocrat amongst his family. '... swore an oath of allegiance and loyalty. Sad indeed are the days when men of supposedly noble blood are so treacherous. This rebellion hurt me deeply, after I have striven day and night to serve you, the people of Caeria. I have upheld your laws and customs, though you are now subjects of Rhenivia. I have protected you from raiding northmen, and the savages who lurk in the forest. I have brought you peace, and this is how the men of the Sanadin repaid me. For shame!'

Someone at the back of the crowd called out in Caerian. Laughter rippled through the audience.

'Find them,' Heirik muttered to the nearest soldier.

The Rhenivian saluted and marched off with two companions towards the heckler.

'People of Etorium,' Heirik called out again, 'I have delivered you Caerian justice and mercy, time and time again, as you deserved. But now is the time to deliver *Rhenivian* justice, which these traitors deserve.' He snapped his fingers at three soldiers beside the platform.

The three strode forward. One carried a great axe and wore a black mask over his face. The other two bore a wooden bench between them. They set the bench down before Heirik and bowed.

'Men of the Sanadin,' Heirik shouted, so that his voice bounced back at him from across the square, 'for your treachery and acts of rebellion, I hereby sentence you to death.'

The crowd gasped.

'Start with the youngest,' Heirik murmured so only the closest soldiers could hear. 'Save the lord for last.'

The Rhenivians hauled a man with a few wispy hairs on his chin from the clump of Sanadin and pushed him to the ground, so that he was bent over with his chest on the bench. The soldiers looked to Heirik.

'No! Please!' Lord Sanadin burst out.

Heirik sat on his stool. 'Begin.'

Without ceremony, the masked soldier hefted his axe into the air and swung it down into the boy's neck. The head dropped clean away. Perfectly executed. Heirik nodded and gestured for his men to continue.

Lord Sanadin screamed. His family lurched about. Some tried to break free, but Heirik's soldiers nudged the condemned back into place at spearpoint. Wails and groans arose from the cityfolk.

'Continue!' Heirik called out.

The soldiers dragged the body and head away and brought another young man, perhaps a few years younger than Heirik, to the bench.

'You bastards!' Lord Sanadin raved. 'You strawhead *bastards*!'

Heirik waved his hand. The axe swung in reply.

Lord Sanadin pushed to the front of his family. He raised his bound fists. 'I curse you, Heirik! I curse you for all time. Death will not relieve you!'

The Thane sneered at the old man and gestured to Daga.

'You shall wander the grey caverns in shame for all eternity. You *filth*! Damn you! Damn you! Damn—'

Daga hopped off the platform and struck Lord Sanadin across the face with the back of his fist. The Caerian collapsed to the ground, moaning and crying.

'Carry on!' Heirik called out.

The cityfolk began to shout and push forward. The Rhenivian soldiers turned outward and held them at bay with spear and shield. The cityfolk threw stones. One hit the platform near Heirik, who was careful not to flinch.

'I said, carry on!' he roared.

One by one, each Sanadin was dragged forth and beheaded. The bodies piled up on the right; the heads on the left. Blood trickled between the cobblestones. The crowd shouted and performed until Heirik had his men drive them from the square.

When Lord Sanadin's turn finally came, the market was quiet and golden in the evening light. The soldiers pulled the blank-eyed lord forward as he hung limply between them. They dropped him on the bench, and he flopped forward with his face to the bloody ground.

The executioner looked up at Heirik, who grinned, sprang to his feet, and bent over with hands on his hips to inspect the old man's face. He waited for Lord Sanadin to say something, do anything, but the Caerian merely lay over the bench in silence.

Heirik frowned, straightened up, and shrugged. 'Well, go on then,' he muttered as he turned away.

The axe fell and lopped off the man's head, much like the others.

After refreshing himself, Heirik joined Razna and his marshals for dinner in the palace dining hall. The Prefect's food poisoning apparently still kept him away. They sat around the table while servants brought boards of grilled lamb and fish, mashed onion and honeyed fruit, with jugs of beer and wine to quaff. Oil lamps filled the room with a lovely glow.

'You were missed,' Heirik told Razna as he ripped meat from a lamb's rib.

'I'm sorry, My Thane,' she replied, between nibbling on a pale strip of fish. 'Next time, I promise.'

'What do you mean, "next time"?' Heirik popped a chunk of meat in his mouth.

Razna turned to him and arched an eyebrow.

Heirik burst out laughing, almost choking on the lamb. A smile broke out on Razna's face as she watched him double over. The marshals chuckled around the table.

The Thane washed down the meat with some sweetened wine. 'Ah, by the gods!'

'So, all the Sanadin are...gone?' Razna asked.

He nodded. 'Root and branch.'

Razna fixed her gaze on the platter as she jabbed a piece of fish. 'And the women?' she asked quietly.

Heirik gnawed on the rib. 'Mmhm.'

Razna chewed on the fish, still looking at her board. She swallowed. 'I never particularly liked Lady Sanadin.'

Heirik shrugged and munched on his meat. He swallowed a cupful of wine. The juices mingled and dribbled down his chin.

A soldier entered the dining hall and bowed. 'Thane Heirik, two people have been waiting to speak with you since this afternoon.'

The Thane wiped his mouth. 'Then they can wait a little longer.'

'Who are they?' Razna asked.

'The smugglers, My Lady,' the soldier replied.

Thane Heirik perked up. 'Oh, in that case, show them in!'

The soldier bowed and left the room.

'This could be interesting,' Heirik told the table.

The marshals nodded in agreement.

A few moments later, the soldier returned with Taerinus and Jeigo Ladistrien. They bowed and stood before the table.

'Well, greetings, you two!' Heirik waved the rib at them. 'I haven't seen you in a long while. What news?'

Taerinus bobbed his head. 'Greetings, Thane Heirik. We have returned from a voyage to Elisdrium.'

'With more beer, I hope. And how is *King* Zjandius?' Heirik asked. 'Shrivelling up in the desert sun, eh?' He grinned and looked around his table. The marshals sniggered.

Taerinus looked at Jeigo, then back at Heirik. He coughed. 'King Zjandius has been quite busy, My Thane.'

'Oh?' Heirik hunched over his board and picked up another rib to bite off a mouthful of flesh.

'He has united all the river princes, Thane Heirik,' Jeigo said. 'His brother is now the Prince of Paeseum.'

Heirik watched them as he chewed on the fatty lamb.

'The sand princes also appear to have allied with him, sir. His army continues to grow... ' Taerinus' voice died away.

'The desert raiders?' Heirik asked Daga. 'The ones who come up the cliff paths to steal my uncle's sheep?'

The marshal nodded.

'And there are rumours he'll ask the Princess of Emzentanis for marriage,' Jeigo added.

Heirik set down his bone. 'What does any of that mean to me?'

He looked around the table at his men, who shrugged.

'If he allies with Emzentanis, sir,' Taerinus replied, 'the flood princes will probably join as well. Probably, sir.' He scratched the back of his head.

Thane Heirik scowled. 'He's going to get married? I drive him from this land, defeat him, humiliate him, and he's going to get *married*?'

'They also say he has some secret fire weapon, My Thane. They say it can—'

Heirik thumped his fists on the table. 'No! I won't stand for it. Daga!'

'Yes, My Thane?'

'I'm sending you on a...a quest.'

Razna rested her hand on Heirik's shoulder. 'What about Sederial?'

Heirik's eyes darted over the table. 'Yes. Yes, you're right.' He looked to his marshal. 'Daga, bring me the Galatani. I have a quest for ***him***.'

CHAPTER SIX

SASIION — AUTUMN'S RISING — 436

Valcero was bored. The palace was quiet, almost lifeless, with King Zjandius away for nearly two months. Terzjin had returned and left the next day with the King and his entourage. The rumour was that Zjandius had gone to beg the Princess of Emzentanis to marry him. 'A bad business,' the palace staff muttered amongst themselves.

Master Maltorus had said nothing to Valcero. Not even a hello or goodbye.

The boy tramped around the courtyard alone. The damp sea wind blew between the walls. He kicked a pebble over the flagstones as he walked.

Master Meretan had sent Valcero outside to give himself peace while he drew and wrote on his papyrus. 'You're being tiresome!' he shouted as he slammed the door in the boy's face.

Valcero wanted to visit Saedelas in the kitchens, but she had been strange lately. Distant. He rounded a corner and found three Elisdrian stableboys squatting on the ground and playing dice.

'A triple and blank,' a boy called as he was about to throw. The dice landed and rolled about to present double-fives, a four, and a one. '*Iabek*!' he swore. 'Next time, I'll bring my own.'

Another boy held out his hand. 'Pay up, Sefti.'

Sefti the thrower scowled and passed him two bronze coins.

'Wouldn't it be safer to bet a double instead?' Valcero asked.

The three looked up at him.

The Caerian boy swallowed. 'I only mean, it's a better chance...'

'So you play then?' the third boy frowned at him.

'Well, not really.' Valcero said.

'So, how do you know the chances?' another boy asked.

Valcero shrugged.

The three Elisdrians exchanged looks.

'Would you like to play?' the third boy asked finally.

'Yes, but I don't have coins on me.'

'Well,' the second boy mused, 'you could borrow some from me.'

Sefti sighed. 'No, don't do that. Not with his loaded dice.'

The second shoved him. 'Loaded dice? I haven't loaded anything except your mother.'

The third snorted. 'You have nothing to give there, Eneb.'

Valcero interrupted before they started fighting properly. 'Could I just watch and learn?'

'You could... ' Sefti squinted at the sky. '... but we're going to watch scorpion fights in the market. Do you have money for that?'

'No. But... but I know about scorpions.'

'Oh yes?' Eneb looked at him with interest as he scooped his dice into a cloth bag. 'What do you know about scorpions?'

Datet lay on the ground, screaming, staring at the heavens. His leg was black and purple.

Valcero swallowed. 'I know which ones are the most dangerous.'

'Which?'

'The smaller their pincers, the more poison they have.'

The boys stood up and started walking towards the palace gate. Valcero walked alongside them, and they did not tell him to go away.

The third boy looked at him. 'Is that true about the scorpion's pincers?'

'Yes, I've seen them,' Valcero said.

'Where?'

'In Nemeket.'

'Nemeket?' Eneb now turned to him. 'The City of the Dead?'

Valcero nodded.

The third bow frowned. 'You did *not* go to Nemeket. No one has been there.'

'I went,' Valcero insisted. 'With Master Meretan and Master Terzjin.'

They passed through the side door at the palace gate and crossed the busy square. The boys stole glances at Valcero.

'So, you live in the Palace?' Sefti asked.

Valcero nodded as he sidestepped a woman balancing a sack on her head.

The third boy chuckled. 'A prince, huh?'

It felt too awkward to ask his name at this point, so Valcero laughed instead. 'No, just a servant like you.'

They pushed through the throng of citizens crowding the street leading to the market. A gap opened, and the four boys filled it. A ring of people had formed in the corner of the market square. They squatted, sat, and stood watching as two men entered the circle, each carrying a wooden box by rope handles. They set their boxes on the ground a span or two apart, undid the catches, and jumped back as the sides fell open. Two small creatures crawled out.

Eneb pointed to two men leaning against the wall. 'Come, let's get closer.'

Valcero followed as they squeezed through the noisy crowd. The little creatures were indeed scorpions—one large and honey-coloured, and the other small, black, and glistening. They scuttled about the circle, as people flicked cloths or poked sticks at them when they wandered too close.

'Hello, boys, come to lose some coins?' one of the men said as they approached the wall.

They were palace guards, though now dressed in ordinary street clothes. Valcero did not know their names.

'Actually, we were thinking of taking some of yours.' Sefti punched one of the men on the shoulder. As they stood together, the similarities became obvious.

'Little bastard.' Sefti's father chuckled and rubbed his shoulder. 'I should toss you into the waterfall.'

'Throw mine off at the same time, would you?' said the other guard, patting Eneb on the back.

The crowd roared as the honey-coloured scorpion pounced on the black, driving its stinger into the smaller body while seizing it in its pincers.

'Ugh!' Eneb's father held out three bronzes. 'I was so sure.'

'Too sure.' Sefti's father pocketed the coins. 'Maybe better luck with the next?'

The scorpion wranglers nudged the two creatures apart with long poles. The black scorpion writhed on the ground. Its owner pushed it back into the box with a pole while the audience clapped. The loser shrugged and bowed before retiring into the crowd.

'What's going on here then?'

They turned to see a woman lugging a jute sack over her shoulder. She grinned at the men and cocked her head at the boys. 'And what will I tell your wives? Corrupting your sons with gambling?'

'Ah, mama, we're just watching.' The third boy went to her and gave her a quick hug.

'Come now, Adjet.' She pinched him on the cheek. 'I know what you get up to with this lot. How many coins did you have on the scorpions?'

'We just got here, actually,' Sefti piped up.

Eneb looked back at the circle. 'We were going to bet on the... little black one, but good thing we didn't.' He shot Valcero a look.

'I meant if the stinger is bigger than the pincers, then the scorpion is more poisonous.' Valcero said. 'I don't know what happens if both parts are the same size.'

They all stared at him now. He tried to smile, but felt like shrivelling up.

'This Caerian has a system,' Adjet explained.

'Is that so?' Eneb's father nodded. 'And where did you learn this system?'

'Uh...'

'He told us he went to Nemeket and saw scorpions,' Sefti said.

'Nemeket?' Adjet's mother flicked her fingers.

'Ah, you're *that* boy.' Eneb's father gazed keenly at him.

Eneb looked at his father. 'So, it's true?'

'You probably shouldn't be talking so loudly about...' Sefti's father looked around. '... that place.'

'You went there with that crazy old man, yes?' Eneb's father said.

Valcero thought for a moment. 'Yes, but Master Meretan is actually not that old. I think he's—'

'You really went there.' Adjet looked at him with new respect. 'Does that mean you're cursed?'

'Quite possibly,' Adjet's mother said. 'He's unclean.' Her gaze softened. 'Who are your parents, boy? Why would they let you go off to a place like that?'

Valcero swallowed. 'They aren't here.'

'Oh, they aren't in the palace?' she asked. 'Are they back in your homeland? In Caeria?'

The boy nodded.

'Oh, you poor thing.' She rested a hand on his shoulder.

'What do your parents do?' Eneb's father asked.

Valcero looked down. 'Uh... a cook and a housekeeper, sir. But in a big hou—a palace, like us.' His eyes prickled. The mother's hand felt warm on his shoulder. He wanted to either hug her, or run away.

'So, who is looking after you here?' Sefti's father asked.

Valcero blinked. 'I suppose, Master Meretan. He teaches me things. But also Master Maltorus! He is teaching me how to fight.'

'Master Maltorus?' Adjet's mother stepped back. 'He's that bodyguard, isn't he? Got a bit of an air about him, but he is a fine one, isn't he?' She winked at Valcero.

The boy stared at her, not knowing what to say.

Eneb's father chuckled. 'Now now, what are we going to tell your *husband*?'

Adjet's mother cackled, and the men joined in. The boys looked from one to the other, except Adjet, who blushed.

'Terzjin Maltorus knows how to use a sword,' Sefti's father said. He patted his shoulder. 'I have the bruises to show for it.'

'Well, in the training yard, at least,' Eneb's father said. 'From what I've heard, he's not so good in an actual fight.'

'Oh?' Adjet's mother and Sefti's father gathered closer.

Eneb's father nodded. 'I heard it from the Caerian guards that he turned to stone and cried when the Rhenivians attacked. They had to drag him from the battlefield.'

Valcero listened. They seemed to have forgotten him.

'He's never actually fought anyone, is what I heard,' Eneb's father said. 'But you didn't hear it from *me*.' He chuckled. 'I want to keep my head.' He glanced at Valcero and winced.

Before the boy could say anything, the crowd rose and clapped. They all turned to see another man enter the ring with a box, larger and more battered than the previous. He set it down and lifted the lid with a flourish. But instead of another scorpion, a striped, tawny creature darted out and crouched on the ground. The crowd hushed.

Sefti nudged Valcero. 'What now, Caerian? The scorpion or the mongoose?'

The surviving scorpion scuttled about the ring, holding its stinger erect. Perhaps the stinger *was* bigger than its pincers, but not by much.

'I think it's a poisonous scorpion,' he replied.

'Well, obviously,' Eneb said. 'It just won, after all.'

'Mongooses are also dangerous,' Adjet said. 'I saw one rip an asp to pieces in a contest here a few weeks ago.'

'So, which should we bet on?' Sefti asked. 'Quick, they'll start fighting in a moment.'

Valcero shrugged. 'I think the scorpion?' He had not seen a mongoose before.

'Hmm, alright.' Sefti said. He took coins from the other boys as Adjet's mother watched and clucked with disapproval. He strode up to one of the betting masters prowling through the crowd.

The fight began as the mongoose paced from side to side. The scorpion raised its pincers and turned back and forth to keep its furry opponent in sight. People cheered the animals on. The boys leaned in and whooped with each feint and near miss.

Valcero wanted to join in, but couldn't. Neither animal seemed worthy of death. He looked past the crowd and noticed people running out of the market square. There was a strange sound, almost lost in the hubbub.

He prodded Eneb.'What's that?'

'What?' The boy's eyes were fixed on the fight.

It came again, louder. A trumpet fanfare, joined with other instruments. Valcero shuffled away from the crowd and peered down the nearest alleyway. People were running to the far end, jostling and craning their necks where the alley opened onto the main street.

Once more, the trumpets blew, too loudly to ignore. The spectators at the fight broke away to investigate. Valcero ran forward and squeezed between two people and the wall. A steady drumbeat overwhelmed the chatter. Musicians blowing a merry tune and clashing cymbals marched down the street, followed by soldiers and the King's lenotare. Then more soldiers, dressed in bronze skull caps and brandishing shimmering sickles. They carried banners and standards edged with gold. A blue falcon and a winding river. The trumpets sounded again. The crowd cheered and clapped.

Then two chariots driven by dainty white horses wheeled into view. King Zjandius rode on the left, and a dark and glittering woman rode on the right. She smiled and waved to the citizens.

They gasped and whispered. 'The Princess of Emzentanis.' 'Nanepti! ' 'The Flood Princess.'

Riders flanked the chariots. There was Terzjin, in shining armour, alongside the King. Valcero drew a breath to shout, but stopped himself. He thought of the gossip from Eneb's father. Before he had another chance, the riders had passed. Now the people screamed and shrank away. The boy gasped and retreated into the alley with them.

Four towering beasts lumbered two-by-two down the street. They filled the breadth of the road. Grey and leathery they were, with skin sagging beneath the rich cloaks and gleaming gold that adorned them. Each creature had a rider atop, who waved a flag bearing the winding river. The beasts had long, sinuous noses that curled in the air, long white horns or teeth—sporting ribbons and copper bells—and massive ears that flapped like sails in the wind. One creature let out a rumbling scream. It rang in the boy's ears as loud as any trumpet.

'What are they?' he asked aloud.

'Elephants, my boy,' a woman said. She pressed herself against the wall and gaped up at them.

Their legs were like tree trunks. Each footfall crunched into the ground. They could crush him without a thought.

The parade passed, and the crowd spilt into the main street to follow. Valcero pressed through the jostling throng to reach the main square, as the parade ended with the two chariots at the palace gates.

A crier came before the pair. 'Attend! King Zjandius of Caeria and Sasiion presents to you, citizens of Elisdrium, Princess Nanepti of Emzentanis, now Queen of all Sasiion and Caeria, as his wedded wife, according to the laws and customs of the two lands. May the gods and people bless them!'

The crowd erupted. They waved rags and tossed flowers at the royal couple. Valcero covered his ears and bent over to push his way to the palace's side gate. The guard ushered the boy through.

He ran up to their apartment to find Colus hunched over his desk with papyrus and a quill.

He sat up and glared at Valcero. 'What's that cacophony outside?'

'Master Meretan! Master Meretan, the King has returned. And he has married!'

'Oh, so it happened after all?' Colus returned to his scroll.

'They also brought elephants!'

Master Meretan jerked upright. 'What? Elephants? Where?'

'Out in the square.' Valcero pointed behind him.

Colus strode to the window and leaned out. 'Where? I don't see them.'

'The main square, Master.' Valcero came up next to him and leaned out the window. 'Ah, there! They were behind the wall.'

The elephants marched around the square in single file, with flailing ears and much trumpeting. The citizens stood well back and clapped the beasts on.

'By the Lord of Life, they are *huge*,' Colus breathed. 'And as the scrolls described. Come, Valcero, we must inspect them properly.' He grabbed a roll of papyrus, a pen, and a pot of ink, all of which he passed to the boy.

'What happens now?' Valcero asked as he followed out the door and down the corridor.

'Great things, my boy.' Master Meretan stopped abruptly and looked down at him. 'And terrible things. Decisions need to be made. The hour won't be put off for much longer.'

'The hour? What do you mean?' Valcero asked.

'King Zjandius can't call himself a king of two lands if he only rules one.' Colus continued walking. 'War is coming.'

CHAPTER SEVEN

SASIION — AUTUMN'S REIGN — 436

More than a month had passed since the wedding feasts, parades, public speeches, and gift giving. Terzjin was practising with his sword in a quiet corner of the palace courtyard, as the late afternoon sun slumped towards evening. A storm had blown in from the sea and lashed the city with rain. A few steaming puddles remained on the flagstones.

He sliced and thrust to the front and behind. He parried at shadows, darted forwards, and sprang backwards.

'Not bad.'

He turned to find Captain Wederet smiling and watching with arms folded. His scars glowed in the afternoon light.

Master Meretan nodded to the older man and resumed his practice. He followed the eight sequences as outlined in the scroll, as he had memorised them. But he felt the Captain's eyes on his back.

Wederet strolled around to face Terzjin. 'Where did you learn these moves?'

Master Maltorus paused. 'I found scrolls in Nemeket.'

The captain pursed his lips. 'I wouldn't trust the writings of ancient warriors too much. If they really knew what they were doing, they would have survived. Battle is the real test.'

'You know better?'

The captain shrugged. 'Some experience.'

'Show me then.'

Wederet smiled and drew his iron broadsword, one of the new pieces from the Elisdrian forges. Without warning, he sprang forward. Terzjin parried the jab and darted to the left. He swung his blade up in return, but Wederet knocked it aside and charged forward into Terzjin's chest. Master Maltorus tried to slash at him, but the captain was too close. He drove his shoulder into Terzjin's face, knocking him backwards.

Terzjin tumbled to the ground, but leapt to his feet before Wederet could land another blow. The captain smiled and resheathed his sword. Terzjin, breathing heavily, glared at him and put his own blade away.

'You have natural talent, boy,' Wederet said, 'and you're certainly quick. But these qualities can make a fighter complacent.'

'I practise daily.'

'Good! But don't follow these drills too rigidly. They could become a cage. When it's life and death, break any rule if you must.'

The sixth bell chimed across the city.

Master Maltorus bowed his head. 'Thank you for your lecture, but now I must attend to my duties.'

Wederet nodded. 'As must I.'

Terzjin strode away, but Wederet kept pace at his side.

'Come, Terzjin,' the captain said, 'we must work together.'

Master Maltorus stared ahead. They entered the palace.

'Tell you what. I'll share everything I know with you,' Wederet muttered as they passed some guards. 'And I'm sure there are things you could teach me. Always be ready to learn, I say.'

Terzjin sighed.

'The day will come when I can no longer serve my princess,' Wederet said.

'Queen.'

'My Queen, yes, but when that day comes, Terzjin...' Wederet grasped Master Maltorus' shoulder and came around to face him, '... I hope I can trust you to protect her.'

Terzjin stared at him.

'And I hope you can trust me to protect your king—as you have.'

Terzjin rubbed his face. 'Such trust takes time.'

Wederet stepped away. 'Of course.' He contemplated the floor. ' I think we are driven by the same kind of... loyalty, Master Maltorus. Do you understand me?'

Terzjin tried to smile. 'I do, Captain.'

Wederet smiled at him in return.

'We should go,' Terzjin said, 'or else we'll be late for the banquet.'

Trust. Such an elusive thing in a house riddled with spies. Terzjin brooded in the corner of the hall, half-concealed in the shadow of a pillar, and watched yet another feast proceed.

There was Zjandius with Nanepti on his arm, holding forth on the grandest couch at the head of the gathering. The Queen laughed and chatted with several flood princes seated along the left side. They were celebrating the triumph against Khemeto—in honour of Admiral Getaelon. Those flood princes had sent soldiers to aid the conquest—and no doubt plundered the wayward city.

Some ship captains sat down the right-hand side at the far end, rough men who seemed unsure of what to say or where to put their hands while dining in a palace. Further up on the King's side lounged his various relatives, including cousin Taeto—quite possibly feeding secrets to the Sasiion princes—and the Dowager Queen Porinia whispering in her son Astulus's ear. *Never* to be trusted.

Lord Corilien sat with his wife and two daughters. He seemed to have taken Zjandius' marriage in his stride and now prodded one of the Corilien maidens to speak to Astulus—still conveniently unmarried. The usual political manoevering. Not something to be concerned about. Probably not.

Captain Wederet watched from the opposite wall. Where did his eyes roam? Everywhere, it seemed. No doubt making observations to share with his princess later. His eyes met Terzjin's, and he winked in commiseration. Master Maltorus nodded in reply.

Servants brought out tray after tray and laid them on the tables amongst the couches. Roasted lamb glazed in honey. Steaming fish. Sides of beef dripping with fat. Jugs of beer and wine. Spiced cakes. Warm bread. Piles of dates, grapes, and figs. Terzjin tried to focus on snatches of conversation—jokes, gossip, bland pleasantries between friends and rivals. Occasional laughter burst out over the musician's pipes, lyres, and bells from the corner.

And here came the man of the hour. Admiral Getaelon strolled through a side door and grinned at Terzjin as he passed. He wore a dark blue tunic hemmed with gold thread, and a wide white overcloak draped over his shoulder and tucked into his belt at the opposite hip.

Terzjin embraced the sailor. 'Congratulations, Admiral.'

Getaelon bowed his head. 'It was a tough journey, but we prevailed in the end.'

'A great success, then?'

Getaelon nodded slowly. 'I would say yes, though...'

'Though?'

The admiral shook his head. 'I've never been in a battle quite like it. The poor bastards...' He sighed and suddenly looked tired.

'There he is!' King Zjandius called out from his couch. 'Come forth, Admiral Getaelon, and dine with us.' Zjandius patted the empty couch at his side as the guests clapped and cheered.

The admiral took his seat while a servant filled his wine cup. He jabbed a slice of lamb from a nearby platter and munched on it with a smile. 'Thank you, Your Majesty, though the honour is yours.'

King Zjandius lifted his cup. 'A toast, to victory.'

The guests lifted their cups in unison. 'To victory!'

'Come, let us eat and make merry,' Zjandius said.

The music resumed, as did the feasting. Getaelon said something, and Lord Corilien and Zjandius laughed in reply.

Nanepti caught Terzjin's eye, but returned to the conversation before he could react.

Another two courses passed before the King tapped his fork on the table for silence. 'And now, Admiral, this feast calls for a story. Please, tell us the tale of Khemeto's fall.'

The guests hushed and leaned forward.

Getaelon inclined his head. 'Well, Your Majesty, it began—as you all know—at the start of Autumn's Rising, when your wonderful new fleet set out from the port here in Elisdrium. By the way, where is our Royal Engineer?' He searched around the gathering.

'Dear Master Meretan does not dine with us tonight,' Zjandius said. 'His work is his true king, and I am but a pretender to the throne.'

The guests tittered in response.

'Well, they are damn fine ships, Your Majesty,' the Admiral said. 'He deserves a feast of his own, if I may say it.'

The King raised his cup. 'To Colus Meretan and the genius within him.'

'To Colus Meretan!' The others cheered and drank.

Terzjin's lip curled. Most of them probably had no idea who Colus was.

Getaelon swallowed his wine and continued. 'We rowed south along the rocky cliffs for many days. The winds served us well until we rounded the desolate cape at the far south of Sasiion. We struggled against contrary breezes for a few days without success. So, we sailed back to a beach where we could take water from a stream and dry our ships. After nearly two weeks, the winds swung west, and we could put out again. We made swifter progress as the coast changed from stone cliffs to empty, barren plains. Provisions are scarce there, Your Majesty, but we were careful with what we had. On a few nights, we met Rugadi nomads and traded for water and fresh game from the hinterland.'

'The Rugadi? Even there?' King Zjandius asked.

'Your Majesty,' a flood prince called out, 'the Rugadi roam wherever they wish in the empty lands between river and flood, sea and mountain. They are a *menace*.'

'It is true, My King,' Queen Nanepti said. 'They have even raided villages near Emzentanis.'

'I hear you all,' Zjandius said, 'but times have changed. Have there been raids since they pledged to me?'

'Well, no ...' the flood prince said.

'Precisely.' The King tapped his fork on the table. 'Please, Admiral, continue.'

Getaelon nodded. 'We sailed along the coast, north and eastwards until we came to the marshlands where the Emzen meets the sea. Our guides were invaluable here, Your Majesty. With their help, we navigated the reedy passages to the isle of Khemeto. They were ready for us, these Khemetese. They must have received warning from spies long before, and no doubt our forced stop on the coast gave them time to prepare. You see, Your Majesty, Khemeto sits on an island shielded from the open sea by a long sandbar, like this.' He used his cup and fork to lay out a map on the table. 'Shallows and sandbars on both sides of the island block most approaches. So, with only a few ships, they can shield all entrances to the lagoon they use as a port. Which is exactly what we found as we sailed to the city.'

'What did you do?' Lord Corilien asked.

The admiral grinned. 'Exactly what we planned, sir. We used the catapults and pots of *tecnaris* that Colus so helpfully designed. The Khemetese withdrew their craft in short order after we set a few alight. And then, once we entered the lagoon, they massed their fleet and tried to overwhelm our ships. But I do not think they could comprehend what we had at our disposal. We flung so much fire at their fleet that they became a funeral pyre in the middle of the lagoon. Thereafter, we rained arrows upon the surviving vessels and rammed them in the traditional way, until all were sunk.

'Once we cleared the lagoon, we turned our attention to the city and prepared to land on the beach. But they covered the sands with soldiers, leaving no safe place to disembark. So we arrayed our boats and used the remaining tecnaris to hurl fire upon the defenders.' Getaelon swallowed and paused for a moment.' There was much screaming. I'm sorry to report that, in the chaos, the palace of Khemeto caught alight and was utterly burnt—as was much of the city alongside the water. It was an inferno, Your Majesty. We had to pull our ships back to avoid falling embers and the same fate.'

King Zjandius stared at the table and nodded slowly. 'A difficult situation, I'm sure. Go on, Admiral.'

The admiral took a deep gulp of wine. The servant stepped forward to refill his cup.

Getaelon nodded in thanks. 'For hours, we stood upon our decks and watched the city burn. We waited for some signal of surrender, but there was nothing. When the fires calmed, we found a safe place to drag our ships ashore and met no resistance on the beach. Instead, we found a young girl with her guards waiting on the sand amidst the smoke and falling cinders. The sole-surviving child of the Prince of Khemeto. You see, Your Majesty, the Prince was on the lagoon when they joined us in battle, along with his two eldest sons, commanding the largest ships. His younger boys and another daughter were trapped in the burning palace when it collapsed. No one remained in command to surrender. The girl said little—just...watched me as the guards explained.'

'And what of her?' Zjandius asked.

'When the flood princes and their armies arrived to occupy the city, they promised to take her north,' Getaelon replied.

'My family in Emzentanis are acting as her guardian,' Nanepti said.

The King nodded. 'Let it be done.'

The feast continued for a few more hours, but Zjandius and Nanepti left early. Terzjin and Wederet escorted the royal couple to their chambers.

'Wederet can stand guard for the first part of the night,' the King said when they reached the doors to the Royal Chambers. He held Nanepti around the waist.

'But, Your Majesty, I always take the first shift,' Terzjin said.

Zjandius smiled. 'Rest, Master Maltorus. You have earned it.'

'They will be safe on my watch,' Wederet said.

Terzjin pursed his lips, then bowed his head. 'As you command, My King.'

He went to the mess hall under the palace and ate his soup alone at a corner table. The hall was loud, with gossiping, singing guards, and other palace staff.

After his meal, Terzjin went to the counter at the front of the hall to leave his bowl and spoon. The girl—Valcero's friend—was there, gathering up dishes to return to the kitchen.

'Saedelas?' Terzjin called out.

She glanced up and gasped. At the same moment, Terzjin flinched as he saw a strange thing, a gleaming light that flared in her eyes. She stepped away.

'Wait.' Terzjin approached her. 'Wait a moment.'

Saedelas gaped at him and backed up against the wall.

'Please, sir!' An old woman marched over. A cook from the kitchens. 'Won't you leave the girl alone, sir! She gets enough trouble as it is from the boys.'

'No, I'm not...' Terzjin looked again at where Saedelas was standing, but she had run off. The hall went silent. Everyone was staring at him. 'Yes, of course. Sorry.' He bowed his head and hurried away.

He went up to his room and stood amidst his things, staring at his unmade bed. Bright moonlight shone into the room, but it was far too early to sleep. Perhaps a walk, then?

Master Maltorus crossed the courtyard and entered a door in the wall. He felt his way up the dark steps to the parapet. Outside, the white walls glowed in the light of the two full moons. He nodded to the guards as they passed. A warm, damp sea breeze ruffled his hair. Down below, citizens wandered between the taverns and their homes. Soldiers patrolled the streets with torches—almost unnecessary in the autumn twilight. Barking dogs and a shouted conversation between two women on their rooftops cut through the dull, ever-present roar of the waterfall. He leaned against the parapet and watched the waters of the Tiana tumble to the sea. The western horizon bore a faint glow under the tall clouds. The sky was not yet black.

The girl, Saedelas. It was not the first time Terzjin had seen that gleaming in someone's eyes. Years ago, while walking on a busy street in Etorium, he had passed a young man going the other way, deep in thought. He had glanced up into Terzjin's face, and the man's eyes had lit up, as if white stars burned inside. Terzjin froze abruptly, shocked. The young man had also stopped, stared at him, then run off into the crowds. And of course, the day he met Valcero, when the boy had tried to steal his coins. The painted lady who flirted with him in the market square. Her eyes had shone too, if only for an instant.

And then that staff fight at the arena, the day he took Valcero. The winner's eyes had gleamed in the same way, or had Terzjin only imagined it?

Master Maltorus strolled along the parapet and into the corner tower. Inside, three guards sat around a fire burning in a small brazier, eating dinner.

'Come, sit with us, Master Maltorus,' one said.

Another guard grinned. 'Tell us stories from the palace. How was the grand feast?'

'Thank you, gentlemen, but I'll keep patrolling,' Terzjin replied. 'As for the feast, it was as grand as you can imagine. Though...' He peered into their stew pot. 'Perhaps it did not quite compare to your fine supper.'

They burst out laughing.

'Next time, gentlemen?' Master Maltorus said.

The guards waved him off as he left the tower and went along the western wall. Halfway along, he stopped and leaned against the stone again. The entire port was spread out far below. The sea shimmered in the moonlight between the dark hulls of the ships—some floating on the water, others dragged onto the sand. The naval fleet, fresh from its conquest of Khemeto, was berthed on the left. To the right lay a multitude of merchant galleys and fishing boats. Lamp lights twinkled from the windows of the port houses, taverns, brothels, and warehouses—merchants counting coins at the end of another day.

Why hadn't he seen that gleaming in Saedelas' eyes until now?

A gentle swell surged past the sandbars and breakwaters into the port. The floating vessels bobbed and twisted at their berths. The moonlight briefly shone on the hull of one particular galley before it returned to the shadows.

Master Maltorus narrowed his eyes. He waited. Another slow swell entered the port. It lifted the vessel into the light, just long enough to reveal an old, worn hull with a painted eye. Not an Elisdrian ship. What colour was the railing? Impossible to tell under the moons. But there was a cabin at the stern. A light twinkled from its door.

Terzjin's heart lurched.

He strode as fast as possible back to his room, stopping only to grab his cloak and sword. He strapped the weapon to his belt and flung the cloak around his shoulders as he marched through the palace. He passed through the palace gate with only the barest farewell to the guards, crossed the square, and hurried down the cliff road.

The few citizens on the road stepped out of his way as he bore down the slope. Snatches of domestic life reached his ears as he passed the curtained doorways in the cliff face—a crying baby, singing, a lyre, an argument. Scents of spiced meat wafted around him.

Master Maltorus slowed to a measured walk as he reached the port. He relaxed his jaw and let his heart go quiet. The streets were busier here, but now he passed the locals without so much as a glance in his direction. No familiar faces. He went through the twisting alleyways and came to the wharf. The air reeked of salt and rotting fish. There it was, the *Dela,* moored at the end of a long wooden jetty.

He crept over the wooden boards. The ship had no gangplank, but was close enough to vault aboard. Some muffled voices came up from below. He trod quietly across the deck and pulled aside the cloth to duck inside the cabin.

Seated at the table, with his head in his hands, was the smuggler Taerinus Ladistrien.

'A long time,' Terzjin murmured.

Taerinus flinched and looked up, but as soon as he caught sight of Terzjin, he slumped. The smuggler's face was grey, even in the light of the oil lamp. Dark pouches hung under his eyes.

Master Maltorus folded his arms. 'I thought I ordered you to report to me in *Etorium*, Master Ladistrien. *And* you are a few years late.'

'I'm sorry, sir,' the smuggler whined. 'I really am. We—I—we had no choice.'

Terzjin glanced around. 'And where's Jeigo? Gambling, drinking, or—?'

Taerinus burst into tears and buried his face in his hands. 'They took him,' he replied between sobs.

Terzjin stepped forward. 'What are you talking about?'

Taerinus sat up and wailed. 'They took him! I had no *choice*, sir. It was "do this thing"—or lose Jeigo.'

Master Maltorus put his hands on the tabletop and leaned over the man. 'What is "this thing"?' His voice went low. 'What did you do?'

The smuggler gazed up at him. 'Forgive me, sir. *Please*. I had no choice. "Bring him here, or lose Jeigo"—that's what they told me.'

Terzjin backed away. 'Who's "him"?'

'Maybe there is time—I don't know,' Taerinus babbled. 'He told me to wait here, to await his return.'

Master Maltorus pointed his finger at the smuggler. 'You stay here. You go *nowhere*.'

'I'm sorry!' Taerinus called out as Terzjin ran away. 'I'm sorry, I'm sorry!'

Terzjin leapt off the deck and sprinted down the jetty.

CHAPTER EIGHT

SASIION — AUTUMN'S REIGN — 436

Terzjin hammered on the door of the port warden's house. The warden opened it, smelling of beer.

Terzjin held up his amulet and pointed to the *Dela*. 'That galley does not leave, do you hear me? By order of the King. On pain of *death*. Do you hear me?'

The man's eyes widened, and he nodded.

'Round up whatever guards you can find and make sure no one leaves that ship. And if anyone tries to board, arrest them. I want them all alive. Understand?'

The warden nodded again. 'Yessir.'

Terzjin dashed off. 'I'll be back shortly!' he called over his shoulder.

He shoved through the alleyway crowds and ran up cliff road to the city. His breath burned, but he would not slow. He did not care who saw him or what they might think. He sprinted.

As he dashed towards gate, the palace guards raised their shields and spears, then leapt aside in recognition.

'Open!' Master Maltorus rasped.

He ran through the courtyard and into the palace. People turned and stared as he raced past. Up the stairs, back and forth, down the corridor, around the corner, and there...

Captain Wederet leaned against the door with his arms folded. He straightened up as Terzjin approached. 'What's wrong?'

Master Maltorus shook his head. 'Open up.'

'What?'

Terzjin pushed past him and through the doors to the royal

apartments. He marched towards the inner doors at the end of the passageway.

'You can't just—' Wederet hurried after him. 'What's the matter?'

At that moment, someone screamed.

Terzjin sprang forward to open the inner doors. Locked. He slammed his body against the wood and fell into the room as it broke apart. He scrambled to his feet and darted around the furniture to the bedchamber.

On the other side of the wide bed stood Zjandius and Nanepti, stiff and wide-eyed in their nightclothes. Nanepti clutched a dagger. Blood streamed from the blade down to her elbow and was spattered across her cotton gown.

Terzjin drew his sword and strode around the bed towards his king.

Zjandius stirred. 'Stop, Terzjin.' He raised a hand.

A body lay on the floor between the king and queen, with blood oozing from wounds in the stomach and chest. A middle-aged man dressed in a brown tunic and cloak, with a beard and curly black hair turning grey. His dark eyes stared at the ceiling. A long dagger lay beside him.

'Are you hurt, Zjandius?' Terzjin asked.

'I'm fine. Put your sword away.'

Master Maltorus sheathed his blade and looked to the Queen. 'Your Grace?'

She shook her head, breathing heavily, gazing down at the man.

'We were sleeping, though not deeply,' the King murmured.

'And that?' Terzjin pointed at the bloody dagger in Nanepti's hand.

'I keep it under my pillow,' she said.

'*What?*'

Nanepti faced him. 'As I told you before, Master Maltorus, I am a princess in a land of princes.' Her hands trembled.

Zjandius moved to put an arm around her shoulder. 'How did he get in?'

'Wederet,' Terzjin muttered.

'Your Majesties, I am *so* deeply sorry.'

They all turned to find the captain at the bedchamber entrance. Wederet took in the blood on Nanepti and slowly shook his head.

'You...' Terzjin advanced on him.

'We bolted the inner door from our side before we went to sleep,' King Zjandius said. 'Calm yourself, Terzjin. Captain Wederet did not let him in.'

Master Maltorus stopped. The balcony doors stood open to admit the sea breeze. 'He must have climbed in, or hid himself here earlier in the day.'

'I failed in my duties, Your Majesties.' Wederet sank to his knees. 'I am not worthy.'

Terzjin faced his king. '*I* should have been here.'

Zjandius shook his head. 'What difference would it have made?'

Master Maltorus knelt to inspect the assassin. The dagger was iron, nondescript, and not of a style he recognised. The belt held no pouch, nothing that could identify the man, no clue where he came from. 'He doesn't look like he's from Sasiion.' But something about his face, his features, seemed familiar. The assassin's eyes twitched. Blood bubbled from his gaping mouth.

'He's alive!' Terzjin leaned closer.

The assassin's eyes focused on him. The lips twitched.

'Who are you?' Terzjin asked in Old Sasiion.

The stranger wheezed softly.

'Who are you?' Terzjin asked again, in Caerian. 'Who sent you?'

The assassin blinked at him.

A feeling touched Terzjin's heart. 'Who sent you?' he asked, this time in Galatani.

The man's eyes went wide. His mouth tightened.

Master Maltorus let his voice turn hard and dark. *'Tell me who sent you.'* Cold fury hummed through his fingers as he dug into the assassin's shoulders.

The man gasped, and more blood spilt from his mouth. 'My King.'

'*Who?*' Terzjin shook him, but the body was already softening in his hands.

The stranger's breath turned ragged, then quiet, and he spoke no more.

'What was that?' Zjandius asked. 'What did he say?'

Terzjin shook his head and stood. 'Not much of anything. But he is—was—Galatani.'

'Which means...'

Terzjin Maltorus gathered himself. 'Your Majesty, let me take lenotare to the port. I will find answers there.'

Terzjin led Taerinus, flanked by two lenotare, into the King's chambers. The rest of the *Dela*'s crew were locked up in the dungeons beneath the palace.

Zjandius and Nanepti sat on their thrones, with a downcast Wederet guarding the corner. More lenotare stood at attention at the walls. The royal couple wore robes, but without their usual court finery. The bell for the third hour had just rung. Braziers along the walls provided soft light.

'Your Majesty,' Master Maltorus announced, 'here is the smuggler.'

'Where is Lord Corilien and Prefect Taeto?' the King asked. 'Astulus?'

'On their way, Your Majesty,' Terzjin answered.

'They should be here,' Zjandius said, then shrugged and beckoned. 'Bring forth the smuggler.'

Terzjin nudged Taerinus toward the thrones. The smuggler stumbled as he walked. He kept his eyes on the long carpet.

'Do you know who I am?' Zjandius asked in Caerian.

Taerinus nodded without looking up. 'Yes, Your Majesty. And you have my deepest apologies.' He bowed low.

'So, you recognise my authority.' Zjandius leaned forward with his hand on his chin. 'And yet you bring an assassin into my—into *our* home. Tell me, what does that make you?'

The Ladistrien shuddered.

'It makes you a traitor,' the King said.

Taerinus dropped to his knees. 'Your Majesty, they gave me no choice. They took my Jeigo hostage and forced me—at spearpoint—to bring the assassin.' He knocked his forehead against the floor and began to sob.

'Jeigo?' The King looked to Terzjin with a raised eyebrow.

'Jeigo Ladistrien, Your Majesty,' Terzjin replied. 'The other smuggler.'

Nanepti leaned over to Zjandius to ask a question. The King murmured a translation of the conversation while Taerinus cried into the carpet.

The chamber doors opened.

'Lord Corilien and Prefect Taeto!' the lenotarus announced.

The aristocrats entered, both with messy hair and hastily dressed. They bowed and assumed their typical places on the side of the room.

Lord Corilien rubbed his face. 'Good morning, Your Majesty. My apologies for arriving late.'

'What is going on?' Taeto asked.

'A few hours ago, an assassin attempted to murder the Queen and me in our bed,' Zjandius explained.

Lord Corilien started. He and Taeto exchanged looks of seemingly genuine surprise. Perhaps trustworthy after all.

Zjandius gestured to the Ladistrien. 'And here is the one who smuggled him into Elisdrium. No need to apologise, Lord Corilien, for we have only begun to question this...wretch. *I* apologise for summoning you both at this hour, but we must establish the truth quickly. Now,' he said to Taerinus, 'get up.'

The smuggler pulled himself to his feet, sniffed, and wiped his eyes with the back of his hand.

Firstly,' Zjandias said, 'who sent you with the assassin?'

'The Rhenivian Thane Heirik, Your Majesty.'

A quiet gasp passed around the room.

'The one who rules in my palace in Etorium?'

Taerinus nodded.

'How many assassins did you bring?'

Taerinus looked up. 'Just that one, sir. I swear it!'

'Are you *absolutely* certain?' Terzjin hissed in the smuggler's ear. 'Consider your answer.'

Taerinus nodded vigorously without taking his eyes off the King. 'Your Majesty, I swear by everything dear. Just him.'

The King sat against the backrest of his throne. 'So, why? Why plot *now* to kill me?'

Taerinus wrung his hands. 'Because... because he is angry with you, King Zjandius. Angry when he found out you planned to marry the

Princess—I mean, Queen.' He bobbed his head towards Nanepti. 'He heard you were uniting all of Sasiion. He said, he said...'

'He said what?' Zjandius asked.

Taerinus swallowed. 'I heard him say that you...were supposed to wither away and die here.'

'Ha.' The King turned to Nanepti and muttered another quick translation. He paused and frowned, then leaned forward again and glared at Taerinus. 'Tell me, smuggler, how did this Thane Heirik know so much about my doings in the Old Kingdom?'

Taerinus coughed. 'Rumours pass back and forth on the trading ships, Your Majesty. A few boats still come through the isthmus.'

The King's jaw tightened. 'Have you, Taerinus Ladistrien, visited Elisdrium in this time? Have *you* passed on some of these rumours? Do not lie to me.'

Taerinus bowed his head and put his fist to his mouth.

'How many times, smuggler?'

Taerinus hunched over and blinked away more tears.

'We should execute you before the sun rises,' King Zjandius murmured. 'Oh yes, the old laws do not protect you in Sasiion.'

'Hear, hear!' Lord Corilien cried.

Taerinus shook his head. His eyes were wide with terror. 'In the name of the Lord of Life, I beg you, Oh King. They will kill Jeigo if I do not return.'

'You are in no position to beg,' Terzjin snapped.

Zjandius folded his arms. '*You* would deserve such a fate, Taerinus Ladistrien. But first, before I pass judgment, you will answer more questions. Answer truthfully, smuggler.'

Taerinus nodded.

'Tell me about this Heirik. What kind of ruler is he?'

Taerinus searched the floor. 'He is a strict ruler, Your Majesty, and violent. Parts of Etorium still lie burnt and ruined—as does Goretonum village. There are damaged cities and towns across Caeria. He dispenses justice, but often harshly. They say people disappear...'

The King nodded. 'How many soldiers does he command?'

The smuggler shrugged. 'Hard to say, Your Majesty. I know most of them have gone home, back over the sea. But many thousands are still camped near Etorium and in smaller groups around the island. Also, the Holy Warriors.'

'Holy Warriors?'

'Of the Corn Mother and the Flood Father, sir. They build temples to the Rhenivian gods in every city and try to convert Caerians to their worship.

'Why do the citizens tolerate all this?'

'They are scared, My King. After what happened to Lord Sanadin and his family...'

'Yes, I know what happened.' Zjandius' face darkened. 'And what of the other aristocrats?'

'They are fearful as well, Your Majesty. The Thane holds Lord Octerian hostage in Goretonum fortress. But Heirik also allows the lords to own and trade in slaves again, to keep them happy.'

King Zjandius scowled. 'Of course he does. And the Aventan?'

Taerinus shrugged. 'Not sure, Oh King. They say Lord Aventan and his family perished in Lastria, but...'

'But?'

'There are only rumours, Your Majesty. Tavern stories shared amongst smugglers.'

'And? Don't be shy to share rumours *now*, Taerinus Ladistrien.'

'Some say at least a few Aventan survived and escaped. Others claim Lord Aventan was never in Lastria when the Rhenivians came, that he had some kind of warning. They speak of bandits in the hills and forests who serve the Aventan and prey on Rhenivians wherever they find them. Some smugglers may pass them food and other supplies, but they do not admit it.'

Zjandius looked over to Lord Corilien.

Corilien frowned. 'It is possible. Sorveo always was a wily old bastard.'

'Interesting,' Zjandius mused. 'So, all Caeria fears and serves Thane Heirik, yes?'

'Not *all*, sir. Heirik has not yet conquered the Nedolian Forest.

'You mean the Torecti?' The King leaned forward. 'The tribes still resist?'

'I know he has sent soldiers into Nedolian, Your Majesty. Many never return. They say it infuriates Heirik. He has ordered the forest burnt, to drive the Torecti into the open where his riders can fight them better.'

'And?'

'The forest does not burn well, My King, though they have done some damage.'

'I've always maintained the Torecti are a plague of wasps,' Lord Corilien said. 'Best not to go banging on their nests. Leave them be in the trees. It gives satisfaction to hear the straw-heads have not yet learnt this lesson.'

King Zjandius settled back in his throne. 'One final question for you, smuggler. What else does Thane Heirik know about me and our work here in Sasiion?'

Taerinus wiped the back of his neck. 'He knows you are building a new cantaris and a new fleet. He knows you are uniting all the princes—and princesses.' He nodded again to Nanepti. 'But he thinks you will remain trapped here forever, that you are not...not strong enough to defeat him, Your Majesty. That is *his* opinion, of course.'

Zjandius stared at the smuggler with a half-smile on his lips. There was a long silence, filled only by the crackling braziers. Finally, he sighed and stood up. 'My lords, I apologise once more for interrupting your dreams. Please, retire now, and we will meet in the proper morning to discuss a plan.'

'Not at all, Your Majesty.' Lord Corilien bowed. 'Glad you're safe.'

'Rest well, cousin,' Taeto said.

They departed the hall.

'You are dismissed, Taerinus Ladistrien,' the King announced. 'You shall remain in the dungeons with your crew while we decide your fate. Take him now,' he ordered the lentotare.

Taerinus shivered as the guards dragged him away. Zjandius explained the rest of the interrogation to Nanepti in Old Sasiion, and Terzjin waited while everyone, except Captain Wederet, left.

'Step forward, Master Maltorus,' the King said.

Terzjin went to the thrones as Wederet joined him.

'Time is running out,' King Zjandius said, now in Old Sasiion. 'We must assume Thane Heirik will send more assassins—or worse—once he discovers his plot failed.'

'I will protect you, Your Majesty,' Terzjin declared.

Wederet stared grimly ahead. '*We* will protect Your Majesties.'

'Of course, but we must do more,' the King said. 'We must strike back and take Caeria. However, we are not ready. Our cantaris is not large enough to defeat the Rhenivians.'

'My King,' Terzjin said. 'We should attack them as they tried to attack you.'

Zjandius frowned. 'What do you mean?'

'Vengeance. Send an assassin to Etorium.'

Zjandius shook his head. 'Absolutely not. That will create chaos that we cannot control. Besides, it is dishonourable and I have enough dishonour weighing upon me as it is.'

Master Maltorus breathed heavily. 'It's what they deserve, Zjandius!'

Nanepti frowned. 'A bodyguard should *not* speak to his king that way.'

'It's alright.' Zjandius put his hand on hers. 'I value Terzjin's honest counsel—as long as it's given *privately*.' He gave his bodyguard a warning look. 'Many do not receive what they deserve, Master Maltorus—whether reward or punishment.'

'Could we not recruit more soldiers and train them up quickly?' Wederet asked.

Nanepti shook her head. 'We cannot afford to ask more from the princes.' She turned to Zjandius. Not quite yet, My King.'

Zjandius nodded. 'I agree. So, it would be best for someone to visit Caeria and find allies already there. And that someone would be *you*, Terzjin Maltorus.'

'Your Majesty, my place is here, to prot—'

'Your place is wherever I need you,' the King snapped. 'Wederet will serve us in your absence.'

Terzjin looked at the captain. 'But, Your Majesty...'

'No buts. He will serve us well, because he now understands the consequences of failure, correct?'

Wederet bowed deeply.

'And Terzjin,' the King continued, 'this will perhaps be your most challenging task ever. Not only do I need you to find allies amongst compromised aristocrats—and aristocrats who may be nothing more than spirits—I also need you to seek help from the Torecti-of-the-Trees.'

'The Torecti?' Terzjin scratched his head. 'Your Majesty, what chance would they help us? They kill trespassers on their land. They do not talk to Caerians, or anyone.'

'Who are these *Torecti*?' Nanepti asked.

'A tribal people who have lived in Caeria since before my ancestors came,' Zjandius replied. 'The Torecti-of-the-Trees remained apart and unconquered after the Sasiion and the Torecti-of-the-Fields became one people. Many wars raged between forest dwellers and Caerians until my ancestors made a pact with them, which brought lasting peace. Part of the agreement was that no Caerian enters their land, and in return, no Torecti enters ours. There has been no contact for more than 150 years.' He blew out a long sigh. 'Now, we must break that pact for everyone's sake.'

The Queen raised an eyebrow. 'An impossible situation, surely?'

'I agree, it is madness,' Terzjin said.

Zjandius chuckled. 'And that is not even the hardest part of the problem. After 150 years without trade, meetings, or any kind of diplomacy, no living Caerian knows their language. And there would be no Torecti who speak our tongue either. Who knows what could happen if you stumble into their forest shouting "Hello"?' He rubbed his face. 'I am unsure *how* you will speak with them, Terzjin, but you must try. We will think of a stratagem before you go, which will be tomorrow.'

'Tomorrow?' Master Maltorus blinked.

'Every day counts.'

A faint thought prodded Terzjin's heart. An old memory. 'Actually, Your Majesty, I know someone who *can* speak to the Torecti.'

'Someone in Caeria?'

Terzjin shook his head. 'No, here in Elisdrium. Perhaps he could go with me.'

CHAPTER NINE

SASIION — AUTUMN'S REIGN — 436

It was morning, and Valcero was with Sefti, Eneb, and Adjet in the great barns, watching the Queen's stablehands feed her elephants. The towering beasts stretched their long trunks between the beams to sniff the air. A stablehand hefted a pitchfork of straw to the barricade. An elephant curled her trunk around the straw to lift it away, and passed the bundle to her smiling mouth. Her tusks knocked against the wooden bars, and a low groan rumbled through Valcero's bones.

The boy crept forward and put his hands on the beams. The closest elephant shuffled about in her pen, which reeked of manure and dried grass. Her ears flapped and brushed his face with warm air.

Valcero chuckled. 'So the Queen takes them into battle?' he asked the nearest stablehand.

Sefti grinned. 'Yes, that's why they call them *war* elephants.'

'It must be terrifying,' Valcero remarked.

Adjet looked up at the beast. 'For the elephants, or for the enemy?'

Valcero shrugged.

The beast regarded him with a dark, long-lashed eye. She seemed sad and wise, or perhaps only curious. She swayed her trunk about and held the tip just above Valcero's arm. The little flap at the end flexed as she tasted the air.

'Can ... can I touch her?' Valcero asked the stablehand.

'I'm sure it's fine,' the Emzentanian replied.

Valcero raised his hand and brushed his fingers against the tip of her trunk—leathery with the odd fibrous hair. She recoiled a little, but then slid her trunk up his forearm. He broke out in goosebumps. She could snap his limbs like kindling.

The stablehand offered him a handful of straw.

'Alright.' Valcero took the straw and held it up for the elephant.

She smelled the grass, then pulled it from his grasp. Her trunk curled inwards, and she flapped her ears as she chewed.

Eneb sniggered. 'You look like you're in love.'

Valcero blushed.

The stablehand laughed. 'There are many days when I feel the same.' He held out another handful of straw. 'More?'

Valcero took the grass and offered it to the beast. As she plucked the grass from his right hand, he stroked her trunk with his left. She lingered under his touch.

'Valcero.'

The boy spun about.

Terzjin smiled faintly. 'Good morning, lad.' Stubble covered his jaw, and dark rings sat under his eyes.

'Good morning, Master Maltorus.' Valcero was not sure whether or not to smile.

Terzjin gazed around the barn and up at the elephants. 'A special place to visit, is it not?'

'I had a short break between my duties,' the boy said, 'so I came here to learn. I'll go back to Master Meretan now.' He made to leave.

'Wait, Valcero.' Terzjin raised his hand. 'I need you to come with me. It's urgent. And Master Meretan is already there, so don't worry about him.'

'Am I in trouble?'

'Gods, no, nothing like that.' Terzjin rubbed his face. 'Actually, we need your help with something. Shall we go?'

Valcero nodded and followed Master Maltorus out of the stable, waving to the other boys and the stablehands as he left.

They crossed the courtyard in silence, past groups of whispering palace staff. When they saw Terzjin approach, they hurried off in different directions.

As the pair reached the side door, Master Maltorus stopped and turned to him. 'Look, I know we haven't spoken much lately.'

Valcero bit his lip and looked through the doorway.

'I've been very busy helping the King,' Terzjin said. 'And I'm sure you've been very busy helping Master Meretan as well. It's a difficult time. I'm sorry, Valcero.'

The boy nodded slowly and stared at the ground. 'It's alright,' he muttered.

Terzjin patted his back. 'But...' He started walking again. '...it seems we'll have plenty of time to catch up.'

Valcero looked up with raised eyebrows.

'I'll explain more when we get there. But first, we need to clean you up a bit.'

Master Maltorus took him into the servants' wing, to a room at the end of the corridor at the bottom of a staircase. He opened the door and ushered Valcero inside. It reminded him of Terzjin's quarters in the palace wall in Etorium, but the stonework was smoother and the window was bigger. The furniture was largely the same—a low, unmade bed, a wooden chest, and a table with a bowl of water. A light beam pierced the rising steam and shimmered against a little bronze mirror.

'You sleep here?' he asked Terzjin.

'Ha! Ideally, yes. Now, can you wash yourself with the water and cloth? Your face and hands at least. I don't think we could present you to the King and Queen while smelling of elephants.'

'King and Queen?'

Terzjin grinned. 'As I said, I'll explain when we get there. Quick please. There's much to do today.'

Valcero frowned and went to the bowl. He splashed warm, lemony water on his face and hair, then rubbed himself dry with the cotton cloth while Terzjin rummaged in the chest behind him.

When Valcero turned around, Master Maltorus had changed from his grey tunic into his royal blue uniform. He was retying his sword to his belt.

Terzjin inspected the boy. 'Good. My turn.' The man splashed his face and hair, then picked up a short bronze blade and scraped it across his cheeks and chin a few times while peering into the dim mirror. He paused and looked at Valcero. 'Do you ever use this?' He waved the blade.

The boy stroked his top lip. 'No, not yet.'

'Soon, I'm sure.' Terzjin resumed his shave. 'Though you should do it more slowly and carefully than this.' He blew the hairs off the blade then splashed more lemon water on his face, wincing slightly. 'I see you've made some friends. That's good.'

Valcero shrugged.

After patting his face dry, Terzjin straightened up. 'Right, let's go.'

Terzjin took him up the stairs, past three landings and several guards, who saluted as they went. The boy had been so high up in the palace before. Terzjin smiled and winked as they strode down a broad corridor to a pair of large wooden doors. The lenotare saluted and admitted them inside.

It was a large chamber, not quite a hall, lit from tall windows to the left. The walls were painted with scenes of ancient hunts, battles, and parties. A royal blue carpet led up to the two thrones on the dais at the end of the room. King Zjandius and Queen Nanepti sat there. Valcero froze, then looked to Terzjin.

'A quick bow is all that's required,' Master Maltorus whispered. He nudged the boy forward. 'Your Majesties,' he announced in Old Sasiion, 'I present Valcero Baradon.'

Valcero stumbled forward and half-bowed, then tried to bow again properly.

'Step forward, Master Baradon,' the King commanded.

No one had ever called him that. Valcero shuffled closer to the thrones. The Queen seemed to be grinning behind her hand. Gold dust sparkled on her skin, though she too looked tired. The boy's heart thudded. Master Meretan stood to the side, in the shadow between two windows.

'Please, Valcero…' The King smiled and beckoned him closer. 'Don't be afraid. I'm sure you're wondering why we summoned you.'

Valcero nodded. 'Yes, Your Majesty,' he added.

Colus stepped closer and examined Valcero with nervous eyes.

Terzjin put his hand on the boy's shoulder. 'Valcero, do you remember when we conducted the funerals in Nemeket?'

'Yes?' How could he forget?

'You said some words during the ceremony?'

The boy thought for a moment. 'The words to release the spirit. It goes like—'

'No need to repeat them here.' Terzjin looked around the room and smiled. 'That would be... unlucky. But what is the language of those words?'

'The language of the Forest People,' Valcero replied.

They all watched him intently.

'Do you mean the Torecti?' Colus asked.

Valcero nodded. 'Yes, sir.'

King Zjandius leaned forward. 'Do you only know these verses, Valcero, or can you speak more?'

'I know more—Your Majesty.'

The King opened his hands. 'Could you... converse with a Torecti?'

It had been so long, not since he was with Praehenna and Aulix. Praehenna. Aulix. But the *King* was asking. 'Your Majesty, I can talk with Torecti. I have spoken with them.'

King Zjandius leaned back in his throne. 'Explain.'

'I... I learned from two Torecti. They looked after me in the Cleotan house for many years. They taught me when I was very little.'

The King looked over to Colus, who shrugged.

'I don't know much of how he lived before he came to my house,' Master Meretan said. 'It is possible.'

The King stroked his chin. 'Most intriguing. So, there have been Torecti quietly living amongst us—even in Etorium—in violation of the pact. I wonder why. Valcero, what were those Torecti doing in the Cleotan house?'

The boy swallowed. 'They were slaves, like me, sir... Your Majesty. Aulix and Praehenna were—are—their names.' Where are they now?

'Aulix. Praehenna.' The King stared into the distance. 'Slaves *would* make sense. Perhaps they wandered out of their forest one day and were caught.' He straightened up. 'Valcero, are *you* a Torecti?'

He blinked and looked around. 'I... I... don't—do not know, Your Majesty.'

The King cocked his head to the side. 'Could you be? Do you know your ancestry?'

'He does not have the typical appearance, Your Majesty,' Colus said. He looked Valcero up and down. 'Wrong hair, complexion, and eyes—if the old writings are anything to go by. Also, "Valcero Baradon" is certainly a Caerian name.'

'Baradon is not a common name, though,' King Zjandius said. He narrowed his eyes. 'I am unsure if I have heard it before, or where...'

'They said they couldn't take me to the Forest,' Valcero almost whispered.

King Zjandius sighed and gathered himself. 'Anyway, no matter. What I must know is that you can *speak* Torecti. So, let us test you, Valcero Baradon. Tell me how you would ask, "What is the weather today?" '

'Oh, um...' The boy cleared his throat. '*Quan ologunum cumo verae?*'

The King repeated the words under his breath. 'Alright, and then how would I say, "Today the weather is very hot"?'

Valcero nodded. '*Cumo ologunus sumsectarum verae.*'

King Zjandius probed him with questions about the words and grammar of Torecti, until eventually he laughed. 'I suppose I am convinced. Colus?'

Master Meretan nodded. 'I have never known the boy to lie, Your Majesty.'

The King shrugged. 'We do not have much choice but to trust his knowledge.' He sighed and clapped his hands. 'Very well. The boy goes with you, Terzjin.'

'Goes?' Valcero looked to Master Maltorus.

Colus went to stand beside Valcero. 'Your Majesty, are you sure this is wise? The Torecti are... inhospitable. And what about the Rhenivians? The boy will be in great danger. Let me go in his stead.'

'You cannot speak Torecti, Colus,' the King replied gently. 'And even if you did, I could not risk losing you. There is far too much for you to do here whilst we prepare.'

Master Meretan put his hand on Valcero's shoulder. 'But you can risk losing this boy?'

Valcero almost jumped with surprise.

'No, Master Meretan. He will be under Terzjin's protection at all times.'

'That is correct, Your Majesty.' Terzjin put his hand on the boy's other shoulder. 'I will guard him with my life.'

Valcero blinked at the carpet.

'Why not have Valcero teach Master Maltorus what he knows, then Terzjin can go off alone?' Colus said.

The King shook his head. 'There is simply not enough time. They must sail with tomorrow's rising sun. Each wasted day increases the chance the Rhenivians learn what happened here and attack again.'

Master Meretan stepped closer to the throne. 'And how will they sail there, Your Majesty?'

King Zjandius grinned. 'I have decided on a fitting punishment for our smuggler. Instead of death, Taerinus Ladisterien will bear them across the sea.'

'Taerinus?' Now Terzjin looked skeptical. 'Your Majesty, I do not think we should trust him. He *deserves* execution.'

The King shook his head. 'I have decided. His ship will draw less attention around Caerian waters. And you can trust him, Terzjin, by making him trust *you*.'

'I do not follow, Your Majesty.'

The King grinned wider. 'In return for Taerinus' assistance, you are going to promise to rescue Jeigo Ladistrien. He will believe you can do it—you have certainly intimidated him enough. And whilst you are at it, if you should come across any *aristocratic* Caerian hostages, you can free them too. Perhaps that will sway some support to us.'

Valcero looked up at Master Maltorus. 'What is happening?'

Terzjin squeezed his shoulder. 'We're going home, Valcero. Back to Caeria.'

CHAPTER TEN

THE SESURIAN SEA – AUTUMN'S REIGN – 436

The sun was still rising as Terzjin stood on the deck and watched Elisdrium recede. The towering cliffs, the palace, the waterfall, all seemed so small as they vanished over the horizon.

Valcero swayed on his feet as he walked over to join Terzjin. 'Will we see them again?'

Terzjin breathed in the salty air and smiled at the boy. 'I am certain we will.'

'I never even said goodbye,' Valcero murmured.

'Who? Your friends?'

'Oh, uh, no. I didn't mean them.' The boy stared at the wooden planks.

'You'll see her again, Valcero.' Terzjin put an arm around his shoulders. 'What did Colus teach you before we left?'

Valcero looked up. 'About the Torecti? He tried to teach me everything. Anything that might help when we meet them.' He looked a bit green in his cheeks.

Master Maltorus guided him to the prow. 'Come, tell me everything he told you.'

They clung to the railing as the ship pitched into the deepening swell. The crew tugged on ropes to guide the sail into position. The cloth snapped and flapped in the rising breeze. Below deck, the rowers chanted an old sailing song to keep time. Their oars dug into the green water and pulled the craft along at a steady pace.

Taerinus was also on deck but strode down the other side as they approached.

The prow sliced through the waves, and Valcero's usual colour returned as the fresh air blew through his hair.

'So?' Terzjin prompted.

'Well…' Valcero coughed and gripped the wood. 'Master Meretan said the Torecti live very differently from us.'

'How so?'

'They don't grow wheat, barley, or vegetables, nor raise sheep, cattle, or other livestock. They hunt, fish, or forage, and don't use wool to weave their clothing. They don't wear much, but when they do, they use whatever they can find—skins and fur, leaves, feathers. Even spider web.

'Spider web?'

'That's what Master Meretan told me. He also said they don't forge metals, not even copper. They make their tools and weapons from wood, bone, and stones like flint or obsidian. In the past, they stole Caerian weapons or received gifts of bronze from us, which they treasure.' The boy spoke as if reciting a lecture—probably the exact manner in which he received this knowledge.

'And what else?' Terzjin asked.

'The cannibalism stories ***might*** be true, but they may have been invented during the wars. There are also said to be Torecti witches who enchant those who wander into their domain. They turn people into animals. Or they put their victims to sleep for a hundred years, so when they awake, there's no one left who might know them. *If* they awake at all. Sometimes, the witches plant trees over the sleepers and imprison them within the roots.

'That's definitely true,' said a crew member working within earshot.

Master Maltorus frowned at the man, then returned his attention to the boy. 'How will we know when we enter their lands?'

A fine spray blew over them. Gulls wheeled overhead.

Valcero wiped his face. 'Master Meretan said they carve patterns on rocks and trees to mark the border.'

The spray refreshed Terzjin. 'And who rules the Torecti? A king?'

'Master Meretan said that no one really knows. Maybe they have clans and chieftains like the Torecti-of-the-Plains did.'

'Anything else?'

'Not really?' The boy shrugged. 'Master Colus asked me to teach him all the Torecti words I know, but that's when you arrived and said it was time to go.'

Terzjin grinned. 'You'll teach me instead, alright?'

The leg across the Sesurian Sea and along the coast of Hebenia Minor was short and uneventful. The wind and waves calmed once they entered the familiar marshes of the isthmus, so the galley relied on the rowers to propel it through the muddy waters. Valcero cheered and spent the time peering over the railing and looking for crocodiles. Even Taerinus seemed to relax and stand in one place long enough for Terzjin to speak with him.

'We're making good progress,' Master Maltorus remarked.

'For now,' the smuggler replied.

They stood side by side, looking at the hazy hills beyond the marshlands. Taerinus chewed on his fingernail. The air was humid and still.

Taerinus sighed. 'I knew it would be you. I just knew it.'

Terzjin looked at him. 'What do you mean?'

'I was sitting in my cabin, waiting for you. I assumed you'd kill me on the spot. I suppose I'm lucky you arrived before, rather than... after.'

'Maybe you *were* lucky,' Master Maltorus replied. 'The assassin wasn't particularly good.'

Taerinus pulled a face. 'Not as good as you, you mean?'

'But how could you?' Terzjin asked. 'How could you bear someone all that way, for all those weeks, knowing what they planned?'

The smuggler hunched over. 'Bearing him? Like how I am now bearing you? Once again, not by choice.'

'It's not the same,' Terzjin said. *There is to be no vengeance*—the King's last words before their farewells at the palace. *Not by you, nor by anyone else's hand.* 'I'm no assassin. Just a bodyguard and a messenger.'

Taerinus scratched the wooden railing. 'I don't really know what you are, sir.'

'What did you know about him, about the assassin?' Terzjin asked.

'Not much. His name was Sederial. Definitely Galatani. He didn't speak much on the voyage. Took over my cabin and ate his meals there. I slept below deck with the rest of the crew. I didn't mind. Preferable to being near him,' he added pointedly.

Terzjin sighed. 'Taerinus, you can trust me, as I trust you. I will find your brother and bring him to safety.'

'My brother?' The smuggler looked up.

'Yes, your brother. Jeigo?'

Taerinus smiled for the first time. 'Oh no, sir. Jeigo is not my brother.'

'He's not?' Terzjin thought for a moment. 'Oh. Oh, I see.'

The Ladistrien grinned and nodded. 'Yes, and I would do anything for him.'

Master Maltorus frowned. 'Even treason? Aiding the enemy? Ferrying an assassin?'

Taerinus scowled. 'They would have *killed* Jeigo if I didn't. Have you ever loved anyone so much, sir?'

Terzjin gazed into the murky water. 'Of course! I mean, well, no, not exactly.'

Taerinus leaned against the railing. 'Of course, the bastards realised this. And of course, that's only half the reason they chose Jeigo as the hostage and me the ferryman.'

'What do you mean?'

Tall, moss-draped trees shaded the ship as it drifted along the banks of the marsh.

'Jeigo was always the braver of us. And he could see it, that Rhenivian thane. Jeigo never really feared him, just as he never truly feared *you*.' The smuggler half-turned to Master Maltorus. 'He told me more than a few times that we should stay away from Etorium and forget about you, sir. Heirik made me take the assassin because he knew I'd be too scared to resist, that I'd be a useful coward.' Taerinus shook his head. 'I've always been a bit of a coward, and Jeigo knew that too. And yet... he took my name.' He wiped his eye.

Terzjin looked around, unable to meet the smuggler's face. 'Well, now you're helping us, helping your King, and I'll get Jeigo back for you. All will be well and history will remember you kindly, I think.'

Taerinus smiled. 'Forgive me, sir, but I don't think *history* will even remember my name. The histories do not record the deeds of smugglers and their lovers, nor bodyguards, and certainly not servant boys.' He gestured to Valcero at the other end of the ship. 'Kings and generals, yes. The children of gods. Perhaps some of the especially beautiful queens and princesses. True heroes, yes, but not the likes of us.'

Valcero whooped. 'I've found a crocodile! It really does look like a log. Come see!'

They passed through the isthmus without incident and struck out for the open sea, but then their good fortune failed. The sailors watched the skies and muttered amongst themselves. Wispy clouds unfurled from the east as the days passed. Contrary winds nudged the ship from side to side. Valcero complained of seasickness and lay curled up on the deck.

'A great storm is coming,' Taerinus told them in his cabin one morning. 'They are common at this time of year, so we must take shelter.'

'Back to Hebenia Minor?' Terzjin asked.

'No,' the smuggler captain replied. 'There's an island close enough.'

The next day, they awoke to see a low shadow on the northern horizon. It was not Temizros, the Ventian island that Terzjin remembered from their voyage to Elisdrium, but similar.

'The locals call it Pergunda,' Taerinus said while they stood at the prow. 'The southern coast is difficult, but we can wait out the storm there. In fact, this is where we hid during the Rhenivian invasion.'

'You were *here* the whole time?' Terzjin examined the approaching island.

Dark, weatherbeaten cliffs, devoid of trees or bushes, dropped sheer into the sea. There was no sign of a village or port.

Taerinus nodded. 'Honestly, we tried to follow your last orders to scout for news around Deria and the islands. But when we reached these waters, we came across the Rhenivian fleet at Mesedrenum. Some of their ships chased us, perhaps thinking we were spies. We had to use all our strength to row—and all our wits and knowledge of wind and sail—to grab an advantage. We came south to Pergunda, rounded the island, and made for that inlet while we were out of sight.'

'What inlet?' Valcero asked. He hung on the railing, pale-faced but trying his best.

'Ah, it's not so easy to see,' Taerinus replied. 'We've used it often in our ... work.'

The sea surged and foamed against the grey coast. Taerinus went to the rudder to steer, while the crew hauled down the sail. He navigated the *Dela* through a cluster of rocks spattered white with guano and up close alongside the cliffs. 'Threading the needle', as the smuggler called it. At his signal, the portside rowers lifted their oars while the starboard side kept their rhythm. The ship turned hard, and pushed by the swell, they glided into a narrow gap in the rock face.

The channel widened and they came into a small, circular bay of turquoise water, surrounded by tall cliffs and a sloping beach of grey sand on the farthest end, where wavelets lapped ashore. The boom and hiss of the sea echoed faintly through the channel. Gulls circled overhead and in and out of their cliffside nests.

They rowed to the beach, then Taerinus ordered his crew overboard to drag the ship onto the sand with ropes. Terzjin climbed down to help. The water was warm, and the sand coarse between his toes. Once the *Dela* was above the tide line, they took down the mast and sealed the hatches. They tied the sail over the deck and carried their goods up the beach, with Taerinus leading.

At the top of the sand, they came to an overhang cave. The crew hauled out jars of oil and bundles of dry kindling from dark recesses, then prepared a fire pit and torches for light. They collected water from a spring trickling out of a nearby crack in the rock. Once they lit torches, Terzjin could see the back of the cave, filled with chests, barrels, and more jars.

'How long will this storm last?' he asked Taerinus.

The smuggler shrugged. 'If we are very lucky, only a few days. But it could be a week or two before the sea calms *and* the ship dries enough for us to set out again.' He went to complete his tasks.

'Dries enough?' Valcero whispered to Terzjin. 'But it's a ship. Isn't it supposed to be wet?'

Only a few hours later, the sky turned dark and the wind rose, shrieking and spinning around the hidden bay. The gulls took shelter in their nests. The rain began as a few drops here and there, but then settled into a torrent. Sheets of water lashed the cliffs. The travellers were warm and dry in the cave, though the flames guttered and flickered with each gust. Later that night, the wind strengthened to a steady howl. Thunder roared and lightning lit up the cliffs as if it were day. Terzjin had never seen such a tempest. And all the while, the rain poured.

Taerinus spent much of the time at the cave's edge before the curtain of rain, staring outside and running his fingers through the falling water.

Terzjin went to join him in the middle of the night. 'What is it? What do you see?' he asked.

'My *Dela*,' Taerinus replied, still gazing into the darkness. 'I need to make sure it's alright.'

'Aren't we sheltered here? I thought that was the point?'

'Keep looking,' the smuggler said. 'Wait for the lightning.'

A flash came. For an instant, Terzjin saw the beached ship, as seawater frothed around it, not quite reaching the prow. More foamy water gushed into the bay from the channel. Then all went dark. Thunder cracked and boomed overhead.

Taerinus stroked his chin. 'I think we'll be fine. The surge isn't quite high enough.'

'You seem... different here,' Master Maltorus remarked. 'Not such a coward as you said.'

'I cannot *afford* to be a coward. Not now,' Taerinus replied. 'And besides, here, away from kings and customs inspectors, I am the master.' He smiled and patted Terzjin on the back before returning to his sandy bed. 'Good night.'

The wind calmed, and thunder moved on sometime during the night. The rain eased to a steady drizzle by morning but lingered all day. The sailors sat in the cave, watching the weather, sleeping, chatting, and later drinking. Valcero paced around. Terzjin forbade the sailors from giving the boy beer or wine.

As the day wore on, the cook stoked the fire and prepared a meal in a copper cauldron. In went onions, dried mushrooms, and strips of salted mutton. The stew simmered for hours. Terzjin's stomach gurgled, so he tried to distract himself by practising sword moves in his mind.

Valcero approached the cook. 'Excuse me, sir, but when will dinner be ready?'

The cook smiled at the boy, saying nothing. Valcero frowned, wandered off to the edge of the cave, and glowered at the rain.

When dinner finally came, they gathered at the fire. Taerinus handed out spoons and clay bowls, and one by one they went over for a dollop of stew.

'Thank you very much,' Terzjin said to the cook when it was his turn.

Again, the cook only smiled and bobbed his head. He was a little older than the other sailors, tall and lean, with long, thinning hair and a bald patch atop his head.

'Does the cook not understand Caerian?' Master Maltorus asked Taerinus.

'Oh no, sir,' one of the sailors replied. 'He understands Caerian perfectly well. After all, he *is* Caerian.'

Valcero sat down with his bowl of stew. 'Well, why doesn't he speak then?'

'Old Entevus here came from Mandonum,' the sailor replied. '*Eo*, Entevus! Do you mind if I tell your story?'

The cook smiled and nodded.

'Alright, Entevus came from Mandonum, that lonely city in the north. One day, Entevus was out on the coast well outside the city walls to do some fishing in a rockpool. And who should come along but some slave traders. *Caerian* slave traders, mind you, so no one thought twice about them wandering the countryside. But these slavers had had a bad week, with few sales or purchases. They needed fresh stock, and then they see *this* handsome fella standing on the rocks with his net.'

The cook winked at the compliment.

'Well,' the sailor continued, 'they took one look at Entevus and netted him for themselves. Of course, the problem is that Entuvus was not a slave. He didn't come from slave stock either. Completely freeborn old Caerian family. And he told them all these things—not that they wanted to hear. They knew if he were to tell everyone this at the slave market, it wouldn't be too much trouble for a warden or prefect to investigate, and the slave traders would be hauled up for kidnapping.'

'Who *can* they enslave?' Valcero asked.

'The children of slaves,' Taerinus answered. 'Foreigners. Criminals.'

'And orphans,' Terzjin said quietly.

The boy looked at the ground.

'So what happened next?' Master Maltorus asked.

'Right.' The sailor nodded. 'They couldn't let Entevus *tell* everyone he wasn't supposed to be a slave. So, they did the obvious thing.'

'Which is?' Valcero asked.

'Cut out his tongue,' the sailor replied.

The boy's eyes went wide. 'What? Can they do that?'

The sailor nodded.

'Could it ... grow back?' Valcero turned to Entevus.

'Tongues don't grow back, boy. Look.' The sailor prodded Entevus.

The cook opened his mouth wide. Apart from gaps in his teeth, there was nothing but a messy, scarred stump in his mouth. Valcero winced and looked away. Everyone else burst out laughing. Even Entevus joined in with a honking chuckle.

'Did you get free when the King abolished slavery?' Terzjin asked Entevus.

The cook shook his head.

'Oh no, this was quite a few years back, sir,' the sailor said. 'What happened was the slavers took him on their ship and sailed all the ways round to Tarbrentum, on their way to the grand slave market in Etorium. They stopped to try get some more slaves on the cheap, you see. When the customs inspector went aboard to check the cargo, he walked past Entevus chained up below deck. But our friend managed to grab the inspector's wax tablet as he passed. You see—what the slavers didn't know—was that old Entevus here knew how to *write*.'

The cook grinned.

'And before anyone realised what going on, he started scratching a message with his fingernail. The traders tried to stop him, but the inspector was curious and made him continue. The whole story came out, and they arrested the slavers. They confiscated the ship, freed the slaves onboard, and I think they ended up punishing the slavers with slavery. Or did they exile them to Deiros?'

The sailor looked to Entevus, but the cook only shrugged.

'How do you know all this?' Terzjin swallowed a final spoonful of stew. It was better than expected.

'Because I was one of the *other* slaves,' the sailor replied. 'Along with Baero here.'

He pointed to another crew member, who waved.

'We were both enslaved for debt,' the sailor continued, 'so, thanks to Entevus, we got out of it. *Unluckily* for Entevus and us was that we were now stuck in Tarbrentum, a long ways from home, with no idea of what to do next.'

'But luckily for them,' Taerinus said, 'Jeigo and I happened to be passing through at the time and were short a few hands. It all worked out rather well.'

The next morning, the sky cleared and the heat returned. Terzjin followed Taerinus out to his ship on the wet sand.

The smuggler patted the hull. It was old and sun-faded, but also solid and intact. Then he climbed up and squeezed the sailcloth. It squelched in his fist. He looked down at Terzjin and shook his head. 'We'll need at least a few days before the ship can sail again. I'm afraid Caeria will have to wait a little longer.'

CHAPTER ELEVEN

CAERIA – AUTUMN'S REIGN – 436

Razna was practising her archery on a hilltop ridge with Heirik. White, puffy clouds marched across the bright sky. A fresh breeze whistled through the dry grass around their feet and rustled the leaves of the laurel tree that shaded them under its branches. Decha and Bulgitha were tethered to the tree and munched on the grass. Razna had a wide view of the hill country. Down in the valley and on the surrounding slopes, the yellow wheat swayed and rippled. A farmer trudged through his terraced field on the hillside, slashing his sickle through the corn.

Heirik walked around her. 'You're getting better and better.'

Razna pulled on the bowstring and stared along the ridge towards an imaginary target. Her arms began to shake.

'See if you can hold it a touch longer,' Heirik said. He nudged her outstretched arm upwards and gently pressed on her shoulders. 'Be careful not to hunch.'

Razna sighed and released the cord with a snap. 'It's too much.'

'No, you nearly have it.' Heirik pulled an arrow from his quiver and passed it to her. 'Come, let's try with the real thing.' He went behind Razna and put his arms around her.

She pressed her back into Heirik's chest. His breath slowed. His hands wrapped over hers to pull back the string and guide her aim towards a target.

'Breathe with me,' he whispered in her ear. 'Relax, my she-cat. Release it as if it were the *littlest* thing in the world.

Razna trembled. 'I'm not ready,' she whispered back.

'You are. Let go.'

Heirik's fingers pried her hand off the feathers. The arrow sprang out of her grasp and flew away. It hit the farmer in the chest, and he dropped into his wheat.

'Excellent.' Heirik squeezed her hand.

Razna's heart thudded. The wind brushed against her ears. She shivered, and Heirik wrapped his arms around her. He was warm.

'We should go,' he said eventually.

Razna put the bow back in Heirik's quiver. As they went to the horses, a faint cry reached her ears.

'What was that?' she asked.

Heirik stopped and looked around. 'I don't hear anything.'

The cry came again. 'There,' Razna said.

Heirik's eyes narrowed. 'The farmer?'

'*Seventer! Seventer!*'

'He's calling for help,' Razna said.

Heirik pulled a face. 'Well, we can't leave him like that. Come on.' He clambered down the slope.

Razna followed him through the golden stalks, heavy with grain. They trampled through the field and came to a halt at the leathery-faced farmer lying on his back, with the arrow still jutting from his chest.

Blood wetted his tunic. His gnarled fingers grasped for the sickle, just out of reach. He stared up at Razna and Heirik, breath coming out in whistles. '*Seventer*,' he croaked and coughed.

Heirik chewed his lip and looked around. There was no one else about, though thin blue smoke wafted from the chimney of the farmer's cottage downhill. Grasshoppers chirped. The old peasant stared at Heirik and tried to say something, but only a little blood trickled from his mouth.

The Thane pulled out his dagger and crouched beside the farmer. He drew the blade across the man's throat in a single motion. 'For the Wolf Lord,' he murmured and wiped the blade on the farmer's tunic.

The old man opened and shut his mouth. Blood pulsed from his neck.

Razna watched the two of them. 'He was innocent, Heirik.'

The Rhenvian Thane stood up. 'He lived in this place. He knew what was going on.' Heirik turned to Razna. 'There are no innocents here.' He gazed into her eyes, as if daring her to say more.

Razna shook her head and turned away. She climbed back up, and Heirik followed. Another column of smoke rose from over the hill—thick and black.

'Let's go!' Heirik called out. 'We're missing out on the fun.'

They rode down into the next valley to a cluster of thatched cottages along a stream, surrounded by pens, fields, and terraced orchards. The houses were burning, lit as the Rhenivian soldiers moved between them with flaming torches. Bodies lay crumpled between the homes. Other villagers, still living, huddled outside the village, shouting and crying.

'Hail, Thane Heirik!' the soldiers cried out as the couple approached.

Heirik leapt off his stallion. 'Tell me you have good news!'

Razna slipped off her mare and went to join him in front of the burning cottages. She tried not to blink as the smoke stung her eyes.

Marshal Grindulf strode forward and bowed. 'We found the rebels, My Thane. All killed, but one.' He waved to the crowd of soldiers behind him.

They parted as two Rhenivians dragged forth a Caerian man by ropes tied to his neck and bound wrists. The prisoner was young, perhaps younger than Razna, and thin. Blood trickled over his swollen, bruised face from a cut on his scalp. He may have been handsome. The soldiers jerked on the ropes, and the Caerian fell to his knees before Heirik and Razna. Ash wafted between them.

The Thane grinned. 'Excellent work.' He folded his arms and inspected the prisoner. 'Last Sanadin, eh?' he said in broken Caerian.

The man spat on his boots.

Heirik bent over and slapped the Sanadin across the face. The young man fell sideways and groaned.

Heirik glowered at his marshal. 'Hopefully, *this time*, the last Sanadin,' he said in Rhenivian.

Grindulf swallowed. 'Shall we execute him here, My Thane?'

'Hmmm.' Heirik straightened up and looked to Razna.

She shrugged.

'No, not here,' Heirik said. He stroked his chin. 'No, let's save him for later. We'll take him to Heiriksreld.'

CHAPTER TWELVE

CAERIA – AUTUMN'S FALL – 436

In the end, it was nearly two weeks before Taerinus declared they were ready to sail—five days of waiting for the ship and sailcloth to dry, and another seven days for the wind to turn in a favourable direction.

Valcero had mixed feelings when they all clambered aboard the *Dela* after their offerings to the Lord of Life. He was tired of stale water, mushroom soup, and being trapped in the hidden bay. But the heaving seas beyond the inlet did not excite him either.

They sailed from island to island, each dark and rocky, sometimes with splashes of vivid green forests on the windward slopes or in deep ravines that opened up to the sea. They stopped at coastal villages to trade for fresh water and food. When they struck out for open water across the Ventian Sea, the boy kept to the prow to breathe the cold air, and as the days passed, he gradually found his sea legs. He had almost forgotten what it was like to be cold.

When the sailors called out 'Land!', Valcero saw only a thin green line on the horizon. They told him it was Caeria, but it could have been anywhere. They sailed north along the outer west coast for two days, using the moons and stars as their guide, not daring to land.

It was still dark when Terzjin shook him awake.

'Up you get, Valcero.'

The boy sat up on the floor of Taerinus' cabin and stretched out his arms. 'Are we at Impona?'

'Not even close.' Master Maltorus gathered up their things. 'The smugglers have found a different kind of port for us. Quickly now.'

He gave Valcero his cloak, sandals and sack, and ushered him out onto the deck.

A chill wind blew off the sea. Valcero tied his sandals and wrapped his cloak around himself to stay warm. The eastern horizon was grey, and the wash of stars was fading before sunrise. The moons provided a little light. The oarsmen rowed in silence below deck, and beyond the wind's whistling and the ship's creaking, there came a distant boom and hiss of waves breaking on rock.

'Keep us turning,' Taerinus muttered to the helmsman from on top of the cabin. The two sailors strained against the steering oar to point the *Dela* north-east.

'How do they know where we are?' Valcero asked Terzjin.

'Because of the Tall Lady over there,' Master Maltorus replied. He pointed across the deck to the west.

Less than thirty spans away, a tower of rock rose out of the ocean swell, higher than the ship's mast. Black cormorants flew around its summit.

'Could we crash?'

Master Maltorus patted Valcero on the back. 'They know what they're doing.'

They drew in towards the land. The sailors pulled down the sail when flashes of foam on the breakers were visible in the dim light. Valcero drank in the rich sea smell. Taerinus remained atop the cabin, glancing back and forth between the Old Lady and the darkly looming coast. The rocky cliffs emerged from the misty gloom.

Finally, the smuggler captain called down to the sailor Baero. 'Hard rowing on the port side. Stop on the starboard.' He leaned against the steering oar

Baero ran to the hatch and relayed the order below deck. The ship began to turn.

'Five strokes on both sides,' Taerinus ordered, once the ship was alongside the cliffs on their left. 'Five strokes, then pull in the oars.

The swell was rough and choppy. Valcero's gut lurched as the ship nosed into a long, narrow gap between the cliff and a lower bank of rock. The cliff jutted outward and blocked off the other end, creating a natural berth. As the galley glided into the space, a plume of sea spray burst over the outer bank and coated them in a fine mist. The sailors braced oars against the cliff and bank and tossed two ropes over a protruding rock to anchor the vessel in place. The *Dela* rocked gently from side to side, sheltered from the raging swell.

Taerinus jumped from the cabin roof. 'This has been one of our favourite spots for years. But we won't stay long. Follow me.'

He led them to the railing, where it almost touched a narrow ledge on the landward rocks. He grabbed the rigging, stepped onto the railing, and hopped onto the ledge.

'You go next.' Terzjin said as he helped Valcero onto the railing.

Taerinus stretched out a hand, and Valcero grabbed it as he jumped across the gap. Master Maltorus followed suit and leapt behind Valcero on the rock.

'I'll lead you to the top,' Taerinus said over his shoulder. 'Follow carefully.'

As Valcero shuffled along behind the captain, Entevus came onto the deck. He smiled and waved at the boy. Valcero raised a hand, then turned to cling to the jagged rock. Wind and waves had honed the ribbons of stone into blades. He scrambled up after Taerinus onto a gravelly path that wound up the cliff, between fragrant bushes and lichen-spattered rocks, and over a few slippery boulders. He turned to look down at the blue sea and the little ship. His head spun.

Terzjin nudged him. 'Don't stop now. Keep going.'

When he reached the top, Valcero found Taerinus sitting on a rock to catch his breath. A dirt track ran along the clifftop, which stretched north and south in an undulating chain that faded into the mist and soft dawn light. This was Caeria. This was home. But it was nothing like the city Valcero had known all his life.

Terzjin came up behind. He breathed in and chuckled. 'Very good.'

Taerinus climbed to his feet. 'We shouldn't linger. You never know who might come along.' He pointed east. 'Just keep walking that way and, I'm told, you should come to Torecti lands within a few hours. Probably before noon at least.'

They contemplated the green slopes stretching ahead. Seagulls soared around them, croaking and squawking.

'Then let's begin, Valcero,' Master Maltorus said. He adjusted the boy's sack to sit more comfortably on his back.

'Will I see you again?' Taerinus asked. 'Will you…?'

Master Maltorus put a hand on the smuggler's shoulder. 'I promised. But if I were you, I'd lie low somewhere quiet along the coast in the meantime—or maybe on Saecros. Then, let's say a month from now, sail to Impona and wait for me there.'

Taerinus nodded.

'I can't promise exactly when I'll see you again,' Terzjin said, 'but wait for us in Impona and we'll finish the rest of our plan. Yes?'

The smuggler bit his lip. 'Alright. Yes, alright.'

'And Taerinus Ladistrien...' Terzjin held out a hand. 'For what it's worth, *I* will remember your name. Thank you.'

The captain grasped his hand. 'Just don't die out there, then perhaps *I* can thank you later. Now go, and may the Lord of Life guide your path.'

They left the smuggler and crossed the track and narrow stretch of grass on the other side. They came to the bushes and pushed between them. The vegetation reached Valcero's waist, but as they progressed up the slope, the bushes rose over the boy's shoulders and above his head, to become gnarled, twisting trees, bent away from the sea wind. As they reached the hilltop and tramped down the other side, the trees straightened and their trunks thickened. The crashing waves quietened to a dull whisper. The green leaves dripped and rustled, and the branches creaked in the breeze. The sea mist rolled through the trees.

'It's so... *wet*.' Valcero whispered as they clambered down the leaf-littered slope into the Nedolian Forest.

Terzjin chuckled. 'We're a long way from the desert now. How does it feel?'

The boy pulled his cloak tighter around his shoulders. 'I don't know. I've never seen so many trees before.' He gazed up at the gloomy canopy.

They entered a stand of coppiced trees and found a faint path that went east through the bracken. Birds trilled, whooped and whistled above. They passed a few clearings with freshly cut stumps and heard the distant knocking of an axe. The mist gradually thinned as they left the coast and the morning light turned golden.

There came another noise, rhythmic and insistent. Hoofbeats on soft earth. Two horsemen cantered along the path towards them.

'What do we do?' Valcero asked.

But Terzjin didn't reply. He froze as the riders approached, head down, with his face hidden under his hood.

'Master Maltorus?' Valcero whispered.

The horsemen wore green cloaks and iron helmets. They carried lances and round, wooden shields. Rhenivians.

'Terzjin, please.' Valcero prodded his arm.

'Just, uh, wait...' Terzjin mumbled. His hands trembled.

The riders halted before the pair. One shouted, but Valcero could not understand the words. He pulled back his hood and tried to smile.

'Who are you?' the other rider barked in rough Caerian.

Terzjin did not reply. His head remained bowed.

Valcero's skin turned cold.

'Who are you?' the rider shouted again.

'Please, sir.' The boy raised his hands. 'My father cannot speak. He...he lost his tongue some time ago.'

The Rhenivian exchanged a look with his companion. 'What?'

'Yes, it's true,' Valcero replied. 'It was an accident.' He mimed a chopping motion with his hand in front of his mouth.

The horseman nudged his steed closer. 'What are you doing here?'

Valcero glanced around the forest. 'We are looking for mushrooms, sir.'

'I don't know you face,' the rider said. He prodded the boy's sack with the butt of his spear.

Valcero licked his lips and pressed his sweaty palms against his thighs. 'We come from a village to the south. We walked here to pick mushrooms because, they say, the mushrooms...are better here.' He swallowed and tried to smile.

The other rider stared down at him, with eyes shadowed beneath his helmet. He had hair the colour of straw and a scraggly beard. His lips twisted in a sneer. 'Forest is dangerous. Bad people live here.' He said something in Rhenivian to his companion, who sniggered. They kicked their horses into a trot and rode off without another word.

Master Maltorus let out a deep, shuddering sigh. He pulled his hood back and wiped his face. 'Thank you, Valcero.'

The boy shrugged.

'That was some quick thinking. Very good. Come, let's go before they return or someone else troubles us.'

They trudged deeper into the Nedolian Forest and splashed through streams filled with dark water and smooth, white pebbles. After a time, Terzjin suggested they stop to eat breakfast. Valcero pulled out hunks of dried bread, cheese and dates. They sat on a boulder carpeted with moss and munched on their meal, listening to the birds. The air was rich with leaf litter and a faint smell like almonds.

'Terzjin?'

'Yes?'

'When the soldiers came...'

'What about it?'

'It was quite dangerous, wasn't it?'

'I suppose it was,' Terzjin replied.

Valcero bit his lip. 'It was a little scary.'

'Mmhm.'

'Were you... were you, uh, *worried*?'

'Of course not,' Master Maltorus snapped.

The boy watched a beetle scuttle over the ground while he chewed his bread.

'I mean,' Terzjin said, 'I know I went a bit quiet back there, but... you know...'

'It's alright.'

'Yes.'

They ate the rest of their food in silence.

'Anyway.' Master Maltorus brushed crumbs off his hands. 'Are you ready to speak Torecti? We must be close.'

Valcero's mind raced. Was he ready? He looked up. 'Yes, of course.'

'Good. I don't know exactly what's going to happen, but I will need your help, Valcero. We must be ready for anything.'

On the voyage, Valcero had asked Master Maltorus what would happen if the Torecti tried to eat them. Terzjin had replied that it was tomorrow's problem, and awaited tomorrow's solutions. Not very helpful. What if Valcero forgot the words? What if he said the wrong word and it got them...? The boy struggled with his last mouthful of dry bread. He reached for the waterskin.

Master Maltorus stood and slung his sack over his shoulders. 'We should keep moving.'

The sun was higher now, though it pierced the forest with only dappled light. After an hour or so, the ground tilted upwards in a long slope. Clouds of gnats danced in the sunbeams. They climbed the hill, sweating in the damp air. And at the top of the ridge, they came to the border.

Valcero went to the nearest tree. 'It's just like Master Meretan said.' A curling pattern was etched deep into the bark all over the trunk. The lines were filled with lime, making them white against the red and green lichen that otherwise coated the bark. He spotted more decorated trees to his left and right along the ridge. They formed a line that stretched off into the forest in both directions.

Terzjin folded his arms and inspected the trees. 'Alright.'

The boy peered down the other side of the ridge. The forest continued, thicker and darker. The trees were even taller—and older maybe—than he had seen so far. He looked back at Master Maltorus. 'What now?'

'Perhaps we should call out a "hello"? Knock at the door? What is the Torecti way?'

Valcero shook his head. 'I don't know.'

'Come on, try something.'

Valcero stood between two marked trees and put his hands to his mouth. '*Sevei!*' he cried out into the woods.

The leaves swallowed his voice.

He cleared his throat and shouted again. '*Sevei!*'

Nothing.

Master Maltorus shrugged. 'Well, here we go.' He led the way down the slope.

They squeezed through the dense, rustling undergrowth. Twigs and dead leaves crunched underfoot. Valcero's breath sounded loud in his ears. The ground flattened out, and they continued for some time. A dragonfly buzzed past his ear.

Terzjin pulled his hood up and slowed to walk next to Valcero. 'I think they are here,' he murmured.

The boy glanced around.

Master Maltorus tapped him on the back. 'Just keep walking.'

'How do you know?' Valcero whispered.

'The birds have stopped singing.'

The trees thinned slightly as they descended into a shallow depression. A nearby stream bubbled somewhere ahead.

Master Maltorus chuckled as they reached the trickling stream between the ferns.

'What is it?' the boy whispered.

'I see one,' Terzjin mumbled. 'Up the slope, over there.'

Valcero could not see anybody.

'Keep your arms out by your sides,' Terzjin said. He raised a hand and waved.

Something moved up on the slope. A figure emerged from the dappled shadows behind a tree—a bare-chested man wearing a leather kilt. Black spirals covered his skin. He sauntered down the slope, bearing a bow and a nocked arrow—pointing down. A quiver of arrows hung on his back. More figures crept out of the shadows, dropped from the trees, rose up from the ferns—ten altogether—and converged in a broad semicircle around the Caerians. Some carried bows. Others bore spears, tipped with flint.

Master Maltorus nudged Valcero with his elbow. 'Now is the time for you to show off.'

'Um...' The boy's heart thudded in his chest. 'Uh...'

'Come now, Valcero,' Terzjin hissed.

The men were all dressed in the same leather kilts and sandals. The same spiralling pattern of black paint covered their pale, sinewy bodies. Their hair was as black as raven feathers, long and tied back. They stared at Valcero with vivid eyes—bright blues and greens.

'*Amaerix...*' Valcero's voice croaked. '*Amaerix enet.*' We are friends? Was that right?

The Torecti crept closer. The ferns rustled behind Valcero. He dared not look.

'Can't you talk?' Terzjin whispered. 'Tell them we mean no harm.'

'I'm *trying*,' Valcero muttered. 'We are friends...' he called out in Torecti. 'We come... we come in peace.' His voice cracked.

The Torecti raised their weapons.

'Oh dear.' Terzjin slipped his hand under his cloak. 'Valcero,' he murmured, 'when I give the word, you run, and you don't look back.'

CHAPTER THIRTEEN

CAERIA – AUTUMN'S FALL – 436

Heirik was rather proud of what they were building in the valley. Heiriksreld. He had chosen the name himself. They sat on their horses on the hill overlooking the construction. 'Do you remember this place?' he asked Razna.

Razna adjusted her shawl that billowed in the wind. 'Mmm. You fought a battle here?'

The Thane nodded and grinned. 'The Caerians mustered to block our march, and we drove them from the field like sheep.' He sighed. 'It was a great victory, and a lucky place to build our new home.'

Razna guided her pale mare forward. 'It seems there's still work to be done.'

Heirik laughed. 'Of course, my she-cat. We'll go and inspect now, yes?'

Heirik whistled to his men and urged his stallion downhill. Razna, their guards, marshals, and others followed. The Sanadin prisoner stumbled at the back, tethered to the last horse by a rope bound to his wrists. His rags were torn and bloody.

Heirik wanted his own hall, built in a more comfortable, more *Rhenivian,* style. He also wanted it to outshine any hall he had seen back home. He had summoned craftsmen —carpenters, weavers and goldsmiths—from across the sea and do their finest work here, along with hundreds of his own soldiers. But the progress was far too slow for his liking. Clearly, it was time to take charge.

The soldiers had thrown up a massive earthen dyke to fully encircle the hall, with space for other buildings, paddocks and campgrounds. The stream that flowed through the valley now skirted the southern boundary of the earthworks. Atop the dyke they had erected a palisade of tree trunks with sharpened tips pointing at the sky. As they approached from the east, Heirik saw men patrolling on walkways behind the palisade. They peered over the wooden barricade and shouted greetings at the newcomers. Marshal Grindulf blew his horn in reply.

A great wooden gate filled the only gap in the dyke. Three black flags hung from the arch, each embroidered with Heirik's silver boar. The doors swung open to welcome the lord of the house and his retinue.

'What do you think?' the Thane asked Razna as they rode through the gateway. He craned his neck upwards and beamed.

'It's massive,' Razna replied, following his gaze. 'You could hold a mighty feast in this space.'

Heirik laughed. 'Oh, we certainly will!'

Daga met them inside. 'Thane Heirik! Welcome.'

He bowed as Heirik and Razna climbed off their horses.

'How is the progress, Daga?' Heirik strode forward and slapped his marshal on the shoulder.

'Good, My Thane. Your hall is progressing well. The stone tower is nearly complete.' Daga looked past them. 'You have a prisoner?'

Heirik glanced behind himself. 'Yes, we caught the final bastard. The Sanadin will be extinguished with him.' He leaned close to Daga's ear. 'If only we had been more thorough and seized him along with the others, eh?'

Daga cringed. 'Of course, My Thane. Once again, I beg your forgiveness. Perhaps we can put him in the tower? We have dungeons at the bottom.'

'Lead the way.'

The marshal took them across an open, muddy tract to a tower of five storeys set against the dyke and covered with scaffolding. Masons and bricklayers were still climbing all over it.

Daga pointed them to the doorway at the base. 'He can go in there, sir. The upper floors will be a strong redoubt—should you ever need it, of course.'

The soldiers dragged the prisoner away into the tower. For later.

Heirik looked over the building and frowned. 'I want it finished by year's end, you hear?'

'My Thane, the walls take time. We need more masons.'

'No excuses, Daga. Get it done.'

The marshal bowed. 'Of course, Thane Heirik.'

'Alright, now show us the rest of my hold.'

Most of the open space was filled with tents for soldiers and workers. Some wooden buildings formed a row along the southern interior of the dyke—workshops for smiths, carpenters and other craftsmen.

'The granaries and stores are still under construction, sir,' Daga said as they walked, 'but they should be complete in the spring.'

Heirik sighed and nodded.

To the rear, Daga showed them a small temple for the Flood Father. Workers were hauling mud from a deep hole to prepare a well for the holy site. Then they crossed a grassy field where soldiers drilled with spear, sword and shield. They completed the circle back to the tower. In its shadow, workers were erecting another temple—this one for the Corn Mother—with a humble, clay idol to worship. Finally, Daga led them to the precise centre of the hold for the jewel of the crown.

'Your hall, My Thane.' Daga waved to the building with a flourish.

It was wooden, as Heirik had specified, and set on a low, earthen mound. The walls were still being built, and the roof was no more than beams, like the ribs of a massive beast. Yet, Heirik could see what it would become. He clapped his hands and strode up the mound to the entrance.

A din of hammers and saws filled the air. A team of carpenters worked on logs in front of the hall, cutting and shaping the planks and beams. They stopped to bow and greet their Thane.

'A hall like this must require plenty of timber,' Heirik said.

Daga came beside him. 'We have just about stripped the surrounding hills.'

'Just about, but not *entirely*?' Heirik asked. They approached the empty doorframe.

'Ah, yes, sir,' Daga replied. 'We left a grove in a valley to the east, as requested.'

'Excellent.' Heirik winked at him.

The marshal smiled and inclined his head.

They walked the length of the hall over the still bare ground. They would have to pound the earth hard and flat and add rushes once the roof was up. There was space for a great fire pit and a raised section where his—no, *their* thrones would sit.

Heirik turned to Razna. 'Here is where we shall hold court. Can you see it?'

She looked around and nodded slowly. 'I see it.' She beamed at Heirik and put her hand in his. 'And where shall we sleep?'

'There at the back,' Heirik answered. 'Correct, Daga?'

'Correct, sir.' The marshal took them under another bare lintel behind the dais and up some wooden steps to a smaller room, where joiners were laying down floorboards. 'It will be warm and comfortable for a lady and her Thane.'

Razna glanced at the open sky. 'But not yet ready.'

'Of course, My Lady.' Daga replied. 'I am sorry for the delays. We have prepared a tent for you.'

He led them out of the hall to a large tent at the rear. Inside, they found a bed, a table, and chairs for dining. Another table was covered with scrolls.

Heirik pointed at the documents. 'What's this?'

'Messages for you, sir,' Daga said. 'Letters, petitions from commoners and aristocrats, that sort of thing.'

Heirik groaned and flopped into a chair. 'Never-ending. Alright, what do I need to know?'

The marshal dug through the scrolls. '*Most* of them are not urgent, Thane Heirik, and can wait for tomorrow. There were a few important ones... like this.' He raised a roll of parchment, sealed with the Corn Mother's mark.

'*Urgh*, what does Frethi want?' Heirik took the scroll and tore off the seal. He unfurled the message and squinted at the writing. 'He... he...'

'My Thane?' Razna stepped to his side and leaned over his shoulder. Her finger traced the runes as her lips moved.

Heirik studied her hand and the look of concentration on her face. He could not help but smile.

'My Thane,' Razna said, 'Brother Frethi would like to know if you can spare a few soldiers and craftsmen to help rebuild the Corn Mother's temple at Etorium. He is shorthanded.'

Heirik sniggered. 'Well, maybe he wouldn't be shorthanded if *he* hadn't sent his Holy Warriors away. In fact, he wouldn't need to rebuild his temple if his Holy Warriors had done their duty.'

The men chuckled.

'But,' Heirik continued, 'I will speak with the Brother when we return to the city. I'm sure we can arrange something. The Corn Mother knows we must right her indignity.'

The attendees murmured in agreement.

'Anything else?' he asked Daga.

'Well...' The marshal lifted another scroll, sealed in a bronze tube. 'There's also a letter from High Thane Getherd.'

Heirik leaned forward and snatched the tube from his hands. He pulled out the letter. 'My Lady?'

'Let's see,' Razna muttered. 'Your uncle, the High Thane of Elborn, sends congratulations for putting down the rebellion and asserting your authority over the Caerians. He says King Randegar also appreciates your efforts and would like to show his thanks by...'

'By...?' Heirik looked up.

Razna clenched her jaw and swallowed. 'By offering his daughter Ranwen as your bride.' She blew air through her nose. 'Your uncle writes that this is an offer you cannot refuse. You are...you are to present yourself in Hustonen in the spring for a union between two great... families.' She backed away abruptly.

Heirik twisted around in his chair and pulled her close. Her heart beat against his cheek. He stared into the distance. 'Everyone,' he spoke finally, 'leave us, now.'

'My Thane?' Daga stepped closer.

'Everyone,' Heirik snapped, not meeting his eye. 'Out.'

The Rhenivians shuffled out of the tent.

When all was quiet, Heirik stood and clutched Razna to his chest. 'They *cannot* do this,' he hissed. 'They cannot. I am Thane here. *I* will choose my bride. I will decide.'

'You can't defy your king, or your uncle.' Razna pulled away. 'Or you will not be a Thane for much longer.'

He shook his head. 'No. No, I chose you, Razna.' He grabbed her shoulders. 'You and only you.'

Razna smiled softly. 'It's alright, Heirik. I understand. This day was always coming.'

Heirik's mouth tightened. He shook his head, without taking his eyes off hers. 'I will fight them all if I have to.'

Razna gazed up at him. 'You really would, wouldn't you?'

He rested his forehead on hers.

She put her hands on his cheeks. 'Of course, there may be a way to stop all this.'

'What do you mean?'

Razna breathed out slowly. 'Well, you couldn't marry this *Ranwen* if you were already married, could you?'

'What are you saying?'

'What do you *think*?'

It was twilight when they reached the forest grove between the two rounded hills. Heirik and Razna carried flaming torches, escorted by Daga, Lithrik and a few of the more loyal soldiers. The couple wore hooded cloaks to guard against the autumn chill and spying eyes.

'Of course,' Heirik whispered to her as they passed beneath the trees, 'we'll get Frethi to redo the rites when we're back in Etorium, just to make it official. He will do it, at spearpoint if necessary. But *this* is the ceremony that will matter.'

Razna squeezed his hand.

They waded through a shallow stream and came to a clearing. The men formed a circle with Heirik, Razna and Lithrik in the centre.

'Bring him forth,' Lithrik ordered.

The last soldiers pulled the Sanadin prisoner through the undergrowth and into the circle. The prisoner was naked except for the ropes around his wrists and the cloth gag over his mouth. Lithrik supervised as they tied the man to a tree. The priest unsheathed his dagger and nicked the Sanadin on his left breast. The prisoner gave a muffled yelp and strained against the cords, as blood oozed down his side.

Heirik and Razna dropped to their knees and pulled back their hoods.

Lithrik scooped up blood with his fingers and went to the pair. 'You come here as faithful servants of the Wolf Lord, his beloved children.' He marked Razna's forehead with blood, then Heirik's.

'Marriage is sacrifice,' Lithrik intoned. 'And a marriage must be blessed in blood to endure against all trials. Do you agree to this union, Heirik son of Heiferth?'

'I do,' Heirik replied.

'Do *you* agree to this union, Lady Razna of Galatan?' Lithrik turned to her.

Heirik looked to his bride. Razna swallowed and gazed at him. She smiled. 'I do.'

'Then make your offering to the Wolf Lord,' the priest said.

The couple arose. Lithrik presented the dagger. Razna looked to Heirik.

He nodded. 'Go on.'

She placed her hand on the hilt. Heirik clasped his hand around hers.

Lithrik stepped aside. 'For the Lord of the Hunt,' he called.

'For the Lord of the Hunt,' the soldiers chanted.

Heirik and Razna advanced as one upon the prisoner. The man squirmed, wild-eyed, and screamed. Piss trickled down his leg.

'For the Lord of the Woods!' Lithrik cried out.

'For the Lord of the Woods,' the soldiers chanted.

They stood before the offering pleading, praying, hesitating for a heartbeat, a breath. Then they plunged the knife together.

'For the Lord of the Night.'

They stabbed again.

'For the Lord of the Night.'

And again.

'For the Lord of Blood.'

And again and again. The chanting and screaming receded. Heirik's heart thundered. His skin prickled. He grinned, face spattered red. And again. He fancied he heard a whispering amongst the leaves. He was here. The Wolf Lord was with Heirik. Blessing him.

CHAPTER FOURTEEN

THE NEDOLIAN FOREST – AUTUMN'S FALL – 436

Terzjin's fingers rested on the leather wrapping of his sword hilt. His eyes flicked between the approaching Torecti warriors. He tried to slow his breath, relax his shoulders, be ready. The Torecti paused several spans away, just beyond striking range.

One of the men, the first whom Terzjin spotted in the forest, stepped forward and examined him. For a brief moment, the Torecti's green eyes gleamed with a pale fire. The man tilted his head to the side. His lips twitched. Terzjin looked to the others. For all but three warriors, their eyes gleamed and flickered. They broke into smiles as they gazed into Terzjin's eyes.

The first Torecti strode up to the Caerians until he was only a few cubits from Master Maltorus. 'Who taught you our words?' He was lean and taller than Master Maltorus. 'Who taught you our words?' He spoke Caerian with a faintly sing-song accent. He looked from Terzjin to Valcero and back again, with smooth, measured movements.

'I…I don't speak your language,' Terzjin replied. He gestured to Valcero. 'Only the boy.'

'They are called…Praehenna and Aulix,' Valcero said. He coughed.

The Torecti man shrugged. 'I do not know who they are. But those *are* names of the *Taurex*.'

He leaned forward and studied the boy, who shrank away, then he turned to Master Maltorus and stepped closer, close enough for his breath to blow against Terzjin's face.

The man's eyes gleamed again. 'Who *are* you?'

'We are messengers,' Terzjin answered. 'Terzjin Maltorus and Valcero Baradon. We come on behalf of King Zjandius of the Caerians to speak with your leader.'

'*Caeri*? Not those with hair of dried grass and fire?'

Terzjin considered the question, then shook his head.

'And where *is* King Zjandius?' the man asked.

'Over the sea.'

The Torecti man stepped away and huddled with his companions.

'What are they saying?' Terzjin whispered to Valcero.

'It's too fast,' the boy replied. 'I'm sorry.'

Terzjin glanced over his shoulder. Another five Torecti warriors stood behind, completing the trap. Two were women, armed and dressed like the men, but with strips of cloth and leather to bind their breasts in place. Valcero followed his eyes and gasped when he saw their breasts. Terzjin rolled his eyes and nudged the boy's head to face forward.

The Torecti finished their discussion and the man returned to the Caerians. 'You will come with us, or leave the forest.'

'We will come with you,' Terzjin said.

'You will walk between us and stay close,' the man said. 'If you fall behind, or try to run away, you may be lost where none can find you. Then you will starve and die alone under the trees.'

Master Maltorus nodded. 'Very well.'

The Torecti formed two lines around them and set a fast pace up the hill.

'Are you alright?' Terzjin whispered to Valcero as they walked.

The boy nodded.

He put his arm around Valcero's shoulders. 'Let's try to keep up.'

The Torecti began to sing as they strode through the forest. The melody rose and fell in a strange mode. The song was repetitive and chant-like. The leaders ahead called out a phrase, and the Torecti at the rear answered. The forest sounds receded as the song gathered volume. Terzjin's head spun and buzzed. For a moment, he felt he might nod off to sleep. But then the song ended.

'You will wait here,' the leader said. He gave orders to the other Torecti, who encircled the Caerians, while he stalked away between the trees towards a village.

There were about thirty buildings, all made of wooden planks and woven branches, roofed with thatch and bark, and perched on stilts above the damp earth. Some were long, others short and box-like. The village was seemingly deserted. The Torecti man climbed some wooden steps and entered the longest, largest house. All was quiet. Their Torecti escort stood at ease around them, waiting.

A face peered from a doorway. Another appeared at a dark window, then retreated into the gloom. A woman leaned out from behind a house. Terzjin heard faint sounds—a giggle and a shushing—from the nearest hut.

After a while, the Torecti warrior emerged from the long house and returned to them. He muttered something to his companions and then spoke Caerian. 'Come with me. You will stay inside for the rest of the day, then speak with our leader this evening. Yes?'

Master Maltorus nodded.

The warriors led them through the village. As they walked, more Torecti burst from the huts. The villagers pointed and stared at the newcomers, whispering together. Children hurried over and ran around the group. Young, old, men and women, they all crowded around to see the Caerians. Some wore leather kilts and cloaks. Others had simple tunics and shifts woven from fibres and stitched with leather. Most walked barefoot, while a few wore sandals of leather and bark. The younger Torecti all had raven black hair that shone in the dappled light, while the older villagers had streaks of silver. Their eyes were pale and bright—ice-blue, bright green like winter grass, some almost yellow like the sun shining through leaves. Many had the gleaming in their eyes. When they saw Terzjin, they smiled and nodded, as if in recognition. The chatter, laughter, and shouts of surprise filled the forest.

The Torecti leader gestured to a small thatched house. 'You will rest in there.'

Terzjin and Valcero climbed into the cramped hut. The thatch gave off an earthy smell. A little light shone through a small window at the back, revealing two mats on the wooden floor, a tray of food, and a bowl of water. The food consisted of cooked forest mushrooms, berries and strips of grilled meat. Without another word, the Torecti shut the wicker door and, judging by the rustling, latched it.

Terzjin peered through the window—barely bigger than his face—and saw the villagers return to their business. They tended fires, sat on the steps of their homes, and carved things from wood or chipped away at pieces of flint and obsidian. Others stood loitering around, talking and laughing.

'Are we prisoners?' Valcero asked.

Master Maltorus sat cross-legged on a mat and examined the meal. 'It seems so. Hopefully not forever.'

The boy sat opposite him. 'Can we trust the food? What if it's poisoned?'

Terzjin shrugged and tasted a mushroom. It was tender and earthy. 'A lot of effort if they just want to kill us.' He chewed. 'Unless they're fattening us up for dinner? I'm joking, Valcero. Only joking. We'll deal with whatever comes.'

Later, when the light turned golden, the steps outside creaked and the door opened to reveal the same Torecti warrior. He now wore a cloth shirt and had washed the painted spirals from his pale skin. 'Come with me now.'

'Could you tell me your name?' Terzjin asked as they clambered out into the evening light.

'You may call me Reito of the Whispering Leaves. This way, please.'

'How did you learn Caerian?' Terzjin asked as they walked. 'I thought the Torecti kept away from our lands?'

Reito chuckled. He led them back to the long-house at the centre of the village. About twenty Torecti were gathered outside. The villagers followed them up the steps to the porch and doorway. Many more were already inside, almost filling the building, apart from a narrow aisle that led to the other end. Two torches burned there, giving a little light in the otherwise gloomy interior. More villagers leaned through the narrow windows. Whispers and murmurs filled the longhouse, then died away as all turned to stare at them.

'Your weapon.' Reito held out his hands. 'It must stay at the door, but do not worry. No one will touch it.'

Master Maltorus hesitated, then undid the sword from his belt and passed it to the Torecti warrior. Reito took it with both hands, examined the sheath, then stowed it on a shelf under the eaves. He guided the Caerians inside and down the creaking aisle. Terzjin gazed ahead, avoiding everyone's eyes.

As they approached the end of the longhouse, an old man appeared from the shadows and sat down on a stool. He had ashen hair, sharp eyes and lean features. He wore a leather kilt and a cloak of shimmering feathers from many birds. Two women joined him at his sides, dressed in cream-coloured cloth gowns and shawls of the wispiest material Terzjin had ever seen, barely visible in the firelight. *They even wear spider web*, Valcero had said.

With a loud voice, Reito announced something to the seated man and the assembled villagers.

'He's introducing us,' Valcero muttered at Terzjin's side. 'He says we come from the sea with a message from the Caerian king.'

Reito turned to them. 'This is Perax, chief of the Whispering Leaves clan and our guardian. You will deliver your message to him.'

'Will you translate for me?' Terzjin whispered to Valcero.

'No, he should probably do it,' the boy mumbled and pointed at Reito.

Terzjin bowed. 'Greetings, Chief Perax. I am Terzjin Maltorus. I speak on behalf of King Zjandius of Caeria.'

He paused while Reito translated his words.

'King Zjandius was forced to leave Caeria when the Rhenivians invaded,' Terzjin continued, 'but he is preparing to return with an army and drive out the Rhenivians. Long have our nations lived peacefully apart, but the King now asks if you would ally with us to rid Caeria of these invaders. Would you help us?'

Reito spoke at length, then Perax waved his arms about and said something brief. He glanced to the side as he spoke, too quick for Terzjin to see where the chief was looking.

Reito spoke. 'Our Chief says that long ago, the Caerians were also invaders. What difference does it make to us—one invader or the other?'

Master Maltorus nodded and licked his lips. 'I understand the history, but that was many centuries ago. Since then, Caeria and the

Torecti have made peace and respected each other's sovereignty. We hear that the Rhenivians have repeatedly intruded upon Torecti lands. That they have tried to burn down this forest. Please, help us, and we will end these troubles together.'

The chief folded his arms and made another comment. His eyes darted to the right again.

Reito gave a wry grin. 'Chief Perax says Caerians have *also* intruded upon our lands recently.'

Terzjin frowned. 'With respect, I am not certain what you mean. If you refer to the boy and me, then—my Chief—forgive us, please. We come only because the situation is desperate—unprecedented, I mean.'

Reito chuckled. 'That is the usual excuse.' He translated for Perax.

'Please tell the Chief that we come *only* to request an alliance,' Terzjin said. 'If his answer is no, then I beg that we may leave unharmed, and I swear our King shall never trouble you nor your people again.' He watched the chief's face.

Perax stroked his bare chin and once more looked over to the side. This time, Terzjin followed his glance to where it landed. A young woman leaned against the wall amongst the villagers, almost lost in the shadows. Coloured beads were woven into her long, straight hair. Her face was obscured, but Terzjin saw her nod, ever so slightly.

Perax sighed and arose from his stool. His feathered cloak rustled. He spoke in a loud, clear voice.

'The chief says that this decision is not his alone to make,' Reito said. 'He says that the other clans must give their words as well. Tomorrow, messages will go out, and the other chiefs shall come and decide together. In the meantime, you Caerians will be our guests. Be at peace.'

As soon as Reito finished, the villagers stood up and all began talking at once as they shuffled and jostled to the door. Terzjin and Valcero stood amongst the crowd, unsure of what to do. Master Maltorus looked around for the young woman, but she had vanished.

Reito went to them. 'Come. We will eat now.'

Outside, they joined a circle around a campfire, one of many throughout the village. They sat and received bowls of pungent broth and pieces of cooked meat on a wooden board. Some kind of bird, as far as Terzjin could tell. Three small children watched the Caerians as they ate, while their mothers whispered and giggled.

Terzjin tapped Valcero on the shoulder. 'Thank you for your help.'

The boy scowled and stared into the flames. 'What help? I didn't need to be here.'

'*Eo*, Valcero. We didn't know any of them could speak Caerian. Besides, I'm glad you're here, whether or not you speak for me. This journey would be far more lonely and difficult otherwise.'

A young girl leaned forward and offered Valcero a piece of meat. The boy said something in Torecti, tried to smile and took the food from her. He bit into the flesh as the girl sat back and giggled.

'See?' Terzjin said. 'You can be useful in more ways than one. We need them to like us.'

Reito sat beside Terzjin and lifted his bowl to slurp up some broth.

Master Maltorus shifted about to face the Torecti man. 'Reito, what did you mean when you spoke about intruders?'

Reito wiped his mouth and shook his head. 'Leave that for now, Terzjin Maltorus. That is tomorrow's thing. Just eat!'

'May I ask another question?'

Reito shrugged as he chewed on some meat.

'What do you see when you look in my eyes? Because, when I look at your eyes and—'

Reito swallowed. 'Perhaps you have some Torecti blood in you. Perhaps the Lord of Life has blessed you in some other way.'

'I don't understand,' Terzjin said.

'Just eat, then,' the Torecti man replied.

They finished the meal mostly in silence, then left the bowls and trays on the ground. They followed Reito and the other Torecti to a bonfire in a large clearing about fifty spans from the village. The people sat on logs arranged around the blaze and fell silent. Terzjin and Valcero stood behind them at the edge of the clearing and watched. The crackling branches sent sparks billowing into the dark sky. Cold stars twinkled above. Distant birds whistled and hooted.

Chief Perax walked into the centre of the clearing and lifted his hands with his back to the fire. He dropped his hands, and the Torecti began to sing.

The voices rose and fell, sometimes quiet, sometimes deafening.

The melody was wild, joyous, defiant. The men, the women, the children—each sang different parts that wove together in lush, unearthly harmonies. They repeated each other, called forth and responded. The fire seemed to burn fiercer, the stars brighter. Terzjin's skin tingled, and a shiver ran up his spine. He blinked away tears. The song reached a crescendo, the voices joined in a sequence of pure notes, then it all ended with a roar. The Torecti clapped and laughed.

Terzjin leaned over to Valcero. 'What were they singing about?'

The boy stared at the villagers as they stood and milled around the clearing.

'I'm not sure,' Valcero said. 'Something about life. Maybe about the Lord of Life?'

'Have you ever heard it before?' Terzjin asked. 'It sounded like...' He shrugged. There was a thought, a memory, something just out of reach.

Valcero shook his head.

Terzjin looked around. The young woman with beads in her hair stood by the trees, only a little way from them.

'Wait here,' he said. He took a step. 'Or, actually, would you come with me? I may need your help.'

Valcero followed Terzjin as he marched over to the woman. She clutched a woven shawl around her shoulders and watched the other Torecti with a smile on her face. As Terzjin approached, she turned to face him.

He stopped and stumbled as if he had collided with a wall. Her eyes flared, as if the very moons shone within them, then dimmed to reveal pale grey. She was short and slender. Her long, straight black hair spilt over her shoulders. Black lines were painted on the milky skin of her cheeks.

Her dark lips parted. 'And you are the one they call Terzjin Maltorus.'

She grinned, and his chest thudded.

'You...you also speak Caerian,' he finally replied.

The woman nodded.

'You, uh, speak it very well.'

She snorted.

Two children, a boy and a girl, ran up to them and said some Torecti words to Valcero.

'Why don't you join them?' the woman said to Valcero.

The boy looked to her, then Terzjin.

'It's alright, go,' Master Maltorus said.

The children took Valcero away, and then Terzjin was alone with her.

'You may call me Illauri,' the woman said. 'Illauri-of-the-Woods. Come, walk with me, Terzjin Maltorus.'

He fell in step with her as she led him into the trees and away from the bonfire. The village noise grew fainter, the firelight softer. The forest was dark, save for moonbeams that shone through the leaves here and there.

Terzjin breathed in and out as slowly as he could, but his heart would not be still. A fire coursed through him. He swallowed. 'I saw you in the longhouse earlier...'

'Mmm.' Illauri ran her hand over the bark of a passing tree. She gazed up at its branches and smiled.

'Chief Perax was looking at you while we spoke.'

Illauri pursed her lips, not meeting his eyes. 'The Chief sometimes listens to my counsel, as he listens to many people.'

'So you are a counsellor, then?'

'I am many things. And what about you, Terzjin Maltorus?' She turned to inspect him. Her eyes seemed to pierce his skull. 'What are you?'

He breathed out. 'I... am many things too.'

'And what are you, here, in our forest? What brings you to us?'

'I am here as an envoy,' Terzjin replied. 'From my King.'

'An envoy. That is good.' Illauri touched him on the shoulder before walking on.

Terzjin put his fingers where hers had been. He felt dizzy. He hurried after Illauri. Where was she leading him? 'Who are you?' Terzjin called out.

The woman glanced over her shoulder as she walked. 'I told you. Who are *you*?'

Master Maltorus caught up. 'When you looked at me for the first time, your eyes glowed. Now, I have seen that gleaming in a few

Caerian people, and many Torecti here in the Nedolian Forest. Could you tell me what it means, *please*?'

'It is a gift from the Lord of Life, Terzjin Maltorus. A gift to be used wisely, or lost. Those of us blessed with this gift can recognise it in others.'

'You see it in my eyes?'

Illauri nodded.

'A gift of shining eyes?' Terzjin said. 'I don't understand.'

'That is just a sign,' Illauri answered.

They reached another clearing, illuminated in silver from the moons.

'Tell me, Terzjin Maltorus, have you ever felt that you are a little different from other people?'

He shrugged. 'Uh, perhaps?'

'You carry a sword. Can you use it well?'

He furrowed his brow. 'I think so, yes.'

'Can you do things that others cannot?'

Master Maltorus examined the leafy ground. 'If I quiet my heart, people seem not to notice me. So, I can walk unseen.'

'A useful trick,' Illauri remarked. 'And tell me, Terzjin Maltorus, have you ever seen the dead walk?'

Terzjin flinched and stared at her. His heart pounded. He swallowed. 'Sometimes.'

Illauri nodded and came closer, close enough that he could feel the warmth of her body.

'There is something about you,' Terzjin said, gazing down at her. 'I feel...'

Illauri put her hands on his cheeks. 'You do not know what you feel, Terzjin Maltorus. It is time for you to go to bed.'

'Wait.' He reached for her hands. 'I have more questions.'

'And we will speak again, soon. Look.' Illauri pointed behind him.

It was the hut where they had spent the day. They were back at the village.

'There is your bed. Sleep now, Terzjin Maltorus, for the forest wakes early.'

CHAPTER FIFTEEN

THE NEDOLIAN FOREST – AUTUMN'S FALL – 436

Valcero dreamed of a great chorus of people singing in the trees. They wore feathered cloaks and sang the sun awake. The music surged to a deafening crescendo.

And then he awoke in the dark. The birds were singing—whistles, whoops, trills, and chirps. He was not in the ship. The hut. They were with the Torecti, of course. Under the birdsong, he made out Terzjin's soft snores somewhere nearby.

Valcero breathed in and out slowly, staring up at nothing. Why was he here? They didn't need him. He wriggled under the blanket and tried to make himself comfortable on the thin mat. His thoughts melted away and he dozed—half-dreaming, half-awake—for perhaps another hour or so.

When grey light snuck through the small window and voices came from outside, he got up, dressed, and pushed the door open. Terzjin groaned and turned over, rubbing his face.

'I'm going to look for breakfast,' Valcero said. 'Would you like some?'

'Mmm, of course,' Terzjin replied. 'I'll be out in a moment.'

A fine drizzle swirled between the huts, but many villagers were walking past with sacks or standing around and chatting, draped in cloaks to stay warm and dry, while their children ran about. A few waved to Valcero, and he waved back. He was probably the first Caerian to see this village in hundreds of years—maybe ever. Master Meretan would kill to be here. The boy smiled to himself as he clambered down the steps. What would Master Meretan be doing this morning? Who would fetch him breakfast while Valcero was away? He had probably found a palace servant to boss around.

A woman approached. 'Morning greetings to you,' she said in Torecti. 'Would you like some food? For you and the man?'

The boy smiled and touched his forehead, as Praehenna had taught him long ago. 'Yes, please.'

The woman laughed.

Valcero blushed and put his hand down. 'Was that wrong?'

'No, no. I did not expect you to know such things.' She smiled and patted his arm. 'I will bring something to eat.'

A thought nudged Valcero's heart. The boy examined the passing villagers. Not one had a tattoo on their forehead, unlike Praehenna and Aulix. Curious. Perhaps they had come from a different village, with different customs?

The Torecti woman returned with two wooden bowls of steaming mushroom stew. Master Maltorus emerged from the hut and ate with Valcero on the steps under the eaves.

'Did you have fun last night with the other youngsters?' Terzjin asked.

Valcero swallowed. 'They showed me a game with a ball, but I didn't understand it.' He scraped the sides of his bowl with the spoon. Some bread would be nice. 'Did you have ... a good talk with that lady?'

'Mmm. Yes. I tried to learn more about how things work here.' Terzjin chewed with his elbows on his knees and stared at the falling drizzle. 'My heart says she may be a witch.'

'A witch?' Valcero turned to look at him. 'Did she do some kind of sorcery or something?'

'Ha!' Terzjin glanced around. 'Not exactly, no,' he muttered. 'But ... we should be careful here.'

Valcero tried to remember what Illauri looked like from last night. She *seemed* normal, as far as he could recall. Quite beautiful, actually. Was that normal for a witch, or were they supposed to be ugly? Or did they use enchantment to *appear* beautiful? He couldn't remember which way the old stories had it.

'Valcero?' Terzjin asked.

'Yes?'

'When you look at my eyes, what do you see?'

The boy blinked. 'I see...your eyes?'

'No, what I mean is, when you look *into* my eyes, do you notice anything...odd?'

Valcero leaned over and peered at the man's face. 'Um, I just see your eyes. They aren't brown, which is a little different, I suppose. But still like eyes I've seen before.'

'So, nothing else then? Nothing happens when you look?'

Valcero frowned and leaned back. 'No. Just a pair of eyes.'

Master Maltorus nodded slowly. 'Makes sense.'

Valcero shrugged.

'Good morning!' Reito walked up to them. 'Have you eaten well?'

Terzjin put his bowl aside. 'We have, thank you.'

'Well, as soon as you are ready, I would like you to come with me,' the Torecti said. 'There is something important that I must show you.'

The Caerians exchanged glances.

'Very well,' Terzjin replied. 'Let me get my cloak, and we'll be off.'

They followed Reito through the village and down a path into the forest. Two more Torecti fell in behind them.

'Please stay close,' Reito called out from the front. 'Once again, do not stray from our path.'

He began to sing.

It was similar to yesterday morning's song. The melody rose and fell in waves. The Torecti behind added a harmony. The song was slow and strange—no words, but sounds without meaning. The tune repeated over and over, until it made Valcero's head spin. The forest seemed to twist and turn around him. He stumbled, but a Torecti grabbed him by the back of his cloak and steadied him.

'We are close,' Reito announced.

The song was complete. The drizzle had passed, and the morning sun peeped through grey clouds. They followed Reito down a steep path that wound between the trees. They heard wood chopping and bleating sheep.

'Are we in any danger?' Terzjin asked.

Reito looked back. 'If you are who you say you are, then you should be perfectly safe.'

As Master Maltorus opened his mouth to ask more, they left the trees and entered a wide field. Yellow wheat danced in the breeze.

Valcero squinted at the sky. 'Have we left the forest already?'

Reito grunted. 'Not exactly. Look.' He pointed over the corn to a distant line of trees. The clearing appeared to be a rough oval, many spans long and across, surrounded by forest on all sides. 'But we are going there.' He gestured to the right, where huts and tents filled the other half of the clearing.

'By the Lord of Life,' Terzjin breathed. 'How could this be?' He ran ahead, down a narrow path through the wheat.

Valcero ran after him. Between the wheat and the village was an open patch of grass. A pole stood in its centre, bearing a scrap of blue cloth. The wind stirred it, revealing some yellow thread.

'Greetings!' Master Maltorus called out in Caerian. 'Greetings in the name of your king!'

Men wandered out from the tents and huts. They gathered on the field, scratching their heads and rubbing their faces. Some wore rough brown tunics, others old blue Cantari uniforms. They were soldiers, Caerian soldiers. Their hair was matted, and their faces poorly shaven. Many smelled of wood smoke and cheap wine. They stood in the strengthening sunshine, blinking and frowning at the newcomers.

Terzjin gazed around and grinned. 'This is a happy surprise!'

They stared back at him with stony faces.

'And you are ...?' a soldier called out.

'My name is ...' Terzjin began. 'Wait, who is in command here?'

'I am.' A man stepped out of the crowd. His blue tunic was in better condition—only slightly ragged on the hem. His thin brown hair was wetted down and his face was freshly shaven.

Master Maltorus strode forward. 'General Divendrion.'

The general frowned and took Terzjin's hand in his. 'Ah, yes. The King's bodyguard, correct?'

Terzjin nodded. 'Terzjin Maltorus. I come from our King, to see what allies we could find in Caeria, but I did not expect you, General. We had no news.'

The general withdrew his hand. 'We had some news of you. Safe across the sea, we heard.'

Terzjin tried to smile. 'But how did you come to be here?'

'We *fled* here,' Divendrion replied, 'and they gave us shelter.' He cocked his head at the Torecti, who waited at the edge of the grass.

Reito stepped forward, and the Caerian soldiers shuffled apart to let him approach.

'They entered the forest pursued by dogs and riders,' Reito said, in Caerian. 'They begged us for sanctuary, and we granted it. At first, they lived by our village, but there was trouble.' He shot Divendrion a pointed look. 'So, we granted them this space where they could live apart.' Reito glanced around the camp and grimaced. 'It was quite a sacrifice to lose so many trees. But we have used the wood to prepare shelter for our children's children, may they come to be.'

Divendrion grunted.

'General,' Terzjin said, 'I come with good tidings. The King has been preparing to liberate Caeria. The time is coming.'

The general nodded slowly. 'Is that right?'

'There is much we should discuss,' Terzjin said. 'Can we talk?'

'Take your time,' Reito said. 'We will be nearby when you need us.'

'They always are,' General Divendrion muttered under his breath. 'Very well, Master Maltorus,' he said more loudly, 'follow me, please.'

The general strode away, and Terzjin followed. Valcero hesitated. The soldiers stared at him, so the boy bowed his head and hurried after. No one told him not to.

They passed through the camp. Men were frying breakfast on a battered old shield. Some soldiers were still sleeping, lying half out of their tents, while others squatted on the ground and stared at nothing in particular. Some tents were nothing more than old cloaks propped up with rusting spears.

Divendrion's hut was at the back, built directly on the ground and roofed with thatch, larger than the others. Inside was dim and cool. Only a little light shone through the doorway and small windows.

'Please, sit.' The general pointed to three stools at the hearth. 'I don't have much food and drink to offer. The bread's still baking. We tend to wake late these days.' He shrugged and sat down.

Terzjin and Valcero followed suit.

The general sucked on his cheek and studied the boy 'And you?'

'This is Valcero Baradon, my assistant.' Terzjin leaned over and patted him on the back. 'He speaks Torecti and is completely trustworthy.'

Valcero gingerly raised his hand. 'Well met, General.'

'Alright.'

'General, can you tell the story of how you came here?' Terzjin asked. 'What happened after…?'

'After *you* all ran away?' Divendrion sighed. 'Well, we ran away too, so can't fault you, I suppose. We tried to hold Etorium, but the strawheads got over the river and broke through the East Gate. They rode up the hill and surrounded the palace, so we couldn't retreat there. They were swarming into the city, and we knew we were done for. Didn't see much point in surrendering, so I rounded up as many of us as we could find—some 500 soldiers—and we snuck out the West Gate with a bunch of civilians in tow, while the strawheads pillaged the eastern districts.'

Divendrion reached for a waterskin hanging on the wall. He unstoppered it and held it out to Terzjin and Valcero. 'Wine? No? Oh, well.' He flung his head back and took a deep gulp, then winced. 'Needs honey. Where was I? Oh yes, we headed off on the Impona road. We were a real mix, you see—cantare, lenotare, palantare, some tirentare who'd somehow missed the boats, along with a few volunteer militia and the citizens. They'd never held a spear in their life, but were hoping we'd keep them safe. Poor bastards.'

Divendrion took a more cautious sip. 'Our plan was to get to Impona or Mandonum—somewhere up north that's easy to defend—and maybe hold out there. But after a few days on the road, we saw a cloud of dust behind us—the Rhenivians in pursuit. Now, we had some horses and chariots to carry whatever supplies we grabbed on our way out. But we were all otherwise on foot, and the Rhenivians were almost certainly on horseback. So, I changed the plan. We'd go to the Nedolian Forest and find a place to hide.

'We left the road and crossed the countryside until we came to a river. The Lebantia, I believe. We found a ford but had to abandon the chariots. The river was too deep and full of rocks. It was slow going, and by the time we were all over, the strawheads were maybe an hour away.'

'What did you do?' Terzjin asked.

The general scratched his face. 'Well, one of my commanders—Gergius, a veteran from the Galatan War—offered to win us some time. I refused, but the old soldier insisted. We asked for volunteers and ended up selecting our hundred best. Gergius—long may we remember his name—told the rest of us to keep running. Wouldn't take no for an answer. We didn't see them again, of course. But the story made its way to us much later, and it seems they pulled together a barrier on the west bank and made their stand. Twice the strawheads tried to cross on their heavy steeds, but Caerian spears sent them back—or floating away downstream.' He gave a bitter laugh. 'Of course, the bastards sent half their riders upstream to find another ford, and then they rode back down and surrounded the Gergius and his men. It was a tough fight, and the Rhenivians prevailed in the end. But, we did get three more days.'

'And then you made it here?' Valcero asked.

'Well,' the general replied, 'not exactly. We didn't sleep easily on any of those three nights, but by the third, we thought *maybe* they had lost our trail. How wrong we were.'

Terzjin leaned forward. 'What do you mean?'

'They fell upon us like wolves in the middle of the fourth night. Half of us were asleep. A bloodbath. But some of us escaped in the dark and fled all through the night under the moons and the stars. We ran and ran, not stopping for water or food, or those too tired to continue. The Rhenivians found us as we neared the forest. Our fallen comrades had left a neat little trail for the strawheads to follow.

'Once we were in the Nedolian Forest, they were close enough we could hear their hoofbeats and their dogs. Their *dogs*, you see. They hunted us like animals. All we could do was run, or collapse and die. We reached the tree line, just as the old stories described it. We were scared, though what choice did we have but to enter? The Rhenivians followed. They didn't know what the markings meant. And then we came to a river too deep to cross, and we were trapped.

'I prepared the remaining soldiers for a final stand—less than a hundred by then. We waited. The Rhenivians never arrived. We heard what sounded like a fearsome battle, and then *they* came out of the trees. Hundreds of Torecti poured down the hill towards us. I screamed for mercy, but they just came on, painted like spirits and ready to cut us to pieces. An out of the fisher's net and into the shark's jaws kind of situation. I begged again, and then *that* one...' Divendrion pointed out the open door. '... that *Reito* sauntered right up to me and spoke in the most perfect Caerian, as if he'd learnt it on his mother's knee.'

'What did he say?' Terzjin asked.

'He said they would give us sanctuary, that we would be their guests, basically. And we were. We first lived beside the village, but yes, it's true as Reito said. Some of the men were a little... too friendly with the local maidens. Not that their advances were entirely unwelcome—actually—but it caused a stink with the chief. I had to have the boys whipped; otherwise, we'd have all ended up with an arrow in the neck. After that, they gave us this patch away from the village. They let us cut down the trees and plant corn for real food, but you could see how much it pained them. We're allowed to go hunting a bit, but not far, or their patrols send us back. So yes, we are guests and the Torecti are determined to follow the laws of hospitality, but it's clear they'd rather we leave their house now.'

'That time is coming soon,' Terzjin said. 'I promise.'

'You mentioned this new cantaris.'

'Yes,' Master Maltorus replied. 'They are well-trained, armed with forged iron. King Zjandius has enlisted all Sasiion in this cause. The new fleet is bigger, with better ships, new weapons. They are tested. He's determined to drive out the Rhenivians.'

'And you have come to tell us all this?'

'Not exactly, no. As I said, we had no idea you were here, but it's a welcome surprise. The King sent me to make an alliance with the Torecti and any other rebels we could find.'

'Did the Torecti say yes?' Divendrion frowned. 'Seems unlikely.'

'Not yet,' Terzjin said, 'but they are planning a meeting in a few weeks' time. The chiefs will gather and decide. I'm confident they'll say yes.'

'Perhaps.' The general swallowed more wine. 'It's a lot of promises to keep.'

'We have a ship waiting in Impona, with a secret cargo of arrow heads, spear tips, and swords. All freshly hammered from the finest Sasiion iron. If you could lend some men, and with the Torecti's help, we'll bring the weapons. It's a gift that will surely sway them to our side, and should also be enough for your cantare. How many live here?'

General Divendrion sighed. 'Our numbers have risen and fallen over the years. Like I said, we were fewer than a hundred when the Torecti took us in. We gained a bit as we found survivors and fugitives. They occasionally let a handful of us in and out of the Nedolian to gather recruits and supplies.' He patted the wineskin. 'Then the Sanadin uprising happened, and many wanted to go and fight. They thought it might be the reckoning, that the tide would turn and Caeria would be free. Others were not so certain. So, we put it to a vote and let the volunteers go. Most died in battle, but a few returned and brought Sanadin cantare with them. Now we are just over 200 men.'

Terzjin clapped his hands. 'Excellent!'

The general scowled. 'Look outside, Master Maltorus. Do you see a cantaris ready for battle? They are tired and without hope. They would be fat as well, but we don't have enough food for that. We have endured defeat, and stories from across the sea will not rouse us. We're trapped here. We'll spend the rest of our days in this clearing and as we die one by one, the trees planted over our ashes will swallow up the camp, and then the Torecti will have their forest back.'

Master Maltorus stood up. 'Caeria *will* be free, with or without you, General. You can help us, restore your pride and honour, and—more importantly—go home. Or you can rot here alone in the forest, as you predict. What would you prefer?'

Divendrion glared up at him. 'Where would we even begin?'

'We have time before the gathering. I'll help you prepare your cantaris—train them and raise their spirits. We'll plan a strategy with the Torecti at the same time. It *can* be done.'

The general fidgeted with the wine stopper. 'I don't know.'

Terzjin paced around the hut. 'Aren't you all *bored*? At the very least, it will give you something to do.'

Divendrion squinted at him. 'Are you serious about all this?'

'Yes!'

'Do not dangle false hope before me, sir.'

Master Maltorus strode over to the general. 'I am not.'

'Oh, gods.' General Divendrion sighed and stood. 'Oh, very well.'

Terzjin grabbed him by the shoulders. 'Yes! Why don't you go and make an announcement?'

The general wriggled free. 'Yes, yes.' He walked to the door, then paused. 'Actually, Master Maltorus,' he said, 'if you seek allies to liberate Caeria, it would be wise to invite some other guests to your gathering.'

'Who?'

'They are rebels,' Divendrion replied, 'but I'm not sure exactly who they are. They keep to themselves, though we've had contact over the years.'

'Go on,' Terzjin said.

'The rumour goes they are some kind of bandit group that grew a conscience, or at least decided that attacking Rhenivians suited them. Either way, they would make useful allies. I can get a message to them via our friends in the towns near the forest.'

Master Maltorus nodded. 'Please do.'

The general stretched and yawned. 'Alright. Now, I must go out and sell a hopeless dream to some hopeless men.'

CHAPTER SIXTEEN

THE NEDOLIAN FOREST – WINTER'S RISING – 436

The weeks passed quickly. On some days, Valcero went with Terzjin to the camp and watched as Master Maltorus trained the soldiers into a new cantaris. Terzjin could shout quite loudly, as the boy discovered. He made them run around the edge of the clearing until the soldiers moaned and collapsed. Valcero also tried to run, but managed one circuit before his sides ached. Terzjin ordered the cantare to carry tree trunks, then drop and pick them up repeatedly. The men grumbled and complained, yet obeyed. Valcero tried to lift the end of a log, but his thin arms strained until he dropped the timber. The soldiers laughed, and Terzjin told the boy to rest in the shade. Valcero blushed and stormed off.

Then, Terzjin went to Impona to meet with Taerinus. He would not let Valcero accompany him. 'Too dangerous,' Master Maltorus had said before striding away through the trees.

Valcero spent the following days playing with the Torecti children and trying to learn their names, their customs, and their secrets. But the children did not want to talk much about anything, except whatever game they were playing at that moment. It was difficult.

When he returned from his adventure a week later, Terzjin came with some cantare pulling carts covered in sackcloth.

Valcero ran up to him. 'Terzjin!'

'Ah, Valcero, good to see you.' Master Maltorus patted him on the shoulder.

They stood looking at each other for a moment while everyone watched.

Terzjin scratched his head, then bent over and embraced the boy. 'Have you been well?'

'Yes, I've been learning all—'

One of the soldiers coughed. 'Master Maltorus, we must take these to our camp.'

'Oh yes. Look, here comes Reito. I'm sure he can escort you.'

The Torecti warrior led the soldiers away, as they hauled the carts, huffing and puffing, over the soft, uneven ground.

'What are they carrying?' Valcero asked.

'Weapons.' Terzjin grinned. 'Everything from the Ladistrien ship. Enough to reequip General Divendrion's men and share with the Torecti.' He turned away and strolled to their hut.

The boy followed. 'How is Master Ladistrien?'

'He was relieved to see me. He thought we were going to rescue Jeigo there and then, and his face fell when I told him, "Not yet". Poor man. They had been berthed in Impona for a while, and I think Taerinus was running out of coins to bribe the port warden. So, we took the *Dela* upriver as far as it could go—past the border and into Torecti lands. They should be safer there, though I think the smugglers are terrified.' Terzjin chuckled.

'I wish I could have come with you,' Valcero said. 'Maybe next time?'

Terzjin flopped down on the steps of the hut and looked around. 'And this forest…' he whispered. 'We reached the northern edge in less than a day. We walked for another *five* days to Impona. Yet, it would take at least four days to sail to Impona from where we landed. It makes no sense.'

'How do you think they do it?' Valcero asked. 'The Torecti, I mean.'

Master Malorus shrugged. 'Who can say? Perhaps we don't know the shape of this land very well.'

'If Master Meretan were here, he'd say to look for the simplest explanation.'

Terzjin smiled. 'He really should be here. He will be so envious when you recount your adventures.'

'Caeri!' Reito strode up to their hut.

'Greetings.' Terzjin stood. 'Are the soldiers back at their camp?'

Reito nodded. 'And I saw what they were carrying. Glittering metal.'

'There's plenty to share with the Torecti, if you want it.'

The Torecti man smiled. 'We shall see.' His expression turned serious. 'But I come about another matter. The chiefs have arrived, Terzjin Maltorus. There shall be a gathering at sunset. They will decide if we go to spill blood, or not. You will make your case.'

Terzjin nodded. 'I see. General Divendrion should also attend.'

'Of course,' Reito replied. 'We will escort him. And your other guests.'

'Other guests?'

Reito's face was carefully blank. 'From beyond the forest. We met them at the border, but we will not bring them here until the gathering.' He frowned at Terzjin and Valcero. 'I trust you will use your judgement.'

'I'm not sure I understand,' Master Maltorus said.

The Torecti shrugged. 'You will see.'

'Do you really need me?' Valcero asked. 'They all seem to speak Caerian.'

The sun was setting as they approached the gathering place.

'Of course I need you,' Terjin replied. 'I need someone I trust.' He lowered his voice and spoke in Old Sasiion. 'I can't always be sure that Reito gives the full story. You can sit at my side and whisper in my ear if he leaves anything out, alright?'

The boy nodded. 'Alright.'

'Good. Now let's be on our best behaviour.'

They came to a new clearing in the forest. The Torecti had set logs in a semicircle to one side. On the other side were five seats, roughly hewn from pale rocks that jutted out of the leaf litter. The Torecti guided them to the logs, where General Divendrion was already sitting.

Reito emerged from the forest. 'I present Chief Ferro, of the Tall Trees.'

An elderly man, clad in a feather cloak, hobbled into the clearing.

They arose to greet him. The chief leaned on his staff and nodded to the Caerians, then eased himself into a stone chair with Reito's help.

Reito looked to the trees. 'Now, Chief Elagius, of the Grey Mist.'

Another feather-cloaked chief entered the clearing and took his seat. He was tall and gaunt, his hair streaked with silver.

'Chief Duella, of the Running River.'

She was a short woman of middling years. The other chiefs stood and bowed as she sat amongst them.

'Chief Seralix, of the Sighing Cedars.'

Seralix was far younger than the others, perhaps younger than Terzjin, yet bore a serious face and a noble air. The chiefs bowed to him as they had done with each other.

'And your host, Chief Perax of the Whispering Leaves.'

Perax entered the clearing, bowed to them all, and said a few words of welcome. Everyone sat, except Reito, who beckoned to someone in the trees. Three hooded figures, escorted by four Torecti warriors, emerged from the forest. As they approached, they lifted their hoods to reveal two young men and an older woman. One of the men—a barely more than a boy—with a thin, pale face and a red birthmark splashed across it, squinted and stared at Terzjin.

Master Maltorus leaned forward and stared at the young man, then the woman. 'By the One,' he whispered.

Reito nodded at the group, then turned to the chiefs. 'I present Lady Hiregeia Aventan and her sons.'

The Aventan bowed to the chiefs, then sat on the logs with the other Caerians. General Divendrion gaped at Lady Aventan in shock.

Terzjin leaned over. 'My Lady… how…?'

Hiregeia Aventan was tall, with greying hair, sharp eyes and a tight mouth on a lined face. She sat straight-backed and nodded in greeting. Terzjin peered again at the young men, who pulled their hoods over their heads and turned away.

'We now begin the gathering,' Reito announced. He gestured to Terzjin. 'Step forward.'

Master Maltorus stood, glanced at Lady Aventan, then turned to face the seated chiefs. He gave much the same speech as he gave Chief Perax on their first evening in the forest. The chiefs watched Terzjin while he spoke in short bursts, with Reito translating.

Valcero looked around the clearing. Some Torecti watched from the edge of the clearing. Behind them, half-hidden in the bushes, stood Illauri. She winked at Valcero. The boy blushed and pretended to study Lady Aventan's gown. The cloth was fine, though the hem was torn and ragged.

'It had gold thread, but I pulled it out,' Lady Aventan muttered. She peered down at him, frowning.

Valcero blushed again. 'Pardon, My Lady,' he whispered.

'In times like this, I can't go parading about the countryside covered in gold.'

Valcero nodded, not sure what to say.

Master Maltorus concluded his speech and waited for a reply.

The Chief of the Sighing Cedars spoke first, waving his hand about.

'Chief Seralix says that in villages close to the border, they hear the knocking of Rhenivian axes,' Reito translated. 'The invaders grow ever more bold.'

Now Chief Duella spoke, her voice sharp and angry.

'Twice now the Rhenivians have set trees afire near Running River lands,' Reito echoed. 'She would have the invaders driven back, out of the forest completely.'

Terzjin bowed and smiled. 'We appreciate your support, Chiefs.'

Chief Elagius coughed and folded his arms. He turned to his fellow chiefs as he spoke.

'Chief Elagius,' Reito said,' maintains that we Taurex have the means to keep the invaders at bay. 'There is no need to waste our lives on adventures beyond the border. He asks why the Taurex should help the Caeri, when you were content to forget our very existence.'

'I... I am not sure what the chief means,' Terzjin replied. 'The Torecti-of-the-Trees are well-remembered in Caeria.'

Reito cocked his head. 'Is that so? According to the pact, Taurex and Caeri promised to meet yearly—on midsummer's day, the first of your month of Summer's Reign—to discuss matters and exchange gifts of friendship. Yet, after some summers, the Caeri no longer showed their faces. We Taurex were faithful to our word. We still come each year to the appointed place and leave our gift to you—on a pile of gifts, now worn and rotted.'

Master Maltorus bowed his head. 'I am sorry for that, sorry to all of you. I cannot account for the actions of past generations.'

Perax shook his head and grumbled something about promises unkept. The other chiefs muttered in agreement, except Seralix, who spoke forcefully.

'What's he saying?' Terzjin whispered to Valcero.

'Seralix says they don't have to trust the Caerians. They only need to ally with us long enough to defeat the Rhenivians, then things can return to how they were.'

'Dear chiefs.' Master Maltorus stood again. 'I cannot change what past kings have or have not done, but I *can* promise Zjandius is an honourable man and will renew the old pact. I have his ear and can pass on whatever message you wish to give him.'

The chiefs regarded him silently.

Lady Aventan arose. 'Perhaps I may speak?'

Reito looked to the Chiefs, then back to her. 'Go ahead.'

Terzjin sat as she drew herself to her full height and gathered her cloak around her.

'I am Lady Hiregeia Aventan. We Aventan are one of the six—no, five—remaining aristocratic families of Caeria. Our roots reach deep in this land. Torecti blood courses through us. I came to tell you what these invaders did to my family and our people.

She paused to allow Rieto to translate her words. She breathed in. 'The Rhenivians struck us first. They beached their ships by our Lastria in the early hours before dawn, in the waning days of the year. We had barely a moment to bar our gates before they fell upon us. Alas, our numbers were too small to hold the city walls when the Rhenivians battered their way inside and flooded our streets. Terrified we were, but I tried to stoke my people's courage.'

'And what of Lord Aventan, My Lady?' Terzjin asked.

Lady Aventan looked down at him. 'My husband was away, hunting in the hills with my elder sons before Fools' Week.' She put a hand on each of the young men. 'The defence of the city fell to me. We tried to barricade the palace as a final refuge, but they broke through without much effort.' She sighed. 'When it became clear the barbarians would enter my house, I had my attendants hide my daughters and youngest son, while I disguised myself as a servant. I planned to survive the battle, and then escape the palace with my family.

'The Rhenivians slaughtered many as they barged in, but rounded up most of us in the courtyard. They demanded to know where Lord Aventan was, where my family and I hid. But my people were loyal, and did not surrender me, though I stood right before the barbarians.'

Hiregeia paused and examined the ground. She flicked away a tear and then looked up, eyes cold and hard. 'They trampled through the palace, shouting, taunting, threatening all manner of obscene things for when they would find us. And they *did* find my daughters.' Her throat tightened, and she swallowed. 'They were hiding on a balcony that overlooks the sea. Hiding with my youngest son—barely a babe—and some loyal cantare, ready to fight to the end. The invaders smashed through the door and made to seize them, but my daughters would not be taken alive. They leapt into the ocean, carrying my son between them. And the Rhenivians thought the servant who leapt with them was me, so they believed I too was dead.'

One of her sons reached up and took her hand. The chiefs exchanged glances.

'For nearly a week, I wandered my halls as a shade of myself. I played the part of a servant in my own house, attending to every drunken demand from the boors who despoiled it. One night, when most had left my Lastria to plague the rest of Caeria, and the rest were sleeping, I crept out of the palace by secret means and left the city to seek what might remain of my family.'

'Did you find Lord Aventan?' Terzjin asked.

Lady Aventan smiled thinly. 'Yes and no. Unfortunately, the news had flown ahead of me. When I found his hunting camp in the hills, my husband had already fallen upon his sword. His rage could not withstand his grief. But I found my two sons...' She squeezed their shoulders. '...and we mourned together. Then we began to wreak our revenge.'

'Revenge?' Reito paused in his translation and turned to her.

'For the past few years, we have gathered anyone we could find loyal to the Aventan, anyone loyal to a free Caeria. We hide in the hills, the forests, and the mountains. We have no great cantaris, but we ambush and sabotage the Rhenivians wherever possible. We never allow them to feel safe in our land.'

Chief Elagius pulled himself to his feet and spoke.

'The chief says that you Aventan already wage war against the invaders,' Reito said. 'You are the natural allies of your King Zjandius, and so the Caeri have no need for the Taurex. You can leave us out of this fight.'

Master Maltorus stood up beside Lady Aventan. 'Good chiefs, please. *Every* ally counts.'

'With respect to you Torecti chiefs,' Hiregeia said, 'but you know not how many Rhenivians there are. Their soldiers are like a flood upon the plain. Our attacks are like a rat nipping on the hooves of a great bull. You may feel safe in your leafy fortress, but they *will* keep chopping and burning until you have neither shade nor shelter to protect you. You can kill a few intruders, yes, but they can bring more from across the sea. Only a decisive defeat will end this invasion.'

Chief Elagius gazed at her while Reito translated.

Lady Aventan's voice rose. 'Believe me, Torecti Chiefs, the Rhenivians are true savages. Barbarians, every one of them. They burn, they break, they steal. They have no honour. They observe no laws of good conduct in war or peace. The ancient treaties mean nothing to them. You *know* this.'

'It is true.' Illauri-of-the-Woods strode into the clearing, speaking Torecti. 'They perform blood sacrifices in the forest, on the very trees themselves.'

'On the trees?' Chief Ferro's voice quavered.

Illauri nodded. 'They slaughter beasts and men to honour their dark gods. Sometimes *even* in the shadows of the cypresses.'

Chief Duella scowled and shook her head. 'Unforgivable.'

'What are they saying?' Terzjin whispered to Valcero.

'She's helping, I think,' the boy muttered.

The chiefs arose and huddled with Reito. Illauri withdrew into the trees.

'Thank you for your assistance, Lady Aventan,' Terzjin said while they waited.

The lady bowed her head. 'I pray it will be enough.'

'And I am sorry for everything you have suffered,' Master Maltorus continued. 'I swear, I will do whatever I can to bring you justice.'

'Fear not,' Hiregeia said. 'We shall have our vengeance against those who assaulted my family. Heirik and Getherd will pay—life for life.'

'Ah, but My Lady...' Terzjin grimaced. 'King Zjandius wants it known that he has forbidden assassination of the thanes. He wants them to stand trial.'

Lady Aventan scowled, but at that moment, the chiefs broke from their huddle and retook their seats.

Reito cleared his throat. 'The chiefs have decided. Though the ancient pact forbids it, they will gather warbands and cross the borders. It is unprecedented, but we will help drive out the invaders. In return, you Caeri must renew your vows to uphold our laws in this land. Do you accept these terms?'

Master Maltorus bowed low. 'On behalf of King Zjandius, we *gratefully* accept. Thank you.'

Reito nodded. 'Then the chiefs will go to their clans and prepare for war and death. We will await word from your king about when to strike.'

'There is no time to lose,' Terzjin said. 'I will return to King Zjandius in the morning with these glad tidings.'

The Chiefs nodded to him and left the clearing in different directions.

'We take our leave as well,' Lady Aventan said.

Her sons arose. The one with the birthmark glanced at Valcero and then at Terzjin. He flinched and turned away.

Valcero looked up at Terzjin, who was staring after the boy with a strange expression on his face.

Master Maltorus blinked and smiled at Lady Aventan. 'Thank you again, My Lady. I hope to see you again soon. Hopefully in Etorium, and under better circumstances.'

'You look just like him, you know. *Quite* uncanny.'

'My Lady?'

'Your father, I mean.'

Terzjin frowned. 'I beg your pardon, Lady Aventan, but you must be—'

'I met him once, many years ago, at the wedding of old King Adomenus.' Lady Avantan searched Terzjin's face, smiling faintly. 'He was there to give away his wife's sister. Of course, you would have only been a babe, perhaps not even born. It *was* a happy celebration. Your father certainly tried his best, but we let him down, King—'

'I am sorry, My Lady.' Terzjin shook his head. 'You must have me mistaken for someone else. My parents... well, my parents, they died not so long ago. In a fire, ten years past. In... Enternis.'

'Really? With a name like *Terzjin*?' Her eyes were locked with his. 'Well, maybe I *am* mistaken. Very well, yes, may we meet again in Etorium, Master Maltorus. We can speak more then. Perhaps you could tell me the tale of how you came from... *Enternis* and ended up in Etorium as a king's lenotarus. I am sure it would be most fascinating.' She nodded at him and glanced to Valcero. 'Farewell.'

The three Aventan walked away, escorted by Torecti.

'What was she talking about?' Valcero asked Terzjin.

'Leave it,' Master Maltorus snapped. He stared after them; his face was pale and tense.

The Aventan son with the birthmark leaned to his mother's ear and whispered. She glanced back at Terzjin, before disappearing into the forest.

General Divendrion shrugged. 'Well, I think I'll be heading home as well. Good night, all.' He left with his own Torecti escorts.

Valcero and Terzjin trudged back to the village in silence.

When they reached their hut, the boy asked, 'Will we eat with the villagers tonight?'

Terzjin shook his head. 'I will go to bed. I must go to the ship early tomorrow, fulfil my promise to Taerinus, and return to the King.'

'And me?'

'You'll stay here in the forest, boy. It's the safest place for you. War is coming.'

'But, Terzjin—'

'I know a better way to Etorium, Terzjin Maltorus.'

They started.

Illauri-of-the-Woods stood behind them with her hands behind her back. She smiled. 'There are other paths to reach the city, quicker than a ship, and... *possibly* safer.'

Master Maltorus frowned. 'Will you show me the way tomorrow?'

'I will show you the way, yes,' Illauri replied, ' but we must leave *now*. This is the moment.'

Terzjin chewed his lip. 'Alright, let me collect my things.' He climbed into the hut.

'Pack lightly,' Illauri called after him.

Terzjin clambered outside again and strapped his sword to his belt.

'Can I come with?' Valcero asked. 'Please?'

Master Maltorus scowled. 'No.'

'Please, Terzjin. I can help.'

'No, you can't.' Terzjin put on his cloak.

Illauri watched them.

'But I want to help you.' Valcero reached for Terzjin's arm.

Terzjin jerked his arm away. 'By the *gods*, child! Listen to me. I promised to protect you, not drag you along everywhere. And I am not your family. So, you will stay *here*. Not with me. Can he stay here?'

'Of course,' Illauri replied.

'There, it's settled. Stay here and behave. I will send for you when it's all over.' Master Maltorus nodded at Valcero.

The boy stood watching them stride away. Laughter and chatter drifted through the trees, but he was alone.

CHAPTER SEVENTEEN

THE NEDOLIAN FOREST – WINTER'S RISING – 436

'You were a little harsh, no?' Illauri remarked as they walked through the forest.

'I don't think so,' Terzjin said. 'It will be dangerous out there, and he's not prepared for it.'

'Are you?'

Master Maltorus grunted. 'Prepared enough.'

'Hmm.' Illauri led him along a narrow path through the trees. Only Telanis shone in the sky, so the way was dim. 'So you have fought many wars before?'

'Well, not many wars as such,' Terzjin said. 'But I have experience in the matter.'

Illauri turned to look at him. 'Have you taken many lives?'

Terzjin breathed in sharply and frowned. 'No. Only once, long ago.'

'I see.' She turned away.

They walked on. The crickets, frogs and nightjars filled the darkness with sound.

He lifts the rock above his head. His thin arms strain with the weight of it.

'Tell me something.' Terzjin broke the silence. 'Did you see the sons of Lady Aventan?'

'Yes, what of it?'

'The older son, the marked one, did you see his eyes?'

Illauri chuckled. 'He has the gift. You want to ask me about that.'

'I do, yes.'

'The lady claimed to have Torecti blood. Perhaps that is why.

Perhaps you do as well, Terzjin Maltorus.' She studied him, and her eyes flared.

His spine tingled. 'I'm sure that is impossible. My family was... not from here.'

'Or,' Illauri continued, 'perhaps not. The Lord of Life chooses as he wills.'

They went in silence for a while. The path began to slope downward.

Master Maltorus peered at her face. 'And? What are we supposed to do with this... gift?'

Illauri glanced up at the multitude of stars and smiled. 'A good question. One could spend a lifetime in search of an answer.'

'What do... do you do with your gift?'

'As little as possible. It is for the best.'

'I don't understand.'

Illauri laughed. 'Oh, but you will, Terzjin Maltorus. You will, in time.'

Terzjin stumbled on a root hidden in the shadows, but caught himself before he fell.

'But to answer your question properly,' Illauri said, 'I tend to the forest, and help those who dwell within it.'

'You helped us at the gathering, I believe. The chiefs listened. Thank you.'

'Oh, I gave no orders.' Illauri put her hand on his shoulder. 'I merely confirmed the lady's words. The chiefs listen to me, yes, but they do not answer to me.'

'Mmm.'

'And what else did Lady Aventan say before she left?' Illauri asked.

'Nothing important. She had me confused with... I take it we're journeying overland to Etorium?'

'In a manner of speaking, yes,' Illauri replied.

'Walking on foot? Are you sure this is quicker than sailing?'

'Yes.' She halted and put a hand on his chest to stop him. She gazed at the stars while Terzjin's heart beat under her touch.

'I appreciate your help, but perhaps this is not—'

'Shh!' Illauri peered ahead into the distance. There was nothing there, save trees with pale branches and dark leaves. She nodded.

'Now, it's time.' She pulled out a strip of cloth. 'Here, I must cover your eyes for this next part.'

'Cover my eyes? No—'

Illauri glared at him. 'Do you trust me?'

Terzjin stared at her. He breathed out. 'Alright.'

She chuckled and reached up to wrap the cloth over his face. She pulled it into a tight knot at the back of his head. The night went even darker. An owl screeched nearby.

'Now, I will take your hand…' Her hand, soft and warm, nestled against his. '…and lead you upon a *very* secret path. For I trust you, Terzjin Maltorus.'

'I am honoured, Illauri-of-the-Woods.'

'Do everything I say. Do not let go of me. Do ***not*** remove the blindfold.'

'Very well.'

Illauri tugged his hand and led him forward. She began to sing. The song was slow and strange, the words wild and unknown. Her voice rose and fell, soft and sweet like liquid honey. The melody haunted Terzjin, like a distant memory, just out of reach, a song of long ago, a dream lost upon waking. A song unending. How long they walked, he could not say. His head spun, and he struggled to find his footing in the dark, but Illauri let him lean on her and steadied him as they went.

Eventually, the air lost its chill and grew warmer, thicker, more damp. A golden light suffused dimly through the fabric.

'Is it morning already?' Terzjin reached for the blindfold.

Illauri slapped his hand down without pausing her song.

Birds called, soft and distant. He breathed a rich reek of leafmould and resin, the wafting scents of nectar-laden flowers. Illauri's song wound to a gentle close.

'Where are we?' Terzjin whispered. He twisted his head from side to side.

'I would prefer not to tell you.'

She led him along for a time, over soft ground that seemed to swallow each step. Then she squeezed his hand. 'Be still for a moment, Terzjin Maltorus.' Her voice was tight. 'Please, do not move.'

They stood in silence. Terzjin listened to the dimmed forest sounds, to the pumping blood in his ears, to Illauri's gentle breathing.

There was something else.

Muffled footfalls approached on the soft earth. Heavy. Deliberate. Master Maltorus' left hand drifted towards his sword hilt, but Illauri squeezed his right, and he stopped himself. It was two feet—he was certain—so not on horseback. A Torecti? A Rhenivian? Who? Terzjin's heart thudded in his chest.

'Do not move,' Illauri hissed.

The footfalls grew closer and then stopped, right before them. The birdsong died away. Something loomed and radiated heat. Its body rustled, as it perhaps leaned closer. Warm breath puffed across Terzjin's face. He smelled damp earth and roots, rain, moss, and sap. He could reach out and touch it, whatever it was, but he dared not.

'Do you trust me?' Illauri asked.

Terzjin licked his lips. 'Yes. I think so.'

'I am going to make a small cut on your hand. Have courage.'

Before he could say a word, Illauri twisted his palm upwards. A sharp pain sliced across it. He bit his lip. Illauri twisted his palm downwards. His hot blood welled up and trickled down his fingers. Each drop thudded on the leaf litter.

The warm breath blew over him again, then whatever it was drew away. The footsteps faded into silence. The birdsong returned.

Illauri breathed out. 'Good,' she whispered. 'Very good.' There was a soft tearing, then she bound his hand with another strip of cloth. 'Now, come. We have not much further to go.'

She led him along for another length of time and resumed her song. The light dimmed once more, and the winter chill returned. Illauri's song diminished to a whisper, then nothing. She stopped, and Terzjin nearly bumped into her. A lone cricket whistled nearby.

She undid his blindfold. 'Only a little way farther.' She sidled away through the trees.

Terzjin blinked. The trees grew tall and tightly together here. He pushed his way through the branches after her. He brushed against the fine, rough leaves and brought forth a pungent aroma. Cypresses. He squinted into the gloom and up at the night sky. 'Where are we?'

'Quiet now,' Illauri whispered, just ahead.

Terzjin squeezed out of the cypresses to join her and stopped short. An old brick wall, encrusted with moss and fern, blocked their path. A faint sound of lapping water and croaking frogs came over the wall. And he tasted a hint of salt in the air. Master Maltorus searched Illauri's face. She stared at him with pale eyes, her face carefully blank. He ran his hand over the rough wall and walked ahead, squeezing through the gap between the wall and trees, until he reached a small archway.

He peeked through. A familiar river flowed past, glimmering in the light of the blue moon Telanis. On the far bank, he spied a grassy field and the dim silhouette of a hill, topped by a fort. Terzjin spun around. A path between the cypresses—some burnt, he noticed—led to a taller stone wall at the back of the grove. A city wall he knew well. Etorium.

Illauri slipped through the trees to stand with him.

He stared at her, wide-eyed. 'How? *How?*'

She put a finger to her lips and smiled. 'You know where to go?'

Terzjin gazed through the archway towards Goretonum. 'I suppose I do. But, still, how—?'

'Good. Then go *now*, Terzjin Maltorus. You do not have too much time.'

'Will you come with me?'

Illauri retreated into the shadows of the trees. 'I cannot help you with this part. I will await you here.'

Terzjin strained to see her. 'Very well.'

'Listen carefully,' she whispered. 'You have little time. You must return before the moon Hirenis rises, or I cannot help you leave this place. Do you understand?'

'I understand.'

'Come too late, and you will not find me here.'

Terzjin nodded.

'Go. Now.'

CHAPTER EIGHTEEN

CAERIA – WINTER'S RISING – 436

Master Maltorus exited through the archway and pulled his hood over his head. He pressed himself against the wall, stilled his heart, and walked like a shade in the pale moonlight. It was as if he had never left.

He paused just before the East Gate. A band of Rhenivian guards carrying fluttering torches marched out and over the bridge. Their boots crunched on the wet paving. As the wooden gate creaked shut behind them, Terzjin took his chance. He crouched low in the shadow of the parapet wall as he crossed the bridge, keeping well behind the soldiers as they approached the village.

The wall of Goretonum lay collapsed in sections of blackened rubble. Campfires revealed the ruined buildings within—burnt and abandoned—where Rhenivians sat amongst them, eating and chatting. One played a lyre while others joined in song. Terzjin darted from shadow to shadow, head bowed, mind carefully blank.

He ducked through a gap in the wall on the other side of the village and scrambled up the grassy hillside, avoiding the gravel track that spiralled up to the fortress gate. The way was slow—steep, bushy and slippery in places. When he reached the wall, he shuffled along the base to the old fig tree that jutted from the stonework. He climbed the bare branches and felt around for crevices between the bricks to place his hands and feet. Master Maltorus scaled the final spans and poked his head over the parapet.

Moonlight bathed the ramparts, all deserted. He hauled himself on top and peered back over the edge. The village below glittered with firelight. Echoes of soldiers rose up to his ears. The night sky glowed as Telanis floated on a bank of clouds, before a ribbon of stars across the heavens. Etorium, beyond the dim river, yet so close, lay sleeping. Lamplight twinkled here and there from windows and alleys winding up the hill. And there, above the jumble of rooftops, at the very top, was his old home, the palace. It crouched dark and quiet.

Terzjin found a shaded wooden ladder set against the wall and descended to an alcove beside a tower. Where would the prison cells be? Under the fort? If memory served him, they were in the wall, on the northern side.

He crept along the courtyard's edge, checking the surrounding windows as he went. Lamplight spilt from a few, while most were dark holes. All was silent. Perhaps the guards were already drunk or asleep. Good. The paved courtyard was empty. Or was it? No, there, in the centre...

Terzjin froze, transfixed, and gaped at...*them*.

They stared back, through the darkness that concealed him. A small crowd, silent, unmoving, watching. They were women, Caerian women judging by their dress, with some children—boys and girls—amongst them. Why didn't they move?

Terzjin lost his fear, or perhaps his wits, and crept to the very edge of the moonlight. They were pale, with shadowed eyes and frowning mouths. The children clutched the women's hands and clothes as they gazed up at him. One woman cradled a baby in her arms. The infant did not cry, did not stir, but only watched him with dark eyes. A woman came to the front of the gathering, a matron with silver-streaked hair and a familiar face.

'Lady...Lady Sanadin?' Terzjin breathed.

She said nothing. Her mouth was a tight line.

Terzjin stepped closer.

Lady Sanadin's neck was bleeding; a long gash ran across her throat. The front of her gown was dark, not from shadows, but from a wash of blood pouring from her neck.

A shiver ran up his back. His scalp prickled. They all bore dark splashes upon their clothes, on their necks, blooming from their bellies and hearts. Even the children. Even the baby.

Avenge us.

Did they say that? Or was it his thudding heart?

Terzjin blinked, and they vanished.

He blinked again, and they reappeared, pressing against him, pale and furious.

Lady Sanadin loomed. *Avenge us.*

Terzjin staggered backwards. 'My Lady...' His heart banged against his ribs.

The Lady's unseen eyes bored into him. *Avenge us.*

He turned and dashed to the wall, not daring to look back. Breathe. Breathe. He pressed his forehead against the cold stone. Calm yourself.

Breathe.

The cold stone...

A memory bubbled up from the deep. Under the bed, hiding. The cold stone of the floor against his chest. His mother also lay on the floor, beyond the bed, her head pressed against the stone. She gazed at him and said something without sound, only moving her lips. What did she say?

Avenge us.

Did she say that?

Terzjin winced. Breathe. Steady. He pushed away from the wall and stumbled towards an open door. The way to the cells—he was certain. Running down the corridor, looking back, seeing his brother, his little brother, held aloft by the leg. And the arm, swinging the child downwards, to the side, to the wall...

Breathe. Terzjin gripped himself in the dark. A breeze blew down the stairs and onto his face. Like the north wind. Cold and relentless. His heart slowed and hardened, into ice.

Master Maltorus tiptoed up the stone steps. His eyes and ears strained into the darkness ahead. On the landing, he found a sentry, fast asleep in a splash of moonlight from a window, slumped against the wall with his head on his knees. Terzjin crept past the man, over his fallen spear, and down the corridor. All the lamps had long since burnt out. He brushed his fingers along the wall. A patch of dim light ahead suggested a door. Terzjin peered through the small grille into the cell.

Silence.

He shuffled to the next cell and looked inside. It was too dark, even with moonlight from a small window within. But he heard faint breathing, slow and regular.

'Jeigo?' Terzjin whispered.

No reply.

'Jeigo Ladistrien?' he hissed, louder this time.

The breathing stopped. 'Who's there?' a voice rasped in the dark. Not Jeigo, yet still familiar.

Master Maltorus thought for a moment. 'Lord Octerian?'

The bedclothes rustled and bare feet padded across the stone towards the door. 'Who is that?'

Terzjin grinned. 'Lord Octerian, I am an agent of King Zjandius. I am here to free you.'

A shadow blotted out the moonlight. 'Don't play games with me. What hour is this?'

Terzjin felt for the bolt and eased it out as carefully as possible. He pulled the door open. 'Come quickly, My Lord. We do not have much time.'

The figure moved aside to let some light fall on Terzjin's face. The old man leaned forward. 'The bodyguard?'

'Yes, My Lord. Terzjin Maltorus is my name. Come, let us leave this place.'

'Where is Zjandius?'

'Still in Elisdrium, My Lord. He's—'

Lord Octerian backed into his cell. 'Still in Elisdrium? Are you *mad*?'

Terzjin blinked. 'Sir? I have good news. The King is preparing a cantaris to liberate Caeria.'

'So?'

'If you just come with me, Lord Octerian, we can—'

'You fool!' Octerian nearly shouted. ' If I escape, my family will die. Leave me be, boy. Don't speak to me of cantari.' The aristocrat pulled the door shut. 'Lock it, will you?'

Terzjin stared through the grille. 'My Lord, what happened?'

'You have *no* idea, none of you. You haven't been here.'

'Take heart, Lord Octerian, please,' Terzjin whispered. 'King Zjandius will return. The day approaches, very soon. And there will be justice—for you, and everyone who has suffered. I swear it.'

Lord Octerian spat. 'Go away, boy. Let me sleep.'

Terzjin leaned his head against the door. 'Be ready, sir.'

No reply came.

Master Maltorus left the old aristocrat and crept further down the corridor. He passed two more cells, both silent and empty, before reaching the end, with one final door.

'Who's there?' a voice whispered through the grille.

'Jeigo Ladistrien,' Terzjin said.

'Fuck.' Footsteps pattered from the door. 'By the gods, they forced Taerinus to take that man. Please…'

'Be quiet!' Master Maltorus hissed through the door. 'And calm yourself. I'm here on *behalf* of Taerinus.'

'What?'

'He's alive and well, luckily for you. In fact, Master Ladistrien has been most helpful, so I came to rescue you in return.' Terzjin teased out the bolt and dragged the door open. 'Come, quickly.'

Jeigo crept forward. 'Is this true?'

Terzjin sighed and grabbed the man's arm. 'We don't have time.'

'I have no shoes, nor winter cloak,' Jeigo muttered as they went along the passage.

'No matter. I'll find something. Be careful here.'

They crept past the sleeping guard, with Master Maltorus ensuring the smuggler did not trip on the spear.

They squeezed along the courtyard wall in its shadow. Terzjin kept his eyes on the wall. *They* were still out there in the courtyard, watching him. He shuddered.

Laughter burst from an upstairs window. They froze.

'Do you know what happened here?' Terzjin whispered. 'What happened to the Sanadin?'

'I heard it,' Jeigo whispered in reply.

'Can you tell me more?'

'I would rather not.'

Master Maltorus found rope piled against the wall. He picked it up and led Jeigo to the ladder, which they climbed in silence. At the top, he glanced around the ramparts—still no sentries. The smuggler was thinner than Terzjin remembered, more gaunt around his face. He wore a dirty, threadbare tunic with a piece of string for a belt. Terzjin tied the rope around a crenellation and tossed the rest over the wall. 'Follow me.' He tugged the rope to test it.

Jeigo peered over the edge. 'You could have just stabbed me in the cell, you know. Quicker and cleaner.'

'You're a sailor, aren't you?' Terzjin poked the smuggler. 'How is this any worse than climbing a mast?'

'These days we pay others to do that.'

'Go back to your cell then, if you love it so much.' Master Maltorus swung himself over the side, his feet braced against the wall. 'Or, follow me to freedom and your precious Taerinus.' He began to descend. When he reached the fig tree, he shook the rope. 'Your turn!'

There was a faint, disgusted sigh, then Jeigo clambered over the parapet and down the wall. He slipped at one point, but clung to the rope, cursing Terzjin's name. With help from Master Maltorus, he grabbed the branches and slid to the ground.

They scrambled down the hillside. Jeigo grunted and swore as thorns and stones cut into his bare feet. When they came to the remains of the village wall, Terzjin made the smuggler wait while he snuck into the Rhenivian camp. He ducked into an empty tent behind a group of soldiers, who sat drinking around a nearby fire. He found two cloaks and two helmets. This would do. He threw one of the cloaks around his shoulders, donned a helmet, and gathered the rest into a bundle.

He returned to Jeigo, only to find a Rhenivian swaying and staggering towards the gap. Terzjin froze in the alley a few spans behind the soldier. There was no one else in sight. The Rhenivian paused at the edge of the firelight. Terzjin gripped his sword hilt, ready to spring forward. After what seemed an age, the soldier fumbled with his trousers. There was a sound of liquid spattering against stones. The soldier tied up his trousers, swung around, and tensed as he caught sight of Terzjin. Master Maltorus swayed his body on the spot. He shrugged his shoulders and grinned. The Rhenivian grinned in return and said something in a slurring voice.

Terzjin chuckled and shrugged again. The man stumbled past, slapping Terzjin's shoulder as he left.

He ran to the gap and poked his head through, looking both ways. Jeigo was hunched against the masonry, eyes wide and clutching a brick in one hand.

Master Maltorus lifted his helmet. 'Let's go.'

The smuggler dropped the brick and let out a long breath. 'By the One.' He put on the cloak and helmet that Terzjin handed over. 'Now what?'

'We stroll through the camp as if we belong here. No stopping. Look straight ahead and follow me.'

They stopped only to grab unattended spears and torches, then left Goretonum through the broken wall.

A breeze from the south made the torches sputter as they crossed the river. The gate guards waved as they approached, but Master Maltorus pointed his torch to the right.

'We're not going to the port?' Jeigo muttered.

'No, we travel by another road.'

The smuggler halted. 'I don't understand. How could the roads be safer?'

'This way, please,' Terzjin whispered. 'We're attracting attention.'

Jeigo glared at him from under the helmet.

'Please, trust me. Taerinus isn't at the port.'

'I *don't* trust you. That's the problem. Where is Taerinus, then?'

Master Maltorus rolled his eyes. 'If I *wanted* you dead, yes, I could have done it in your cell. Far simpler, don't you think? Taerinus is safe. He's with your ship, berthed where the Rhenivians cannot find it.'

Jeigo snorted and strode forward. They turned right and followed the path between the river and the wall. As they approached the grove, Terzjin glanced over his shoulder. No guards on the walls, nor following.

'Toss your torch into the river,' Terzjin said, as he threw his away. 'In here.' He led the smuggler through the gate into the cypress grove.

'What are we doing here?' Jeigo looked around. 'A strange time to honour spirits, no?'

Illauri stepped out of the shadow between two trees.

Jeigo sprang back. 'By the *gods*!' He flicked his fingers.

'Fool, she's not one of the dead.' Terzjin almost laughed. Almost.

'This is him?' Illauri asked.

'Jeigo Ladistrien, this is Illauri-of-the-Woods. She is assisting us.'

'Illauri-of-the-Woods...' Jeigo furrowed his brow. 'You are Torecti, aren't you?'

She nodded.

The smuggler turned to Master Maltorus. 'Well, this plan grows ever stranger.'

'We should leave now,' Illauri said.

'Yes...' Terzjin looked up at the cypresses—tall, dark silhouettes against the starry sky. A puff of wind whispered through their branches. What did it say? What did the dead say? He sucked in a deep breath. 'There is one more task.'

Illauri frowned. 'What?'

Terzjin put his hands together. 'Please, wait for me here.'

Illauri shook her head and stepped closer. 'Terzjin Maltorus, no—'

'I won't be long. Just wait.' He backed out of the grove before she could say another word.

Terjin ran along the wall, keeping to the narrow shadow, back to the bridge and the eastern gate. Another patrol was crossing as he neared. Perfect. Master Maltorus slowed to a walk and stilled his heart. His tongue floated in his mouth, his eyes drifted to the ground, and his breath flowed like the gentlest zephyr.

As the patrol approached the gate, he fell in at the back of the group. None of the soldiers noticed. The gates groaned apart, and they trooped inside. Terzjin followed until near the Bakers' Square, then sidled into a dark alley. He dropped the helmet and cloak, and jogged northwards through the twisting streets. He paused and hid three times as patrols marched along the larger cross-streets by the arena. But before long, he was in the northern districts, near the old quarry turned citizens' assembly, clotted with grass and weeds.

He gazed up the hill to the back of the palace. He was here on the King's business. Zjandius would want him to gather news, and that's what he would do. It would be a waste otherwise to be in Etorium and not look. Wouldn't it? That was all he was going to do—just...look.

Terzjin climbed the hill, past small caves with shrines to minor spirits and old gods, past tombs from the early days—broken and abandoned to rats and vagrants. He squeezed through thorny bushes and scrambled over jagged rocks. And his thoughts began to wander as he went.

Another rocky hillside came to mind, unbidden and unwanted. He tried to push it aside, but there it was.

The palace recedes as he stumbles along a thin gravel path through the hills. Black smoke rises from the rooftops. The old man hurries him, not letting him linger or look back.

'What is your name?' the old man asks.

The boy tells him.

'Wrong!' the old man replies. 'Forget that name. Leave it buried here. You will take my name. For everyone we meet on the way, you are my grandson.'

'Where are we going?' the boy asks.

'South,' the old man says. 'South and then across the sea if we can. We will see whom we can find of your family.'

Terzjin wiped his eyes. What was the old man's name?

The palace wall loomed over him at the top of the slope, far too smooth and high to climb. The pale stone glowed in the moonlight. But there, behind a cluster of gnarled laurel trees at the base of the wall, was a way in—if he remembered correctly. Master Maltorus pushed through the branches and squinted into the gloom. He found the low archway and the old, all-but-forgotten door set back in the shadows.

Terzjin ran his fingers up and down the wood until he found the long slit where the planks had warped apart. He drew his sword and slid the blade into the gap, blunt edge up. He carefully raised his sword until it caught the latch on the other side. He lifted higher, pushed the squeaking door open, and entered.

He shuffled along the narrow passage and into the store rooms, all without light. His fingers touched jars and pots, wooden barrels and woven jute sacks. The next door was where he remembered. It was supposed to be locked, but the palace servants usually forgot. Thankfully, their habits had not changed. Terzjin pushed it open and listened. No footsteps, no voices. No patrols down here. He followed the wall to the end of the passageway and found the stairs leading up.

Master Maltorus poked his head outside and scanned the palace courtyard. How many years had it been? Some soldiers loitered at a fire, a few more guarded the gate, and there should be patrols on the walls. He crept to the back of the palace. With the help of some woody old ivy, he scrambled up the wall that enclosed the gardens. After treading along the top of the wall and finding all the old holes in the rotten brickwork, he was soon up on the palace roof. He kept to the shadows, out of view from the ramparts, and scrambled over the tiles to the next rooftop—just as he remembered sneaking about at night as a child.

But it was not all he remembered.

For days—who knows how many days—he and the old man trudge through the hills. They hide in grottos and groves at night, and sometimes during the day when hoofbeats thunder nearby. The boy cannot remember the old man's face. The man always walks in front, so the boy recalls best the grey cloak covering the round shield on his broad-shouldered back. He has a spear, too.

Master Maltorus shook his head. The balcony was just above. He hauled himself up the wall and shimmied along the ledge until he could stretch out, grip the balustrade, then vault over the top. Here he was. Zjandius would want him here. Of course he would.

He pressed on the double doors, which came apart, just a little. Terzjin waited for a noise, a shout, anything. He squeezed through the narrow gap and into the royal apartment. He let his eyes adjust to the gloom.

Over his beating heart, he heard slow, regular breathing. Terzjin padded closer to the bed, to the left side. Zjandius' bed. His king's bed. The strip of moonlight revealed a man sleeping on his back, covered by blankets up to his chest. A young man, younger than Terzjin had expected. Perhaps the same age as him. Dark, curling tattoos covered the man's pale neck and shoulders.

The young soldier lies on his back, his legs under the screaming horse. He glares up at the boy, with pale blue eyes on a freckled face crumpled in pain and fury. His helmet has fallen off to reveal hair like straw. He shouts at the boy. Blood and spit fly from his mouth. Over and over he shouts. Then he speaks with words the boy can understand. 'We will find you. Wherever you go, we will find you.' He grins with red teeth. He actually smiles as he lies there, looking up at the boy. The boy stares down at the man, then squats and puts his fingers around the rock. The grey stone is rough against his skin.

Master Maltorus drew his sword. So, this was Thane Heirik. He crept nearer, until he leaned over the Rhenivian. The young man bore a faint smile on his lips, as if he were having a pleasant dream. Master Maltorus lifted his blade above his head, point down, dangling above the thane. The weight of it dragged on his arm.

Avenge us.

But there were two sets of breathing. Just beyond the moonlight, on the other side of the bed, lay another. A young woman, with dark hair spilt across her pillow. The sword shook in Terzjin's hand. He stared at her, then at the man, then her again. His ears rang and hummed. She stirred and shifted to her side. Terzjin's blade swayed and caught the moonlight. The reflected beam flashed on her face. Her eyes flicked open, staring right at him. They gazed at each other for a long moment.

She screamed.

Terzjin backed away from the bed.

She screamed again.

Heirik sprang up and shouted at Terzjin. Master Maltorus dashed out onto the balcony. Heirik crouched beside the bed, hauled out something, then stood and hurled it at Terzjin. Master Maltorus leapt off the balcony as the axe whistled past and struck the stone balustrade with a dull clang. He slammed onto the tiles below, grabbing his sword before it slid away. He rolled down the roof and clambered to his feet to limp to the edge. A shout and a stream of Rhenivian curses came from behind. He looked back and ducked as the axe flew overhead into the gardens below.

Bells and cries rang out across the palace. Terzjin slid off the roof and onto the wall, dropped to the ground with a wince and hobbled to the cellar doorway. Yells and screams came from behind. He leapt through the door and slammed it shut, plunging himself into darkness. Boots hammered on the courtyard outside as he sheathed his sword and stumbled down the steps to the passageways.

Where was the store room? Which way?

The door creaked open, and torchlight flickered down the stairs. After lurching back and forth, Terzjin found the storeroom and closed the next door behind him. He felt his way through the narrow passage between the jars and reached the postern door. Heavy footsteps echoed through the passages. He scrabbled for the latch and pulled the door open. He closed it as quietly as possible, using his sword to hold the latch up until the door was shut.

He tore down the hillside, not caring what branches and thorns scratched him. He tripped and fell, then pulled himself up again. The East Gate was too far, so he ran north through the alleys and market gardens. By the Lord of Life, the North Gate was open. A trio of guards joked and laughed as they waited for their shift to end. Terzjin crouched and panted in the shadow of a well. The soldiers stopped their chatter and pointed to the palace as the faint ringing reached their ears. Master Maltorus darted from shadow to shadow in a wide arc until he reached the city wall. He tried to calm his heart as he slid with his back against the bricks towards the open gate, but his blood boomed in his skull.

A soldier happened to glance over and spotted Terzjin. He shouted and pointed. Master Maltorus sprang forward and out through the gateway to sprint east along the wall. Running footsteps were not far behind, but fear and madness clamoured through his limbs, and Terzjin sped on. His spit tasted of blood. The soldiers fell behind. As Terzjin reached the eastern side of the walls and the winding river drew close, a silver light glowed on the horizon. The moon Hirenis was rising. Run. He grunted and strained towards the approaching grove. His thighs ached, his breath burned, but he did not stop.

Terzjin slid and fell through the archway. He picked himself up and bent over, gasping for air. 'Illauri?'

The shadows between the trees were still and silent.

Terzjin grimaced and straightened up. 'Illauri? Jeigo?' His sweat chilled on his skin.

No one replied—no Torecti, no smuggler. Only the faint singing of crickets in the otherwise empty grove.

CHAPTER NINETEEN

CAERIA – WINTER'S RISING – 436

Razna waited in the middle of the throne room, wrapped in a shawl and surrounded by Heirik's personal guard, three rows deep. Only a single brazier burned, so the hall was dim and cold. The soldiers shuffled and coughed and avoided her eye. Good. Let them feel shame.

Heirik's voice drifted through the open door, rising louder and louder until he burst into the room, wearing only his trousers and followed by a handful of wide-eyed soldiers. He clutched his long axe and gazed around the hall as if the assassin were lurking in a corner. His ranting and swearing slowed to a halt, and he stood there, breathing heavily.

Razna pushed through the huddle of soldiers and ran to him. 'My Thane, my love. Any news?'

Heirik scowled and shook his head. 'The bastard slipped away, through a door at the back of the palace *that no one told me about*.'

He rounded on the nearest group of soldiers. They cringed and shrank back out of axe range.

Heirik's shoulders slumped, and he turned to Razna to wrap an arm around her. 'He could have killed you. I don't know what I would have—'

Razna pushed away. 'Don't be silly, Heirik. He was after *you*. If I hadn't screamed, you'd be a dead man.'

Heirik frowned. 'I would've fought back,' he mumbled.

She snorted and shook her head. 'Think now. *Who* sent him? That's how you discover where he fled.'

The Thane shrugged. 'The bandits? The aristocrats? Yet another Sanadin who slipped the net. The king…' He looked at Razna.

She nodded. It seemed obvious.

Daga ran puffing into the throne room. 'My Thane, I have…difficult news.'

Heirik sighed. 'What now?'

Daga swallowed and caught his breath. 'The marshal at Goretonum sent a message. A prisoner escaped.'

Heirik's face darkened. 'A prisoner? Lord Octerian?'

The marshal shook his head. 'No, sir. He's been asleep the whole time, apparently. But the smuggler, sir, he's gone. No sign of him or how he got out.'

Heirik clenched his jaw until the cords of his neck popped out. Razna held his arm and squeezed gently.

'Search the harbour for the smugglers' ship.' Thane Heirik said. 'If you find nothing, send soldiers along both coasts and arrest *anyone* suspicious within a day's ride of the city. Also, bring me the fort marshal. And whoever was guarding the cell.'

The sun was rising by the time Daga returned. Razna had the men open a few shutters. The golden beams passed between the pillars and pierced the dusty air. Heirik sat on his throne, now dressed and toying with his axe, with Razna beside him. She stifled a yawn and tried to look as coldly furious as her husband when Daga brought forth the two soldiers.

'So, you mean to tell me the smuggler escaped from his cell without anyone noticing?' Heirik murmured. 'Did he climb through the window?'

'No, My Thane,' the marshal replied. He clutched his helmet at his chest as he spoke. 'The window bars were untouched. Besides, the window is too small for someone of his…size to squeeze through—not to mention, too high.'

Heirik cocked his head. 'So…he dug out, then?'

The marshal coughed and exchanged glances with his guard. 'No, Thane Heirik, there is no sign of anything like that.'

'Ah, so he used some kind of... witchcraft to spirit himself out of the fort. Perhaps he turned into a raven or an owl and flew from captivity that way? Hmm?' Heirik leaned forward.

The two men shrugged and cowered before their Thane.

'Or...' Heirik held up his axe and inspected the edge. 'Perhaps he had aid and left through the door.' He glared at the soldiers. 'That seems most likely, yes?'

'Probably, yes, My Thane.' The marshal nodded and studied the ground.

Razna turned to Heirik. 'Surely, My Thane, the guard would have seen or heard something suspicious? *He* must have something to say.'

Heirik raised an eyebrow. 'Well?'

The guard bowed and fidgeted. 'I saw nothing, sir. Didn't hear nothing either.'

'How's that possible?' Heirik asked. 'Did you let him out?'

The guard shook his head vigorously and mumbled a reply.

Heirik thumped the axe butt on the stone floor. 'Speak up!'

The guard stared at the carpet and trembled.

The marshal put his hand on the guard's shoulder. 'Sir... he, he may have fallen asleep at some point during the small hours of the night. Tiredness after a long day. It could happen to any of—'

'He... fell... asleep.' Heirik whispered. He stroked his chin. 'Very well,' he announced to the hall. 'Guards...' he gestured to the men from Goretonum. '... take these two back to the fort and lock them in the smuggler's cell. Perhaps *they* can find a way out before sunrise tomorrow.'

Heirik beckoned to Daga as the guards escorted the men out. 'Tomorrow morning, have them both whipped and beaten in the courtyard. Then execute them there, and make sure all the soldiers watch.'

Daga bowed and stepped away.

Heirik stroked his axe. 'So, now we return to the question. Who was this assassin? And who sent him?'

'It was almost certainly Zjandius, My Thane,' Razna said. 'An act of revenge.'

A murmur of agreement rippled around the hall. Razna smiled to herself.

'But what kind of revenge?' Heirik said. 'Revenge because Sederial was successful? Or revenge after Sederial tried and failed?'

'I suspect the latter,' Razna said. 'The smuggler vanishing on the same night is too much of a coincidence. Taerinus betrayed you, Heirik. Perhaps he handed Sederial over to the Caerians and they tortured the plan out of him.' Hopefully.

Heirik frowned. 'Senderial does not strike me as a man who would surrender so easily. No, I believe he was caught in the act and died fighting. May the gods honour Sederial.'

The gathered Rhenivians echoed the blessing. Razna mumbled along. A horrid little man. About as horrid as the one who stole into their bedchamber. She remembered his face, caught in the moonlight. Come to think of it, he looked rather Galatani as well. Perhaps a deliberate choice?

'Has there been any news from Elisdrium?' Heirik asked the assembled men. 'Any sighting of the smugglers?'

Daga shook his head. 'No, My Thane. Their craft hasn't been seen in many weeks, but we are scouring the coasts as you commanded.'

Heirik leaned back and tapped his fingers on the head of his axe. 'I think this *King Zjandius* has grown too comfortable in his desert. He marries princesses and sends assassins against me—the coward. Enough.' He arose. 'Daga, how many boats do we have ready to sail?'

'Some thirty or so, My Thane.'

Heirik nodded. 'Very well. Fill those vessels with the very best soldiers we have—every last ship. Find some navigators who know the way to Elisdrium and have the fleet ready within a day or two. We shall attack this Zjandius where he believes himself safe.'

'Thane Heirik,' Daga said. 'Is this the best—?'

'There won't be enough men, brave as they are, to capture this Elisdrium,' Heirik continued. 'No matter. Come upon their city with speed and cunning, surprise them, break and burn whatever you can. If a chance arises to kill the king, seize it. But if not, no matter. Strike fear into their hearts, see the lay of their land, and return. Meanwhile, we shall prepare a full host to end this absurdity.'

'As you wish.' Daga bowed and departed.

Heirik extended a hand to Razna. 'Come, My Lady. I'm hungry. Let's go to breakfast.'

Razna took his hand. They walked out of the throne room with bodyguards close behind.

Heirik turned to them. 'No, leave us. I won't fear these Caerians anymore.'

Once they were alone in the corridor, the Thane turned to Razna and took both her hands in his. 'In truth, I *am* a little afraid—for you,' he whispered.

Razna sighed. 'Heirik, I told you. I'm not their target.'

'I know,' he said, 'but I don't trust the Caerians. I don't like you spending time with any of them, not even that tutor of yours.'

Razna frowned. 'I will not stop my lessons, Heirik.'

Heirik gazed into her eyes and grinned. 'You are so stubborn, my she-wolf.' He released her hands. 'Very well. Then I have a little gift for you.'

'Oh?'

He pulled back his cloak and brought forth a sheathed dagger on a leather belt. 'Something to keep you safe.'

Razna took the dagger and pulled it out of its sheath. The blade was iron, in the Rhenivian style, with gold inlay in the hilt. She turned it about to catch the light. 'Very pretty.'

'And deadly when it needs to be,' Heirik replied, 'so it should suit you well, yes?'

Razna kissed him. 'Thank you.'

CHAPTER TWENTY

CAERIA – WINTER'S REIGN – 436

Terzjin snuck into Etorium at the rear of another patrol, then slowly made his way back to the northern districts. The streets and alleys were thick with Rhenivians banging on doors, shaking beggars awake, shouting and hunting for the assassin—or someone who could be the assassin, if necessary.

He came to the old rubbish heap as the night sky yielded to dawn. It was a grassy mound with bits of roof tile, rotten wood and bones sticking through the soil. He walked past the mound and over a small field of bushes and overgrown grass, where horses occasionally grazed, to the city wall and a possible refuge. Some brickwork had crumbled away at the base of the wall, creating a small cave. A faint glow filled the hollow.

Terzjin crouched and tried to scramble inside. A pile of glowing coals was all that remained of the fire. The hole smelled of sweat, woodsmoke and rotten food. Metal flashed in the corner of his eye, but Master Maltorus grabbed the thin wrist before it could plunge the knife into his neck.

'Ah!' A reedy voice. A familiar voice. The arm thrashed about in his grip.

'Alectus?' Terzjin said.

The arm stopped moving. A face entered the light, a young boy, younger than Valcero, but painfully thin with dark bags under his eyes and streaks of dirt across his face. The boy scrutinised him. 'Master Terzjin?'

'So, you remember me, Alectus.'

'Of course, sir! I still have your silver coin. For tracking the boy to the Portsiders.'

'You haven't spent it?'

Alectus grinned. 'I spent our other coins.'

'Our?' Terzjin's eyes adjusted to the gloom. At least six other children crouched inside, all wide awake now and staring. Boys, girls, some impossible to tell—of various ages and all dressed in rags. And one—by the gods—one of them had eyes that gleamed with pale fire when he looked at Terzjin. That boy flinched and retreated into the shadows.

'Well…' Master Maltorus blinked, then took a coin from his belt bag and held it in the firelight. 'How would you like to earn another?'

Alectus leaned closer. His breath smelled of onions. 'What's the job?'

'Let me spend the night—and perhaps the day—in your little home, quietly and peacefully. You can pretend I'm not here. What do you say?'

The children looked at each other.

'Some soldiers came past,' a young girl announced. 'They shone their torches into our cave.'

'Did they now?' Terzjin said.

'They tried to kick me,' a little boy said, 'but I got out the way.'

'I can make sure they don't bother you,' Terzjin said, 'and give you this silver coin, as long as you all promise *not* to tell anyone I'm here.'

Alectus smiled. 'Alright.'

Terzjin crawled into the hollow and the children wriggled aside to make room. He wrapped his cloak around himself and tried to sleep, but pieces of brick and stone dug into his back. The children whispered and fidgeted in the dark. His thoughts chewed at him.

How could he have been so foolish? He disobeyed his king—well, *nearly* disobeyed Zjandius. How could he return? The Ladistrien were on the other side of Caeria. The Nedolian Forest was nearly two weeks' away on foot. Stupid, stupid, stupid. And even if he could find a way to Elisdrium, how could he face Zjandius now? He had ruined everything. The Rhenivians will work it out. They would know Zjandius was alive, that he was coming. They will prepare for the attack. Zjandius will lose, and it will be entirely Terzjin's fault.

Idiot.

He thought back to the bedchamber, to the bed. If he had intended to do *it*, he should have done it. Losing his nerve was worse than doing it. Coward. *Weak*, foolish coward. What was the point of his training if he couldn't act? He knew what the lenotare said behind his back. He knew. And they were right. What's the point of beating bumbling guards with blunt swords and sticks when he couldn't fight for real? He was a joke, a fraud. Useless. Useless...

Terzjin is lost, alone. In the forest, stumbling about. He could try calling for Illauri, but why? She thinks he is a joke. Shameful. The trees crowd around and claw at him. Strange figures watch him through the leaves, behind the trees. Endless black eyes. Moss and leaves. Dark, lichened horns twist and curl amongst the branches. They watch him. His hand itches.

Terzjin awoke with a start and winced. His back ached. He grunted and twisted onto his side. Weak winter sunlight shone on the ground outside. The hole.

'You talk in your sleep,' the young girl said, squatting beside him, biting into a chunk of bread. Her hair was thin and wispy. She sniffed.

'What did I say?' Terzjin croaked through his cracked lips.

'Nothing that made much sense.' It was the boy with the glowing eyes. He was tall and gangly with sloping shoulders. His hair was dark and wild. Freckles and acne scars covered his face. He hunched against the wall with his arms around his knees and watched Terzjin intently as his eyes flashed. He tensed.

There was no one else in the cave. City sounds drifted in on the cold breeze.

'Could I have some of that bread?' Terzjin asked.

The girl hesitated, then tore off a piece and handed it to him. The bread was stale, but chewable. He wolfed it down.

'Perhaps some water too? Please?'

'I'll get it.' The boy spoke with a cracked voice. He grabbed a copper cup and crawled out of the hollow.

The girl studied Terzjin. 'Who are you?' she asked eventually.

'No one special.' He pushed himself into a sitting position.

'Where are you going to go?' she asked. 'You can't stay here forever.'

Master Maltorus shrugged. 'I don't know. Where is Alectus and the others?'

'They went out a long time ago,' the girl replied, 'to look for food and coins. And to get warm in the sun.'

Terzjin nodded.

The boy returned with a full cup and passed it to Terzjin.

'Thank you,' Master Maltorus said. The water was cold and almost fresh. He smiled to the boy.

'Mmm.' The boy sat at the entrance and avoided Terzjin's eyes.

'We should also go look for food,' the girl said.

'Here's an idea.' Terzjin withdrew two more silver coins from his bag. 'How about you go buy food for everyone? So we can eat better tonight?'

The girl snatched the money from his palm. 'Alright.'

The children scrambled out of the hole and left Terzjin alone with his thoughts.

The day crawled by. Master Maltorus lay in the cave and tried to sleep, but sleep would not come. He watched a millipede crawl through a gravel landscape. Outside, the long grass waved in the winter wind. He gazed about, not really seeing anything. What was the purpose of him? What use did he serve?

When sleep finally took him, Terzjin dreamed of the rock in the desert. He stands atop it, but then the rock shudders and a dark hole splits open beneath him. The rock collapses into rubble and dust with a deep, moaning roar. And Terzjin awoke and stared up at the brickwork.

When he could no longer stand the ache in his bladder, he slithered out of the cave and limped to the bushes to relieve himself. He hurried back inside before anyone could see him, ashamed.

The children returned when the shadows had grown long. They brought a grilled fish—slightly ragged from the carrying—a bread loaf, a block of hard cheese, and wooden bowl of cooled mushroom soup.

'Not bad.' Terzjin said.

Alectus and the others fetched bits of wood to make a fire—this time, outside the hollow. The wood was damp, so the fire gave off more smoke than flame, but warmed them nonetheless. They sat around the flames and shared the food, chewing on their supper and staring into the glow. There were, in all, seven children.

Terzjin sat closest to the hole and kept his hood up. He blinked and tried to lean away from the smoke. 'You have gathered quite the gang, Alectus.'

Alectus munched on a sliver of fish. 'Hard times,' he said. 'Some came from Goretonum, after the fire.'

'My house burnt down,' a boy said.

'And your parents?' Terzjin asked.

'I don't know,' the boy whispered. He kept his eyes on the flames.

'What are *you* doing here?' the girl asked. The same girl, of course.

Terzjin swallowed a mouthful of bread. 'I made a mistake, a stupid mistake. I shouldn't even be here.'

'It's alright,' the girl said. 'We all make mistakes.' She leaned over and patted his knee. 'Maybe *none* of us should be here.'

Terzjin's lip curled up.

They ate in silence for a while. When the soup came to Terzjin, he held the bowl up to his mouth and slurped. It was ice cold and nearly tasteless.

'Have you heard any news today?' Master Maltorus asked the group. 'Any rumours floating around Etorium?'

'They're searching the city for a criminal,' Alectus said. 'He escaped, or something.'

'Oh?' Terzjin said. 'What else did they say about this...criminal?'

'They say he's a slim young man of average height to short, has dark curly hair, and a thin face,' the girl recited.

'Is that so?' Terzjin said.

'Yes, they are arresting everyone they find who looks like that.' The girl watched him.

'And they're offering a reward to anyone who helps catch him,' the boy with the gleaming eyes said. 'Ten silver coins.'

'I see.' Terzjin gazed at the dying flames. 'Well, I don't have ten silver coins, but I'd give everything I have to make sure they don't see me, mistake me for this... criminal, and arrest me.'

'Oh, don't worry about that,' the girl said. 'We won't help the Rhenivians. We *hate* the Rhenivians.'

Alectus nodded. 'They're bastards.'

The boy with the gleaming eyes glanced at him, without quite making eye contact.

'Well, that's good to hear,' Terzjin said.

'And then what will you do when you have no money left?' Alectus asked. 'Will you come beg with us? Or are you good at stealing?'

Terzjin smiled wanly and shrugged. 'I'm not sure, exactly. I must leave Etorium.' He bit his lip. 'I'm supposed to sail across the sea.'

'They've stopped all the ships in the port,' another girl said. 'They're checking if the criminal is on them.'

'Not *all* the boats,' Alectus said. 'Not the Rhenivian ones that the soldiers are going on.'

Terzjin frowned. 'What do you mean?'

'They say the ships are going to Sasiion, to kill the king.'

Master Maltorus rubbed his brow. Of course they were. 'Can you discover more about these boats tomorrow, Alectus? I'll give all the coins I have left if you help me—I mean it.'

The boy with the gleaming eyes leaned forward. 'The coins will be for all of us?'

'Of course!' Terzjin replied.

Alectus grinned. 'We'll see what we can find out.'

One by one, the children crawled into the hole and fell asleep. This corner of the city was nearly deserted, save for a drunkard who stumbled past at a late hour and peered at Terzjin. 'Don't leave him behind,' the drunk mumbled. His face was vague in the darkness.

Master Maltorus glared at him, and the man stumbled off. Terzjin sat alone by the fire until the embers turned dark and his eyes drooped. He dragged himself inside, careful not to bump any sleeping children, and wriggled into an open hollow to pass out into a deep and dreamless sleep.

Or, nearly dreamless. He found himself wandering a dim forest at dawn, or maybe sunset. The golden air feels thick, and he struggles to push through dense undergrowth and tangled branches draped in curtains of lichen. Strange figures spy on him through the leaves. Whispers float past his ear. A bird—shimmering blue with long, curling, rustling tail feathers—hops from branch to branch overhead.

'Illauri!' he tries to call out, but the sound dies in his throat.

'I am here,' she whispers, loud and close.

Terzjin swings around to find her. There she is, passing between the looping vines and striding towards him.

'Illauri, I have missed you,' he tries to say.

'Listen to me.' Her whisper booms and rattles through him. She clutches his face with both hands and pulls him close, so that he is gazing deep into her grey, burning eyes. 'Listen to me, Terzjin Maltorus.'

How did he find his way back to the Nedolian? Did he walk or did he ride?

'Am I dreaming?' Terzjin asks. His heart thuds.

Illauri smiles. 'Yes, you are. But listen to me, Terzjin Maltorus!' She shakes him.

'Alright, I have listened,' Terzjin replies.

Illauri groans. 'Not yet you haven't.'

A distant tree topples, as if an invisible hand has pushed it over. It rustles and creaks as it falls. The trunk crashes to the ground with a resounding thump. Another tree groans and tips over.

'Quickly now,' Illauri-of-the-Woods whispers. 'Go back to the grove tonight, after midnight and before Hirenis rises. Do you understand? Repeat it.'

More trees fall around them, each one closer than the last. The ground shakes. The roots throw up mud and leaves as they tear out of the damp earth.

'Repeat it,' Illauri hisses.

'Back to the grove,' Terzjin mutters. 'After midnight and before—'

A shadow falls across Illauri's face. He turns around as a tree drops on them with a thunderous roar.

Terzjin jerked awake. Daylight filtered into the cave.

'You were talking again,' said the girl with the wispy hair.

Terzjin sat up. 'What did I say?'

She shrugged. ‘It was all mumbling. Anyway, here’s breakfast.’ She gave him stale bread from last night and a cup of wellwater. ‘I have to go now. Farewell!’ She crawled out of the hole and was gone.

Terzjin gnawed on the bread and stared at the ground. What did he say? The dream was melting away like morning mist.

The second day passed much like the first. Terzjin remained in the hollow and tried not to think about anything. He tried practising sword moves in his mind’s eye, but it felt like a useless exercise, a child’s game. His limbs were heavy and his heart dulled. He lay on the ground, wrapped in his cloak for warmth. He no longer noticed the smell of piss and rotten onions.

The children arrived in the early evening with two loaves and skewers of grilled mutton wrapped in cloth.

‘Did you use the money?’ Terzjin asked.

Alectus grinned and chewed on some meat. They sat in a circle in front of the hole around the fire, while clouds blew in from the west and darkened the sky.

Master Maltorus sighed. ‘Any news about the Rhenivian vessels and where they’re going?’

Alectus nodded. ‘They are definitely going to Sasiion, to a city called Elis … Elisder …’ He scrunched his face.

‘Elisdrium?’

‘Yes, that’s the one. And they are sailing tomorrow, with the morning high tide and north wind at their back. That’s what I heard the sailors say.’

‘Are they now?’ Terzjin scratched his cheek. An idea took shape in his heart. ‘And will they need rowers for these boats?’

Alectus shrugged. ‘I only know they’ll be carrying lots of soldiers.’

‘Where are these ships berthed?’

‘In the marsh next to the Port District,’ another boy replied. ‘They’re pulled up on the sand.’

'Excellent.' Master Maltorus pulled a chunk of meat off a skewer and passed it on. 'Thank you all for your help.' The mutton was cold, but still juicy.

'What are you going to do, then?' Alectus asked.

'I'll rise early tomorrow,' Terzjin said, 'and go see these ships for myself. Perhaps I'll sail with the soldiers to Elisdrium. I will try, at least.'

Alectus nodded as if it all made sense.

A cold wind arose, and the children crawled into the cave to huddle and sleep. Only the boy with the gleaming eyes remained outside with Terzjin, as a few stars appeared between the gathering clouds. The boy sat poking at the coals with a stick.

'What is your name?' Terzjin asked.

'Rufeo,' the boy replied. He rested his chin on his knees.

'A good name.' Terzjin leaned back against the wall. 'And where do you come from, Rufeo? The city?'

The boy glanced sideways at him with narrowed eyes that flared then dimmed. 'Why do you want to know?'

'Just curious. I wondered where your family might be from, that's all.'

Rufeo stabbed the embers. 'They're all gone.'

'Oh.'

Rufeo sighed, looked at him, then looked away again. 'Your eyes. Why do they...?'

'Light up?'

Rufeo nodded.

'Your eyes do too, you know?'

The boy sat up straight. 'They do?'

'Oh yes. Has no one told you?'

'No.'

'Have you seen anyone else like me before?' Terzjin asked.

'Hmm, maybe once or twice. I'm not sure.'

'There are not many of us about,' Master Maltorus said. 'Or at least, not in these parts of Caeria.'

'But *why* does it happen?'

'Well, they say it's a gift from the Lord of Life.'

Rufeo frowned. 'A gift of *what* exactly?'

Terzjin sighed. 'I asked the same question.'

Illauri. The memory of last night's dream opened like a flower. Terzjin examined the strip of bloodied cloth still wrapped around his palm. He looked up at the heavens. His skin prickled. 'What time do you think it is?' he asked.

'I don't know,' Rufeo said. 'I haven't heard the tenth bell yet.'

Terzjin stood. 'I need to go somewhere, just to see something, just in case...'

The boy stared up at him. 'In case of what?'

'Rufeo, we'll speak more about this when I return. About these gifts, I mean. I have questions for you. And maybe you have for me. Yes?'

The boy shrugged. 'Alright. See you later.'

CHAPTER TWENTY-ONE

CAERIA – WINTER'S REIGN – 436

Terzjin ran from alleyway to alcove, always in the shadows. He considered passing through the North Gate, but the long walk down the river path was too exposed. Could he fight off a troop of Rhenivians? Perhaps not now. Perhaps not ever. So, he took the same crooked ways south through Etorium's streets.

The tenth bell tolled. He could slow down. There was time.

When he arrived at the East Gate, he waited in a doorway for a patrol to set out. The eleventh bell rang. There was still time.

When a patrol finally came, Terzjin slipped out and joined them at the rear. He kept his heart calm and quiet. If his tricks failed, he would be dead. So be it. A fitting end, perhaps. But the Rhenivians did not notice, and Master Maltorus parted with them as soon as he cleared the gate.

The frogs sang in the riverbank reeds in a rising and falling chorus. The sedge shook in the winter gusts that whipped along the wall. The gateway to the grove was unguarded.

Terzjin leaned his head through the archway. There was no sound of breathing, shuffling feet, or a sign of guards lying in wait. Only the cypresses stood as tall, silent sentinels. He stepped inside.

'Illauri,' he whispered, barely more than a breath.

Nothing. The cypresses creaked with the wind. The twelfth bell tolled faintly over the wall.

Terzjin crept closer to the trees. 'Illauri?' he whispered again, as loud as he dared. Perhaps it was only a dream. Perhaps that would be best.

He jumped.

Illauri stepped away from a tree, as if she had been invisible and watching him the entire time. She strode up to him, eyes gleaming, mouth set in a hard line.

Master Maltorus smiled. 'Illauri, I wasn't certain if—'

She slapped him on the cheek. His face rang.

'I trusted you,' Illauri hissed. 'I told you what to do and trusted you would do it.'

Terzjin held his cheek. 'I'm sorry. I needed to do—'

'Oh, and did you accomplish what you *needed* to do?'

'No, not exactly.'

Illauri shook her head. 'Do you have any idea what is *needed*?'

Terzjin slumped. 'I don't know.'

'Foolish boy!'

'Where's Jeigo?'

'He is with his people,' Illauri replied. 'At their ship. There was much rejoicing.'

Terzjin nodded.

Illauri sighed. 'I am sorry for hitting you. I should not have done that.'

'I ... probably deserved it.'

'Never mind.' She pulled a strip of cloth from her belt. 'We should leave, immediately.'

'Wait.' Master Maltorus raised his hands. 'I have a plan. I must return to my king, and I have found a way. I'll go tomorrow by ship.'

Illauri shook her head. 'No, you will come with me.'

'Illauri, listen. I've given you enough trouble. It's best I go my own way. I'll sail—'

She gripped his arm. 'No, you listen, Terzjin Maltorus. If you do not follow me, I can never help you again. In fact, we will never *meet* again. Do you understand?' She glared up at him.

Terzjin stared back at her and breathed out. 'Very well.'

Illauri covered his eyes and pulled him by the hand into the fragrant grove. She began to sing. It was a sad and lonely melody, a song for a cold, clear night, full of long, high notes that tumbled and fluttered. Terzjin's head spun. The ground slipped and twisted beneath his feet as he stumbled along beside her. After a time, the air grew warmer and still. The same golden light suffused through the cloth, and Illauri's voice faded into silence.

'Can I take it off?' Terzjin asked.

'No.'

'Please, I'd like to see where we are.'

She squeezed his hand. 'I am not certain I trust you. Besides, there are things here best left unseen, and I need you to remain calm.'

'But where is *here*?'

Illauri kept silent as she guided him. Master Maltorus stretched out his other hand. His fingers brushed against rough bark. A warm tree. A bird sang in the distance.

Illauri sucked in a breath. 'You can never share what I tell you here. These are deep secrets.'

'I swear it.'

'Well then. What do you know of the underworld?'

'The spirits of the dead pass through it.'

'A grey and gloomy place,' Illauri said, 'or so I am told. Well, you may think of *this* place as the…overworld. The source of all living things, a realm of the yet-to-be-born. The roots of all fates are here, if you know where to search.'

'What does it look like?' Master Maltorus turned his head from side to side, straining his ears for a clue.

'It appears to me as a forest,' she replied. 'That is all you need to know.'

'Will you draw my blood again?'

'You have already earned your passage. We should not be…interrupted on this journey.'

Terzjin's skin tingled. 'And who would interrupt us?'

'Enough secrets for one night. Be silent now.'

Illauri-of-the-Woods resumed her song. For a time unknown, they walked as she sang, until the golden light faded.

Illauri pulled the blindfold from Terzjin's face. They were in a forest, dark and dense, but the trees were different—tall, thick trunks wrapped in vines—and the air was damp and warmer. He peered up to see the stars, but the leaves blocked his view.

'So this is your gift?' Master Maltorus asked Illauri. 'Your secret forest ways?'

She smiled and nodded.

'And the other Torecti can walk these paths too?'

'Those with the gift, yes, though none can walk quite as far as me,' she said. 'Of course, it is not *such* a secret. Do you not know why your cypress groves are planted outside your city walls?'

Terzjin stared at her open-mouthed.

She laughed and shook her head. 'You Caerians! You love to make scratchings of your memories, but you have forgotten so much of your own history.'

She strode ahead, and Terzjin followed.

'I'm not Caerian, actually.'

'Oh?' Illauri glanced at him, then ducked under a branch along their path. 'Then tell me about yourself.'

'I'd prefer not to.' Terzjin said. 'The past is gone.'

'Not entirely gone for you, Terzjin Maltorus. *They* linger, yes?'

He scowled at her back. How dare she? 'Where are you taking me, anyway?' he asked. 'To Taerinus and Jeigo? To the ship?'

'No.'

They entered a small clearing where a tree had fallen some time before. Ferns grew thickly around what was left of the trunk. Crickets and cicadas whirred and whistled amongst the leaves.

Terzjin stopped. 'Where are we going then?'

Illauri pushed through the undergrowth ahead. 'You will see, Terzjin Maltorus.'

Master Maltorus folded his arms. 'No. Enough mysteries. Tell what you mean to do with me.'

Illauri looked back at him and smiled. 'Be patient, Terzjin Maltorus. Come, we have a little way to go.'

The blood rushed to his face. 'No!' He let his fury pour into his voice, turning it cold and strange. '*Tell me what I want to know*.'

Illauri stopped and turned fully to glare at him. 'You believe you have power over me?'

'Uh, no, I meant only that...'

Something moved in the corner of his eye. Terzjin shifted to look as a bird swooped out of the canopy and into his face.

'Eo!' Terzjin waved his arms, but the bird had already flown off.

Illauri advanced upon him. 'You think you can command me?'

Another bird flew at Terzjin's eyes and darted away.

'Did you see that?' Terzjin cried out. 'The birds...'

The air rushed through the leaves. A swarm of fowl, large and small, fell upon Terzjin, pecking, scratching, and beating him with their wings. He covered his face with one arm and waved the other about, trying to drive the creatures away. And then, as suddenly as they appeared, they were gone, fluttering back into the trees.

Terzjin breathed heavily. 'Did... did you do that?'

Illauri folded her arms.

The undergrowth rustled. Something heavy galloped through the forest. Master Maltorus drew his sword. A great wild pig, tusked and bristling, crashed through a thicket and careened towards him. Terzjin leapt aside as the pig galloped past and away into the bushes with a squeal.

The clearing fell silent again.

Terzjin gasped for breath. He stood and pointed his blade at Illauri. 'You mean to kill me, don't you?'

'Don't be foolish, boy.'

A snake reared out of the ferns only a span from Terzjin's side. It flared out its hood and hissed at him, baring pale fangs. He turned to face it, sword at the ready.

'There are forces in this world you do not understand, Terzjin Maltorus,' Illauri said. 'Forces that mere strength cannot match. Put away your blade, boy. If I wanted you dead, it would have happened already.'

Terzjin glanced at her, then back at the snake. It watched him, unblinking. He swallowed, lowered his weapon, and returned it to its sheath. The snake dropped to its belly and slithered away through the ferns.

'I'm sorry,' Terzjin said. He could not quite meet her eyes.

Illauri chuckled. 'Were you really going to cut me down with your sword?'

Terzjin searched the ground and shrugged. 'No. I don't know. Probably not.'

'Have you ever taken a life?'

Terzjin looked up. 'Only once.' His hands shook.

Illauri sat on the fallen tree. 'Tell me about it. Tell me your story.'

'Why do you want to know?'

Illauri patted the wood. 'Because a tree with rotten roots can fall without warning.'

'And you want to know if my roots are rotten.'

'Perhaps.' She shrugged. 'Best to know now, so we can prepare the tree before the storm arrives. So, come, tell me about your roots.'

Terzjin sighed and leaned against the trunk next to her. He gazed up at the stars. 'I am not Caerian. I was born across the sea in Galatan. When the war came, and the Rhenivians fell upon our land, they came to our house, our... our palace to take my family.'

'Palace?'

'Yes, because...'

Say nothing! Tell no one!

He drew a long breath. 'Because my mother was the queen, and my father the king.'

'I see.'

'I don't remember seeing it, but they dealt with my father and sisters first. I did watch them catch my mother. I was hiding, but I escaped before I saw what they would do to her. I did nothing to stop them. Nothing to help her...'

Avenge us. Did she say that?

Illauri put her hand on his shoulder.

'I saw them... hurt my brother as I ran away. They chased after me, but I hid again. Then someone found me. An old soldier, a loyal servant of my parents, took me from the palace into the night. We walked along mountain tracks. We hid in the valleys. He said we would go south and across the sea. He told me to take his name.'

What was the old man's name? And then the memory finally came back to him.

Terzjin.

'But we were followed,' he continued. 'The Rhenivians tracked us through the countryside. They sent riders and a dog. And, one day, they caught up with us on a rocky hillside. The old man fought them off with his spear and shield. He killed two, but they wounded him. He told me to run, run away fast. So I tried, as the last Rhenivian slaughtered him and rode after me, but I was small and slow. Then the horse fell—slipped on a rock or something—with the rider trapped beneath. The man was screaming. Cursing my name. Crying for help, I think. I walked back. He shouted at me. I stood over him, frozen. He said he would find me, that *they* would find me, no matter how far I ran. They would always find me. And I was angry…and afraid.'

Terzjin swallowed and shivered.

'I picked up a heavy rock and I…I…dropped it, on him. But he screamed. So, I picked it up again, and…' Gods, his face…

Illauri squeezed his shoulder.

'After, I took the old man's sack and whatever food I could find from the riders, and I carried on walking.'

'How did you know where to go?'

'Oh.' Terjin blinked. 'I don't recall exactly. Someone was there on the path, I think. I can't picture their face…they…they pointed the way, said to follow the moon Telanis.' He rubbed his face. 'I came to a city by the sea, called Deria. And I remembered we were supposed to go over the ocean, so I stowed away on a ship on the beach. But sailors found me hiding in the bottom and pulled me onto the deck. There was water everywhere. No land. They wanted to toss me overboard, and I was terrified. But the captain said that I could earn them money instead. He kept me from the crew and put a copper band around my neck. When we came to another city—Etorium—they put me naked on a platform in the slave market. People prodded me. I didn't know what they were saying. A man came to the market and took me away. I think he paid the captain, but I'm not sure. He wrapped a cloak around me and hid my face.'

'He knew who you were?'

'I never thought about it, but I suppose so.' Terzjin smiled sourly. 'Apparently, I look very much like my father. Anyway, the man took me up the hill to the palace and left me in a room. Night had fallen. Another man came in, dressed in fine clothes. He spoke in Galatani and asked for my name. I told him, and he said I must never say it again, that I must forget that name and bury it deep in my heart. So, I told him I was Terzjin, and he said that was better.

'Then, I saw a woman standing at the door. "Mother!" I called out. Somehow, she must have survived, I believed. Somehow, she had found her way here, and we were together again. But when she stepped into the room, into the lamplight, I saw it was not my mother, but someone so similar, so much alike. She cried and rushed forward to embrace me. She whispered in Galatani and told me I was safe. But the man pulled her away and told her she must never hold me, nor speak to me with our tongue. There were spies everywhere, he said. They could not risk angering the Rhenivians.'

Wherever you go, we will find you.

'So he, King Adomenus, took the copper band from my neck and put me with the *lenotari*—the palace guard—where I became their servant. They taught me how to fight—and I was good at it. There was another boy in the palace, only a year older than me, and we played together sometimes in the courtyard and gardens. When Adomenus found out, he forbade me from fraternising with this boy, his son, but I believe Queen Elatuë spoke up for me. Later, I was allowed to spend time with Zjandius—as his servant. I never spoke to the Queen again after that first night, until she sent for me and Zjandius, years later. She was lying in bed, very sick, near death. She held our hands and told us to be strong. She told me to protect her son, and that he would protect me.'

'As family should,' she whispered in Galatani, close to their ears, with wheezing breath.

Terzjin sniffed. 'After Queen Elatuë passed, the King married again, but the new Queen, Porinia, never cared much for me. She said I should know my place. That it was not proper to be so familiar in royal company. I don't believe my uncle ever told her who I truly was. So I lived in the walls, away from them, and attended to my training. And when the old King died, and Zjandius gained the throne, I became his bodyguard.'

'He trusts you,' Illauri said.

Terzjin looked away. 'I hope so.' He wiped his face.

Illauri leaned over and held Terzjin while he trembled.

Eventually, she let go and stood up. 'Well, Terzjin Maltorus, you have been wronged by so many and suffered so much. And there is nothing you can do to erase any of it.'

Terzjin looked up at her. 'Nothing?'

'It is under your skin and in your bones.'

'What would you counsel me to do then?'

'What you know to be right. What is necessary.' She smiled and took his hands. 'Plant the seeds of something better and help it grow. Come, Terzjin Maltorus. Dry your eyes and get up. You have a little way further to go.'

Illauri led him out of the clearing and onward through the forest. The birds began to sing. The ground sloped downwards, and the trees thinned. Here and there, they passed stumps and other signs of woodcutters. They found a dirt path and followed it until the tall trees parted enough that he could see straight down to the greying, pink horizon.

There was the sea, glittering with the light of the two moons. The water lapped ashore on a white, sandy beach. Somewhere, faintly ahead, he heard voices calling out, in Caerian, Sasiion, and some other, vaguely familiar language.

Terzjin looked around the forest and felt the warm, damp air. 'This is Hebenia Minor, isn't it, near the shipbuilding camps? And there is the Sesurian Sea.'

Illauri shrugged. 'I believe your destination lies over the water, but your path leads beyond my sight and reach. Good luck.'

Terzjin marvelled at the sea ahead and looked to Illauri. 'Thank you.'

She inclined her head.

Terzjin thought for a moment. 'Illauri, if we are parting here, could you do me a favour?

'Yes?'

'Please, ask the chiefs to prepare for war, to begin the raids as soon as possible. I'll make sure the Caerians arrive before the end of Spring's Fall.'

She smiled. 'I can do that. Is there any other message you wish to pass on?'

'No, that's all. Thank you.'

A frown flickered over her face before she nodded. 'Before you go, tell me one more thing. Who are you?'

'You know who I am—Terzjin Maltorus. The King's bodyguard.'

Illauri shook her head. 'No, who *are* you?'

He breathed out. 'Very well, if you insist. I am... Prince Heleziel, named after my father, and the last of the royal blood of Queen Irdegal.' The names sounded foreign on his lips, somehow wrong. Even unburied, they remained dead.

Illauri put her hands on his shoulders. 'No, who are you *truly*?'

'I don't understand.'

Illauri chuckled and stepped away. 'Alright. When you know the answer to that question, seek me out, and we will speak more about such matters. But—for now—farewell, Terzjin Maltorus.' Her eyes gleamed in the predawn light.

Terzjin raised his hand. 'Farewell, Illauri-of-the-Woods.'

But Illauri had already turned from him and was sauntering off into the trees, singing to herself.

Terzjin trudged alone down the path towards the sea, and reached the sand as the sun began to rise.

CHAPTER TWENTY-TWO

THE NEDOLIAN FOREST – WINTER'S REIGN – 436

Valcero had no choice but to stay in the village, so he tried to learn more about the Torecti. Master Colus would have approved.

He watched them cook, chip arrowheads, and carve wood into all manner of things. In the evenings, he followed the children into the longhouse to hear stories from the elders. By the glow of the burning torches, they told legends of Torecti heroes he had never heard of. They recounted the tale of Forest Cat, who stole fire from the Sun and gave it to the people to keep them warm, but the flames singed her fur and soiled her nose and paws with soot. He learnt about the Lord of Life, who shared secrets of food and medicine from plants, and the Lord of Death, who taught people how to make tools and weapons. He heard how these brothers fought until their mother Earth grew tired of their battles and tossed them into the sky to live with their father, the Sun, and all their sisters, the stars. And after dinner and stories, Valcero sat amongst the villagers while they sang their night song and the bats flitted overhead.

'Do you always sing when you walk through the forest?' he asked Senno, a young Torecti boy, while eating lunch around the fire.

'We do not *always* sing,' said Amia, one of the girls.

'The songs help us find the secret paths, the shorter ways,' Senno replied. He grinned. 'Otherwise, it would take forever to go anywhere.'

'Alright, but how does that work?' Valcero said.

Senno frowned. 'I do not understand.'

‘The song shows the way,’ another girl answered.

Valcero peered at his meat. Definitely not a person. Probably not. He popped it in his mouth and chewed. ‘And what about the song you sing every night? What is that for?’

‘To drive away the dark, of course,’ Senno answered.

‘But the dark does not go away when you sing,’ the Caerian said. ‘It is still night.’

The Torecti children stared at him.

‘Sorry,’ Valcero added.

‘There is more than one kind of darkness.’

They all turned to see the lady, the maybe-witch, at the edge of their circle.

‘Illauri!’ The children leapt up to hug her.

Valcero stood with his hands behind his back.

Illauri wrapped her arms around the children and grinned at Valcero. ‘You ask many questions, Caerian,’ she said in his language.

Valcero blushed.

‘That is nothing to be ashamed of. There is nothing wrong with asking questions, if you are willing to listen to the answers. Come, walk with me.’

The other children returned to their meal. They seemed unafraid of Illauri. Perhaps she was safe. Perhaps. Valcero nodded and followed her away from the fire and towards the edge of the village.

‘Has Terzjin come back?’ the boy asked.

Illauri shook her head. ‘Terzjin Maltorus is already on the way to his king.’

Valcero frowned. ‘He went to Sasiion? Oh.’

‘He rescued the Caerian,’ Illauri said. ‘He was successful, in the end.’

‘He didn’t say farewell.’

She put her hand on his back. ‘You will see Terzjin again, when the time comes. He cares for you, Valcero.’

The boy shrugged her hand off his back.

They went on in silence.

‘Your family name is Baradon, correct?’ Illauri asked.

‘Yes, that’s right.’

‘Baradon...’

Valcero watched her face. 'Do you know my name?'

'No, not yet. But I am sure you will make it a name worth knowing.' She smiled. 'Now, you have questions?'

Valcero bit his lip. He wanted to ask if she was a witch, but... if she were not a witch, she would be insulted by the question. But also, if she *were* a witch and he asked her, well, anything could happen...

Illauri winked and burst out laughing. The boy went cold. Could she read his heart? He blushed and stared at the ground.

'Come, Valcero Baradon,' Illauri said. 'You wanted to ask about our songs. About why we sing them?'

He studied the trees. 'You said there was more than one kind of darkness. What did you mean?'

'Hmm, well, we sing at night to keep the Lord of Death sleeping in his cave. It is best he does not roam. We Torecti serve the Lord of Life. When our ancestors wandered the world without home or hope, the Lord of Life took pity and brought us to this island. It was a dead, ashen land, with mountains that spewed fire and smoke. The Lord of Life made it a garden for us, so we sing his songs in thanks and observe his laws. Well, we Torecti-of-the-Trees do. The Torecti-of-the-Fields forgot *their* songs.'

'And when you sing while walking through the forest?'

Illauri smiled slyly. 'That is one of our most precious secrets. But...' She pointed ahead. '... let me show you something else.'

The villagers were hewing and scraping timber into long planks for a new hut. Reito was among them. He looked up and waved to Illauri and Valcero. Others were tying bundles of reeds to prepare a roof. In front of the house, a third group was decorating a sapling with lime and garlands of flowers while they quietly sang. They smiled and raised their hands in greeting, then continued singing.

Illauri pointed to this third group. 'What they are doing?'

'They're praying?'

'Something like that,' Illauri replied. 'Who are they praying to?'

Valcero shrugged. 'The Lord of Life?'

Illauri shook her head.

'Their ancestors?'

She laughed. 'Why would they do that? Their ancestors are long passed.'

'I don't know then,' the boy said.

'They are honouring their *descendants*,' Illauri explained. 'The Torecti unborn. The villagers are building this house for their children—and their children's children. All preparation for the Torecti-to-be.'

Valcero watched Reito, bent over a plank, pushing his edged flint up and down the length of wood.

'I thought Reito was a warrior?' Valcero said to Illauri.

The Torecti man laughed. 'Only when I need to be, my lad. Most of the time I am busy like this.'

Illauri put her hand on the boy's shoulder. 'There is great honour in this work.'

Valcero examined the Torecti's bare necks. 'You don't use slaves to build houses?'

Illauri frowned. 'Slaves?'

Reito said something in Torecti.

'Ah, we do not have such a thing amongst our people,' Illauri said. 'You could not... *own* a Torecti any more than you could own a cloud. It is not our way.'

The Torecti began assembling windows. They locked pieces of wood together to make a frame, while also stretching a yellowish-white sheet between them. Once the Torecti had bound the frame, they tore off the material that protruded from the edges. A long strip wafted to the ground.

'May I?' Valcero reached to pick it up.

'Of course,' a woman said. 'Keep it.'

It was smooth, almost like papyrus. He rolled the strip and stowed it in his pouch. Something to show Master Meretan.

Valcero turned to Illauri. 'And what about your shawl? What is it made of? Spiderweb?'

Illauri glanced at the translucent cloth wrapped around her shoulders and giggled. 'No, but you are not too far from the truth. It is a woven gossamer, yes, but from a caterpillar's cocoon. Perhaps you will see it in the spring, if you stay for a while longer.'

They carried on walking.

'Have you ever left this forest?' Valcero asked. 'Is that how you learnt Caerian?'

'I did visit the outside once, when I was very young,' Illauri said, 'but it was later, when I made a friend who taught me. She is gone now.' Illauri's face clouded over.

'I'm sorry.'

'Now, I have a question,' Illauri said. 'How did *you* learn to speak Torecti?'

'Uh, from Aulix and Praehenna, who looked after me, when we... lived together. They came from the forest, but they never spoke about it. I hoped they'd be here, but...'

'The forest is big, Valcero Baradon. There are many villages.'

'They told me they couldn't go back, but they never said why.'

'Oh?' Illauri furrowed her brow. 'Well, I am sure they had a good reason. Look! There is one more thing to show you today.'

They came to a small clearing amongst the tall trees. In the centre, under the gentle sunlight, grew a young sapling only slightly taller than Valcero. Its trunk and branches were pale and thin. A few leaves, as red as flames, hung from its branches—a burst of warm colour in the otherwise green forest. A leaf dropped off and drifted to a crimson pile on the ground.

'Have you seen a tree like this before?' Illauri asked.

Valcero shook his head.

'The sap is sweet, you know? You can drink it, and it will sustain you through the bitterest months of winter.'

The boy tried to imagine drinking sap.

'Here is a secret, Valcero. In this forest, in this gift from the Lord of Life, one can find every kind of tree that grows in the world.'

'Every tree? Truly?'

Illauri smiled.

Master Meretan would call that nonsense, but Valcero was not so sure.

She put her hand on his shoulder. 'I do not tell you these things to entertain your curiosity, Valcero. I want you to see what treasures we have. We Torecti are going to fight to protect what is precious to us, for ourselves and all those to come.'

CHAPTER TWENTY-THREE

SASIION — WINTER'S REIGN — 436

Terzjin arrived in Elisdrium more than a week later. After reaching a camp and waving his royal medallion in the foreman's face, he secured a place aboard the next ship to Sasiion. But contrary winds and threatening clouds had worried the captain, so they waited a few days.

While striding up the cliff path from the port, Terzjin passed two women lugging baskets of fish and gossiping in Old Sasiion.

'Calls himself Emperor now, they say,' one woman muttered to the other as she wiped her brow.

'What does that even mean?' the second asked.

'I don't know. Probably nothing really,' the first woman cackled. 'Certainly doesn't change the price of fish.'

The other sighed. 'Or the weight.'

Terzjin stopped next to them. 'Excuse me, but I heard you talking about an emperor?'

The women frowned at him and hurried off.

Master Maltorus shrugged and continued up the steep road. When he reached the palace, the guards recognised him immediately.

'Welcome back, sir!' A guard thumped on the wooden door. 'The Emperor will be pleased to see you, I'm sure.'

'The Emperor?' Terzjin asked.

The guards smiled and waved him through.

He found Zjandius Vaecerion in the gardens atop the palace. Zjandius was strolling along the flower beds with his hands behind his back while an advisor walked alongside, explaining something.

Queen Nanepti sat on a couch under the awnings before the cloisters, with two servants in attendance. She waved to Terzjin as he crossed the lawn, and he smiled and bowed in reply.

Master Maltorus came to Zjandius and bowed again. 'Your Majesty!'

Zjandius turned to him and beam. 'Ah! Look who it is. We have been awaiting you most anxiously.' He patted the advisor on the shoulder. 'We shall continue this discussion later, yes?'

The advisor bowed and backed away. 'Of course, Emperor.'

Terzjin raised an eyebrow. 'Emperor?'

Zjandius chuckled. 'Yes, uh, we decided that "King" was no longer sufficient. I am the ruler of two lands now. And if I am to be known as The Last King of Caeria, why not *also* be known as The First Emperor, no?'

Terzjin smiled. 'Congratulations, *Emperor*.' He bowed.

'Although yes, yes, we still need to take back Caeria and all that,' Zjandius said, 'but my heart says the day is coming.'

'Well, I have news about that,' Terzjin said.

'Come! Let us retire to the shade and talk. It is good news, I hope?' Emperor Zjandius led the way to the awning, but then stopped and turned to him. 'Oh, but I have good news of my own. Terzjin, I am to be a father!'

'What?'

Zjandius beamed. 'Yes! Nanepti is with child. And if the Lord of Life wills it, the surgeon says we shall have a son or a daughter by the end of next Autumn's Rising. We discovered it only a few days ago.'

Terzjin looked to Nanepti.

She smiled and nodded. 'My diviners predict a daughter.'

Zjandius chuckled. 'Mine say a son.'

Terzjin laughed and flung his arms around Zjandius. 'What news!'

'Ah, now...' Zjandius tensed and prised himself away from Terzjin. 'You cannot just touch your Emperor in front of everyone.' He stepped back and glanced around the courtyard. 'It is not proper, Master Maltorus.'

Terzjin blushed. 'Oh. I am sorry, Your Majesty.' He bowed again. 'Congratulations, Emperor.'

'Thank you, Master Maltorus. Now, come sit and give us a report.'

Terzjin joined them under the awning and took a cup of sweetened wine from a servant. 'Your Majesties, I have good news from Caeria. We met with the Torecti at one of their villages. They—'

'There he is!' Colus Meretan came hurrying through the garden towards them. 'You're back.' Colus huffed and wiped his brow. 'Tell me everything.'

The Emperor coughed.

'Tell *us* everything, I mean,' Colus said. 'Your Majesty.' He bowed quickly and dropped onto the couch beside Terzjin. 'And where is Valcero?'

Zjandius rolled his eyes and smiled.

'Uh, Valcero is fine,' Terzjin replied. 'I left him with the Torecti. It's the safest place for him right now. Safer than sailing back here.'

'You left the boy with *them*?' Colus frowned. 'But what if they eat him?'

'Oh, no,' Terzjin chuckled. 'The cannibalism is just a tall tale. Truly, Valcero is safest there. The Torecti guard their forest well.' He tried not to think about how he spoke to Valcero before they parted.

Zjandius leaned forward. 'But will they help?'

Terzjin nodded. 'Their chiefs gathered and elected to join us against the Rhenivians.'

'So, Valcero was helpful as a translator, then?' Colus asked.

Master Maltorus smiled. 'Yes, he helped quite a bit, but as it happens, at least a few Torecti speak our language.'

Zjandius frowned. 'Oh?'

'They would not tell me *how* they learned Caerian, but I suspect a few have spent time amongst our people. Perhaps as farm labourers or traders.'

Colus nudged Terzjin. 'And how about how they live? What do they eat? Do they live in houses, or...?'

'Master Meretan,' the Emperor said, 'there will be time for your debriefing later. For now, I must know what they can do for us.'

'The Torecti will wage war against Rhenivians wherever they find them in the forest and nearby,' Terzjin said. 'They are wary of venturing far from their trees, but they should begin their attacks soon, before the end of the month. Ah, but Your Majesty, I nearly forgot *another* piece of good news. '

'Yes?'

'General Divendrion lives.' Terzjin grinned. 'He and some soldiers escaped into the Nedolian Forest—a few hundred in total. They live under the Torecti's protection, though they are chafing to return home.'

Zjandius smiled. 'That is welcome news. And eases my conscience a little.'

'To be honest, Majesty, the Caerians had somewhat gone to seed, and abandoned hope. But I spent time with them to refresh their training. And then, of course, there are the Aventan.'

'Tell me.'

'At least a few survived the invasion through cunning and stealth. Sadly, Lord Aventan perished, along with some of his children. Lady Aventan leads the family now. She hates the Rhenivians with a passion. They organise raids and ambushes to harass and frighten the invaders. She came to the gathering and pledged to assist us. I believe we can trust them to play their part.'

The Emperor stroked his chin and nodded.

'What about the hostage smuggler?' Nanepti asked.

'I rescued him from the fort, Empress,' Master Maltorus answered. 'Lord Octerian was there as well...'

Avenge us.

Terzjin blinked and swallowed. 'But he did not wish to leave. He fears what the Rhenivians might visit upon his family were he to escape.' Terzjin looked to Zjandius. 'But I am certain he will support us when we return.'

'Sailing to and from Caeria, visiting Torecti, training soldiers, and rescuing a smuggler from Goretonum,' Zjandius said. 'You have been busy! To be honest, I did not expect you so soon.'

'Your voyage back must have been speedy,' Colus remarked. 'Perfect winds, I take it?'

'Ah, yes.' Terzjin said. 'I snuck aboard a ship bound south to Hebenia Minor. The weather was perfect, as you say.'

Nanepti's eyes narrowed. 'Is that the full story?'

Zjandius looked between them.

Master Maltorus stiffened. 'For my voyage...yes, Empress. But, there is some bad news I must relay.'

'What is it?' the Emperor asked.

Terzjin swallowed. 'I believe Thane Heirik is sending a force to attack Elisdrium—some thirty ships. They may only be a few weeks away.'

'What?' Zjandius sprang up. 'Why now?'

'Uh, perhaps Jeigo's escape angered them. Or perhaps he received word that the assassination failed.'

The Emperor sighed. 'Terzjin, you should have begun with this! I must speak with Admiral Getaelon immediately. With me, Master Maltorus.' He strode away.

Terzjin hurried after him.

'This is a test I hoped we could postpone a little longer,' the Emperor muttered, half to himself.

Master Maltorus walked behind as they left the courtyard and made for the stairs.

'Are we ready?'

'Your Majesty... Zjandius...' Terzjin said as they descended the echoing staircase, 'there is something else.'

Zjandius paused on the landing and looked back at him.

Terzjin rubbed his temples. 'It is possible I may have... provoked this attack.'

The Emperor frowned. 'How?'

'The night I went to Goretonum, I also... went into Etorium, to the palace.'

'What?'

Terzjin swallowed. 'I... I mainly just went to see, to learn more of their plans.'

'Terzjin...'

'They slaughtered the Sanadin. Did you know that? Even the children.'

'What did you do, Terzjin?'

'They sleep in your bed, Zjandius.'

Zjandius stepped closer. 'Did you...?'

'No, no. I didn't. I mean, I considered it. I could have, but...'

The Emperor gazed at the ceiling and blew out a long breath. 'Master Maltorus, I said *no vengeance*. I explicitly forbade you from—' He stopped himself and glanced around.

‘They woke up, Your Majesty. They awoke and saw me in the room. I fled. There was no blood spilt, I swear it.’

Zjandius shook his head. ‘And if they hadn’t awoken? What then?’

Terzjin looked at his feet and shrugged.

‘Eo! *How* could you disobey me?’

He looked up at the Emperor. ‘They have killed so many, Zjandius,’ he whispered fiercely. ‘So many hurt. So many lives destroyed. *Someone* has to deliver justice.’

Zjandius gripped him by the shoulders. ‘And they *will* receive justice—true justice. I swear it to you.’ He looked his bodyguard in the eyes. ‘But Terzjin, the time has come to decide. Is your loyalty with the living, or with the dead?’

Terzjin stared at his Emperor, then bowed his head. ‘I’m sorry.’

Zjandius sighed and squeezed his shoulders. ‘Save your apologies. Come. We must prepare for whatever trouble you have brought.’

CHAPTER TWENTY-FOUR

CAERIA — WINTER'S FALL — 436

'You have learned so much, Lady Razna.' Her tutor Nerea smiled as she spoke in Caerian.

'Thank you,' Razna replied, 'but you flatter me.'

'No, truly, My Lady. I have not seen another learn to read and write Caerian *and* Galatani simultaneously—a real achievement.'

Razna examined her ink-stained fingers and the parchments that lay about on the table. She could not deny at least a little glow of pride. She had finished translating the old Caerian poem, *The Sacrifice of Leiga*, into Galatani. 'An interesting tale, but I'm not sure I liked it.'

'Oh, why is that, My Lady?'

'Well,' Razna began, 'I don't believe the gods would punish Leiga simply for loving the fisherman instead of the priest—especially if the priest is clearly unworthy of her affection. And it seems the gods cursed the priest just as much. It makes no sense.'

'Hmm,' Nerea mused. 'A fair point. Some claim the poem has changed over the years, which may explain inconsistencies. And, of course, priests are a stock villain in old Caerian stories.'

'Why is that?'

Nerea cleared her throat. 'They brought ruin to the Old Kingdom. When the first Caerians fled Sasiion, the King barred all priests from the ships. Thus, the survivors forgot the old deities. We honour the Torecti Lords of Life and Death, sometimes your Galatani gods as—'

Razna leaned back in her chair. 'After yet *another* temple has been burnt down, do you think you Caerians will ever adopt the Flood Father and Corn Mother as your own?'

Nerea squirmed a little. 'Well, My Lady, I…'

'I'm not Rhenivian, remember. You may speak plainly.'

The scribe furrowed her brow. 'It is not certain, Lady Razna. The people may need some time, uh…'

'They'd probably appreciate a leader who didn't impose gods upon them, no?'

Nerea nodded and smiled. 'That is probably true.'

'Thank you, Nerea, most helpful. I will pass on your advice to the Thane.'

She swallowed. 'Oh, My Lady, I would not presume to advise Thane Heirik on such matters. Please don't take it as—'

Razna reached out and put her hand on the scribe's. 'Peace, Nerea. I won't put you in any trouble. No, I appreciate you far too much.' She smiled and patted the woman's hand. 'I'll tell him as if it were my own idea.'

The scribe bowed her head and chuckled nervously. 'Thank you, Lady Razna.'

'And is this why the people have abandoned the Baker's Square? Because of beliefs from these Torecti?' Razna said. 'They don't set up market stalls, nor hold any of the usual gatherings. They haven't even set up their bonfires for the festival.'

Nerea turned pale and grimaced.

'In fact, I'm told almost no one enters the square anymore, especially after the sun sets. Ever since the…executions.'

'Please, My Lady, I am not sure if it is my place—'

'Nerea…' Razna held the woman's hand tightly between her own until her tutor blushed. '…you have been a wonderful teacher to me. I'd like you to be more than that.'

'Lady Razna?'

'I need an advisor. I know your words and letters, yes, but I must also understand your customs, if I am to *help* lead Caeria. Could you be that advisor?'

The scribe nodded.

'I will need your honest counsel, Nerea, even if that means sharing difficult truths.'

The scribe swallowed. 'Yes, My Lady.'

'Now, explain why people shun the square.'

Nerea took a breath. 'They see it as a cursed place. According to the ancient Torecti pact, we must not murder or execute anyone on this island. We must also burn the dead and scatter the ashes to the elements, releasing the spirits on their journey to the underworld. Especially when a person dies violently. There are exceptions for war, but even then, rituals must be followed.'

'And if not?'

'The spirit will haunt its place of death for all eternity,' Nerea said. 'It will trouble anyone who crosses its path.'

Razna nodded. 'Thank you, Nerea. Again, you are most helpful.'

The tutor smiled weakly.

'I will do what I can about this matter,' Razna said. 'I'll make sure the square is cleansed. I promise this.'

There was a knock at the door.

'Come!' Razna called out.

A Rhenivian guard opened the door. 'Lady Razna, Thane Heirik summons you urgently.'

Heirik was pacing the council room when she entered. Daga and a few other marshals sat around the table and watched him nervously.

'What is it, my love,' she asked her Thane.

'The forest savages.' Heirik stopped and slapped a parchment on the table. 'They're attacking everywhere.'

'You mean the woodcutters' camps?' Razna asked.

Heirik thumped the table. 'No, I mean *everywhere!*' He sighed and looked up at her. 'Sorry. No, I mean they are raiding beyond their borders, even beyond the forest. From the north near Impona, to the south, near Dolemios. Within a week, they have attacked estates, camps and forts at least ten times—that I know of. Riders keep arriving with new messages from all over the west.'

Razna sat down. 'Are they trying to invade?'

Daga shook his head. 'No, My Lady. They attack and kill only Rhenivians near the forest, it seems, then vanish back into the trees. In some places, they pile the bodies and set them on fire before they leave.'

'They are following their rituals,' Razna said. 'They burn the dead here.'

'What does it matter?' Heirik slumped into his chair. 'Why are they attacking? Why *now*?'

'I'm told such a thing has not happened in 200 years since their treaty,' another marshal said. 'They say these savages have kept to themselves for so long the Caerians have all but forgotten them.'

'Perhaps they attack because *we* have violated this treaty,' Razna said.

Heirik frowned. 'What?'

'The executions, My Thane.' Razna swallowed. 'Perhaps they attack because of what happened here in Etorium. Executions violate their laws.'

'How would they even know what happened?'

Razna shrugged. 'Perhaps they have spies in the city.'

The Thane stood. 'It's my right to deliver justice as I see fit.'

'The Torecti don't respect your authority,' she said.

Heirik smiled. 'They will. I'll lead a host against these savages.'

'How large a host?' Razna asked.

Daga now spoke. 'It may need to be very large, sir. The reports say they attack in bands of a hundred or more. If they can attack everywhere at once, they may have an army of thousands.'

Heirik's lip curled. 'Let's see how they fare against Rhenivian hooves.'

'Thane Heirik ...' Razna arose. 'Let's tell the people that you march to protect them from these savages. We need to start winning their support.'

Heirik pulled a face. 'Why?'

Razna circled the table. 'Because you are their leader. And fear and love can bind to forge loyalty.'

Razna rode out beyond the western gate to see off Heirik and his host—some 500 riders and perhaps 2000 more on foot—assembled on the road. Their iron glinted in the winter morning sun. A fresh breeze whipped up their banners.

Look at me now, Mother. Look at me now, Father.

She brought her mare Decha up to Heirik, who sat atop his Bulgitha. 'I should be coming with you,' she said. 'You know I can fight.'

Heirik grinned. 'I know, but I need someone trustworthy here.' He took her hand. 'Grindulf will help with the soldiers, but *you* are the lawgiver while I'm gone. I've made it known.'

Razna bowed. 'I am honoured, My Thane.'

He squeezed her hand. 'You honour *me*, my she-wolf.'

She lifted her head. 'But think on this while we are apart, Heirik. You could be more than a thane.'

'What do you mean?'

She pulled Decha closer to press her thigh against Heirik's. 'We are married now, my love,' she whispered.'We must be ready for when your uncle and king find out. Wouldn't it be helpful if we could use Caerians to fight for us?'

Heirik frowned. 'I couldn't fight my only family. And certainly not with a host of cowards.'

'*We* are family now, my love,' she said in his ear, 'and it's time you grew out of your uncle's shadow. Come, win these Caerians' love and loyalty, teach them to be true warriors, and *you* could become their king.'

Heirik turned to look at her properly. 'And you their queen?'

Razna smiled. 'Of course.'

Heirik stared into the distance, then eyed her again.

'Think on it,' she said. She leaned over and kissed him.

'I'll see you soon, Lady Razna,' he said. He twisted away and blew a sharp note on his horn.

The soldiers cheered and roared.

'Be safe.' She caressed his hand.

Heirik winked. 'The Wolf Lord protects me.'

Razna watched them march away for a while, then trotted back into her city.

CHAPTER TWENTY-FIVE

SASIION – WINTER'S FALL – 436

Two weeks had since Terzjin returned to Elisdrium. Rumours of an imminent attack swirled through the markets and mansions of the city. Farmers reaped their winter crops quickly and early, while nervously eyeing the plain over their shoulders. Lenotare patrolled the palace walls night and day, straining their eyes into the ocean horizon for the first glimpse of a raiding fleet. The tirentare sat poised in their portside barracks, ready to put to sea at a moment's notice.

Today was a long-shadowed, yet warm, winter's morning in the palace courtyard. Master Maltorus was trying to teach the guards some drills he had learnt from the ancient Sinotan manual.

'No, try twist and pivot on your heels,' he explained to a Caerian lenotarus.

The man smiled and wobbled stiffly.

Terzjin shook his head. 'Uh, try shifting your weight from one to the other. Like this.' He turned and swung his sword down over his head, then sliced across to where he started.

The watching soldiers stumbled out of range.

'Do you follow?' Terzjin asked.

They smiled sheepishly and looked at one another.

Master Maltorus sighed. 'Shall I show you again? Perhaps slower this time? See, up and over like this, *while* I'm twisting and pivoting, then down, cut across, and shift back. Alright?'

They watched blank-faced.

'And our shields, sir?' a Sasiion guard asked.

Terzjin thought for a moment. The scroll didn't really explain that. part.

'Master Maltorus!'

A palace servant ran over to the group. 'Master Maltorus, please, come quick!' She bent over and put her hands on her knees.

'What is it?' Terzjin looked around. 'The Emperor?'

The servant shook her head and gasped. 'No, sir. The kitchen. There's trouble in the kitchen.'

Master Maltorus frowned. 'The kitchen? Surely a problem for the cooks to sort out?'

The soldiers chuckled.

The servant straightened up. 'There's been a fight in the kitchens, sir. A stabbing. The girl asked for you, sir. Please, come quickly, before there's any more trouble.'

'The girl?' Terzjin sheathed his sword. 'Show me.'

It was noisy, but instead of clanging pots and shouted orders, Terzjin heard arguments, wails, and banging as he entered the dim kitchen below the palace. A crowd of servants crouched in a tight circle on the floor between the tables, while another huddled at the larder entrance. They shouted through the closed door and hammered their fists on the wood.

Master Maltorus nudged his way through the first crowd. 'What's going on here?'

They backed away, revealing a slender young Sasiion man lying on the floor. His otherwise grey tunic was drenched dark with blood. It pooled on the flagstones around him. Two servants remained hunched over the man, pressing rags against his stomach to staunch the flow. The young man's face was grey. His eyes fluttered, then he passed. The servants gasped and moaned.

A kneeling cook turned to glare at the larder door. 'Curse you, child! May your soul *rot*!' She burst into tears.

The men at the larder resumed their banging. One slammed his shoulder against the door.

'Leave her!' the head cook cried out. 'Leave the girl.' She pointed at the dead boy. 'You know what he did, what he wanted to do.' She ran to the door and tried to push the men away.

The kitchen erupted in shouting as both sides argued.

'Enough!' Terzjin roared. '*ENOUGH*!'

They fell into shocked silence and stared at him.

Master Maltorus felt tired. 'You?' he said to the head cook. 'You are in charge, yes? Alright, explain.'

'Sir.' She bowed. 'Enlet here...' She pointed to the body. 'Gods give him peace, though he doesn't deserve it, Enlet, the boy, tried to have his way with one of my girls, sir. I've told him off about it before. Many times, sir. He pesters them, sir. Well, he followed her into the larder and had her trapped there. She screamed. And then another of my girls ran in with a knife and he tumbled out like this and, well...' She gestured at the boy on the floor.

Terzjin looked to the door. 'And there?'

'They've barred it from the inside, sir,' one of the men replied. 'They won't come out.'

'Hardly surprising,' Terzjin muttered. 'Alright,' he said, 'let's see. Step aside.'

The servants shuffled away from the door.

He pressed his ear to the wood. Silence. He knocked. 'It's Master Maltorus. Can you open, please?'

There was a pause, then a faint rustling. Terzjin waited. Something scraped over the stone floor inside, and the door cracked open. A small face peered out. She was Sasiion. Her eyes were red and her cheeks were streaked with tears.

'Are you hurt?' Terzjin asked.

The girl stared up at him for a moment, then shook her head.

'May I come in?'

The girl glanced back into the larder, then up at him again. She nodded and stepped aside to open the door wider. It was dim inside, lit only by a single oil lamp on a shelf. The room was crowded with barrels, sacks, and clay jars.

Master Maltorus asked the girl. 'What's your name?'

'Nanepti,' she replied.

Terzjin smiled. 'Like the Empress.'

Nanepti, the servant, shrugged.

'Who else is here?'

Nanepti pointed to the corner. Half hidden behind a barrel, crouched another girl. She clutched a long bronze carving knife in a trembling hand. She looked up at Terzjin, and her eyes flashed.

'Saedelas,' Terzjin said.

She stared at him. Her face was ghostly.

'There she is!' a man shouted from the doorway.

The servants crowded at the larder entrance, all craning their necks to peer inside.

Terzjin looked to Nanepti again. 'Did he hurt you? The boy outside, I mean.'

She wiped her eyes. 'He tried to. But she...' Nanepti glanced at Saedelas. 'She stopped him before he could... do anything.'

Master Maltorus nodded, then addressed the assembled servants. 'Can any of you here say that Nanepti has done wrong? Has she committed any crime?'

No servant spoke, but a few shook their heads.

'Very well.' The king's bodyguard gestured to the head cook. 'I leave in Nanepti in your care, yes? Alright.' He nudged the girl on the shoulder. 'Go with the cook. You'll be safe with her. And if *anyone* should trouble this Nanepti,' he announced in a loud, cold voice, 'in any way, you will answer to me.' He pulled aside his cloak to reveal the sword at his side. 'Do you understand?'

They stared at him sullenly and nodded.

'Good. Now shut the door and leave us in peace.'

Once they were alone, Terzjin sat on the floor with his back against the wall. 'Saedelas,' he whispered.

She gazed at the floor while squeezing the knife handle. It dripped with blood.

'Saedelas,' Terzjin said again.

She looked up at him. Her whole body shook.

'Are you hurt?'

She bit her lip. 'No.' She breathed out. 'Will... will he be alright?'

Terzjin shook his head.

Saedelas dropped the knife 'I.. I didn't want to, but...' She buried her face in her knees and sobbed.

Terzjin put his hand on her shoulder. 'What happened?'

She sniffed and wiped her face. 'I was cutting meat in the kitchen. I heard Nanepti scream, and I knew what was happening. Enlet...he's tried with me before, and her, and others. I knew what was happening, and I didn't think. I just ran in here. I tried...I tried to pull him off. But he turned to hit me in the face. He missed and I just...' She looked at the knife and began to sob again.

Terzjin held her.

She gulped and pulled away. A tremor passed through her body, and her teeth chattered. 'I feel so cold.' She stared at her shaking fingers. 'Why do I feel so cold?'

'It means you have a good heart,' Terzjin replied. 'Be glad of it.'

'I'm so sorry,' she whispered. 'I'm so sorry. I never really wanted to...Never.' She hid her face.

'He was going to do a terrible thing, yes?' Master Maltorus said.

Saedelas sniffed and nodded.

'And you stopped him. Good. You can take comfort from that.'

She lifted her head and stared at him, wide-eyed and shocked.

Terzjin sighed and leaned against the wall. 'I meant only that...Look, it's a terrible thing, no matter the reason. I understand how you feel. Truly, I do. Sometimes, we must do terrible things to protect ourselves or those we care about. But...I can't pretend I have any answer for it, or wisdom that justifies it. I...' He rubbed his face. 'I don't know.'

The girl slumped against a barrel. 'What will happen to me?'

'You can't stay in the kitchens,' Master Maltorus replied. 'You'll come with me and we will find a safer place for you.'

Terzjin helped Saedelas to her feet. When he opened the door, the servants all leapt into action, as if they had been busy the entire time. Only the pool of blood remained on the floor. Saedelas shivered when she saw it.

He wrapped his cloak around her. 'Just follow me. Follow me. That's right.' He guided her to the stairs, where the head cook was waiting. 'I'm taking her up,' he told the cook. 'She'll find another job.'

The head cook nodded. 'There'll be trouble. His family...They'll demand a blood price, but considering the circumstances, probably not high.'

'I'll take care of it,' Master Maltorus replied. Once again. 'Let the staff down here know that Saedelas is under my protection. As is the other girl, Nanepti.'

They left.

'Where is Valcero?' the girl asked as they climbed the stairs.

'He's in the forest,' Terzjin replied. 'Safe with the Torecti.'

'I wish I could have gone.'

'Oh. Well...' Terzjin scratched his neck.

Upstairs, he found Captain Wederet guarding the doors to the royal chambers.

'The Empress feels poorly and is resting,' Wederet said. 'I believe the Emperor is downstairs.'

'Actually, Captain, I came looking for *you*,' Terzjin replied. 'This is Saedelas. She's been working in the kitchens, but needs a new position.'

Saedelas stared at the floor.

'Do you think there's room for her in the Empress' staff?' Terzjin asked. 'She's a quick learner.'

The Captain frowned at her. 'She's the one who stabbed the cook?'

Saedelas' lip quivered.

Master Maltorus snorted. 'You know already?'

Wederet shrugged. 'News travels up the stairs very quickly in this palace.' He eyed Saedelas again. 'I don't know if I like the idea of it. I have to think of Her Majesty.'

'She was defending her friend,' Terzjin insisted. 'She's no assassin.'

Wederet frowned.

'Please, Captain. As a favour to me. And I believe the Empress, of all people, would understand.'

Wederet chewed his lip until his face softened. 'Alright. I'll speak to the chambermaids. She'll need to clean up a bit, though. Can't smell of onions up here.'

Saedelas wiped her face.

Terzjin shook his hand. 'Thank you, Captain. I appreciate it. Please, keep her safe.'

A bell rang from downstairs. The two bodyguards looked at each other.

Terzjin sighed. 'What now?'

Terzjin found Emperor Zjandius in one of the lower reception rooms. The open shutters let in the sun. Admiral Getaelon and one of his captains were already there.

'Your Majesty?' Terzjin bowed as he entered. 'Is everything alright?'

The admiral patted him on the back as he passed to the throne.

'Master Maltorus.' Zjandius nodded. 'We have news, finally. Admiral Getaelon, if you please?'

Getaelon beamed. 'It seems fortune favours us, for once. Captain Helention here sailed to the isthmus and brought back word from passing traders. The Rhenivian fleet was lost.'

'Lost?' Master Maltorus looked from the Emperor to the admiral, then remembered himself. He stepped to Zjandius' side and tried to listen.

'Remember a few weeks back, when we had that bout of drizzle here in Elisdrium that blew in from the west?' Getaelon said. 'Well, apparently that was the edge of a mighty storm on the Ventian Sea.'

'I remember it well, Your Majesty,' Terzjin remarked. 'It delayed my crossing.' His heart skipped. *If you do not come with me, I will never help you again. In fact, we will never meet again.*

The captain nodded. 'You were lucky, sir. They say it was a once-in-a-generation tempest. Floods and wind ravaged the islands. But most importantly for us, the storm caught the Rhenivians before they could reach a safe port or place to beach. The waves smashed every ship and drowned nearly all their men. The few survivors are stranded on an island. The raiding party is gone, Your Majesty, their navy destroyed.'

Zjandius settled in his throne and breathed out. He gazed out the window, then looked to Master Maltorus. His face was tight, his jaw clenched.

Terzjin nodded.

Zjandius blew out a long sigh. 'Admiral, ready the fleet. Terzjin, send for my generals. We are going home.'

CHAPTER TWENTY-SIX

THE NEDOLIAN FOREST — SPRING'S RISING — 437

Valcero sat on a rock and held a leaf to the light. The warm sun shone through it, to reveal its branching veins. He tossed the leaf and sighed as it drifted to the ground. A fine carpet of white flowers poked through the leaf litter. Here and there, tall lilies of blue and purple swayed in the breeze that passed through the trees. The days were longer now. The weeks of drizzle and rainstorms had given way to dappled sun and warmth that pierced the damp.

Each day seemed much like the last, or the next. How long had he been in the forest? Had Fools' Week come and gone? Was he in the new year? Was he a year older? The Torecti did not seem to record the days, and Valcero had not thought to make his own count.

The trees loomed over the boy, crowded around, hemmed him in. How he longed to see the edge of the world, whether desert sands, dark seas, or grassy hills. Where was Terzjin? Colus? Saedelas? Valcero sighed again.

The boy slid off the rock and took up his long stick. He gripped it in one hand and practised what he remembered Master Maltorus had taught the cantare. Swing, thrust, jab. Swing, thrust, jab. If only he had a shield.

Distant voices brought him out of his thoughts. He propped his spear against a tree and trudged through the forest.

The warriors—men and some women—gathered along a river in a deep gulley, undressed, and entered the icy waters to wash the paint and dirt from their bodies. And the blood, of course. Valcero tried not to stare at the women, or at least, not let anyone see him staring.

The warriors sang as they washed, while the villagers watched in silence from the ridge. He had witnessed this scene countless times in the past month.

'Valcero!' Amia ran up to him.

Valcero jumped and blushed. 'Hello!'

'Where have you been?' she asked him.

The boy gestured vaguely behind himself. 'Just...walking around.'

'Come eat with us.' Amia punched his arm. 'It is lunchtime.'

'Wait.' Valcero looked at the warriors down the slope. 'Why are they singing?'

'Oh.' Amia followed his gaze. 'Well, they sing for forgiveness.'

'Forgiveness? What did they do?'

The girl frowned. 'Do not be silly. They went to war. They beg forgiveness from the Lord of Life.'

The warriors climbed out of the water and dried themselves with cloths in patches of sunlight along the riverbank.

Valcero stared at them for a moment longer. 'Ah. Of course.'

He followed Amia and the other Torecti back to the village, where mats and bowls of food were already spread out in the space between the huts. He sat with Amia and some other children. They munched on spring berries, strips of roasted bush pig, and parsnips cooked and ground to a paste.

'Where is Illauri-of-the-Woods?' Valcero asked Amia.

She shrugged while slurping water from a wooden cup, then swallowed. 'She comes and goes.'

'I heard she is with the Tall Trees clan,' another girl said.

'Will any of you go to fight?' Valcero asked the older children around him.

'Why?' a boy asked.

'I do not know.' Valcero shrugged. 'To protect your lands? For the honour of your people?'

The boy thought for a moment. 'I do not think so. There are already lots of warriors. And I am sure the war will be over before I am old enough.'

'Do you not *want* to fight?' Valcero asked.

The boy shook his head. 'Why? Do you?'

'Maybe. I can do it, you know.'

‘Oh?’ Amia leaned over and pinched his thin arm.

Valcero twisted away from her. ‘Actually, Master Terzjin Maltorus trained me. I learnt a lot from him.’

The children exchanged looks.

‘Maybe you can,’ Amia said, ‘but do you need to? The forest is already protected.’

Valcero bit his lip. ‘I am going to join the next raid. You will see.’

After lunch, he left the circle and found Reito sitting on the steps of his hut, while an older woman attended to a deep cut on his shoulder. She mashed a dark paste on a bark board, then smeared it over the wound with her thumb, muttering to herself. Reito flinched and grimaced as she worked.

‘What is that?’ Valcero asked in Torecti.

The man glanced at the paste. ‘Dried moss and mushrooms, I believe.’ He looked to the woman, who nodded without pausing her work. ‘It keeps the wound clean and helps it heal.’

‘How did the raid go?’ the boy asked.

‘Fairly well, I suppose,’ Reito replied. ‘We lost someone, distant kin of mine, but this is the nature of things.’ He studied his hands.

‘Reito, could I join you? On the next raid, I mean.’

The Torecti man looked up at him. ‘Of course not.’

‘Please, Reito. I want to help. I *can* help.’

The man shook his head. ‘If you want to help, gather berries and roots from the forest gardens. Or build huts with us. And there is always cooking to be done.’

‘But I can do more than that,’ the boy insisted. ‘I want to fight. Terzjin Maltorus trained me. He taught me everything.’

Reito sighed. ‘Terzjin Maltorus asked us to protect you, Valcero, and we shall honour our promise.’

Valcero scowled.

The woman wrapped a linen cloth around Reito’s shoulder and under his armpit, then finished with a tight knot.

Reito smiled. ‘Listen, lad. Your time for fighting may come, but it will be when you are older. For now, learn to live in the forest. You have been with us for some time. My heart tells me this could become your home.’

The boy looked around. ‘But I’m not Torecti,’ he said in Caerian.

The woman inspected her handiwork. Reito smiled and patted her hands before she left.

'You could become one of us.' Reito switched to Caerian as well. 'The clan can adopt you, make you one of the Whispering Leaves, if you like.'

'Adopt me?'

The man nodded and held out his hands. 'There's family here for you. And I've seen how you spend time with young Amia.'

Valcero blushed and inspected his feet.

Reito chuckled. 'You'd be most welcome. Consider it.'

Valcero looked up. 'I want to be a warrior.'

The Torecti frowned. 'No, Valcero. Do not ask me again.'

As the afternoon shadows lengthened, Valcero asked the Torecti if they would take him to the Caerian camp for a few days. Reito escorted him, singing along the forest paths to the open field, where green shoots poked up from the dark earth. Reito exchanged some whispered words with a cantarus amongst the tents. They glanced at the boy while they spoke.

Reito turned to leave. 'I will come for you in a few days, Valcero, if all goes well for me. Please, do not be angry.' He waved at the sky. 'Enjoy this wide open space for a while, then return to us with a lifted heart.' He bent over to look into Valcero's eyes. 'We have all grown very fond of you.'

The boy nodded and tried to smile. 'Thank you, Reito.'

The Torecti man embraced him and walked off into the trees.

Valcero followed the cantarus to General Divendrion's hut. The camp still smelled of piss and rubbish, but the men strode around with purpose. Their armour and gleamed in the afternoon light.

Divendrion met him outside his hut. 'Ah, so you've come to lend your services, have you?'

Valcero saluted, or at least did what he thought was a salute. 'General, I have come to pledge myself. Please, sir, take me into your cantaris.'

Divendrion's mouth twitched.

'I can fight, sir.' Valcero stood as tall and straight as he could. 'I have been trained by Master Maltorus. The very best, sir.'

'Oh no, not this.' General Divendrion shook his head. 'I've already heard about all this nonsense. Terzjin wanted you safe and out the way. I'm certainly not going to disobey him.'

Valcero's face fell. 'Please, General. I *want* to fight the Rhenivians with you. Just give me a chance.' He blinked away tears. Not now. Now would be the worst time.

The general sighed and put his hands on the boy's shoulders. 'Look, son. I admire your spirit. And we certainly need more soldiers. But you are too young, too untrained. Plus, you need a bit more meat on your bones, huh? You would be in the way. Doesn't mean you can't fight in the future.'

'When, sir?'

'Help us in the camp. Assist the men and learn from them. There's lots to do here, starting right now.'

And so, Valcero did help. He stoked fires and stirred bubbling stew pots. He polished armour and shields. He carried bundles of cloaks and helped sharpen spear points and swords on the whetstones. He stoked the fires again at sunset and ladled stew into bowls for the soldiers to slurp upon. He sat with the cantare as they ate, trying to keep up with their jokes and banter, always laughing too late. They shared some wine with him. It burned Valcero's throat and set his head spinning.

When the stars and moons shone at their brightest, General Divendrion beat the drum for bed. Valcero stumbled to a tent the General had set aside for him. He lay in a bundle of blankets and listened as the camp gradually fell into silence, overwhelmed by the crickets and frogs singing from the forest. Sleep took him eventually.

It was another bang of the drum that jolted the boy awake. He waved his hand in front of his face, but could see nothing in the perfect dark.

'Get up! Up!' The general's shouts echoed around the camp. 'Awake and prepare yourselves!'

The men grumbled in their tents. The birds began their chorus. Valcero poked his head through the flap and felt about on the dewy ground for his sandals.

General Divendrion strode past bearing a flaming torch. 'Ah, Valcero. Good morning.'

The boy tried to get up on his knees and salute. 'Sir!'

The general chuckled. 'You can stay in your tent and sleep a little more, son. Get up at sunrise and help prepare breakfast for our return.'

'Yes, sir.' Valcero retreated into the tent, but did not sleep.

He put on his sandals. Master Maltorus would understand. He would, wouldn't he? Valcero pulled out the short sword he had hidden under the thin mattress yesterday evening. He strapped the sheath to his belt. He would show Terzjin what he could do. Terzjin would be pleased deep down. Of course, he will be angry at first, and then he will grow impressed and... proud. Yes, he will be proud.

The boy pulled aside the cloak and lifted the breastplate from the heap. It was quite heavy, come to think of it. He tugged on the cords along the sides. Should he untie them, or just slip the whole thing over his head? Which was front? He wrestled with the armour in the dark as many feet passed his tent. He was wasting time. He dropped the armour and put on the helmet. A little big, but it would be alright. He threw the cloak around his shoulders and clipped it into place. And finally, the shield. He lifted the mattress and hauled it out. Which hand—left or right? Either way, it also felt heavier than the night before. No matter. Too late now.

He poked his head outside. The cantare were shuffling between the tents towards the field. Some held torches to light the way. Valcero scrambled out of his tent and hurried after them in the shifting shadows. He grabbed a spear from a rack and kept his head low. His heart thumped. He pulled the cloak tight around his chest.

'Come on!' A captain shouted at him and other stragglers. 'Hurry up, or get a whipping!'

Valcero ran into the back of the column.

'Form up!' General Divendrion ordered from somewhere ahead.

The men jostled around him, standing shoulder to shoulder in rows of five, muttering and shivering in the gloom.

'Ah, here they are,' whispered the soldier in front.

Bare-chested Torecti warriors, painted with swirling patterns, strode along the column on either side and took up positions. They carried bows and arrows in bark quivers, held spears in hand, and wore bone daggers tied at their hips. Valcero saw faces from the village. He hunched over and stared at his feet.

'Douse the lights!' Divendrion barked down the line.

The cantare jabbed their torches into the dirt and dropped them, until only the moons provided some weak light through the clouds.

'Stay in your lines,' another voice called out in accented Caerian. It was Reito. 'If you wander or fall behind, you will be lost!'

'By the One,' a cantarus whispered behind Valcero, 'Every time!'

'They think we're children,' another muttered.

'Forward!' the general shouted.

Row by row, the men marched into the trees with the Torecti at their sides. Once they were all under the branches, the warriors of the Whispering Leaves began to sing the now familiar melody. The song echoed and rang in Valcero's ears. The soldiers walked tightly around him, close enough that he could hear their breathing. A shield knocked his back; their shoulders bumped against him. The ground seemed to slip and slide away from his feet. The song rose and fell as the sound surged through his blood and buzzed through his skull. It filled him with warmth. He could fight. He was brave. He knew it.

CHAPTER TWENTY-SEVEN

CAERIA – SPRING'S RISING – 437

And then, the song faded. The cantaris continued through the forest in a steady march as the trees began to thin. The soldiers did not speak. All Valcero could hear was pants of breath, feet stomping on the damp earth, jingling armour and rustling cloaks, a crow cawing in the trees. The knocking of a woodpecker.

They halted without warning.

'Stop, stop.' The whispered order passed back through the ranks.

The Torecti and Caerians crouched in the undergrowth. Valcero copied them and glanced over the helmets. A grey, pre-dawn light suffused the forest under a cloudy sky. The ground dropped away, out of sight. General Divendrion and Reito were upfront, each standing behind a tree and peering ahead.

Reito turned back and signalled to his warriors. They loped forward, remaining bent over, spears held low.

'Forward, keep low, ranks of ten.' A new order murmured from Caerian to Caerian.

The men crept forward and reassembled themselves as they went. Valcero stumbled into what he thought was the right place. No one seemed to mind. They were too busy staring ahead. The men passed out of the forest, save for two Torecti who climbed into the trees, perhaps to keep watch.

The soldiers poured down the slope in a narrow gulley clogged with bracken, down to a valley stretching left and right between the green hills. The Torecti warriors slipped ahead through the vegetation with barely a rustle. The fronds whipped across Valcero's face as he pushed up his helmet to look properly. A villa lay to the left, partly hidden from view as they descended the hillside. The valley was otherwise filled with fields, orchards, and bare-leafed vineyards along a thin, dark river.

They gathered in the bushes at the bottom of the slope. A thrill coursed up Valcero's spine. If only Terzjin could see him now.

Reito inspected the Torecti and Caerians, and his eyes fell upon Valcero. The boy quickly turned away.

Reito yanked the helmet off Valcero. '*Cunestia!*' He slapped the boy across the head. 'What are you doing here?' He turned to General Divendrion. 'What is he *doing* here?' he hissed.

The general swore and strode to them. 'I didn't bring him!' he whispered harshly. He glared at Valcero. 'I ordered you to stay at camp, boy. '

Valcero's cheeks burned. Everyone was staring.

Divendrion pulled open Valcero's cloak. 'By the Lord of Death, you're not even wearing armour. Do you want to die out here?'

The boy pointed at the Torecti warriors. 'They aren't wearing bronze,' he mumbled.

The general raised his hand as if to hit Valcero. 'Do not tempt me.' He turned to Reito. 'You have to take him back.'

The Torecti man looked around and up the slope. He shook his head. 'We do not have time. I cannot. We must attack now, all of us, or call it off. What do you say?'

Divendrion groaned. 'Damn you, boy. Alright, we attack. And *you*...' He jabbed Valcero in the chest with his finger. 'You keep behind.'

Reito pulled aside three warriors, two men and a woman. 'Stay with Valcero,' he ordered in Torecti. 'Let nothing happen to him, do you hear me?'

They nodded and surrounded the boy.

'At least keep this on.' The general dropped the helmet back on Valcero's head. It slipped to the side, lopsided. 'Ugh.' Divendrion shook his head and shrugged. 'So be it.'

At Reito's signal, they stalked towards the villa through the bare orchards. A stone wall surrounded the inner gardens of the great house, interrupted by a half-open gate where a couple of Rhenivians sat dozing. The Torecti loosed two arrows without warning or ceremony, and the sentries keeled over. The warriors swarmed towards the wall, scaling it without effort. They crouched on top, fired arrows into the grounds, then dropped over the other side. The Caerians broke into a run and made for the gate, with Valcero and his protectors a few spans behind.

A horse whinnied somewhere within the walls. A shout rang out.

'Form up!' General Divendrion barked.

The Caerians roared in response as they burst through the gateway. They lined up in a shield wall, spears fanning out. Valcero peered over their shoulders into the camp.

The Rhenivians were screaming and shouting, running in every direction between their tents. The Torecti rolled through like a wave, hurling spears, shooting arrows, slicing and stabbing with daggers. Without stopping, the warriors slashed the throats of waking soldiers as they tried to sit up in their beds. It was only a game, surely?

Some Rhenivians rallied. They threw axes and spears at the Torecti and swung their swords, but the forest people dodged their blades and dealt death in return. The Caerians roared again and charged into the camp, ramming their spears at the invaders. There was blood and more screaming. Valcero gaped at it all.

'Come, boy,' the woman warrior tugged at his cloak. 'Come, we cannot linger.'

Three tall Rhenivians dashed at them, half-dressed, screaming and yelling, waving long axes above their heads. Valcero shook. His blood turned cold. The warriors dispatched two Rhenivians with arrows. The third came too close, so the woman warrior loped towards him, iron dagger ready. He swung his axe down, but she slipped aside, danced behind him, and swooped low to slice his ankles, then spun around to slit his neck from the front. The man sagged to the ground.

Valcero's head spun. His teeth felt loose in his jaw.

'Quickly now,' a warrior muttered in his ear. 'Breathe.' He nudged the boy forward.

They ran along the wall, keeping clear of the fighting, towards the villa. The grounds must have been a garden once, before the Rhenivians set up camp. There were remains of long lavender hedges, now squashed and torn up. A heap of ash lay on a square of paving, the remains of a bonfire. A Fools' Week bonfire. So the new year had come.

'It was my birthday,' Valcero muttered.

The Torecti woman pointed ahead. 'Look.' A handful of Rhenivians threw open the front doors and fled inside.

A Torecti man whistled to three companions. They turned and nodded. As one, the four converged on the doors and entered the house in pursuit.

'We will wait here,' the woman said to Valcero.

The boy looked up at the villa. There was something about it, something so familiar. His heart pounded from fear, but also something more. 'I know this place.' He had to go inside. He had to see. He dashed for the house.

'Stop!' The Torecti shouted.

But Valcero pushed through the doors into the dim hallway. Screams came down the passage. He crept past the statues and busts lining the walls. He flinched as footsteps thumped and creaked through the wooden ceiling above.

'Valcero!' The woman warrior called after him.

The three Torecti crept inside behind him. They gaped at the plastered walls and tiled floor.

A woman's shriek echoed around the corner.

'How *dare* you!' a man shouted, both outraged and fearful, somewhere ahead. That voice...

The boy peered around the corner and gasped.

Master Cleotan, much as Valcero remembered him, stood with his arms spread, as if to block the Torecti who strode towards him and his family. Mistress Cleotan crouched behind, clutching the dear, sweet twins, now taller. And of course, cowering behind her was Tenerus Cleotan. The gangly boy was nearly a man.

Valcero swallowed and tried to breathe normally. He stepped around the corner and towards his old masters. He felt weightless, dizzy. He felt... everything.

The Torecti raised their spears.

'Stop!' Valcero called out in the warriors' language.

They all looked at him.

'They are sheltering invaders here,' a warrior replied.

'They are *Caeri*, like me,' Valcero said. 'No *Caeri*!'

'We must find all the invaders,' the warrior insisted.

'How many Rhenivians are in the house?' Valcero asked Master Cleotan in Caerian.

'Who do you think you are?' the man spat. 'You come in here, in my house, attack my wife and children.'

'They won't harm you,' Valcero said.

'I don't believe you!'

Valcero Baradon pulled off his helmet. 'They will not harm you... sir. Do you remember me?'

They stared at him blankly.

'It's just a boy,' Mistress Cleotan said.

'It's *him*,' Tenerus leaned out from behind his mother and pointed. 'He was one of ours.'

'What?' Master Cleotan squinted at Valcero.

'Yes, Papa, you released him when the king banned slavery. He's called Valcero.'

Realisation dawned on the man's face. 'Ah, so you've come for revenge, have you?'

Valcero shook his head.

'Well, you are nothing.' The patrician jabbed his finger in the air. 'You can take what you want, but you are *nothing*.'

Valcero's fist tightened around the spear.

The warrior woman came to his side. 'You know them?' she asked.

'I was their...' the boy began to reply. 'I... yes, I know them.'

She held her dagger out at her side. 'Are they bad people?' she murmured.

The Cleotan huddled, staring at the iron blade. The twins' eyes were widest.

Valcero sighed. 'They... no, no, they cannot hurt us. Not now. Leave them, please.'

Master Cleotan glared at the boy. 'You are nothing more than a bandit, consorting with savages.'

'And you consort with Rhenivians,' Valcero shot back.

His old master grimaced, white-faced.

'We had no choice,' his wife wailed.

'Then tell us how many are upstairs.'

Master Cleotan eyed the intruders. 'Five soldiers. And there's the marshal in the bedroom.'

'They say six invaders,' Valcero said in Torecti.

A warrior chuckled. 'At least. Alright.' He signalled to four companions, and they pushed past the family and up the stairs.

'We should leave,' Valcero said to the other warriors.

He turned his back on the Cleotan and followed the Torecti towards the front door. But here, cowering in the shadows of another passageway, were two more people. A man and woman, both marked on their foreheads, grey-haired and trembling.

Valcero blinked. He stepped towards them. He held out a hand.

'My boy.' The man came into the light. Aulix. He peered at Valcero. 'My boy, I cannot believe it.'

'How are you here?' Praehenna crept forward with her hand at her mouth. 'Where have you been?'

Valcero reached to hug them, then saw the copper rings around their necks. 'They made you slaves *again*?'

Aulix smiled weakly. 'We had no choice, lad. Nowhere else to go.'

Screams and shouts came from upstairs. The Cleotan stood rooted in the hallway.

Valcero looked to Aulix and Praehenna. 'Come with us,' he said in Torecti.

'We can't, love.' Praehenna replied.

'Don't worry about them.' Valcero jerked his head towards the Cleotan. 'Just come with us, please.' He reached out to take their hands.

'No!' The Torecti warrior woman seized Valcero and pulled him away. 'They are *telotulae*.' She pointed at the tattoos on their foreheads.

'What?'

'Outcasts, lad.' Aulix looked pained. 'We are exiled from the forest.'

Another Torecti spat on the ground. 'Child killers.'

'What?' Valcero struggled in the woman's grip. 'No!'

There was another scream, followed by a thump above their heads.

Praehenna shivered. 'It was an accident, Valcero. We did nothing, I swear.'

'It was our boy, our little baby.' Aulix's face turned ashen. 'He never awoke.'

'We always loved you, Valcero.' Praehenna wiped her eyes. 'We would never hurt you. Never!'

A horn sounded upstairs. They looked up. It blew again, but was cut short. The Torecti warriors glanced at each other.

'We must leave now.' The warrior woman dragged Valcero away. 'Come, boy.'

Praehenna tried to touch Valcero's cheek, then jerked her hand back and pressed it to her mouth. She sobbed and fell to her knees. Aulix crouched to hold her.

'No, please. No.' Valcero dropped his spear and shield and strained towards them.

'Shhh,' the woman whispered in the boy's ear as she dragged him away. 'They are unclean. Leave them.'

They came outside into the dawn light. The battle was over. Torecti and Caerians had gathered all the Rhenivian bodies into a heap and were adding pieces of wood and smoking coals to make a funeral pyre. Valcero's stomach lurched. He wiped his eyes with his cloak and gazed at the house instead.

Five dead Caerians and three Torecti lay on the ground. Their companions were wrapping them in tent cloth and lifting the bundles onto their shoulders.

'All taken care of in there?' Reito asked the warriors around Valcero.

They glanced at the boy. 'All taken care of,' a man replied.

General Divendrion inspected the wrapped bodies and strode over to Reito. 'We should get back to the forest. I don't like that they blew their horn.'

Reito nodded and whistled to his men. Divendrion called to his. They trooped out of the estate grounds and along the track towards the hills, as a plume of black smoke began to rise behind them. An orange glow burned under the clouds to the east. The Caerians chatted amongst themselves as they walked; the Torecti went in silence.

Valcero trudged amongst them. Did Praehenna and Aulix truly kill their child? No, it couldn't be. Could it?

'Shh!' Divendrion held up a hand.

The cantare paused and fell silent.

'Did you hear that?' the General asked Reito. 'Thunder?'

Reito cocked his head to one side. 'Drums?'

Valcero heard it too. A distant rumbling, growing louder.

The general glanced about the valley. 'No. Hooves.'

Reito stared past him down the road and cursed. 'Run!' he shouted in Torecti.

'Run!' The general shoved his men towards the hills. 'Run!'

Scores, maybe hundreds, of riders thundered down the road towards them, lances lowered and axes waving overhead. The Rhenivians roared and screamed and blew horns as they galloped.

The Caerians and Torecti fled through the orchards, almost tumbling over each other. Valcero dashed behind. He glanced over his shoulder. A handful of warriors lined up against the oncoming horde and fired arrows into the throng. Some riders fell, but the Rhenivians smashed through the line of Torecti and turned about to pursue the rest.

As he sprinted, Valcero's cloak caught upon a branch and yanked him backwards. He screamed. His heart seemed to burst from his chest. He wriggled out of the cloak and ran on. They were leaving him behind. He strained to catch up. Lord of Death, spare me. Hoofbeats drummed in his ears. Lord of Life, save me. A spear flew past his head. Help. He tripped and fell into a ditch along the orchard's edge.

His leg hit a rock, but he couldn't scream. Cold, thick mud choked his mouth and nose. His fingers clenched the ooze. His body froze. The shadows of horses flew overhead. Hooves hammered the earth around him. He waited for iron to pierce his back. He wet himself.

He was going to die.

He was dying.

Lord of Death, guide me.

And then, the horses passed. The galloping faded. The shouts and whistles grew distant. But Valcero could not move. He shivered in the mud, locked in place. Somewhere, a dog barked and howled. He sucked in a breath and coughed out the earth. He slithered out of the ditch on his belly and looked about. All was quiet. The valley seemed deserted. Flames leapt up from the pyre, higher than the garden wall. He looked up the hill. There was no one in sight. He stood, but immediately collapsed onto his hands and knees. His back spasmed and arched, and last night's supper spewed out. He broke down crying into the splash of vomit. Where was Terzjin? Terzjin would help him. He would always help him.

The boy coughed and spat, then wiped tears, mud, and puke from his face. He could go back to the house. Praehenna was there. Aulix was there. They would help, look after him. Wouldn't they?

No, his heart said. The Cleotan would kill Valcero as soon as he crossed the threshold. He must find a way back to the Torecti, back to their forest.

He sniffed and swallowed and hauled himself to his feet. His leg throbbed. He limped up the hillside into the bracken. The sword was still at his waist, banging against his leg. It could be useful. He may need to defend himself.

Don't be ridiculous, his heart said. They were all right about you. That blade is worse than useless in your hands. It only marks you as an enemy to any Rhenivian who may find you. You *idiot*.

He untied the sheath from his belt and flung it into the braken. He didn't deserve it anyway. He continued uphill, slowly and painfully. No Torecti awaited him at the top. They had forgotten him. Of course. Valcero hobbled into the forest with his back to the rising sun, hopefully in the right direction.

He was shivering. He stopped to rest against a tree and clutched himself.

And then two Rhenivians rode into sight from around the trunk. They flinched in their saddles and trotted forward. Valcero wanted to run, but his legs failed him. His heart failed him.

One of the soldiers shouted. Something in Rhenivian.

'I don't understand,' the boy muttered.

They screamed at him.

Valcero burst into tears. 'I don't understand!'

They looked at each other, and then again at the boy.

'Who are you?' the other man asked.

'They are all dead.' Valcero sobbed. 'They killed all the men and they burnt them.'

The soldier looked at his muddy, torn tunic. 'You are from the estate?'

The boy stopped crying. His heart drummed in his chest, but an idea came. He wiped his face. 'I work for the Cleotan, yes. Please don't hurt me. Please.'

'You are a servant?' the first soldier asked.

Valcero sniffed and nodded.

'Good.' The second soldier slid off his horse and pulled a length of rope from his pack. 'You will work for us now.'

CHAPTER TWENTY-EIGHT

CAERIA – SPRING'S RISING – 437

The soldiers bound Valcero and forced him to march ahead of their horses over the course of the day, until his head spun from hunger and thirst. They stopped only to toss him a chunk of bread and let him kneel at a stream. They joined more Rhenivians with a horse-drawn cart of Caerian captives, who sat grim-faced and silent. The next day, they reached a camp amongst wooded hills, some distance from the edge of the Nedolian Forest.

'This is what you will do,' a soldier announced in Caerian as they rolled through the stockade gate. 'You will build what needs to be built. You will dig what we tell you to dig. You will obey, you will say, "Yes, sir", and you will live. Do you understand?'

The camp was a tiny city of cramped huts and tents crowded within the wooden walls and interspersed with muddy alleyways. The only open space was the paddock on the eastern side, where the Rhenivians kept their horses.

The soldier whacked his spear against the cart. 'I said, do you understand?'

The Caerians nodded and muttered in agreement.

The soldiers herded them off the cart and towards a rough, wicker-walled hut with other Caerians , all wearing copper neck rings.

The Rhenivians took the newcomers one by one to the smith, who attached the rings. They held Valcero's arms, and the boy stood numbly as the smith hammered the pin into the back of the ring.

'You are not a slave,' a soldier told him. 'This is just so you don't run away.'

He had forgotten how uncomfortable the ring was, how the metal pressed against his throat.

Valcero spent each day much like the last. They hauled wooden poles from one end of camp to the other, they dug latrines in the muddy earth, and he passed bales of hay over the fence to the slavering horses, surrounded by clouds of flies. He cooked, he scrubbed, he polished.

After sunset, they hunkered in the hut on the earthen floor, passing a bowl of gristly stew from mouth to mouth and gnawing on old bread. The boy woke up screaming in the middle of the night, from nightmares of blood and iron hooves.

The Rhenivians rode out at sunrise each morning, leaving the camp in relative peace. By nightfall, they galloped back inside and demanded dinner. Valcero ran with cups of beer and wine when summoned, to avoid a cuffing. If the Caerians were too slow when lifting logs and digging pits under the daytime sun, the foreman whipped them with flicks of a long willow switch.

At night, Valcero lay on his back on the cold ground, while the wind blew through gaps in the crude hut. He prayed for Terzjin, or the Torecti, to find him, to rescue him. Any moment now, he would hear the attack, the screams, the clang of metal, then Terzjin would burst through the door and set him free. But the moment never came. Master Maltorus didn't know where he was. The Torecti thought he was lost—or dead, most likely. They weren't coming. He was alone. This is what he deserved for trying to be a warrior. This was his prize for failure. His thoughts turned until he fell into a miserable, fitful sleep, ending when the guards thumped on the wicker walls to repeat another day.

One evening—he was not sure when—the horsemen rode into camp, dragging a man at the end of a long rope. He was nearly a corpse, yet still breathing. A Torecti man, judging by the paint on his skin. Valcero could not recognise the smeared, faded patterns—waving lines like seaweed, or grass billowing in the wind.

The Rhenivians dragged the captured warrior to a junction between the huts and tied him to a pole. His face was swollen and bruised, while blood dripped from cuts all over his body. He hung off the pole while the Rhenivians laughed and whipped him. The next day, they threw water in his face, then untied and dragged him to a large tent. All the Caerians could hear his screams and groans. The cries went on for an hour or more, until they dragged him out and retied him to the pole, more battered and bloody. This went on for two days.

When the guards sent Valcero for a bucket of water one quiet morning, he passed the prisoner.

The boy glanced around and crept over the bound man. '*Sevei,*' he whispered.

The Torecti man looked up and squinted at the boy with one open, swollen eye.

'What is your name?' Valcero whispered.

'Who are you?' the Torecti replied with a croaking voice. 'You speak my tongue.'

'Valcero,' the boy said. 'I lived with the Whispering Leaves clan. Do you have news of them?'

'News?' The warrior laughed and broke into a coughing fit. 'The news seems bad, my boy. Do you not think?'

'I am sorry,' Valcero said. 'Can I do anything?'

'A little of that water, please.'

He lifted the bucket to the man's mouth.

The Torecti gulped water and coughed again. 'Could you untie me?'

The boy examined the knots. 'The rope looks tight, but I can try.'

'Try then, do.'

Valcero reached out with his fingers.

'Ey! What are you doing?'

The boy recoiled and spun around.

A Rhenivian strode towards him, brandishing a spear. 'What is this?'

Valcero backed away. 'I'm sorry, sir. I'm sorry. Just giving him some water, sir.'

The soldier struck him across the face with the spear shaft. 'You. Do. Not.'

Valcero dropped the bucket to shield his head, but the blows came too quickly.

'I'm sorry, sir. I'm sorry!'

'Get out of here!' the guard snarled. He hit Valcero again.

The boy grabbed the bucket and scrambled off, receiving another blow across his back as he fled.

'Stay away!' The soldier roared after him.

Valcero limped back to the well to scoop up more water. He received another blow across his back when he was late delivering it.

The other slaves saw him wince and hobble through the camp.

'Come here, lad,' an old woman said. 'Let me see.' She brought him to a gap between the tents out of the Rhenivians' view.

Valcero bent over with hands on knees while she peered down the back of his tunic.

'Ah, don't worry, lad. I'll find herbs and fat to rub on the bruises.' She patted his shoulders. 'Don't worry.'

Valcero stood up. 'Thank you, but don't get into trouble for me.'

She held his hands. 'Best keep your head down, boy. Know your place, yes?'

'Yes.'

The next day, the Torecti prisoner was gone. Died, the slaves gossiped. Or perhaps murdered in the night.

What if I had helped him? Valcero wondered. Where would he be now? Another failure, his heart told him. You idiot.

CHAPTER TWENTY-NINE

SASIION – SPRING'S RISING – 437

Terzjin stood with Zjandius on the plain outside the walls of Elisdrium, with the sea breeze in his hair. Thousands of soldiers fidgeted behind them under a forest of pikes and rippling banners, gleaming and flashing in the rising sun. A regiment of war chariots, a contribution from the flood princes, clattered alongside to their place at the flank. Four rumbling war elephants and their handlers, the pride of Empress Nanepti. Slingers from Tergad, archers from Paeseum. Light infantry from the little villages and other small cities, armed with round shields, spears, and bronze sickles, shuffled in their places.

And of course, beyond the cantare and assorted warriors, the multitudes of wagons, mules, quartermasters, servants, cooks, engineers, smiths, carpenters, fletchers, tailors, and other camp followers also waited for the order to move.

A sea of people, ready to march.

Master Maltorus followed the Emperor in front of it all as Zjandius said his goodbyes. First, he stopped at Taeto Vaecerion, who smiled and bowed.

'Govern well, cousin,' the Emperor said. 'I leave Elisdrium once more in your care, and now all Sasiion as well.'

'As you command, Your Majesty,' Taeto replied. 'I shall guard it well.'

Zjandius nodded and walked on, now stopping before his half-brothers—Merius, Prince of Paeseum, and Astulus—as well as Dowager Queen Porinia, who had come to see them off.

'Brother,' Zjandius said.

Merius raised his eyebrows and smiled. 'Majesty.' He bowed.

'Govern well, Prince Merius. And should the Rhenivians grow vengeful, you will need to meet them at the northern borders. At Emzentanis, or wherever.'

Merius bowed again. 'Of course, Your Majesty.'

Zjandius turned to Porinia, who sat on a shaded palanquin. She arose as he drew near.

The Emperor smiled. 'Queen Porinia, I am glad to find you here.'

'Your Majesty.' She inclined her head.

'Will you come to Caeria on the second voyage?' Zjandius asked. 'With the rest?'

'*Will* there be a second voyage?'

Zjandius sighed. 'A fair question, My Queen. I hope so, if the Lords and the One allow it. I undertake this war with the intent that there shall be—for all of our sakes.'

Porinia looked from side to side. 'I am not sure I have the strength to cross the sea, Your Majesty. I feel age creeping upon me. I may stay here with my boy...' She patted Merius' back, '... and live out my days with sand in my hair, shrivelling in the sun.'

Zjandius smiled. 'Well, My Queen, Etorium will always be waiting. Vaecerium will always be waiting. They are your homes too, always and forever.' He swallowed. 'We... we haven't always...'

'No, we haven't.' Porinia said.

'Well, in case there is no second voyage, or...' Zjandius coughed. '... or we don't meet again. For some other reason...' He held out his hands.

The dowager queen hesitated, then put her hands in his. Zjandius squeezed them, then bowed and gently kissed each in turn.

Porinia watched him with a strange expression on her face, then leaned forward and kissed Zjandius on the forehead. 'Your father would be proud,' she whispered, then straightened up and proclaimed, 'Now go, Your Majesty. Honour us. Honour all Caeria. May the Lord of Life keep you and the Lord of Death forget you were ever born!'

Zjandius grinned and nodded. He strode on, now with Prince Astulus in tow.

Porinia blinked and wiped her eyes. 'And take care of my son!' she called out.

'Of course, My Queen!' Zjandius called back and put his arm around his half-brother.

Terzjin walked behind.

And then they came to the end of the line. Empress Nanepti sat in her own palanquin, draped in fine, white cotton and flanked by guards and attendants, including Saedelas and Captain Wederet. Nanepti went to Zjandius as he stopped before her.

'My Emperor,' she murmured.

'My Empress.' Zjandius kissed her on the lips, long and slow.

The soldiers cheered and whistled.

The couple parted, then embraced for a time, foreheads pressed together. They whispered to each other. Zjandius stroked her belly.

Finally, the Emperor stepped away and addressed her bodyguard. 'Protect her well, Captain!'

Wederet bowed low. 'With my every breath and every beat of my heart, Your Majesty!'

'I will send for you,' Zjandius said to Nanepti, 'when the time is right. Wait for me.'

She smiled. 'Go well.'

Wederet caught Terzjin's eye and winked. 'Show them hell, my boy.'

Master Maltorus nodded and smiled in return. He looked to Saedelas amongst Nanepti's servants. Her eyes gleamed, and she raised her fingers to give a discreet wave.

Zjandius turned to face his cantaris. 'Well, a speech?' he muttered. 'Hmm, no, perhaps not.' He strode forward and stepped aboard his waiting chariot.

Terzjin hurried to join him and take the reins.

Merius boarded his chariot to the left.

'Your Majesty!' Lord Corilien saluted from his chariot on the right.

Colus Meretan waved from his wagon, surrounded by his engineers and their contraptions.

The Emperor signalled to his herald, who waited on horseback nearby. The herald raised his brass trumpet to his lips and let forth a long, sonorous note. The army roared and cheered. Spears banged against shields. Merius and Lord Corilien stirred their horses into action and rode off to lead their respective flanks. The lenotare on their own chariots wheeled into formation around their emperor. Captains and generals shouted orders across the field. Like a lumbering beast, the cantaris turned about and began to move.

Master Maltorus drove the emperor's chariot westward, behind the army, right to the cliff edge. Below, spread out on the shimmering sea, the great, white-sailed fleet lay waiting. The herald galloped up from behind.

'Sound it!' Zjandius commanded.

The herald blew again on his trumpet. A moment passed, and another trumpet echoed up from Admiral Getaelon's ships. Oars raised and dipped in salute. Sails grasped at the wind and billowed. The eyed vessels lurched and turned north. They were off.

On the advice of the diviners, who had found only ambiguous auguries, and the old captains who scanned the skies with furrowed brows, Emperor Zjandius and Admiral Getaelon had decided on the most cautious route possible. The fleet sailed light and empty, hugging the coast while the cantaris marched alongside on land. They went north through the dry country—slowly but surely—past the sea cliffs and onto the flatter, sandy coast.

They reached the northern point of the Sesurian Sea, where the red mountains touch the water near Heropis. Five hundred Rugadi and their horses camped at the foot of the mountains and greeted the marching forces with water, dates, and fresh game.

The sand prince Hemadir presented himself to the Emperor with a deep bow. He hugged Terzjin. 'I am coming with you, Master Maltorus. I want to know this land of grass and trees over the sea for myself. I want to see how fat my horse will get from eating all that green stuff.'

The Rugadi led them along the narrow coastal paths and into the long valley that stretched northwards. They wished the sailors well as the fleet continued its voyage, now bearing south along the eastern coast of Hebenia Minor to the isthmus.

The cantaris went north, then west. The Rugadi found the best passes through the dry mountains, the secret wells and springs in shaded, rocky recesses, the lush pockets in the valleys where beasts could feed and the army could rest.

The way was slow. Ox wagons trundled up and down the winding paths. Their wheels often jammed on the dusty rocks, or they threatened to tip over the cliffs and tumble down the thorny slopes. Master Meretan cursed, swore, and threatened eternal torment to anyone who might lose one of his precious siege engines. But, somehow, they made their way through each jagged range that barred their passage. And, one fine afternoon late in the month of Spring's Reign, they came over the final pass and glimpsed the ocean again, washing against a greener shore.

They turned north, through groves of olives and almonds and onwards over long days to the old city of Deria, with its whitewashed walls overlooking the turquoise sea. Terzjin's heart fluttered at the sight of it, to be in this place once more.

Prince Esioret of Deria rode out with his retinue to Zjandius's tent, where the Emperor awaited on his wooden throne. Esioret greeted Zjandius as an old friend, which—Terzjin suspected—was not entirely heartfelt. Prince Astulus, Lord Corilien, and Prince Hemadir all attended the meeting. Esioret eyed the sand prince as he entered.

'Emperor Zjandius, welcome.' Prince Esioret bowed deeply. 'You honour us with your presence. The old friendships endure.' He was a middle-aged man with only tufts of silver hair over his ears, dressed in a white tunic under a finely woven blue robe. He opened his hands with fingers festooned with rings and jewels.

Zjandius arose to greet his one-time vassal. 'Thank you, Prince. Your hospitality is most appreciated. However, I am told you have other guests who may not welcome our visit.'

'Ah.' The Prince's face turned serious. 'The Rhenivians. Yes, they were not too happy when your cantaris appeared on the horizon, Your Majesty. They ordered me to prepare for a siege.'

'And yet here you are.'

The Prince grinned. 'Well, after so many years, there were only about 200 of their soldiers in the city. My Derians rioted and forced the gates open. The Rhenivians panicked and fled when you were less than a league away.' He turned to the open edge of the tent and waved in a vague direction. 'They have returned to their kingdom.'

In fact, a faint cloud of dust hung over the northern hills as he spoke. The road to Galatan.

The Prince grimaced, 'I suspect they will come back soon—with friends.'

'We will protect your city,' the Emperor said, 'if we are here when the Rhenivians return.'

'You will not stay here for long, Your Majesty?' Various emotions flitted across the Prince's face—relief, hope, and worry.

Zjandius sat down. 'No, My Prince. Our destination lies elsewhere. We shall await our ships in the shade of your walls, if that would not bother you.'

'Oh no, of course not, Emperor. You are our guests. The Prince bowed again with a flourish.

'Excellent,' Zjandius said. 'We will defend your city as long as we are here. But, should the Rhenivians come after we are gone, well, perhaps it would be best that you prepare for a siege all the same.'

CHAPTER THIRTY

CAERIA – SPRING'S RISING – 437

Heirik rode into the next camp with a grin on his face. Another day of hunting forest savages. His axe was notched from a few of their bones. A pity he hadn't felled more, but the sly cowards always melted away before his riders could get close enough. Well, they were getting better at catching the vermin, that's for sure. Now, the savages had barely a moment to attack before his men rode them down.

'Welcome, Thane Heirik!' The soldiers gathered around him and the other riders. 'Good hunting, My Thane?'

'Excellent indeed!' Heirik reached into his saddle bag to lift a severed head by its long, dark hair.

The Rhenivians roared and cheered. They were winning. One by one, they would wipe out these *Torecti,* and the whole island would truly belong to him, Thane Heirik. He will accomplish what these useless Caerians never could.

Heirik tossed the head to a soldier. 'Pop that on a spear, would you? Leave it at the gate to mark our victory.' He dropped off his horse and grimaced. A long day. 'Bring me water,' he called out. 'I will wash, then we feast!'

The camp marshal led him to a tent. Inside, Heirik peeled his blood-spattered jerkin away from the cut across his chest, then pulled off his trousers. An elderly woman hobbled in, lugging a bucket of well water, and blushed at the sight of him.

'Set the water down there,' he ordered, 'then take this for cleaning.' The woman bowed, then scuttled out of the tent with his dirty clothes before he could dismiss her. She looked as if she were pretty once, perhaps as pretty as Razna. But time and poverty had shrivelled the old bag's skin and left her worn. The copper ring around her neck did her no favours either. Heirik sniffed. How he ached for Razna right now. She should be here. What was she doing at this moment? Perhaps learning her reading, or maybe entertaining Lady Eledan and the Prefect's wife through gritted teeth. He smiled and splashed cold water over his face and the wound on his chest. She'd be so much happier here.

Once he had washed and dressed in fresh trousers, a clean woollen tunic, and a cloak, with hair freshly greased and eyes sooted, he went to the hall. It was evening, and the camp was bathed in a warm light that made it beautiful to his eyes. So much better than all that cold Etorian brick and stone. His new hold would be *even* better. It would be the finest, the envy of all Rhenivia. The thanes would journey far to Heiriksreld to sit at his table, drink his beer and sing his praises. Soon. Very soon.

The camp hall was dim inside, with smoke that pricked the eyes. The servants hurried to light oil lamps and stoke the fire to brighten the place. He salivated at the smell of charred meat and fresh beer.

'My Thane!' The soldiers rose from the long table and clapped as he walked past. They reached out to thump his back and fuss over him, leading him to the head of the table, before his throne, draped in a wolfskin cloak, a gift from Uncle Getherd. His favourite axe lay across the throne's armrests.

'Please, all of you, be seated,' Heirik called out to his men. 'Welcome, and be merry!' He sat, and they all followed suit.

Some musicians started up a tune on drums and pipes, some kind of sour, Caerian melody. Supposed to be cheerful, but not quite right. He needed better musicians from the homeland. *Another* thing to organise.

The servants brought a board of lamb roasted in honey and set a cup of Rhenivian beer at his side, without even being asked.

He grinned and smacked his lips. 'Let's eat!'

The feast began in earnest. They joked, drank a steady stream of wine and beer, sang war songs, and swapped tales. His visiting marshals told him of the heaps of forest savages they had felled, of the traps they had set, and all their heroic feats against the foe. Heirik stood and regaled them with his own day's deeds. The men listened, silent and rapt.

'I cornered this forest chieftain against the wall of a farmer's barn, like a fox pinned against the henhouse. He had his women come at me to scratch with their blades and fingernails. Their women can fight, I must say. Anyway, the women attacked me, defending their chief. But I knocked them down, one by one.' Heirik mimed each swing of his axe. 'The old fox cursed me in his tongue. I mean, who knows *exactly* what he said, but it certainly didn't sound like praise!'

The soldiers laughed.

'So,' Heirik continued, 'I went in with my axe, and he gave me a bit of a scratch...' He patted his chest, '...but I brought him low. Don't worry; there're no hard feelings. Look, I even invited him to the party!'

He pointed as one of his men brought in the head on the spear and danced with it around the hall.

The Rhenivians burst out laughing and thumped the table as they cheered. 'To our Thane!' They raised their cups. 'Long live Thane Heirik! Hurrah!'

Heirik beamed and raised his own cup to gulp beer. Of course, he had left out a little bit. The Torecti man—chief or not—had already been limping and gushing blood after fighting off three of Heirik's best, and killing them in the process. No need to go into *all* the boring details. Just brings down morale and all that.

The feast continued for a few hours while they emptied barrels of beer and platters of meat. The songs grew more slurred and the tales more rambling. The firelight glimmered and danced around them. Eventually, Heirik pulled himself to his feet.

'I need to piss,' he announced.

The men sitting around didn't seem to hear. They were too caught up in their own deeply important conversations, sleeping facedown on the table, or whatever. Heirik stumbled out of the hall and into the narrow alleyway. The stars gleamed in long streaks. The night air was sharp and chilly so far from the sea. Heirik rounded a corner and looked for a spot to empty his bladder. He undid his trousers and sighed as he aimed a stream against the wooden wall. He finished, and just as he fumbled to retie his trousers, he heard a cough to his right.

He swung his head around.

'Good evening, Thane Heirik.' The voice came from the shadows, speaking Caerian. 'I am sorry to bother you, but may I have a word?'

Heirik frowned and squinted down the alleyway that ran between the hall and a wicker hut. 'Who's there?'

Something moved in the darkness. A figure stepped into view, wearing a black cloak and a hood. The hood fell back, revealing an older man with long grey hair, a sharp nose, and dark eyes. He gazed at Heirik with a calm, yet watchful expression. 'I beg your pardon, Thane Heirik, for we have never been formally introduced. But I come here tonight to offer you news.'

Heirik leaned against the hall. 'Who are you?'

The old man smiled and bowed. 'I am Sorveo Aventan. Lord Sorveo Aventan, to be precise.'

Heirik stood up straight and frowned. 'I thought you'd have died by now,' he said after a moment.

The old man chuckled. 'I thought so too, Thane.'

'How do I know you are Lord Aventan? You could be anybody.'

'Well,' the old man replied, 'what would I gain by meeting you and pretending to be him if I were not?'

Heirik's hand closed over the dagger hilt at his side. 'Very bold of you to creep alone into my camp like this.'

Lord Aventan nodded. 'It certainly would be.'

Heirik's eyes flicked from side to side. He couldn't see anyone else. Or hear them.

The old aristocrat watched him with the ghost of a smile on his lips. 'But I am quite serious, My Thane. I did not come here tonight to battle—merely to talk.'

'About what, then?'

'A warning, Thane Heirik. King Zjandius is returning to Caeria. He intends to arrive before the end of Spring's Fall, with a new *cantaris* freshly trained and equipped for fighting Rhenivian soldiers. He wants his kingdom.'

Heirik looked around and scowled. 'Why are *you* telling me this?'

'To prepare you,' Lord Aventan replied. 'These Torecti attacks are all part of his plan, to spread your forces and keep you away from Etorium, so they can capture the inner-coast cities and gather strength.'

Heirik folded his arms. 'Obviously, I don't trust you. Why would you ... betray your king by revealing his plans?'

'A fair point,' Aventan said, 'but the days of the Vaecerion are done. That family ruled this land for centuries, only to lose it. We cannot cling to the past. I must look to the future and be practical, despite my pain.' His face clouded.

'Pain?'

'My wife. My children,' Lord Aventan muttered. 'All dead.'

'Ah.' Heirik opened his hands. 'My Lord, I promise you, we never wanted to harm your family. It was *always* our plan to capture them alive. We would have treated them as hostages with all the honour they deserved, I swear it.'

Lord Aventan sighed.

'It was a horrible mistake, My Lord. A tragedy.'

Aventan smiled gently and nodded. 'I believe you, My Thane. War is always full of such tragedies.'

They regarded each other for a moment.

Heirik rubbed his head. 'Forgive me, Lord Aventan, but I'm still surprised you would share such secrets with me.'

The old man smiled wanly. 'Ah, my boy, I am tired of hiding in the shadows. I would like to come back to the light. I can help you win over the Caerians, far better than Lord Eledan or Octerian ever could. But first, you would need to defeat Zjandius.'

'And you offer to help?'

The lord nodded. 'We certainly can. I have gathered a small *cantaris* of my own. They are fiercely loyal to me. And through me, they would be loyal to you.'

The bandits in the woods. 'I think I've met these soldiers of yours.' Heirik pulled a face.

'Ah, yes, my apologies. As I said, war is full of little accidents.' Lord Aventan took a step forward. 'It is all in the past now, Thane Heirik. I will provide these warriors to aid you, but still, I am not sure it would be enough.'

'Not enough?'

'Here is my advice, Thane—call upon your Uncle Getherd. Ask him to bring reinforcements. Together you will certainly defeat Zjandius Vaecerion, and end his little campaign.'

Heirik sucked on his tongue. 'I'm not sure I want my uncle's help. Perhaps I don't need your help either. I will defeat these forest people, and then Zjandius. My men are handling the fight.'

Lord Aventan sighed. 'With respect, Thane Heirik, your men are lying to you. They are *nabolestan*.'

Heirik scowled. 'What's that mean?'

The Caerian smiled. 'Would you prefer we speak Galatani? I am told you know it well.'

The Thane shrugged.

Lord Aventan switched languages. 'Your men are *outmatched*, My Thane. While you have certainly won great victories as you move from camp to camp, the news elsewhere is not as good. The Torecti attack all along the borders of the Nedolian Forest. For every savage your soldiers kill, five to ten Rhenivians die in return. Every day, you lose soldiers, and your marshals are too afraid to share this truth. They send honeyed words instead. This all makes you vulnerable for when the Caerians return—and they will.'

'I sent a force to attack King Zjandius in his desert city,' Heirik said. 'They will tell me the truth of what you say.'

'Have you heard from them, Thane Heirik?'

He said nothing.

Lord Aventan nodded. 'I suspect they have suffered defeat, and the Caerians are now on their way. I suspect your heart tells you the same. Trust me, send a letter to High Thane Getherd and ask him to come with an army. Zjandius does not expect this. You will catch him unawares and *crush* him.'

Heirik looked at the old aristocrat in his black cloak. 'And should Zjandius arrive on these shores, how could you help me?'

'You tried to have him assassinated, yes? I have it on good authority that your plot failed. But my Aventan would not fail. No, My Thane, they would solve the problem of King Zjandius very efficiently.'

'And what would you like in return, My Lord?'

'As I said, Thane Heirik, I wish to come back into the light. A seat at your table. Peace between our people. Certainty. These simple things.'

Heirik stared at him, musing for a while. Then he stepped nearer and offered Lord Aventan his hand. 'Perhaps we can work together.'

The lord smiled and shook his hand with a firm grip. 'To the future, My Thane.' He let go and turned away. 'We shall speak again soon.' In a moment, the man slipped behind the hut and into the shadows.

Heirik strode after him and peered around the corner. There was no one there.

CHAPTER THIRTY-ONE

CAERIA — SPRING'S RISING — 437

Valcero breathed out slowly. He shifted on his bedmat to try another view through the gap in the wickerwork. A thin strip of moonlight crossed his face. The older man, supposedly Lord Aventan, had walked out of sight. And the younger man—Thane Heirik, apparently—had followed. Valcero froze. The Thane stomped back through the muddy alley and paused beside the hut, swaying on his feet. All he had to do was glance down, and he would surely see the boy spying on him through the wall. Valcero dared not move. The man muttered to himself and wandered off.

Valcero slid backwards onto his stomach and rolled over to stare at the dark ceiling, surrounded by soft snores. What happened out there? Was that truly Lord Aventan? He thought back to the gathering in the forest, when Lady Aventan recounted her story. Didn't she tell everyone her husband was dead? But now he was out there, alive and saying his *wife* was the one who was dead. What did it mean?

The Aventan are lying, his heart said. They are lying to everyone and playing their own game. What game? What else did the two men talk about? If only he understood Galatani...

A stick jabbed Valcero awake. He jerked about.

'Up, you lazy worm.' The guard stood over him and spat on his chest. 'Get up!'

The boy scrambled to his feet and stumbled out into the morning light. Did he dream the conversation? Could it be real?

He joined the other Caerians at the kitchen tent to queue for morning broth. The soup was perhaps two days old and beginning to turn. Valero forced down the sour liquid and ate some bread to distract himself. Praehenna and AulixCould they kill a child? He tried to picture Aulix doing something violent, but his heart could not imagine it. Praehenna had never even smacked him.

The guards marched along their line. 'Latrine duty! Get to it!'

Valcero trudged through the camp to the smelliest corner next to the paddocks. He took a spade and found a place next to the old woman, who had wasted no time and was already thrusting her spade into the mud. The horses milled around in the paddock, swishing their tails to ward off the flies. Swarms of them rose from the stinking earth and buzzed over his face, seeking the spit at the corner of his mouth, or the tears from his eyes. He tried to brush them off while digging, but it was a futile battle.

A tall Rhenivian, wearing a black and green cloak pinned at the shoulder, strode past to the edge of the paddock, along with some soldiers. The man leaned against the wooden fence and glanced around with an irritated face. He rapped a beat on the wood with his knuckles. His eyes were dark blue and intense. It was the same man from last night.

Valcero pointed. 'Who's that?' he whispered to the old woman.

'That's Thane Heirik,' she whispered back. 'Put your hand down, boy!' She grabbed his arm and nudged him back to his spade. 'You don't want his attention. Keep your head down and dig, yes?'

The Thane's eyes landed on Valcero. The boy quickly turned away and jabbed at the ground.

Someone shouted nearby. Valcero stole a glance. Another Rhenivian hurried to the paddock, while struggling to tie his cloak and put on his helmet. Thane Heirik said something to him in a sarcastic tone. The newcomer bowed his head and stammered. Heirik cut him off with more curt words, then held out a bronze message tube. He said more, and Valcero was certain he heard 'Getherd' and 'Lastria'.

'What do you think they're doing?' he murmured to the old woman.

She glanced to the side. 'I don't know. Sending messages, but it's none of our business, boy. Just dig.'

The soldier tied the tube to his belt, then climbed into the paddock and took a saddle and reins from the fence. He slipped the ropes and thick cloth over onto a horse, clambered up, and rode out where soldiers held the gate open. He cantered past the huts and tents, out of sight.

Thane Heirik watched the soldier ride off and muttered to his attendants. They nodded and bowed, then left one by one. When Heirik was alone, he turned back to the paddock and whistled. A huge black horse neighed and tossed its head, and trotted over to Heirik. The Rhenivian stroked the animal's snout, then put his head against the beast's face. He whispered words, and the horse snorted in reply.

None of it was a dream.

The next day, they sent Valcero to deliver beer and bread to the Thane's hall. He carried the tray inside, keeping his head low.

'*Eglor.*' The soldiers snapped at him and waved to an empty place on their long table.

Valcero hurried over and set the tray down. The Rhenivians huddled around a blank parchment and seemed to be struggling with writing on it. They had started a message with what were probably Rhenivian runes. A man leaned over the table and jabbed at the parchment with his finger.

Another looked across and saw the boy. '*Haalik!*' he shouted and pointed to the door.

Valcero cringed and ran to the doorway. He paused. They were still arguing over the pen and scratching out lines of text from the letter.

The following days passed in a similar fashion. The Rhenivians rode out at dawn to hunt and battle Torecti, while Valcero worked under the spring sun to dig fly-strewn latrines, carry water and hay for horses, and drag lumber for huts and the palisade wall. By dusk, the Rhenivians returned, bloodied and slightly fewer in number. Valcero ran back and forth with more buckets of water and rags, while men screamed and moaned in their tents. Sometimes, the blacksmiths went in bearing rods of glowing iron, and the soldiers screamed even louder.

Later, the boy carried caskets of beer and platters of meat to the hall, while men feasted and drank. One soldier gave Valcero some scraps of meat from his platter and patted the boy's head. Valcero shoved the meat into his mouth between the hall and the cooking fires, before the cook could see him. Later, they tossed him into the slaves' hut, shivering and still hungry, to sleep and wait for the next day—and for it all to begin again.

The boy lay on his mat and felt around in his belt bag. He rubbed the Torecti's window material between his fingers. It was smoother than papyrus, almost like parchment. Probably would take ink. Master Colus would probably like it—if he ever saw it. The Torecti weren't coming to save him. Terzjin wasn't coming either. Valcero might die here, whether from hunger or being beaten—or worse. He scrunched the paper in his fist and tried not to cry.

He awoke the next morning and drifted through the morning tasks. The Caerians muttered and chattered around him. The guards shouted and taunted in his ear, distantly. He sipped dirty water and a mouthful of broth. He followed the other slaves around the camp, as if he were one of a line of ants in the dirt.

'Boy!' A hand shook his shoulder.

Valcero flinched and glanced around.

The old woman snapped her fingers in his face. 'Wake up, boy!'

Valcero blinked at her.

She pushed a tray of steaming lamb shanks into his hands. 'Take this to the hall. It's for Thane Heirik, so be quick and don't drop anything.'

Valcero stared at the food and then at her. He nodded.

The old woman sighed and rubbed his head. 'Don't look the Thane in the eyes. Just go in quietly, set down the food, and be off without a fuss.'

Valcero carried the tray into the hall. The Rhenivians were once again arguing over parchment at the table.

Thane Heirik was with them. He spoke in Caerian. 'Report on the grain. How many ships to leave from Etorium?' He waved at the parchment on the table and nudged one of his men towards it.

The soldier cringed, stammered, and shook his head. Heirik pressed his fists into his forehead and groaned. He shoved the soldier aside and stormed over to his throne. He flopped into it and scowled at his men, then caught sight of Valcero frozen at the doorway. He flapped his hand impatiently.

The boy bowed his head and stumbled forward. He put the tray on the table while they all watched him, then made to leave.

'Stop, boy,' Heirik barked.

Valcero paused, his eyes fixed on the floor.

'You are Caerian, yes?' the Thane asked.

Valcero gave a slight, quick nod.

Heirik snorted. 'Like a scared little mouse boy.'

The soldiers laughed.

Something broke inside Valcero. His cheeks burned. 'How may I serve you? Thane Heirik?'

'Can any of you slaves write?'

He swallowed. 'I can write, sir.'

'You?'

Valcero looked up.

Heirik leaned on an armrest with his chin propped on his hand. He grinned in amusement.

'I was taught, sir.' Valcero cleared his throat. 'I can write Caerian.'

Heirik stood and strode over to Valcero. He loomed. 'Let's see.' He guided the boy to the parchment with a hand on Valcero's back. 'My first scribe is dead, and they say my other scribe is too sick to get out of bed, so you will do it.' He glared at his men. 'This lot are useless. Be sure you are not useless, eh?' He pushed the reed pen into Valcero's hand. 'Write my words.'

Valcero dipped the pen into the cup and waited. His hand shook, and ink drops fell onto the table.

Heirik rapped the wood. '*Agh*, boy. Do not be such a shivering mouse. Write my words and I will not gut you.'

'Yes, sir.'

Heirik cleared his throat. 'Wait, first you write my name at the bottom here. Write my name—Heirik, son of Heiferth, Thane of Caeria. That is your test.'

Valcero breathed out and bent over the page. He scratched out the name and title as best as he could with Caerian letters. He straightened up. 'Sir?'

Heirik leaned over. 'Hmm. Well, it looks right. I can't read the scribbles anyway.' He sniggered, as did the other Rhenivians.

An idea, dark and seductive, arose in Valcero's heart, like a bubble escaping from the depths. He trembled.

'No shaking, boy,' Heirik snapped. 'You must write neat words, or she will not understand, eh? Alright, now start up top there. Hail, Lady Octerian of Enternis.'

Valcero dipped the pen again and wrote *Hail, King Zjandius of Caeria*. He waited for a reaction, a slap on the head, anything. His heart pounded.

Heirik continued. 'I want to know how many ships from Enternis have grain from last year's harvest.'

Valcero wrote, *I know of your plan to return to Caeria. I have sent word to my uncle Getherd.*

'How many more grainships for the rest of this season?

He will come to Caeria with an army. Bees buzzed in Valcero's head, almost drowning out the Thane's words.

'You must stop loading this grain. Keep it in your granaries until I give new orders.'

They sail to Lastria. They plan to unite and outnumber you. Beads of sweat ran down Valcero's back.

'Send your reply to Etorium, where I will receive it.'

Be warned, King Zjandius, and prepare yourself.

'Now read it to me,' Heirik ordered.

Valcero swallowed. He repeated the Thane's words as best as he could remember.

'Hmm, close enough.' Heirik flapped the parchment in the air, then rolled it up, pushed it into a bronze tube, and closed the lid. He snapped his fingers at the other Rhenivians. One of them hurried over with a small copper pot from the fire.

Heirik pushed the top of the tube into the pot to coat it with glistening beeswax. He made a fist and pushed his ring into the wax. 'This part I do myself.' The Thane took the pen and scratched runes onto the seal. 'To... Lady... Octer... Octerian... In Enternis. There. All done.' He waved the tube at his men. 'Now, go find a rider for me.'

Valcero coughed. 'I can take it to a rider, sir.'

Heirik frowned at the boy. Valcero tried to keep his face steady. His fingers rubbed against his damp palms.

'Very well.' The Thane passed the tube to the boy. 'Go quickly to the paddocks and find someone there.'

Valcero bowed and tried not to run as he left the hall.

'Oh, and boy,' Heirik called after him, 'do not lose that message, or I'll cut you up myself.'

Valcero stopped and turned back to the Thane. 'Yes, sir. No, sir.' He bobbed his head and left through the door, while the Rhenivians laughed.

He strode through the camp looking left and right. No one seemed to pay him any attention. He folded his arms to hide the tube and ducked into a narrow gap between two tents. He rubbed the soft wax with his thumb until the runes were erased, while leaving the Thane's seal—a boar's head between two ears of corn—untouched. A burst of laughter made him flinch. Valcero glanced about. No one saw him. He scratched new words into the wax with his fingernail. *To King Zjandius in Elisdrium*. He added *via Etorium*.

Valcero tucked the tube up his sleeve, then went to the storehouses and took a waterskin and sack. He filled the sack with bread and hard cheese, then went to the well to scoop up water to fill the skin. He trotted over to the paddocks. The other slaves were digging pits while some guards supervised. One Rhenivian leaned against the paddock fence, away from the others. He was young and red-headed, with a thin beard, and one of the few who could speak Caerian, which Valcero knew because the guard had shouted at him more than once. Perfect.

He approached the Rhenivian. 'Sir?'

The guard scowled. 'What?'

Valcero held out the tube. 'Thane Heirik wants you to deliver this message. It has to go to King Zjandius in Elisdrium.'

'Elisdrium?'

The boy tensed. 'Uh, in Sasiion. It has to go to Sasiion. Elisdrium is a city in Sasiion,' he babbled.

The guard threw up his arms. 'What? How am I supposed to do that? Swim there?'

Valcero wet his lips. 'He says you must take it to Etorium and arrange a ship.'

'*Arrange* a ship? Just like that?'

The boy's heart began to beat faster. 'I don't know, sir. The Thane just told me to tell you that. He... he said you must take it to Etorium first, and then go from there.'

'I'll find out what he really meant.' The guard stepped away from the fence.

'No, sir! He said you have to leave immediately. Those were his strict orders, sir.' Valcero held out the waterskin and sack. 'Please, sir, it's urgent.'

The guard examined the items, then the boy's face. 'Well, it looks like it, I suppose.' He squinted at the message tube. 'What's this? Doesn't look like runes.'

'Oh, it says "To King Zjandius in Elisdrium via Etorium", sir. It's in Caerian, in case you need to pass it to any Caerians along the way.'

The guard snatched the skin and sack from him. 'I will ***not*** be doing that.' He sighed and looked around the camp. 'I have to leave right now?'

Valcero nodded. 'It's very urgent, sir. Very important message. And it's a secret, sir.'

The guard shook his head and muttered in Rhenivian. He vaulted over the paddock fence and went to a grey mare rooting in the churned mud. He led the horse to the fence, threw on a saddle and reins, tied the sack and skin to the saddle, then mounted the horse. Valcero dragged the gate open, and the messenger rode away.

Valcero pushed the gate shut and breathed out. It was done.

'Where've you been?' The old woman came over. 'Come, boy. We have work to do.'

It was only while digging a new pit that a thought flashed through Valcero's heart. Heirik expected a reply to his letter. What will happen when he doesn't receive it? Would he send another message, or go to Enternis and discover that his letter never arrived? And what if the rider decides to turn back to camp for any reason? He will talk to his companions, won't he? He'll talk to the Thane. Of course he will. Someone will hear about the letter and it will get back to Thane Heirik and he'll realise that Valcero tricked him and...

Valcero wanted to vomit. Stupid stupid stupid stupid.

CHAPTER THIRTY-TWO

CAERIA – SPRING'S RISING – 437

After a week, Heirik decided it was time to move to the next outpost. They had foiled at least one raid on a woodcutters' camp and driven off the Torecti after the savages had killed everyone at the other. A partial victory, at least.

'We'll go south,' Heirik announced in the hall at dinner. 'It's a three-day ride, and who knows, maybe we'll have some hunting on the way.'

His soldiers raised their cups and cheered.

The next morning, they were up before sunrise. The slaves were handing over bundles of food to his soldiers and generally getting in everyone's way. His riders lead their steeds from the paddock in a long, chaotic line to the gate, where Heirik waited on his stallion Bulgitha, with long mane and flicking tail.

'Come on, you lot,' he shouted. 'Get a move on. I want to be at full gallop before the sun gets too high.'

Daga walked out the gate with his dappled horse, still looking a little grey and gaunt of face as he led the beast. Dark rings lay under his eyes.

Heirik leaned over. 'Daga! Have your bowels finally stopped betraying you?'

Daga smiled and bobbed his head as he passed.

Once the host was out of the camp, he turned to the marshal staying behind to keep the peace. 'I'm relying on you,' Heirik said.

The marshal—he couldn't remember the name—smiled weakly up at his Thane. 'We shall serve you, My Lord.' He looked around at the departing riders. 'Though perhaps it would be better to keep a few horses here?'

Heirik snorted. 'Nonsense. The savages never venture this far, so a hundred or so men should be plenty. But don't you just hide away here in the camp. Should the local Caerians become restless—for any reason—you march out and remind them who their masters are, yes?'

The marshal stood to attention. 'As you command, My Thane!'

Heirik took the host southwards along a dirt road. He decided to keep close to the forest for the first day. And behold, for there *was* some hunting to be done.

Heirik peered into the distance with his hand shielding his eyes. 'You see the smoke?'

The plume rose straight up from behind the rocky hills.

'Aye, My Thane,' Daga replied. 'Should we ride fast over the ridge?'

Heirik shook his head. 'No, let's rather make for ... there. Over there, down that valley. We'll cut off the savages as they retreat to the trees. With me!'

At his command, the riders broke into a gallop in tight formation behind their Thane. They poured into a long valley of grass and scattered trees, and raced along the stream that ran through it. Heirik could not help but grin. His heart beat with the horses' hooves. His blood sang.

They burst through a scrub thicket and into a broader valley with forest at the far end. The savages were already sprinting for the trees.

'Chase them down!' Heirik roared. 'Trample them!'

The Rhenivians formed a wedge and gathered pace. Long threads of spittle flew from his stallion's snout. He lowered his lance at the fleeing foe. One turned to him and hurled a spear Heirik's way. The Thane leant aside and let the spear shoot past. Someone screamed behind. Too bad.

'Ride on!' he shouted.

The Torecti scattered before his wedge, so that the Rhenvians sliced between them. Heirik slowed and turned to the right to catch the savages already closest to the woods. They fought like fiends, these forest people. They tossed spears and arrows into his throng, even as they backed away towards the trees. Rhenivians fell here and there, but so did the savages, and more to come, if he could help it. Heirik struck one to the ground as he rode past her and threw his spear to bring down another. He swung his axe through the skull of a third. Gods, his father would be so proud.

The axe caught in the man's head, nearly yanking Heirik from his horse, but he righted himself and rode on.

They came up to the forest's edge—tall trunks and wide branches with ferns spilling out between the roots. The savages paused at the tree line to fire arrows and cover their companion's escape. Thane Heirik snarled and raised his shield to block an arrow. The savages slipped into the wood as Bulgitha brought him under its eaves and reared up.

Heirik gripped the horse's flanks between his thighs. 'Halt! No further!'

The others pulled up on either side, beasts and men both panting.

'Should we chase them?' Daga called from down the line.

The savages ran deeper amongst the trees, almost lost to sight.

'No,' Heirik called back. He looked back at the bodies scattered about the valley. 'We have done enough.'

The riders rode back across the valley to a small Rhenivan camp. The thin fence was all but torn down, as were the tents within it. The savages had done their usual work—a heap of bodies, mostly Rhenivians, burning fiercely.

A low groan caught Heirik's attention. He swung off his horse and searched about the wreckage until he found a soldier, wallowing in his own blood that muddied the earth around him.

The pale man clutched at his own torn stomach and blinked. 'Thane Heirik?' he croaked.

Heirik knelt at his side. 'Hush now. Are you in pain?'

The dying man swallowed and nodded.

'Go to the gods,' Heirik whispered. 'We have avenged you.' In one movement, he drew his dagger and sliced through the man's throat. Heirik cradled the fallen soldier's head until he was sure the ghost was gone. Then he stood up over the body. 'May the Corn Mother and Flood Father welcome you into their eternal halls,' he said.

His soldiers repeated the words.

'And the Wolf Lord,' Heirik murmured.

They travelled onwards and a few hours later, when the sun neared its peak, they came upon a farmhouse set amongst a few small fields of grain and vegetables. Geese waddled about at the farmhouse door as Heirik rode up. The windows were shuttered, but a wisp of blue smoke arose from the chimney.

'Open up!' Heirik called out in Caerian.

The door creaked ajar, and a middle-aged man with balding hair and a rough tunic leaned out. 'We don't have anything!' he shouted. Then he caught sight of Heirik—spattered in blood—and the rest. He blanched. 'Sir, I...'

'We are hungry,' Heirik snapped. 'And thirsty. Your Thane demands hospitality.'

'Well, uh, My Lord, I...' The farmer wrung his hands and looked about. 'We are poor, sir, and do not have much, you see.'

Heirik pointed his spear at the geese. 'These will do.'

The farmer looked pained. He hesitated at the door, then crept towards the birds. 'As you wish, My Lord.'

'And water and wine too, thank you.' Heirik said.

A shutter rattled. Heirik glanced at the window and saw a small child peering at him through a gap. He winked, and the face shrank away. The farmer tried to herd the geese into their pen at the side of the house.

'Hurry up,' Heirik said. 'Or do you need help?' He skewered a fowl with a flick of his spear. 'There.'

The farmer flinched as the other geese scattered, honking and flapping their wings.

The farmer and his family took an age to slaughter, pluck, gut and grill the fowl, so the Rhenivians eventually took over. The meat was tough and the wine sour. When they had finally eaten their fill and set off again, the sun was lower than Heirik wanted. They rode for a few hours more and found a convenient hilltop to camp upon for the night. Trees dotted the slopes of the wedge-shaped hill up to its rocky crown, but a flat, open shoulder halfway up was the perfect space to eat and lay down their heads. They found an old shepherds' camp there, with stones arranged into a firepit against a rockface.

While the other horses munched on the grassy hillside and the soldiers tramped about to gather firewood, the Thane inspected his stallion. Bulgitha walked through the long grass with an ever-so-slight limp. Heirik ran his fingers through the horse's long, dark mane and patted his flanks. The coat had lost some of its sheen, and dull patches revealed where hair was falling out.

Heirik tore up a fistful of grass and fed it to his horse. 'Ah, Bulgitha, my friend,' he whispered, 'are your best days behind you?'

The stallion took the grass with warm lips and snorted in reply.

Heirik stroked Bulgitha's snout and gazed into his dark eyes. 'Can you carry me a little further before the Corn Mother takes you? I will honour you, my friend. I'll bring you home to the fields of your birth, to lie with the best of your herd. You shall rest under the stars of the wide Rhenivian sky, forever.' He pushed his forehead against the beast's. 'I promise.'

It was grey twilight by the time the soldiers started the fire. They brought out bread and salted meat from the camp, and other bits and pieces they had taken from the farm. Not quite a feast, but it would do. They sat in a circle and ate, drank, and joked.

Heirik leaned against his pack next to the fire, with a cup of beer in one hand and a strip of meat in the other. 'So, who killed the most today?'

'Surely you, My Thane?' called out a soldier who perched on a rock on the other side of the fire.

'Nah,' Heirik replied, 'Not my personal best. Only three, I think. How about you?'

'I managed two, My Thane,' the soldier said. He leaned over and grabbed a companion by the shoulders. 'Gafi here managed six!'

Gafi, a scruffy-looking fellow with wild brown hair and a shaggy beard, sat cross-legged on the ground. He hunched over and grinned sheepishly at Heirik. The others clapped and stomped their feet.

'Very good,' Heirik said. Six seemed a bit much. Boastful.

'My Thane,' piped up Daga from Heirik's left. 'I've two men here who both managed five, though one of them has paid a little price.' He pointed to a soldier sitting behind him.

Despite the poor light, Heirik made out the rags wrapped around the man's head, stained dark from blood that still trickled down his face. The man nodded to his Thane. The soldiers cheered, and some went over to pat him on the back and shoulders.

'Yes, yes, very good,' Heirik said when the applause died down. 'Just be careful next time, eh?'

'I managed four,' a voice called from the group.

'Me too,' said another.

Heirik raised his cup. 'To *all* of us. To our victories. To our glory.'

The soldiers raised cups, wineskins, and bits of meat into the air. 'To us! To victory!'

Heirik drained his cup and set it down. He grunted. 'Excuse me, good men.' He clambered to his feet and strolled away from the fire and around a pale boulder at the edge of the slope. He found a tall cedar sprouting from the rock and reaching toward the darkening sky. He undid his trousers and aimed a stream of piss against the trunk. He listened to the crickets and the soldiers' voices bouncing off the rocks. He gazed down the hillside, patched with bushes and grass and spindly trees. An odd smell hung in the air.

What was Razna up to right now? Perhaps Daga could read her last letter to him later, when the fire was still bright but most of the men had fallen asleep. Heirik finished and tied up his trousers. He should send her a reply. Yes, as soon as they arrived at—

Something slammed upon his shoulders and knocked him to the ground.

The air burst from Heirik's lungs. He pushed against the earth to raise himself, but arms snaked around him and pinned him down. He grunted and thrashed and sucked in a breath to call out, but a hand shoved a ball of wool over his mouth and nose. The wool was wet and smelled terrible. Sweet and terrible. His head swam...

He was being carried, face down, lurching down the hill. The grass brushed his cheeks as he swayed from side to side. Many hands gripped his arms and legs. Another arm was wrapped around his waist. He heard laboured breathing and footsteps lightly crunching through the dirt.

Someone called his name distantly. There came a shout, some echoes of Rhenivian voices.

Heirik reached for his dagger.

'He's awake,' a voice whispered in Caerian.

'Quick.' Another voice, down by his feet. 'Give him some more.'

'Hurry.'

'Who are…' Heirik mumbled. He grasped his empty scabbard. He tried to wriggle out of their grip.

A hand pulled his hair and jerked his head up. Another hand shoved the wool back in his face. A swarm of purple flies danced over his eyes. He spun. His limbs grew heavy. Sleep was swallowing him. Where…? why…?

'Faster!' a voice hissed somewhere.

Heirik stopped swaying, or so it seemed. They pressed more wool into his mouth and bound the wad in place with a rag. It tasted of sweet fire—bitter too. They dropped a hood over his head. Only dancing sparks to see, swiftly fading. The hands raised him up, floating forward. Then he settled over some large, warm body as ropes wrapped themselves around him. A horse. His horse? That would be nice. They would ride away together.

'Go now!' another voice whispered. Always whispering.

The horse began to run, and the darkness took him.

CHAPTER THIRTY-THREE

CAERIA — SPRING'S REIGN — 437

Razna awoke with sickness in her stomach. She sat up in bed, alone, and looked around the dim royal chamber. Morning light and faint sounds of an awakening palace came through the balcony doors. She swung her feet off the bed, and her belly heaved. She yanked the chamber pot out from under the bed and emptied her guts into it. Her suspicions were confirmed. Now is not the time. Really not the time.

Afterwards, she wiped her mouth and stood. A soft knock came from the door.

'Enter!'

One of the mousy servant girls scurried into the bedroom and began fussing around, making the bed and laying out dresses and robes for Razna to choose. 'What would My Lady wish for breakfast this morning?' She avoided Razna's eyes.

'I'm not sure.'

'Perhaps some mushroom soup, My Lady?'

Razna's stomach churned. 'No, no. Just bread and water today.'

'As you wish, My Lady.'

The servant helped her into a long, cream dress pinned at the side, with a blue robe draped across her shoulders. She did up her hair in the Caerian fashion, using the dolphin comb to hold it all in place. When she was ready, Razna followed the servant downstairs to one of the private rooms where she preferred to take her meals when Heirik was away. While she sat and waited for her food, Razna tapped her fingers on her belly, lost in thought.

A secretary entered the room with a wax tablet. 'Good morning, Lady Razna. How are you?'

'Oh,' she looked up. 'Well enough, though I may have eaten something rotten.'

'Oh, dear,' the clerk said. 'Shall I fetch the apothecary, My Lady?'

Razna shook her head. 'Perhaps later. What business do we have today?'

The secretary read out a list of petitions, legal cases, and other matters, while two servants entered with trays of food, including mushroom soup. Razna rolled her eyes. She had definitely said no to mushroom soup. She tore off a chunk of bread and nibbled at it. Too dry. She managed a sip of water, but only just.

'...so there we have it, My Lady. When shall we begin the hearings?' The clerk looked up from his tablet with a hopeful smile.

Razna rubbed her forehead. 'We may as well start now, I suppose.'

She made her way to the throne room, where Prefect Suletonius was already waiting at his table of scrolls. She nodded to him and sat on the smaller throne beside Heirik's.

'A busy day, I believe,' Razna observed, in Caerian.

The Prefect nodded. 'You look a little pale, Lady Razna. Should we postpone?'

She forced a smile. 'No, no. Let's not keep the citizens waiting, shall we?'

The first matter was a land dispute. There seemed to be so many of these lately. It was not a difficult case, however.

'After listening to your stories,' she told the farmers, 'I shall award the property to this gentleman over here. However, you, sir...' She gestured to the other farmer. '...deserve compensation for being misled. I will instruct the treasury to pay out thirty silver coins for your troubles.'

The second farmer sighed and considered the judgment for a moment, then bowed. 'Thank you, My Lady. I accept your justice.'

The next case was another land dispute, but more technical in nature. Razna felt her heart wandering as the Prefect read through the details and introduced the opposing parties—two women. Something about a marriage, a death, and an inheritance gone awry. She didn't really care, to be honest. The two women started arguing.

Razna leaned over to the Prefect. 'What's your opinion on this one?' she murmured.

Suletonius cleared his throat. 'The precedents are quite clear, My Lady. If no new will was written up when the landowner died, then the daughter receives the estate, not the new wife. The daughter was clearly named in the old will.'

Razna turned back to the women. 'Very well! You,' she said to the daughter, 'are to receive the property, according to your father's testament. However, we cannot ignore the marriage. So, *you*, My Lady, are entitled to payment from the estate. What would be a fair sum?'

The women started arguing again.

Razna banged her hand on the armrest. 'Silence!' She winced, then recovered. 'I will have silence. Was there a dowry in your marriage, madam?'

The older woman bowed. 'Yes, Lady Razna. Fifty silver coins.'

'Hmm,' Razna mused, 'then you shall have that, and half again. Seventy-five silvers in total.'

The younger woman gasped.

Razna frowned at her. 'Is that a problem? You'll earn that back very quickly from your new farm.'

The young woman flinched and bowed. 'No...yes, My Lady.'

'You are very fair, Lady Razna,' the Prefect murmured as the women left the hall.

'I have to be,' Razna replied. 'They rely on me. Alright, who's next?'

'Uh, perhaps a delicate matter.'

'Yes?'

An elderly man, bent-backed and leaning on a stick, now presented himself. He wore a threadbare tunic and broken sandals. A marshal followed, accompanied by two young Rhenivians. The boys eyed Razna and bowed their heads.

'The charge is that these two soldiers robbed this man down in the Port District,' Suletonius said. 'Show Lady Razna, old father,' he commanded the Caerian man.

The man tottered about on his stick and twisted his arm around to tug on his tunic, revealing purple bruises on his upper back.

'Thank you, old father,' Razna said.

The old man turned to face her again and bowed clumsily.

'Is there any other proof?' Razna asked.

'Yes, two witnesses already testified,' the Prefect replied.

The marshal sighed and gestured to the soldiers. 'I found money in their beds, Lady Razna. They say it was a fine. He tried to attack them first, they claim.'

Razna considered the gnarled man and the tall boys with their fuzzy beards. 'Firstly, return the money to the victim. Secondly, seize an equivalent sum from the soldiers' possessions and give it to this man as compensation. And thirdly...' She pointed to the soldiers. '... a hundred lashes—each—for these two.'

The two young soldiers looked up, angry and confused.

'My Lady,' the marshal began, 'perhaps that's a little—'

Razna leaned forward and scowled. 'We could make it 150 lashes if it is a little.' She tapped Heirik's throne and switched to Rhenivian. 'How are *we* supposed to rule this land if you turn the people against us? We must set an example, understood?'

The marshal bowed his head. 'Aye, it shall be done, Lady Razna.'

'My apologies to you, old father,' Razna spoke in Caerian again. 'Is there anything else I can do?'

The elderly man smiled and bobbed his head. 'Nothing, My Lady. You are most kind.'

The marshal was ushering them out of the hall when Daga strode in, flushed and sweaty.

Razna's heart skipped. 'What are you doing here?'

He approached the thrones and bowed. 'Lady Razna, I must speak with you at once. In private.'

Razna gripped the armrests. 'Now?'

Daga nodded. His face was tense.

The Prefect coughed. 'Uh, there are five more cases for this morning...'

Razna stood, holding the armrests to steady herself. 'Later. I'll see to them later. With me, marshal.'

They left the hall and climbed the stairs to a reception room. Razna ordered the servants out and then turned to Daga. 'Just tell me, is he alive?'

He looked pained. 'I don't know, My Lady.'

'Don't know?' Razna's voice rose to nearly a shriek.

'They took Thane Heirik—bandits or rebels, I'm not sure. They kidnapped him from our camp. By the time we realised what had happened, they had ridden off with him into the hills. We tried chasing them, but we lost the trail in the dark. I am sorry, My Lady.'

'You're sorry?' Razna hissed. '*You're sorry?* That is ***not*** good enough.'

She jabbed him in the chest, and the Rhenivian staggered backwards.

'Are you not a servant of the Wolf Lord?'

'Yes, My—'

'Are you not a hunter?'

Yes, Lady Razna...'

'Then *hunt*.' Her eyes blazed. 'You hunt for your Thane. Take whatever men you need. Use your hounds. And you ***find*** him, Daga. For all of our sakes.' She stepped backwards, breathing heavily. 'And you destroy whomever you find holding him. Is that clear?'

Daga nodded.

Razna folded her arms. 'Who else knows?'

'Only the men in our party, My Lady. I kept them outside the city, but word will spread. And there is the other matter...'

Razna narrowed her eyes. 'What other matter?'

'Thane Heirik never told you?'

'What matter, Daga?'

The marshal swallowed. 'Apparently, Thane Heirik received word that the Caerians are coming back. Their king is bringing a host, soon, perhaps before the end of spring. He had me write a letter to his uncle, High Thane Getherd, asking for help.'

Not now. Now is not the time. 'How big of an army?'

Daga shrugged. 'No one knows. Perhaps when our men return from their raid across the sea, they can tell us.'

'Those soldiers are gone,' Razna snapped. 'Or haven't *you* heard? Lost in a storm amongst the islands.'

Daga's eyes went wide. 'No, how can that be...?'

'I sent a letter to Heirik. Didn't you get it?'

'We move from camp to camp, My Lady. Perhaps the messenger missed us.'

'And will High Thane Getherd be coming to Caeria as well?'

Daga nodded. 'I believe so.'

Not now. Now is not the time. Razna groaned. 'We're too scattered. We should recall the hosts in the west. Summon everyone from across Caeria and gather them here. Obviously, Zjandius will come for this city first.'

'My Lady, that won't be necessary. We are winning in the west and have plenty soldiers in Etorium. We defeated the Caerians before. Our horses will trample them once again.'

Razna balled her fists. 'Your Thane left me in charge.'

Daga bowed his head. 'Of course, Lady Razna, but I must also do his bidding. If we abandon the west, we only embolden the savages.'

Razna glared at him. 'Zjandius would not return if he did not intend to win.'

'And he will not, Lady Razna. With the High Thane's help, we will have more than enough to crush the Caerians. Please, trust me. Grindulf is here to prepare any defences you may need.' Daga bowed his head. 'My Lady, I should leave. I will find Thane Heirik, I swear it.' He went for the door.

'Don't return until you have a better story to tell,' Razna said.

Her stomach throbbed and churned. She sent for her most trusted guards and told them to await her in the courtyard. Meanwhile, she went upstairs to change into a white shift and a brown shawl. Then she left the palace to find her guards.

Soldiers, servants, and cityfolk streamed in and out of the palace gates and crowded the courtyard. Glints of water from last night's rain lay between the cobblestones. Puffs of white clouds drifted in the otherwise blue sky. The two guards snapped to attention when they caught sight of her.

'Come,' she said. 'You will escort me to the apothecary.'

The men exchanged looks, then bowed to her.

Razna draped the shawl over her head and shoulders. They walked through the tall gates and across the palace square before passing down one of the quieter, shaded alleyways.

The streets rang with shouts and chatter. Beggars, porters hauling sacks and jars, and other assorted cityfolk bumped past them as they descended the steep, twisting alleyway between the looming buildings. The cookshops and food stalls were preparing for the lunchtime rush, and woodsmoke stung Razna's nose. Someone was grilling fish nearby, grilling it with seaweed. The stench brought slimy seashore rocks to mind and made her guts leap into her throat.

'Wait...' Razna coughed and ducked around the corner into a side alley. She bent over and vomited onto the paving.

The guards crowded over her, too close, with their greasy hair and sweated clothes.

'My Lady, are you alright?' one asked.

'Yes, just...' She nudged them away and stood up again, wiping her mouth on the edge of her shawl. 'Let's continue.'

They reached the shop at the bottom of the alley.

Razna stepped onto the threshold. 'Wait outside,' she ordered the guards.

Inside was dim and cramped. A wooden table served as a counter, behind which the apothecary fiddled with pots, sacks, and jars of herbs, roots, powders, and potions, stacked on shelves up to the low ceiling.

He turned as the door squeaked. 'Ah, My Lady, welcome!' He bowed and stepped up to the table. 'Will it be the usual?' He reached into a pouch and pulled out a fistful of dried leaves.

Razna leaned against the doorframe. She drew a breath. 'Uhhh, no, not this time.'

'Oh?'

She bit her lip. 'Perhaps something...else, just to soothe my stomach...for times like this. To restore my appetite.'

The apothecary dropped the leaves back in the pouch and beamed. 'I have just the thing, My Lady. And allow me to give my congratulations!'

CHAPTER THIRTY-FOUR

CAERIA — SPRING'S REIGN — 437

When Heirik awoke, he was rolling from side to side on the back of a cart that bumped and squeaked over rough ground—or so he guessed. A hood covered his face, but he could hear the wheels rumbling beneath him, kicking up stones that clattered against the bottom of the cart. Two sets of hooves clip-clopped on the road, and sunlight dimly shone through the rough fabric of the hood. His mouth was gagged, and his wrists and ankles throbbed from chafing ropes. His legs were numb. His back ached against the wooden boards.

Heirik tried to sit up, but his head bumped against something, a cover on the cart perhaps. He tried again, and a fist struck his head.

'No.' A low voice said, somewhere nearby.

Heirik snarled and thrashed about, trying to loosen his bonds. There was a rustle, then someone pressed the wet wool onto his face. He choked. The sickly scent flooded his nose, and he fell back into sleep.

Heirik awoke again, still lying on the cart, now still. It was cold and dark. His head ached and his bladder burned. He groaned.

'He's awake,' someone muttered in Caerian.

'I suppose we'd better...' another voice replied.

Someone climbed on the cart, and pulled Heirik into a sitting position. A cool, metal edge pressed against his throat.

'You move, you die,' the voice spoke. A hand reached under his hood and pulled off the gag.

'You pieces of...' Heirik croaked.

They shoved something into Heirik's mouth. A waterskin. He gulped the liquid, then choked and coughed.

'More,' Heirik said.

They put the bag to his mouth again, and he tried to drink more slowly.

'I need to relieve myself,' Heirik announced as soon as he had drained the skin.

'You can piss yourself,' a man replied. 'We don't mind.'

They chuckled. At least three voices.

'I am going to destroy each one of you,' Heirik said. 'And then I will hunt down everyone you love and feed them to my hounds.' He grinned. 'No! Actually, I will hunt down your families *first* and feed them to my hounds, while you watch. I will show you such pain and despair as you have never known.'

'I don't see you doing much of anything when you can't even see where you're going, dear Thane.'

Heirik gritted his teeth. He tried to pull his hands apart, but the ropes merely cut deeper into his skin. Curse them. May they rot. May the crows peck out their dead eyes. Curse their mothers. Curse them...

'Help!' Heirik shouted in Rhenivian. 'Help me! Help! I am Thane Heirik!'

His voice echoed faintly in the cold night air. No one moved, nor said a word.

'Help me, please!' Heirik called again, now in Caerian. 'They have taken me! Help! Anyone!' He sagged forward, weak and dizzy. His voice echoed back from somewhere distant.

'Oh, don't stop, Thane Heirik. Maybe someone will hear you—eventually.' A snigger.

Heirik sat up straight. 'Where are you taking me?'

'Never mind about that, *My Thane*. Sleep now, and your journey will end, soon enough.' Two pairs of hands pushed him onto his back.

Heirik was starving, but he would not beg.

Another two days, more or less, passed by. Eventually, they fed him chunks of stale bread and more water, without untying his hands. When his bladder could hold no more, he wet himself. They made no comment about the stink. The cart rattled his skull until he felt sick. At some point, they shoved the stinking cloth in his face and his wits left him. The throbbing pain receded as they lifted him from the cart and over the back of a horse, or was it a mule?

It seemed only a moment, then Heirik jolted awake.

They had splashed icy water over him. The hood was off and he was inside a dim room, sitting on the floor and leaning against a wooden post. He spat out water and blinked. A tall, narrow window in the drystone walls let in a shaft of bright light. The roof was made of wooden beams and thatch.

A woman, tall and grey-haired, stood before him, with her hands behind her back. She wore a long, white dress with a grey shawl draped over her shoulders. She examined him with cold eyes, her mouth set in a frown. Beside her stood a young man, probably a few years less than Heirik, holding a dripping bucket. He was also tall and bony, with a red birthmark across his lean face that became clearer as Heirik's eyes adjusted. He wore a dark, nearly black tunic, and a hooded cloak, also black or dark grey.

Heirik tried to lunge at them, but his hands were bound to the pole behind, as was his neck. 'My uncle is going to be very angry when he finds me,' he said in Caerian.

'I'm sure he will be,' the woman replied. Her voice was brittle and elegant, like the aristocratic ladies who hung about the palace in Etorium.

Heirik smirked. 'You should let me go now. Perhaps he will show mercy.'

The woman nodded. 'Perhaps.'

The young man looked from her to Heirik. Something of his face resembled hers. There was something else, something familiar in his stance or maybe the overall shape of him.

'May I at least know who has made me their guest?'

'There shall be a proper introduction later,' the woman replied. She nodded to the boy—her son most likely—and they left the room, bolting the heavy door behind them.

Heirik leaned against the pole and listened to the wind whistling through gaps in the stones. His head throbbed. Curse these people. But he would have his vengeance. Patience.

Some time passed, and the bolts unlocked. The door opened, and a silver-haired man entered. Someone else closed the door.

'I had a feeling you were going to show your face.' Heirik grinned up at Lord Aventan. 'This seems like your handiwork.'

Lord Aventan regarded him in silence. He was dressed in a long robe, grey and slightly dirty. 'I thought we had reached an understanding, Thane Heirik,' the aristocrat finally said in Galatani.

'Oh, we had, My Lord, though I don't remember *this* part of our deal.'

'You sent a letter to your uncle, as I suggested,' Lord Aventan continued, 'All well and good. But then you sent *another* letter, to Zjandius Vaecerion.'

Heirik narrowed his eyes. 'What are you talking about?'

Lord Aventan leaned forward. 'That was *not* part of our plan. Why did you do that?'

'You are mistaken, My Lord Aventan. I did no such thing.'

'What did you write in that letter?'

'I wrote no letter to Zjandius.'

'I ask the question again. What. Did. You. Write?'

'I wrote *nothing*.'

'Tell me what you told him.' Lord Aventan stepped closer.

'Listen, you old fool,' Heirik snarled. 'I have *never* written a letter to King Zjandius. Why would I do that?'

'Stop lying.' Lord Aventan glared and drew a bronze dagger from his robes. 'We know that the day after you wrote to Getherd, you *also* sent the letter to Zjandius. We know which camp you were at. We know which rider carries the message.'

Heirik laughed. 'If you know so much, why don't you know what I supposedly wrote in this letter?'

The lord straightened up and sighed. 'We pursued your horseman, but unfortunately, he rode too fast.' He ran a fingertip over the point of the dagger. 'We will catch up with him eventually. But why not save everyone—and yourself—some trouble and tell me what you wrote?' He crouched and pressed the blade against Heirik's thigh.

The Rhenivian tensed, but tried not to let it show. 'Wrote? I can't write Caerian. I barely *speak* your stupid tongue.'

Lord Aventan pushed the blade through the cloth and into Heirik's skin, just a finger width deep. He dragged the blade slowly down Heirik's leg. The Rhenivian gritted his teeth. He would not scream. He would not.

'I didn't write *anything*,' Heirik growled. 'Listen to me.' His breath came light and quick.

Lord Aventan sat back on his haunches. 'There is no point in lying.'

'I'm not lying.' Heirik thought quickly. 'The only letter I sent that day was to Lady Octerian. It was for grain supplies, by the gods. I had some slave boy write it. I'm not lying. Your information is simply wrong, Lord Aventan.'

The lord studied his face. 'What is this slave boy's name, then?'

Heirik rolled his eyes. '*Obviously,* I don't know their names.'

The Caerian aristocrat regarded him for a moment longer, then stood. 'We shall speak further, but in the meantime, think of a better story. A more *honest* story.' He turned and strode to the door as it opened for him.

'What are you worried about, anyway?' Heirik called after him. 'Do you think I told your king about your treachery?'

Lord Aventan paused, without looking back.

'Ah, that's it, isn't it?' Heirik grinned. 'This is all just you panicking over nothing.'

Aventan's fist clenched around the dagger.

'Why? Do you think the Caerians have a chance against us? Fear not, Lord Aventan. We shall defeat them, with or without your help.'

The lord stalked out without another word.

Perhaps an hour later, when the blood had clotted on Heirik's thigh, the door swung open and the young man entered with a bucket of water in one hand and a platter of bread and hard cheese in the other. 'You can eat and wash,' he said in Caerian.

The Thane's eyes followed the boy around the room. He was not quite as tall as Heirik. He had a sword at his belt, but it would take a moment to draw if he had to. The boy set the bucket and platter on the floor before Heirik and walked around behind him. Heirik felt the knots loosen at his wrists, and his hands prickled to life.

Heirik stretched his arms ahead. His hands were purple and swollen. 'What about my neck?' he said. 'Can't do much with my head tied up, can I?'

The boy paused, then loosened that cord as well.

The Thane leaned forward and sighed. 'Thank you.'

The boy sniffed. He walked past Heirik towards the door.

As soon as the Caerian's back faced him, Heirik pressed his palms against the floor and launched himself to his feet. Ah, but his feet—still tied at the ankles. Never mind. He lunged at the boy's neck and sword arm.

But the boy darted to the side and punched up into Heirik's neck, quick as a snake.

Instant pain.

Another fist struck his side. Heirik gasped. The boy swung a leg into the back of his knees, toppling him off his feet. Heirik's forehead hit the cold stone. The boy kicked him in the ribs, in the stomach, and finally, the patient vomit spilt forth. Heirik rolled over, with puke and blood mixed on his face.

The boy tapped the tip of his sword under Heirik's chin. 'Wash, and eat. Do you understand?'

Heirik grinned up at him. The boy left the room and locked the Thane inside.

Heirik felt much better after a meal and a splash of water on his face. It was a good sign that they were now feeding him. Perhaps this misunderstanding would end with an apology and a horse to send him home. Of course, he was still going to kill them all, later.

Heirik peered through the narrow window, barely wide enough to fit his arm through, and saw nothing more interesting than the stone wall of another building. He had untied his legs and now hobbled about, trying to restore life to his limbs without tearing the long scab on his thigh.

The door opened again. Five men entered, all dressed in black with swords drawn. They spread out in the room. Heirik tensed. Perhaps he could just get one sword and even the odds. But if they all fought like the boy...

One of the men smiled coldly and held up a dripping rag in his other hand. A familiar sweet smell wafted to Heirik's nose. The man raised his eyebrows and cocked his head.

The Thane sighed and dropped his shoulders.

'Back against the pole,' the man ordered. 'Sit down. Yes, like that.'

Heirik glowered at the man with the rag as the others bound him, even tighter this time. They left the room, and the woman entered.

Heirik sniffed. 'Oh, it's you again. Tell me, good mother, who are you in all this...mess?'

She folded her arms. 'I am Lady Hiregeia Aventan,' she replied in Galatani.

He laughed. 'Impossible!'

She smiled and shook her head.

'A *new* Lady Aventan? How quickly the old man mourns and remarries.'

She looked down her nose at him.

Heirik stared up at her. 'Lady Aventan died. She jumped into the sea with her children. I saw the water take her body.'

'You saw a body. Not *my* body, Thane Heirik.'

It made a strange kind of sense. No wonder old man Aventan had seemed so willing to forgive.

Her smile turned bitter. 'But yes, the sea did take my daughters, and my youngest son.' She stepped closer. 'They were precious to me,' she whispered.

Heirik frowned.

'You do not remember me, do you?'

'What do you mean?'

'I was there.' Lady Aventan stared at the ground. 'I was in the courtyard, while you barbarians ransacked our great house and corralled us like sheep. Your uncle held his axe above my head, like a butcher.' She pulled out a dagger. 'What message did you send to Zjandius Vaecerion?'

Heirik sighed. 'Not this again. I told Lord Aventan—'

'You told Lord Aventan lies.'

'Lies?' Heirik chuckled. 'You accuse me of lying, but it is you lot who are full of trickery and deceit. When I get out of here, when my uncle comes, oh, there shall be *such* a reckoning...'

'Get out of here?' Lady Aventan smiled. 'You do not even know where you are, boy.'

Heirik grinned. 'We're in the mountains, aren't we?'

Her face went blank.

'Oh, come on, it was not so difficult. It's cold at night, windy all the time, and there's no one around. So, what is this place?' He looked around the bare room and then at her again. 'Your summer palace?' he sneered.

Lady Aventan crouched and tapped the blade against his other thigh. She glared. 'What did you tell Zjandius Vaecerion?'

Heirik's heart began to flutter. 'I can see how scared you are. It's in your eyes. It must be in your blood, too, seeing as how you all skulk in the shadows. How your children take the coward's death.'

She slapped him across the face.

Heirik sniffed and grinned. 'It's a pity they jumped, don't you think? Just imagine if we'd got our hands on them, eh?'

Her jaw clenched and her eyes blazed with cold fury. Her knuckles turned white on the dagger hilt. Heirik readied himself. She stood.

He breathed out and smirked. 'What? No torture then?'

'No,' she mused, staring down at him. 'No, we are going to send another letter to your uncle Getherd instead.' She gestured to someone beyond the open door.

The young man—apparently one of the surviving Aventan sons—strode in, carrying a bronze bucket by a handle. This time, it was full of red coals instead of water. He set the pail down next to his mother, and she plunged the dagger blade into the coals. She stood up, watching them smoulder.

Heirik also eyed the coals. 'And what is this letter going to say? Will you beg for forgiveness?'

'Not exactly,' Lady Aventan replied. She waited for a long while, then nodded to her son. He picked up the dagger, now smoking, with a piece of cloth and walked behind Heirik, out of sight.

The Rhenivian scowled. 'I told you, Lady Aventan, I did *not* send any message to your king.'

She crouched in front of him. 'You know, I think I believe you, Thane Heirik.'

The boy grabbed Heirik's hand.

Heirik clenched it into a fist. 'What are you doing?'

He felt the boy pry his fingers apart.

'Stop that!' Heirik snapped. He struggled against the pole. 'No. No. No!' He looked to Lady Aventan. 'Stop him! No!' He would not scream. He would not.

'Will *you* beg for forgiveness?' she sneered.

The burning blade sliced into his flesh.

Heirik screamed.

CHAPTER THIRTY-FIVE

CAERIA – SPRING'S FALL – 437

The Field of Bees hummed as the insects flitted and bumbled from blossom to blossom. Purple, yellow, white and red—the field was awash with colour. The field also rumbled with thousands of soldiers and their marching feet. They covered the field in dark formations, blotting out the sun for the grass beneath.

Terzjin inspected the soldiers' faces. They leaned on their pikes and peered with tense, eager eyes over their shields at what lay ahead. The city of Etorium. The walls and the hill, crowned with its palace. Home. He looked to Emperor Zjandius on his horse. Zjandius swallowed and tried to smile. He was pale and sweating.

In the end, the fleet arrived at Deria before the Rhenivians did. As the first galley beached on the shore, Admiral Getaelon strode through the surf and greeted them with a smile and bow. The voyage had been easy for the most part. The ships waited out a storm in the lagoons of the isthmus for a few days, then continued on their coastal route. Along the way, they picked up stories from locals about marooned Rhenivians, but the fleet wasted no time in hunting down survivors. With much vigorous rowing, they cruised along the northern side of Hebenia Minor and up the coast to Deria.

Prince Esioret waved them off from the beach, no doubt relieved to see them go. The crossing was brief and trouble-free, thanks to a lucky wind sent by the Envoy to drive them home. They sailed into the inner gulf of Caeria, and went up the coast past Tarbrentum. No Rhenivian galleys interrupted their voyage.

It was at the lagoon of Jaeterium that the Emperor decided they should disembark. Zjandius dropped to his knees and kissed the sand as he stepped ashore, followed swiftly by the other Caerians who had long missed home. Many salty tears were shed that morning, then wiped away for the work ahead.

The cantaris surrounded Lord Corilien's former city, and the few hundred Rhenivians garrisoned there surrendered without a fight, under pressure from the citizens. Another bloodless victory, they crowed to each other.

Lord Corilien and the Emperor entered Jaeterium and recruited more cantare to bolster their numbers. Grey veterans and their sons reached under their beds and into their rafters to haul out dusty shields, helmets, spears, and greaves. All in all, they rounded up another 300 men in a matter of days, then marched north on the Etorian road.

They came up on the east bank of the River Haepastis. The Rhenivians had received word of their arrival and had erected barricades between Goretonum and the river, barring their way to the bridge. The palisade bristled with spears and soldiers peering over. The cantaris halted, and the Emperor debated the way forward with his generals. They elected to attack from the north, where they would have more space to manoeuvre.

The cantaris skirted the hill of Goretonum, keeping enough distance to avoid arrows from the fort, then entered the Field of Bees from the east. Here they arrayed themselves, facing the city ahead, and the mass of Rhenivians who stood in their path.

'Are we ready?' Zjandius asked the other leaders. He had abandoned his chariot for a horse outfitted with stirrups—a gift from Prince Hemadir.

Terzjin sat on his own horse beside his Emperor, while the lenotaris remained on foot, four rows deep around them.

'As ready as we could hope to be,' Lord Corilien answered. He stood in his chariot and gripped the reins.

Colus ran over, panting heavily. 'I need more time! The engines are not yet set up, and we haven't been able to measure ranges yet.'

'Then move faster,' the Emperor insisted. 'And Master Meretan, *nothing* is to hit Goretonum or Etorium. Is that clear?'

Colus nodded before hurrying back through the ranks to his contraptions. Engineers crawled over them—hefting beams into place, adjusting ropes and bolts, shouting and arguing all the while.

The sun blazed overhead. Sweat trickled down the back of Terzjin's head from under his helmet.

'Alright.' Zjandius breathed. 'Hemadir, take your riders out on our right flank towards the river, but not too close in case they fire arrows from the walls. If you can get near enough to the bridge to shoot a few arrows their way, do it.'

Hemadir saluted and stirred his horse. He rode off and whistled to his riders, who broke into a canter towards the western edge of the field.

'Lord Corilien,' Zjandius ordered, 'bring up the light infantry and other skirmishers. Let us see if we can goad the Rhenivians into action. Astulus, keep the elephants back. I do not like how restless they are.'

The beasts were rumbling, trumpeting, and shuffling about, so much that even their riders were struggling to calm them.

The Rhenivians began to sing. The words were muffled and foreign, but the mood was clear. They struck their axes and spears against their shields. They roared. In reply, the Rugadi danced forward on their horses and skipped backwards, taunting the Rhenivians.

Terzjin shivered as memories flashed through him. He saw the black banners emblazoned with red boars that tipped and swayed as the Rhenivians grew more agitated, more battle-hungry. He breathed in and out, desperate to banish the shades.

Under Lord Corilien's command, the slingers and archers of Sasiion dashed forward and let off a volley. The cloud of missiles soared, dipped, and whirred into the defenders. The Rhenivians shouted and cursed. They spilt over the dyke and barricades towards the Caerian forces. A horn blew somewhere. The wooden fence toppled forward, and a mass of riders poured onto the fields. They broke into a gallop, hurtling towards the Caerians, with footmen running behind.

The Caerian archers, slingers and skirmishers sent another volley in the riders' direction.

'Fall back!' the order rang out along the line.

The light infantry sprinted through the gaps as the lines of cantare closed up behind them.

The riders thundered closer, waving spears and shields. They screamed curses and threats. They formed a wedge, a spear of spears hurtling ever nearer.

'First shields up!' the captains ordered.

The front cantare raised their tall shields, forming an iron wall.

The foam flew from the horses' mouths. The ten ranks between him and the Rhenivians seemed a thin and pitiful barrier all of a sudden. He fingered his spear.

'Courage all,' Zjandius called out.

The horses kept coming, like a storm wave barreling ashore, smashing everything in its path. The red boar was painted on each rider's shield. Terzjin's leg began to shake.

The horses were only fifty spans away—no, forty. They drove hard at him and Zjandius. Nothing would slow them, nothing could—

Crack crack crack.

They whistled overhead—dark shapes too quick to track.

A ball of fire boomed amongst the Rhenivians, then another, and another. They screamed and wailed. The footmen flailed and scattered, wreathed in flames. The leading riders slowed and glanced back, but the mass pressed them ever forward, ever closer.

Another *crack* from behind.

Fire exploded before the riders, flinging several from their steeds. The tip of the wedge split apart. They tried to ride around the flames. The charge lost speed, but the horses remained riled, unstoppable. The rear pressed upon the front. They closed upon the Caerians.

'Ready yourselves!'

'Now, now!'

'Shields up!'

'Pikes up!'

As one, the cantaris lifted and locked their shields together. They raised their pikes forwards and upwards through the shield notches, as a forest of thorns sprouting from an iron wall.

The horses baulked and whinnied at the oncoming pikes. They tried to turn aside, but momentum drove them onto the shield wall. The armies crashed together, iron upon iron, flesh upon flesh.

Horses screamed. Men screamed. Spears snapped. Bones snapped. The front rank buckled. Cantare fell, trampled underfoot. The second rank took their place, bringing shields down to repair the wall, jabbing their weapons at the Rhenivians. As pikes splintered, the cantare passed fresh ones forward.

The skirmishers loosed more javelins and arrows over the lines and into the Rhenivian mass. The horsemen were stuck, crushed between the cantaris and their own foot soldiers behind.

'Sound the advance!' the generals called.

'Advance!' The order rang out everywhere.

The cantare began to tread forward, one shuffling step at a time. They stabbed their pikes into the enemy. They stepped over their comrades, over mangled man and horse. The Rhenivians swung their axes and swords against the shield wall and staggered backwards. A smattering of foot soldiers bolted for the barricades.

'Flanks!' The generals shouted.

Two sharp trumpet blasts. A rumbling. From the left, Astulus and the charioteers burst out onto the field. From the right, Hemadir and the Rugadi galloped forward and around. Between them, they trampled, stabbed, and scythed a bloody harvest.

The field emptied. The bees had fled. Black smoke hung over burnt grass. The flowers were shredded, the earth scarred. A triumph.

CHAPTER THIRTY-SIX

CAERIA – SPRING'S FALL – 437

Night had fallen. Razna watched the fires from the palace wall with Daga at her side, torch in hand. Two great bonfires blazed like twin suns out beyond the city on the Field of Bees.

The light shimmered in Razna's eyes. 'They are burning the dead,' she murmured.

'One for their fallen, the other for ours,' Daga said.

'*How?*' Razna asked. 'You said we would crush them on the field.'

The marshal bowed his head. 'They were better prepared this time, Lady Razna. Better equipped, better trained. They hurled fire.'

'We could have discovered this before the battle, yes?' Razna's voice was icy.

'Yes, Lady Razna. Forgive me, My Lady.'

Smaller lights flickered around the fires, and in the village and on the hill of Goretonum, now lost.

'How many soldiers remain?' Razna asked.

'Not many, My Lady. It was a massacre.'

'And Grindulf?'

Daga shook his head.

'Do we have enough to defend the city?'

The marshal sucked on his teeth. 'With the cityfolk at our side, perhaps yes. But now... Already, a few of our guards have been attacked in the streets.'

'Where are the Prefect's guards? They should be keeping order.'

'Most have gone home. The rest are locked away with Suletonius behind his mansion walls. We sent messages, but he does not reply.'

Razna ran her fingers along the parapet. The stone was solid enough, though slippery and worn. She pressed her hands against the wall to keep them steady. 'Could we hold the palace at least?'

'There's enough food, My Lady. But the Caerians probably know secret ways to enter.

'They already have,' Razna muttered.

'We would be trapped, unless help came quickly.'

'The High Thane, you mean?'

Daga nodded.

'Because it seems that Thane *Heirik* remains unfound.'

The marshal flinched. 'I'm sorry, Lady Razna. I truly am. We have scoured the island.'

'Not good enough.'

'If it is any comfort, My Lady, I believe Thane Heirik lives. We would have found his... him by now if not, I am sure of it.'

'That is no comfort, Daga. '

'My heart tells me that he's alive, Lady Razna.'

'*Your* heart knows nothing.'

Daga's shoulders sagged.

Razna gazed at the fires. 'We were building something here, you know. A new kingdom. But they didn't understand, did not appreciate what I was trying to do. They are so *ungrateful*, so...' She drew in a sharp breath and the words died in her throat. It was precisely the sort of thing Mother would have said.

Daga looked to her. 'My Lady, I am so sorry.

She dug her nails into the stone and then turned away. 'Come!'

The marshal followed Razna down the stairs to the palace courtyard. About a hundred soldiers stood, sat and huddled in groups around campfires on the paving. The men arose as they noticed Lady Razna inspecting them. The courtyard fell silent.

She breathed out. 'Here's what we're going to do.'

'Anything you command, My Lady.' Daga leaned closer. 'Anything at all.'

'Gather your twenty best riders,' she said. 'They are to set out immediately, in all directions, to send word to every camp, fort, and garrison in Caeria. The rest of the soldiers in Etorium must prepare to leave tomorrow morning.'

'What is the message?' Daga asked.

'All are to gather at Heiriksreld.'

Her marshal nodded and smiled. 'Very well.'

Razna tilted her head towards him. 'I want you to ready your horse and mine—now,' she whispered, 'and horses for two guards.'

Daga looked at her, then bowed.

An hour later, while both moons gleamed in the heavens, Razna and Daga cantered out of the palace grounds and down the hill towards the west gate, with her favoured bodyguards in tow. They rode down quiet, empty streets, though lamplight shone through many shutters.

'Open up!' Daga cried as they approached the gate.

The Rhenivians hurried forth to pull the gates apart, and the four riders barrelled out into a gallop, without a farewell or backward glance.

CHAPTER THIRTY-SEVEN

CAERIA – SPRING'S FALL – 437

Dawn came over the city of Etorium, colouring the rooftops pink and gold. The Field of Bees lay at peace, save only for soldiers' tents and the smoking heaps of the funeral pyres. Most of the cantaris now camped in the ruins of Goretonum village, having commandeered what the surviving Rhenivians had abandoned as they fled across the river and into the city. Terzjin took in the view of it all from the wall of the surrendered fort. He dared not look back into the courtyard. They still lingered there.

Avenge us.

Emperor Zjandius stood next to him, dressed in his finest purple cloak over a clean white tunic and a gleaming breastplate. A breeze rustled his hair. 'I never quite believed it. But here we are, on the doorstep.'

Terzjin smiled. 'Nearly there.'

'Good morning, Your Majesty!' Lord Octerion strode along the ramparts. He was thinner and hollow-eyed compared to the old days, but he was shaven, dressed in robes and armour, and had his hair oiled. He smiled and bowed.

Zjandius smiled in return. 'Good morning, My Lord. I trust your new accommodation was more comfortable?'

'It was. Thank you, Emperor,' the aristocrat replied. He came to stand beside Zjandius and look over the parapet. 'All quiet, eh?'

'Indeed,' Zjandius said.

The gate to Etorium was firmly shut, but no one patrolled the walls, as far as Terzjin could see.

'And those ships?' Lord Octerian pointed to the south, where the vessels crowded the estuary.

'The new fleet,' Zjandius replied. 'Admiral Getaelon awaits my signal. Well, shall we go down?'

They rode out of the fort and down the hill. Soldiers rose and saluted as they passed. Lord Octerian inspected the new cantare, with their tall shields, long pikes, and iron armour. He gaped at the elephants in their pen amidst the camp. He grinned and embraced Lord Corilien, his old friend and sometime rival from across the gulf.

Zjandius led them to the Field of Bees, where soldiers were pounding the funeral cinders into a fine powder with mallets. The Emperor, lords, captains and generals dismounted to observe in grave silence.

'You killed a lot of the strawheads, I see,' Lord Octerian muttered, as the soldiers completed their work.

'Yes, but we lost a number too,' Zjandius replied. 'More than a few from Sasiion, who will never see their home again.'

Lord Octerian sighed. 'I must confess, Your Majesty, I believed that I faced a slow, lingering death in that cell up the hill. Hope had fled my heart. And for my family, I may as well have already passed from this world.' He gazed up at the sky, with the sun on his face. 'I never thought I would stand here again.'

Zjandius put his arm on the old man's shoulder. 'You shall see your family in short time, Lord Octerian. My ships will bear you home to Enternis as soon as it is safe. The tide has turned.'

Lord Octerian nodded and wiped an eye.

The soldiers filled sacks with grey ashes. They would carry one third up to the ramparts of Goretonum and surrender it to the wind.

'Is there still no sign of anyone on the walls?' Emperor Zjandius asked.

'No, Majesty,' a general replied. 'All deserted.'

'Then we shall scatter the second third in the Haepastis,' the Emperor ordered. 'If anyone watches, I want them to see that we do things the lawful way.'

The cantare saluted and prepared more sacks.

Zjandius went forth to the riverbank with the soldiers and an escort of lenotare, as well as Master Maltorus at his side. The soldiers worked in pairs, one holding up a long shield to cover the other who carried a sack. The lenotare formed a phalanx before their Emperor, and peered watchfully between their shields as they tramped over the field.

When they reached the Haepastis, the soldiers poured hissing ash into the water, which had borne so much over the centuries. The powder sank in cloudy whorls before swirling away downstream to the sea. Zjandius reached into a sack and tossed a handful into the river. Terzjin did the same, then studied his grey palm. Hundreds of people, lives, memories, hopes and fears—hundreds of names now reduced to a dull powder. Who would remember them all? He knelt and washed his hand in the cold water.

They returned to the heaps, where other soldiers now dug the remaining ash into the soil—the final third gifted to the earth.

'We shall plant two cypresses here,' Zjandius announced. 'One for ours, and one for theirs. But first, we must claim our city.'

They mounted their horses and returned to camp. Colus waited with his engineers and the catapults, which they had now set up amongst the tents.

Emperor Zjandius inspected the activity. 'Is this the best place for these devices?'

'Absolutely.' Master Meretan nodded. 'No need to be any closer, Your Majesty. We are getting better at doing the calculations. More accurate at least—if not faster.' He glared at one of his assistants.

'Well, try not to get too carried away, please,' the Emperor said.

'Of course,' Colus bowed. 'I calculate we can knock the gate down with stones. No tecnaris will be needed. And, it would be good to test the engines against a fixed target.'

Zjandius stroked his chin. 'I'd prefer that we did not. Have the Rhenivians prepared any defences?'

Master Meretan pulled out his Sasiion telescope and put it to his eye. 'Nothing on the walls, Your Majesty. Take a look.' He handed the device to Zjandius. 'Ah, the other way around.'

'Oh.' Zjandius examined the telescope in his hands and smiled, then turned it and peered through the bronze tube again. 'Quite marvellous.' He returned the artefact to his engineer. 'And could you make more of these, Master Meretan?'

Colus grunted. 'I am still trying to determine how it works. But I will... Your Majesty. I have been mostly occupied with calculating catapult ranges, but it is slow going. These engineers do their best, but I need my real assistant.'

Terzjin chuckled. 'A battlefield is no place for Valcero. The boy is out of the way for now, Master Meretan, but he will be helping you soon enough.'

Colus grunted again.

Terzjin had not thought of Valcero in days. No, weeks. The guilt caught him by surprise. But Valcero was probably fine, perhaps playing with the Torecti children, learning how to climb a tree or something. Probably fine. He would fetch the boy once this business was done, and they would talk, and it would all be... fine again. Yes. Yes, it would.

The sound of approaching horses broke his thoughts. Hemadir rode up with two Rugadi in tow. He stopped next to Zjandius and gave a quick bow. 'Your Majesty. Our scouts have returned. They caught sight of Rhenivians at dawn on the west bank of the river, some on horses and others on foot. They move northwards.'

'Oh?' Zjandius frowned.

'Perhaps they are going to a crossing.' Lord Octerian said. 'Maybe to catch us by surprise?'

Hemadir grinned. 'It would be a foolish plan. My scouts estimate a few hundred Rhenivians, at most.'

'I am told they built a stronghold to the north,' Zjandius said. 'Perhaps they travel there. But then...' He turned to the gate. 'Is the city abandoned?'

All eyes went to Etorium and its silent walls.

Zjandius blew out a breath. 'Very well. Prepare the cantaris. Colus, ready your catapults. With *stones*, mind. Do not burn down my city.'

Master Meretan nodded and went to the siege engines. The generals yelled orders, and the cantare formed up, before the bridge and in a long flank on the northern side, should Rhenivians attempt a surprise. Once the engines were loaded, Master Meretan looked to the Emperor for a signal.

Zjandius glanced at the gate, then donned his helmet, as did Terzjin and Lord Octerian. The army fell silent. The Emperor raised a hand and gazed across the bridge. He bit his lip. His hand wavered, about to drop.

A trumpet sounded from somewhere behind the gate.

The soldiers looked at each other and murmured. Tiny figures suddenly appeared on the towers over the gatehouse. Their armour twinkled in the morning light.

'Hold fire!' Zjandius shouted. 'Wait, Master Meretan!'

'Holding fire!' Colus called back.

Zjandius nudged his horse to the side and trotted over to Colus. Terzjin followed close behind on his steed.

Zjandius held out his hand. 'Lend me your telescope, Master Meretan.' He surveyed the wall. 'They do not look like Rhenivians. Yes...black cloaks.' He returned the telescope to Colus. 'It's the palantari. They have the gate.'

'Meaning?' Colus asked.

The Emperor smiled. 'Let us wait a moment longer.'

The army stood in restive silence, looking to Etorium.

The trumpet sounded once again, and the gate doors cracked open. There was a rustling and clinking as the cantare readied their shields and pikes for whatever might appear.

In the event, it was a man dressed in a white robe striding out on foot, escorted by two palantare with round shields and spears.

'Ah ha!' Zjandius grinned. He cantered away through a gap in the lines towards the bridge.

Terzjin hurried after, along with a trio of lenotare. 'Wait, Your Majesty!'

It was Prefect Suletonius, of course, clutching the silver mace, and looking a little more grey-haired. He swallowed as the Emperor rode up to him.

'Your Majesty.' He bowed and presented the mace. 'Etorium is yours, Ki—Emperor Zjandius Vaecerion.'

Zjandius dismounted and stood before Suletonius. He passed his helmet to Master Maltorus. 'Thank you, Prefect.' He took the mace and inspected it. 'I am told you did the Rhenivians' bidding. That you served Thane Heirik.' His eyes roved over the man's face.

Suletonius held his gaze. 'I served *Etorium*—Your Majesty. I protected the people as best I could. I kept this city standing.'

The Emperor looked past him, then smiled and bowed his head. 'You are quite right, Prefect. And I thank you.' He held out his hand.

The Prefect hesitated, then shook it. A faint cheer rose from the city walls, followed by trumpets, both dwarfed by the roar of the soldiers waiting across the river.

The parade began with a company of cantare bearing polished shields and tall pikes, followed by Hemadir and his Rugadi on prancing horses. The citizens lined the streets and gawked at the strangers from across the sea, with their lithe mounts and shrouded faces. Ranks of familiar lentotare marched behind, clad in cloaks of royal blue and holding aloft banners of the Vaecerion falcon embroidered in silver and gold. Trumpeters and drummers marched after them, playing a fanfare that thrilled the blood. Then came the Emperor, riding his chariot with two white horses, and Terzjin at the reins. Zjandius wore his old crown of golden laurel leaves, and sported a purple cloak that wafted behind him. He raised his hands in greeting.

Some citizens clapped and cheered. Others tossed petals as the Last King and First Emperor passed. But many merely watched, their faces worn and tired. Hungry, bitter faces. Those who had been left behind, and somehow endured.

Close behind rolled the flood princes' chariots, driven by plumed stallions. Then more cantare, and light infantry from Jaeterium escorting their Lord Corilien. And the final surprise—the four war elephants of Empress Nanepti, sounding their own fanfare. The Etorians gasped and screamed at the alien beasts, creatures from tales of old. Even the weariest citizens could not help but point and gape.

The parade marched through the city, past the empty Bakers' Square and onto the royal street, where they turned and proceeded up to the palace. The rest of the lenotare had hurried ahead and opened the gates to welcome them home.

Zjandius wasted little time and called an assembly in the throne room. All the generals and captains arrived, as well as Admiral Getaelon. He grinned and hugged Terzjin amidst the throng. The room buzzed with hundreds of voices.

Hemadir found Master Maltorus and embraced him as well. He leaned close to Terzjin's ear. 'So, this is your old house, eh?' The sand prince gazed around the hall.

Terzjin nodded. 'For much of my life, yes!' he shouted into Hemadir's ear. 'Though it looks a little threadbare. The Rhenivians seem to have stolen many treasures.'

'It's *almost* as impressive as the palace at Elisdrium. Or Paeseum?' Hemadir winked and nudged him.

Terzjin grinned. 'Needs *more* falcons!'

The Prefect entered with more members of Etorium's most prominent families. There were a few old and familiar faces, and many younger strangers, who glanced nervously at Zjandius Vaecerion before his throne.

At a nod from the Emperor, Prefect Suletonius struck his mace against a pillar. 'Attend! Attend! All hail your Emperor!'

The crowd roared as Zjandius bowed and sat. Master Maltorus pushed through the crowd to reach his place behind the throne.

Zjandius sat and raised his hands for silence. 'Thank you all. I am honoured—and relieved—to sit on this chair once more. Tonight, we shall feast to celebrate this victory, but I am told my... previous tenants stripped most of the larders and made off with my best wine. So, please forgive the poor hospitality I will offer.'

Some laughter echoed about the hall.

'But first,' Zjandius continued, 'to business. I thank Prefect Suletonius for his service to Etorium in my absence. And I thank the citizens of Etorium and Caeria for their loyalty to me. You have suffered much. I have seen your ruined houses, the burnt trees, the despoliation. I cannot imagine the hardships you suffered.'

The patricians, matrons, and merchants nodded gravely as Terzjin looked over them. They seemed well-fed and well-scrubbed. Where were Alectus and the other children who lived in the wall? And Rufeo, the boy with the glowing eyes? Did they watch the parade?

Zjandius gazed down at his hands, then sighed and continued. 'I am sorry that I could not defend you as your King. I failed you. I abandoned you all.'

The audience coughed and shuffled their feet.

'But as your *Emperor*, I vow to rebuild this city, rebuild our land, and restore the freedom and dignity of the people of Etorium—and all Caeria.' He stood. 'I swear this to you, by the One, and by the Lords of Life and Death.'

The people burst into cheers.

Zjandius smiled and waited for the noise to fade. 'Now, what news of the Rhenivians? What of Thane Heirik?'

Suletonius cleared his throat. 'Your Majesty, we cannot be certain. The remaining soldiers in Etorium fled the city before dawn. I am told Lady Razna, who was ruling the city in Heirik's stead, left last night. We believe they ride to the new city Heirik has been building. They call it *Heiriksreld*.'

Emperor Zjandius raised his eyebrows. 'A new city?'

The Prefect shrugged. 'Well, perhaps more of a fort. I am told it is mostly made of wood, in the Rhenivian style.'

'Alright, but what about Heirik?' Zjandius asked.

'He has not been near Etorium in a few months, after he went west to campaign against the Torecti. There are many rumours, Emperor. Some say he is dead...'

'Hah!' Lord Octerian grinned, while more than a few Caerians clapped.

'But others say,' the Prefect continued loudly, 'others say he was kidnapped and is held somewhere. Perhaps by bandits.'

Zjandius glanced at Terzjin. 'Or the Aventan?' he muttered.

Master Maltorus shrugged.

Suletonius looked at them wide-eyed. 'The Aventan?'

Aventan? The citizens whispered the name amongst themselves.

'Never mind about that.' Zjandius raised his hands for calm. 'Please, Prefect, continue.'

'Hmm, alright, yes.' Suletonius adjusted his robes. 'Well, gossip abounds, Emperor.'

'Yes?'

'The word is that High Thane Getherd sails to Caeria with a fresh army.'

The hall broke into a hubbub.

The Prefect banged his mace. 'Attend!'

Zjandius' face turned dark. 'Is there proof?'

'Well, Your Majesty,' Suletonius replied. 'We found this.' He rummaged in his robes and brought forth a message tube, spattered with dried blood. 'Addressed to you.'

Zjandius took the tube and inspected the wax. 'The seal is broken. Is this Heirik's mark?'

'My apologies, Emperor. We did not break it, but yes, it is his mark. Some palantare found it on a Rhenivian soldier in the Port District. They came upon the body in an alley, along with robbers who must have killed him moments before. The brigands dropped the letter and fled as our palantare approached. We suspect the soldier was seeking a ship to reach you, Your Majesty.'

Zjandius studied the bronze tube. 'It does have an instruction to send to Elisdrium... Very well.' He pulled out the parchment and began to read silently. He put the letter on his lap and grimaced. 'Indeed, it says Heirik has summoned his uncle, but is it true? *Why* would he warn me? It could be a ruse to sow panic.'

A woman stepped forward and bowed—a palace scribe, Terzjin recalled. Nerea. Yes, that was her name. 'I can confirm it, Emperor. Lady Razna discussed the matter with her marshals in my presence.'

'It is written very strangely,' Zjandius mused. 'As if by a child's hand, and almost as if it were in two voices.'

'Lady Razna and a few of the marshals learned our language,' Nerea said, 'although those men were not very skilled.'

Zjandius smiled at her and bowed his head. 'Thank you, Nerea. For *all* your work.'

She blushed and retreated into the crowd, who eyed her with curiosity.

'Most likely, Heirik dictated it,' Suletonius said, 'for I never saw him write a word.' He covered his smile with his hand.

Zjandius studied the parchment. 'By the Lord of Death...' he muttered. 'Admiral Getaelon?'

Getaelon came before the throne and bowed.

'Admiral, how quickly can you prepare the fleet for another voyage?' Zjandius asked.

The admiral pondered the question. 'In a day or two, Your Majesty, should the winds and the Envoy favour us.'

'You have a day, Admiral. Prepare half the galleys—the remainder shall remain here. You are to sail to Lastria and see if this rumour is true. You will sink any Rhenivian ship you find. Use all the stores of tecnaris you need. And then, Admiral, you are to sail on across the sea to Rhenivia.'

Getaelon nodded slowly. 'I see, Emperor.'

'And when you reach our enemy's shores, you will find and destroy any ships there as well. Anything that could float and bear a Rhenivian soldier and his horse, you will ram it, burn it, and reduce it to driftwood.'

Getaelon grinned.

'And you will continue along their coast,' Zjandius said, 'as far north as you can go. Spare the common people—they are not our enemy—but anyone who fights against you, or may even try, well, you will destroy them too. You will shut the seas for Rhenivia.'

The admiral bowed low. 'Understood, sir.'

Long after the assembly, and the humble feast, long after Zjandius had retired to bed not drunk enough on sour wine, after Master Maltorus had stood in vigil at his Emperor's door, and after the lenotare had come to relieve him, Terzjin found his old quarters in the wall once again. By the light of the flickering torch, it was even meaner than he remembered. The room was stripped nearly bare, apart from the bed with its worn, now-sagging mattress, and reeked of another man's odour. But it was his again. Terzjin ran his hands along the cool stone wall, closed the shutters, then doused the torch flame and, using his cloak as a blanket, he wriggled into a deep and dreamless sleep.

CHAPTER THIRTY-EIGHT

CAERIA — SUMMER'S RISING — 437

Razna arrived at Heiriksreld a couple weeks' later, grim and grey of face. Her stomach ached from both hunger and nausea. She had grown to hate her horse, Decha. The mare's stink, her relentless flies, the way she jolted Razna's bones and guts as she bounced over the hills and rough tracks—all intolerable.

They had stopped at Vaecerium on the way—not even long enough for her to sleep in a real bed—but only to gather more supplies for the ride. The servants had seemed slower, less quick to bow and serve. Perhaps they had already heard the news and awaited their old master's return. Razna should have ordered Daga to burn down the villa. That would have shown them.

The falling sun cast long shadows over the valley where Heiriksreld lay. Daga blew his horn as they rode towards the gate, and the guards blew theirs in return. The tall gates swung open to receive them and, as Razna slid off her pale mare onto the dusty ground, she finally allowed herself a moment to breathe.

'Lady Razna.' A resident marshal—she forgot his name—bowed and took her horse. 'Welcome to Heiriksreld. How was your journey?'

'Difficult,' Razna muttered. 'I want to rest.'

'Of course, please follow me.'

Razna and Daga trailed the marshal through the maze of tents towards the hall. The soldiers were packed into any open space and jostled for their dinners around the cooking fires. Some stood and bowed as she passed. Others squatted on the ground and merely glanced at her, either not knowing or caring who she was.

The hall's roof was on, and the walls and doors were in place. The eaves had elaborate carvings here and there, but many lengths of wood remained bare, as were the great double doors.

'Everyone is preparing for war, My Lady,' the marshal explained as they approached the entrance. 'We shall finish the hall once we have time and peace again.'

'I understand,' Razna replied. She examined the shadowed roof. 'Thane Heirik will be so pleased.'

The marshal glanced at Daga and then at her. 'Yes, Lady Razna. We shall please him.'

The long, bare hall was deserted, save for a few Caerian servants turning a pig over the fire. They bowed.

'Will My Lady take dinner with the rest of us outside?' Daga asked.

She shook her head. 'I'll have meat and water in my quarters. Don't disturb me until sunrise.'

The servants left a board of dripping pork and a jug on a table in her room at the back of the hall. Razna tore off strips of meat with her fingers and gobbled them down by the light of an oil lamp. She felt satisfied for the first time in days. The soldiers laughed and argued outside. Some sang and played music.

Later, she undressed, climbed into the wide bed, and tried to sleep. Even on this warm night, the sheets felt cold. She ran her hand over the empty space beside her. Was he well? Was he...?

The wooden walls, floor, and ceiling pressed on her, as if she were lying in a pine coffin.

The next morning, Razna forced down porridge and went out to meet Daga and the other marshals. She let her gown hang loosely. The men were gathered around a table in the hall, under a shaft of light from the chimney. Daga had unrolled a map of Caeria on the table and pinned it with some wine cups.

'How many soldiers have arrived so far?' Razna asked.

'Some three and a half thousand, Lady Razna,' a marshal answered. 'With more coming in every day. From the east, from the south west and the south east.' He pointed at each part of the map in turn, 'A few have arrived from Impona and Mandonum to the north.'

Razna tapped on the northeast corner. 'And Lastria?'

'Ah, none as yet,' the marshal replied. He scratched his head. 'We thought perhaps High Thane Getherd ordered them to stay...'

Razna leaned forward. 'What?'

'He has arrived in Caeria, or so we heard, My Lady,' another marshal said. 'He waits in Lastria while his ships bring more soldiers across the sea.'

Razna scowled. 'Why was I not informed?'

The marshals looked at each other. 'We thought you knew already, Lady Razna,' one ventured.

She pulled Daga away from the table. 'We need to speak. Privately.'

They went outside under the shade of the porch. Soldiers and servants hurried past in the sun, on their errands.

Razna drew Daga close. 'We cannot have Getherd coming here and taking over,' she whispered. 'This is Heirik's land, and I must protect it for him. Do you understand?'

'I understand, My Lady.'

She sighed and looked around. A few Rhenivians were eyeing them. Something squirmed within her, and she grimaced. 'We must take charge. We'll invite him here, as *our* guest, before he sends orders. So, we ride to Lastria.'

'And the Caerians?'

'How long before they get here?'

Her marshal searched around. 'They will need time to bolster their host. We outnumber them for now, especially if the High Thane joins us. But we may have only a month or two to prepare.'

'Then we shall ride quickly.'

The other marshals came outside, while more soldiers gathered before the hall.

The marshal of Heiriksreld stepped forward. 'My Lady?'

'We must leave again,' Razna announced, loudly enough for all to hear. 'We go to meet High Thane Getherd and escort him and his army here.'

'So we'll have a *real* leader in charge again?' someone piped up from the field.

She swung around. 'Who said that?'

'Where's Thane Heirik?' another soldier called out.

Daga marched to the edge of the porch. 'Thane Heirik is delayed in the west. He'll return soon. Lady Razna rules in his name in the meanwhile.'

The soldiers muttered and grumbled, as Razna's heart began to thud. They stared at her with suspicion, contempt, perhaps even a little lust. And there were so many of them.

'She's not even one of us!' a young soldier piped up. He put his hands on his hips. 'How can we have a Galatani order us about?'

Razna strode down the steps, right up to the boy. He sneered. She grabbed his wispy blonde beard and yanked his head down to hers. The soldier yelped in surprise.

'You are safe here because of me,' Razna snarled. 'If you do not accept my rule, then leave. Go wander beyond the walls and see how you like it. Perhaps the Caerians will show you hospitality, huh?' She jerked on his beard.

'I—I'm sorry, Lady Razna,' the soldier squealed, bent over. 'Forgive me.'

The men burst out laughing.

Razna released him and surveyed the gathering. 'Your Thane made *me* lawgiver in his absence,' she called out. 'I will not disappoint him. I shall keep you safe and lead you to victory, whatever it takes. Would you disappoint your Thane?'

'No, My Lady!' the crowd roared.

A thrill rippled up her back. 'I ride now to welcome High Thane Getherd and bring him here. Together, with our Thane Heirik, we shall defeat these Caerians, once and for all.'

The Rhenivians cheered.

They left later that day, once more on jolting horseback.

Daga insisted on an escort, some thirty riders. 'We cannot afford to lose you too, Lady Razna,' went his argument.

She gritted her teeth and accepted the soldiers and their crass behaviour, and the horse that stank and threw her stomach about.

They rode fast for two weeks without incident, passing a convoy of Rhenivians heading to Heiriksreld and not much else. Daga opted to avoid Algados and any large towns. They rested in lonely places, such as on hilltops with clear views of the surrounding countryside. Each night, the soldiers slept in shifts, so a third were always awake, keeping a nervous eye on the shadows beyond the campfire.

They reached the mountain pass above Scetana and rode for a few more days down onto the plain before Lastria.

The city was as she remembered from all those years ago when she first set foot on this island, on *her* island. The palace overlooked the sea and the city from the rocky cliff, and the whitewashed houses spilt down the hillside to the bay. A mass of Rhenivian tents sprawled over the fields beside the walls. Getherd's boar banners flapped in the sea breeze.

'Raise your Thane's mark,' Razna ordered the soldiers as they approached.

The riders lifted their flags and blew their horns. They reached the edge of the camp, where an unfamiliar marshal rode out to meet them.

'On behalf of Thane Heirik,' Daga announced, 'Lady Razna is here to welcome High Thane Getherd to Caeria.'

The marshal looked her over while he chewed on something. 'Is that so?'

Razna sat up straight and glared at him. 'Where is the High Thane, marshal? I have much to discuss with him.' She spoke with her best Rhenivian.

The marshal chewed, swallowed, then spat a blob of gristle onto the dirt beside his horse. 'High Thane Getherd is expecting Thane Heirik. But if you're here, then I suppose you'll find him up there.' He pointed a thumb over his shoulder.

They rode through the gates into Lastria and up to the palace. The soldiers led Razna through the hallways—tidier than she remembered—and into a courtyard, lined with beds of herbs and spring flowers wilting in the summer sun. There, under the shade of a gnarled olive tree, sat the High Thane, holding court on a stool.

He was much the same, though his beard was whiter, and his face a little more lined. His blue eyes were as cold and piercing as ever. He frowned as she approached.

Razna bowed. 'High Thane Getherd.'

'And you are?' The Rhenivian nobleman folded his arms.

'Lady Razna, High Thane. We met before...'

Getherd cocked his head. 'The mistress? Is this some kind of joke? Where's my nephew?'

Daga came beside her and bowed. 'Thane Heirik is away, My Lord. He went west to battle the savages. Lady Razna has been ruling in his stead.'

Getherd sighed. 'Has she now? Does this explain his mess?'

'Thane Heirik trusts me, My Lord.' Razna tried to keep her voice even. 'I have served him—and Rhenivia—faithfully for years. I have made Etorium his loyal stronghold. We have—'

'And how are you faring with that?' Getherd raised an eyebrow. 'Why are you here, and not in Etorium?'

'We had to withdraw from the city, High Thane, but—'

'Unbelievable!' Getherd shook his head. 'That nephew of mine. Could never keep his trousers up, and this is what happens. Now, look...' He stood and brushed past Razna to address Daga. 'I must speak to Heirik. Where is he?'

'Uh, sir...' Daga glanced between Razna and Getherd. 'Thane Heirik is... um...'

'Can we speak in private, High Thane?' Razna asked.

The old man swung about. Razna had to stop herself from backing away.

'What do you want a private chat for?' He smirked down at her. 'I'm not interested in whatever you have to hawk. No time for whoring, girlie. This is serious business.'

The men sniggered around her. She clenched her fists and drew herself up to her full height. 'My *Lord*, Thane Heirik has been kidnapped.'

Getherd frowned. 'What?'

Razna nodded. 'He was taken by the enemy. My men are hunting for him as we speak. In the meantime, *I* have been preparing our defences. We are marshalling at Heiriksreld.'

Getherd looked around. 'How did this happen? *Where is he?*'

'Our foes are cowards, My Lord,' Daga said. 'They do not fight with honour. They fell upon our Thane in the night while we were in the countryside, and carried him off like sneak thieves.'

'Is he even alive?' Getherd shouted.

'We believe so,' Razna replied.

'*Believe?* You do not know?'

'Sir, our best trackers are pursuing them through the wilds,' Daga said. 'There is no…body. He lives, My Lord. We are certain of it.'

'Agh.' The High Thane rubbed his face.

Razna breathed in. 'My Lord, I invite you to join us in Heiriksreld. With your help, we can defeat the Caerians and find Thane Heirik.'

'Oh, you *invite* me, do you?' Getherd leaned down into her face. His breath stank of beer and old meat. 'No. No more of this nonsense. *I* am in command. We await my ships to deliver the remainder of my host. Two more voyages, and we'll be at full strength. Then I'll march on Etorium and deal with the Caerians, *again*. And you…' he pointed at Daga, '…will make sure all Heirik's men join me along the way.'

Razna stepped closer to him. 'High Thane!'

Getherd waved her off. 'Enough of your yapping. Get out, or be thrown out.'

She trembled. 'High Thane Getherd, please, I must insist…'

He scowled and advanced on her. 'I said—'

A Rhenivian horn blew from somewhere nearby. The sound echoed around the palace walls, sending a flock of pigeons into flight. The gathered people looked up and around. The horn blew again.

A soldier ran into the courtyard, panting. 'My Lord! Our ships!'

Getherd beamed. 'Excellent!'

'But…High Thane…' The soldier stopped for a breath. 'Another fleet approaches. Up the coast, sir, from the south.'

Getherd frowned. 'Rhenivian ships?'

The soldier shook his head.

The High Thane grabbed the man by the shoulder and shoved him forward. 'Show me.'

The soldier led him and the other marshals into the palace. Razna looked to Daga, who shrugged.

'Come,' she muttered.

They strode through corridors to another doorway leading outside, this time to a balcony on the cliffs above the sea. Getherd and his men huddled on the narrow terrace and peered at the horizon. The waves crashed against the rocks below, leaving foam in their wakes. The salty air cleared Razna's head.

A marshal pointed eastwards. 'There, sir, look!'

A cluster of red-sailed ships bobbed on the vivid blue water, driven by wind and oars towards the shore.

'They're ours.'

'Yes, I recognise them.' Getherd shielded his eyes from the sun and squinted to the south. 'And the others? There?'

They looked rightwards over the bay and the harbour, where another fleet—white-sailed—came rowing fast along the rocky coast.

'They look Caerian in style,' a marshal answered, 'though perhaps bigger than what I've seen before.'

Getherd shrugged. 'So?'

'They are heading for the bay, I think,' a soldier remarked. 'Maybe they're trying to block our ships.'

The High Thane grunted. 'Let them try. They have half our number, at best, if my old eyes are right. We'll sail right over them.'

'They have fire, High Thane,' Razna spoke out.

Getherd turned and glared at her. 'What are you doing here?'

Razna scowled. 'Listen to me, My Lord. Can you warn your boats? The Caerians have devices that throw fire and—'

'What nonsense you speak, girl.' Getherd turned back to the sea. 'What nonsense did you pour in Heirik's ears, hmm? Now, leave before I toss you into the water myself.'

Razna turned to Daga.

'It's true, sir,' Daga said, but too softly to hear above the booming waves.

All eyes were on the Caerian vessels as they cruised into the bay and turned out towards the open sea, where the Rhenivian galleys bore down upon them. The High Thane was right. The Caerians were utterly outnumbered.

'What a gift for the Flood Father.' Getherd folded his arms.

All the Rhenivians leaned over the parapet, eager for the carnage. The red-sailed ships gathered in a tight arc, ready to swallow the white sails. Scores of soldiers crowded the beach outside the city to watch the battle unfold.

The Caerians bobbed in the bay while tiny figures ran about their decks. A trumpet sounded faintly as the Rhenivians closed in. Then, black dots shot off from the Caerian vessels, trailing smoke threads through the air.

'Are those arrows?' a marshal asked his companions.

Crimson, orange and yellow flowers blossomed along the line of Rhenivian ships. Tall flames leapt over the decks and masts. A volley of distant booms reached the watchers' ears. They gasped.

More fire popped over the drifting Rhenivian line. Thick, black smoke billowed over the red sails and the now red hulls.

'By the gods,' someone murmured.

Getherd fixed his eyes on the sea battle and gripped the parapet.

The Rhenivian ships floated towards the Caerians, breaking formation. Was that distant screaming, or seagulls? Some of the Rhenivian galleys turned towards the open sea, rowing away from the foundering vessels. Two burning ships collided. Another caught an untouched boat as it tried to pass. The flames spread. Oars tangled. Ships were spinning slowly in the swell.

And then Caerians nosed forward, rowing hard. They fired swarms of arrows, rammed their bronze prows into the hulls of the flailing Rhenivians, reversed, then turned about to ram some more. Again and again, they tore into the red-sailed sea craft, tilting and sinking under dark smoke. Soldiers, as small as ants, leapt from the burning boats into the blue sea, lost under the waves.

The Rhenivians on the balcony stared in quiet horror, muttering curses and glancing at Getherd for his reaction. Who could say how long they watched, how long before every Rhenivian ship was sunk? Not a single vessel reached the shore.

The High Thane spat into the sea. 'Leave us.' He pointed at Razna. 'You. Stay.'

The rest, including Daga, shuffled through the doorway and out of sight, leaving Getherd and Razna alone on the windy balcony. The Caerian fleet turned south.

Getherd breathed heavily. His eyes blazed. His face was dark.

Razna licked her lips. 'High Thane, I can serve you. I know these Caerians. I know their ways, how they think. I can offer you counsel. I will—'

Getherd slammed his fist against the parapet. 'A thousand of my best warriors, lost to the waves. Another thousand now wait like fools over the sea for ships that will never arrive. Do you understand? Do you?'

'We can defeat them, My Lord,' Razna insisted. 'Together, we—'

'Enough!' Getherd snarled. 'Who do you think you are? There is no *together*. You are a peasant whore. You are *nothing*. My nephew's plaything, a distraction. How *dare* you even think to speak to me.'

'I'm carrying Heirik's child!' Razna shouted. She pulled the front of her robe tight to reveal the bump.

The High Thane blinked. 'Is this true?'

'Yes. If anything happens to Heirik, this child inherits all that is his, yes?'

'A bastard inherits nothing.'

Razna shook her head and smiled. 'Heirik is my husband.' She patted her belly. 'This is his lawful child.'

Getherd's eyes went wide. 'You did *what*?' He stepped towards her.

Razna bumped up against the parapet. 'My Lord, you need me.'

'When?' He loomed. 'I heard nothing about this from Frethi, or Agluf. I *told* Heirik he was to marry—'

Razna gripped the bricks. 'The Corn Mother and Flood Father were not involved...'

The High Thane froze and stared at her. 'Oh, by the gods, you did not...' He backed away and shook his head. 'Is this... is this why they sent the Holy Warriors home? Did you...' He spun about and groaned. 'I never believed it. Oh, you stupid, *stupid* children. Did he not understand my plans? The alliances you have ruined?'

Getherd contemplated Razna, the parapet she leaned against, the crashing waves far below.

Razna's heart boomed in her ears. Her hands went cold. 'Please, My Lord, wait. Wait. It was all Heirik's idea. I love him. I'm loyal to him. I couldn't say no.'

A soldier popped his head through the doorway. 'High Thane?'

The old man turned on the man. 'What. Now?'

The man cowered. 'A message, My Lord. From Thane Heirik.'

Getherd looked at her, then back at the man. 'Where?'

'This way, My Lord.' The soldier retreated inside.

Getherd left. Razna gazed down at the foamy rocks. She held her belly. So be it. She hurried after the Rhenivians into the palace.

She found Getherd sitting under the olive tree in the courtyard with his attendants. Another soldier waited, clutching a bronze tube.

'So, how did you come by this message?' The High Thane said. 'Where's my nephew?'

The soldier bowed. 'I met a stranger on the road to Lastria, sir. A Caerian. He stopped me as I rode and gave me this letter. He insisted it was for you and ... ' He glanced at Razna, ' ... the lady.'

Getherd shot her a look and held out his hand. 'Well, hand it over.' He examined the tube. 'I don't see my nephew's mark.'

'The messenger insisted it came from the Thane, sir.'

Getherd grunted and broke the seal. He drew out a parchment, unrolled it and squinted at the text. 'I can't read this. What writing is this?'

Razna went to his side. 'High Thane, it's Galatani. I can read it.'

Getherd frowned at her. 'Now, why would Heirik send a message in Galatani?' He sighed. 'Oh, very well.'

Razna took the letter and cleared her throat to begin reading, as Getherd dropped the tube on his lap, and something rattled inside.

The High Thane shook it. 'What's this?' He tipped the container over. A finger, bearing a gold ring, dropped into his hand. He started, and the piece of flesh fell to the ground.

Razna gaped at the finger.

The soldiers gasped and cursed.

Razna steeled herself. She would not be sick. Not now.

Getherd leaned over and picked up the finger. He held it in his palm and poked at the ring. The engraved boar and corn were clear to see. The finger ended in a stump of blackened, clotted flesh.

She would not be sick. She would not be sick.

'You had best read that letter now, *Lady* Razna,' Getherd said, in a voice of ice, still gazing at the piece of his nephew.

'Yes. Yes, High Thane.' She swallowed and examined the writing.

'Greetings, High Thane Getherd and Lady Razna of Galatan,' she began. 'We hold your beloved Thane Heirik captive. He is alive and in good health, apart from the…' She coughed. '…sample we send as proof of our claim, and our sincerity. If you wish to receive him in continued good health, proceed at once to the first crossroad south of the pass of Scetana, where you shall receive further instructions. Negotiations will be conducted in person and concluded in the same meeting. Bring at least five talents of silver and be ready and willing to discuss other terms that may arise. Come alone or do not come at all.' Razna trembled.

'Who sent it?' Getherd asked, not looking at her.

She breathed out. 'It's signed by Lord Sorveo Aventan, of Lastria.'

A gust of sea wind blew through the palace courtyard, rustling the branches of the old olive, while the Rhenivians whispered and looked at each other in shock. Getherd gazed at the ground, lost in thought. Razna tried not to look at the finger.

The High Thane roused himself and snatched the parchment from her. He inspected the seal at the end of the letter and nodded. 'It was doomed to happen,' he muttered. 'Foolishness. Pure foolishness.' He sighed. 'Very well. You lot.' He snapped his fingers at some soldiers. 'Get all the silver coin or whatever you can find in the palace. If there isn't enough, go down into the city and extract what we need. Be quick about it.'

'Aye, My Lord!' the men shouted and dashed away.

'The rest of you…' Getherd waved at them. 'Prepare my host. We leave after lunch.'

'And me, High Thane?' Razna asked.

Getherd rounded on her. 'What about you?'

'I can help, High Thane.' She held his gaze and willed herself not to shrink away. 'I want Heirik freed as much as you, sir. I know something of these Aventan. At the very least, should they send another letter, I will read it for you.'

Getherd scowled. 'I *should* have you executed, for many reasons. But, yes, you shall come with me, and we shall see what use you serve.' He stormed away without another word.

Razna watched him leave, and smiled.

CHAPTER THIRTY-NINE

CAERIA – SUMMER'S RISING – 437

Valcero coughed himself awake. The cough wouldn't leave his throat. It came upon him in the night, in the middle of the day, when he tried to sleep in the sweaty hut, when he tried to eat stale bread and grisly broth. It seized him when he dug latrines he no longer smelled, and when he hauled logs that raked his fingers with splinters. The cough burned his chest, where his skin stretched tight over his ribs. For many days, his heart had fluttered at the call of the sunset horn, dreading that the Thane would ride in with the returning soldiers, seeking the treacherous boy. But now he no longer feared that Thane Heirik would come back to gut him—or exact some other horrible punishment. He was too tired.

'Up, up!' the guard yelled into the hut. 'Arise and get to work!'

The slaves rolled over and groaned, but did not linger, lest they get the whip. Valcero trudged to the back of the line for his dull porridge. He swallowed without thought. He trudged to the paddocks to feed the remaining beasts, thin as they were.

'Where are you off to?' a guard shouted at him.

Valcero blinked and bowed his head. 'To feed the animals, sir.'

The guard cuffed him over the head. 'Stupid boy. Don't you listen? New duties.'

The boy looked up. 'Sir?'

'Load the wagons. All food from the stores. Go now.'

Valcero found the other slaves already at work near the gates, heaving sacks and jars onto a set of three carts. He joined the line and went where he was told.

'What's happening?' one of the Caerian men whispered to another.

'Not sure,' the other slave replied. 'But I heard we're leaving. All of us. Everyone.'

'What?' A woman leaned into their little group. 'They're abandoning the camp?'

'Seems like it.'

'But what does that mean?' asked the first slave as he dumped a sack onto the nearest cart.

'Search me.' The other slave passed him another sack and grunted. 'Don't even know where we're going.'

'I could do with something fresh to look at.' The woman passed an amphora to Valcero. 'Don't you think so, boy?'

Valcero shrugged and hauled the amphora onto the wagon. He coughed.

The next day, the guards awoke the slaves before dawn and herded them to the gate, where they joined the Rhenivians—a few on horseback and more on foot—and the mule-drawn carts. They put a heavy sack on Valcero's back with chafing ropes. The wagons already creaked and groaned under their baggage.

The convoy went eastwards along a dirt track that wound between the wooded hills and across a countryside of yellowing grass and dark green scrub. Each day was a slow march under the burning sun, a short break for lunch, where the soldiers claimed all the shade along the road, more marching with the sun blazing against their backs until the orange glow of dusk, then the business of cooking dinner and erecting the soldiers' tents. Valcero lay on the dusty ground under the stars with the rest of the slaves and tried not to cough. The soldiers guarded in shifts.

Valcero's worn-out sandals broke on the sixth day after they left the fort. He walked barefoot over the hot, stony ground. And after the second thorn pierced his foot, he was reduced to limping under his pack. He slowed to the back of the convoy.

'Hurry up!' A guard prodded the boy onward with the butt of his spear. 'Move!'

Valcero turned to face the soldier. 'Please, sir. I need sandals.' He lifted a foot to show the cuts and bruises on his sole.

The guard laughed. 'I am not a shoemaker, boy. Keep walking.'

After another two days of walking and pushing carts over gullies and pits in the eroded track, they met another Rhenivian convoy coming down a north road. They were heading in the same direction, so the two groups merged. During the lunch break, Valcero lay under a wagon with some other slaves to escape the sun. He coughed and listened to their chatter.

'Oh, so you don't know where we're going then, do you?' a Caerian man from the other camp muttered to a slave from Valcero's group.

'No, they don't tell us anything.' The slave passed a waterskin to the newcomer.

The man rolled onto his stomach and took a sip. 'It's some big fort the strawheads are building over in the east, near Algados, or so I heard. All the Rhenivians are moving there now, apparently.'

'Ah, but Mesentius,' a slave woman whispered from under the next wagon, 'you have to tell him *why* we're moving. That's the best part.' She grinned.

'Of course!' The slave named Mesentius nodded and passed the waterskin to the next man. 'We were listening to our bunch of soldiers gossiping one evening by the fire. They didn't want us to hear it.'

'Hear what?' The man holding the waterskin wriggled closer.

Mensentius glanced at the Rhenvians under the trees, then looked at everyone listening to him and smiled. 'They're assembling because King Zjandius has returned.'

Another slave spat on the ground. 'Never. He ran away and is ***not*** coming back.'

'It's true,' the woman under the wagon insisted. 'I heard them myself. The King came back with a cantaris and has already chased the Rhenivians out of Etorium.'

'They're trying to keep it secret,' Mesentius said, 'because they're afraid of what we might do.'

'What would we do?' another slave asked.

'We could run away,' a man said—a slave from Valcero's camp who lay beside the woman.

'How would that work?' the woman frowned. 'Aren't you forgetting?' She tugged on her neck ring.

'I'd take my chances,' the man murmured.

'We should be ready,' Mesentius whispered, 'for when the moment presents itself.'

The next day was the hottest of the summer so far. Although they set off before sunrise, Valcero's back turned slick with sweat under the sack. After the tenth or eleventh hour, the bright light ached his eyes and burned through his hair into his scalp. His head began to throb.

'May I have water?' he whispered to a Caerian woman walking beside him.

'Only a mouthful, mind. I don't know when they'll let us stop to gather more.'

Valcero took the waterskin and tossed his head back to swallow.

'That's enough!' The slave woman snatched the water and hurried forward.

The boy coughed and wiped his mouth. His temples thumped with each step.

When the break came, he had to sit against the cart with the sack over his head for shade, because there was no space under the wagons. But his arms were too weak to hold up the pack for long, and he was forced to submit to the sun. He gnawed on a lump of bread. So King Zjandius was back in Caeria. Were Master Meretan and Maltorus here as well? What did it matter? They didn't know where he was. They had probably forgotten all about him. Probably too busy to think about Valcero.

When the guards resumed the march, Valcero could barely put one foot in front of another. No one would share their water. Dark spots danced before his eyes. It felt as if two great hands were squeezing his head and trying to tear open his scalp. His stomach churned, as if he might lose his scrap of lunch.

Late in the afternoon, he heard a trickling from around the bend in the road ahead. A stream wound across the track and down a narrow gully lined with bushes and trees.

'Please, sir, I need water,' he rasped at the nearest guard.

'Hmm?' The man barely glanced at the boy as they marched.

'Please, sir.' Valcero's lips cracked.

Would the guard care if he keeled over and died? Would he even notice? What did it matter? Valcero dropped his sack and stumbled to the stream, where he fell to his knees and scooped up handfuls of water. It was muddy, yet cold and refreshing.

The guard strode over to him. 'What are you doing?'

'Just a moment, please, sir...' Valcero splashed more water into his mouth.

'Get up!' The guard grabbed the back of the boy's tunic and hauled him to his feet. 'What are you doing, you worm?' the guard screamed in the boy's face, spraying spittle.

The convoy had halted. Everyone was watching.

'Sorry, sir,' Valcero gasped out.

He heard running footsteps.

'*Ech!*' another guard called out. Another soldier further ahead shouted in Rhenivian.

The man tossed Valcero aside. 'Stop!' he yelled.

Five slaves—Mesentius and some others—ran along the stream towards a cluster of laurel trees on a craggy ridge. Someone blew a horn, but the Caerians only sprinted faster. Three riders, spears held high, galloped from the head of the convoy in pursuit. The rest stood frozen—Valcero included—and watched every moment. The slaves nearly gained the ridge, but the riders crashed through the bushes and over the stream and cut off the slowest four.

The horsemen turned about and knocked the Caerians down, trampling them under hooves and forcing them to their knees. The watchers gasped and sighed. The farthest slave, Mesentius, scrambled up the rocks out of the horse's reach, but a rider hurled a spear after him. It pierced Mesentius' back, and he tumbled off the ridge without a cry. The other horsemen leapt from their mounts to hack and jab at the remaining four with swords, spears and axes. A woman screamed. Valcero flinched and looked away.

The guard seized the boy again and shook him about. 'You are making tricks!'

'No, sir!' Valcero shouted. 'Just thirsty! Please—'

The Rhenivian threw Valcero to the ground and kicked him in the back, in the stomach, in the head. The boy yelped and curled into a ball, but the kicks did not stop until another guard ran over and dragged his companion away. The guard spat on him and stormed off.

Rough hands lifted Valcero to his feet. 'Careful, boy,' the second guard said. 'Don't make him angry.'

When the day's march ended, and the stars began to wink in the sky, the Rhenivians tethered the remaining Caerians in a ring, with each slave's feet bound together and tied to the next. The Caerians sat on the ground away from the campfire, with only dry bread for dinner. Valcero lay on his side, clutching his bread to his chest, staring at nothing, saying nothing, while his body ached. The firewood popped and cracked. The captives whispered amongst themselves.

'They're going to kill us, aren't they? By the Lord of Death, we're going to die out here. Look at them. That's what they're talking about.'

'No, they won't.'

'Of course they will! Listen to them. I know Rhenivian.'

'Yes, but they won't kill us.'

'They still need us to carry their things.'

'So what happens after the journey is done? What then?'

A long silence.

'Look at their faces. They're frightened. And so am I, quite honestly.'

'Oh, be quiet. What's the point of this?'

The whispering died down after a time. Crickets and cicadas sang in the brush. Valcero gazed unseeing, until a tiny movement caught his eye. A little field mouse had come scurrying out of the dry grass towards the camp. The boy kept still, barely breathing, holding back his cough. The field mouse had rust-brown fur and three white stripes along its back. The creature crept forward, within a cubit of

Valcero. It paused and sniffed the ground, then rose onto its hind legs to smell the air.

Valcero dug his fingernail into his bread, broke off a piece, and flicked it to the mouse. The little creature darted back a bit, then sniffed and crawled closer, close enough to touch—if the boy dared. The mouse took the bread in its paws and sat on its hind legs to gnaw on the morsel. Its whiskers twitched. Pinpricks of firelight danced in its dark eyes.

Boy and mouse regarded each other for a long while.

Then Valcero's cough burst out of his throat, and the mouse dashed into the grass, out of sight, as quiet as a thought.

CHAPTER FORTY

CAERIA – SUMMER'S REIGN – 437

When Getherd and Razna reached the crossroads beneath Scetana, with the High Thane's host of thousands in tow, they found a soldier tied to a tree with his mouth gagged and a scroll tube in his bound hands. The Rhenivian was pale and near death. Dried blood covered his jerkin and trousers from a gash at his side.

'They ambushed us on the road from Lastria,' he mumbled. 'I was the only one they spared.' He shook and collapsed while Getherd took the scroll.

The High Thane frowned at the message, then passed it to Razna. 'What does it say?'

Razna glanced over the parchment. It was the same Galatani script—certainly not Heirik's hand. 'We are to take the road to the northwest, up the valley to the ridge. Apparently, there is an open field up there where negotiations will be conducted. And they remind us to go alone.' She waited for Getherd's response.

The old High Thane scowled at the ground, then squinted at the mountains to the northwest. The slopes were dark and hazy under the summer sun, blanketed in cedar forest with some outcrops of pale sandstone reaching into the empty sky. The soldiers surrounded him in a respectfully wide circle.

'How can I trust these Aventan?' Getherd murmured.

'You cannot, High Thane,' Razna murmured in reply. 'But they have Heirik. What choice do we have?'

'Hmm.' Getherd narrowed his eyes and breathed out. He turned and whistled at two marshals.

The Rhenivians strode forward.

'You,' Gertherd pointed at the first, 'shall pick out a hundred of your best riders, and go up the other side of this valley. Don't seek out trouble, but fight if you must. Look for this meadow and watch over it from a discreet spot. Use your horn to signal if you have problems. And you...' He pointed at the other marshal. '...will pick out twenty of *your* best riders and escort us up this road to whatever *negotiations* await.'

'High Thane,' Razna said, 'the letter—'

'I don't care what the letter says.' Getherd spat on the dirt. 'I'm not riding alone with bags of treasure into an obvious trap. If these Aventan are so desperate for my silver, they won't mind if I bend their rules a little.' He smiled to himself.

'But I will be riding with you, sir,' Razna said. 'It's what we agreed.'

Getherd's smile turned sour. 'I don't see you being much use if we're attacked, *Lady* Razna. But, yes, you should come along. Perhaps the presence of a woman in your... delicate situation will stay their hands. Perhaps you could declare your love for my nephew and melt their hearts. Or perhaps not. Come on then—we leave now.'

The bulk of Getherd's host set up camp at the crossroads, while the larger detachment trotted off to the other side of the valley to find a path to the mountain top. The High Thane went up the road with Razna and his escort.

The road rose gently through grassy meadowlands to dense, shoulder-high scrub, then tight ranks of cedar that pressed close along the track. The shade and sighing wind cooled them. The riders glanced from side to side as they travelled through the shadowy forest. All they could see were birds flitting between mossy trunks, and a family of wild pigs that trundled away as soon as they were spotted.

At times, the track went so narrow that they were forced to ride in a single file. The soldier ahead of Razna clutched his spear in one hand and his reins in the other, ready for an ambush.

'What about these forest savages, these Torecti?' one of Getherd's marshals asked.

'They only dwell in the Nedolian Forest in the west,' Daga replied while riding beside Razna. 'Far from here.'

A branch fell somewhere in the forest, and the Rhenivians flinched on their horses. But there was no one about. A false alarm.

As the sun descended and the forest became even gloomier, the party stopped to camp. They gathered kindling to build a fire in a clearing and prepared a meal. Most of the soldiers formed a ring around the camp and drew lots to keep watch through the night.

'No one is to enter or leave this circle until daybreak,' Getherd ordered.

He sat hunched over on a tree stump, gnawing on a leg of lamb, with Razna, Daga, and a few of his marshals sitting close by.

'So, why haven't you dealt with these Aventan already?' Getherd asked.

'We didn't know they still lived, My Lord.' Razna nibbled on her own strip of lamb on the rib—quite burnt, to be honest. 'They have been in hiding since we came to Caeria.'

'Heirik mentioned ambushes and assassinations, though.' Getherd eyed her over his hunk of lamb and chewed noisily.

She nodded. 'Yes, there were attacks, but we believed them to be the work of bandits. We did what we could to prevent them.'

The High Thane frowned and sucked meat from between his teeth.

'Sir,' Daga said, 'we questioned peasants, used hounds to track them, even…eliminated villages we suspected of sheltering rebels. But these Aventan are very cunning. They eluded us for years.'

'Clearly, you didn't do enough,' Getherd said. 'You should be ashamed that they could pluck my nephew from amongst your company.' He chewed some more. 'I am ashamed for him.'

'The Aventan know these lands far better than us.' Razna pulled a piece of lamb off the rib. 'We are still learning its ways.'

The High Thane grunted.

They ate in silence next to the crackling fire. An owl hooted nearby.

'You think they could be watching us at this moment?' Getherd muttered.

Razna peered into the shadows between the pale trees, beyond the iron circle that shielded them. 'Almost certainly.'

Getherd roused them early after a quiet night, and they soon mounted their horses and returned to the road. The track grew steeper and zig-zagged up the forested slopes. Razna slapped mosquitoes off her skin every few steps as they hummed around her ears.

When they stopped for a break, the High Thane took Razna aside. 'When all this is sorted out,' he muttered, 'the first thing you and Heirik will do is go before Brother Frethi and make your vows. I'll drag you there if I must.'

She bowed her head. 'Of course, High Thane.'

'I don't care what blasphemies have bound you two together. You shall kneel before the Corn Mother, and you will marry Heirik the *proper* way. Understood?'

'Yes, My Lord. It is proper.'

'Hopefully, you bear a son. Let at least one good thing come from this mess.'

'Of course, High Thane. I shall pray on it.'

'Hmph.' Getherd turned away and went to his horse.

Razna stared at his back—Uncle Getherd's back—and smirked.

After a few hours, the track flattened out, and they could hear the sound of rushing water, which grew into a roaring as they went. The track dipped steeply, and the trees thinned to reveal a river, bubbling and surging over a cliff above the valley of trees. And there, on the precipice on the other side of the fall, stood Heirik and the Aventan.

'Attend!' Getherd called out in Rhenivian.

His soldiers sprang forward to encircle their lord, their horses jostling against Razna on her mare until she was right beside Getherd. The men raised their shields and held their spears ready.

The Aventan surrounded Heirik and watched the newcomers in silence. Heirik had his arms behind his back and rope around his torso. He was pale and a little gaunt, but stood tall amongst the

Caerians and broke into a grin at the sight of his people. When he locked eyes with Razna, his grin became a beam of joy, and her heart fluttered. She smiled and raised a hand.

'Clever bastards,' the High Thane muttered.

She followed his eyes to the riverbank lined with polished white rocks like giant eggs. The same rocks filled the river bed, along with long strands of green slime undulating in the swift current.

'Could we charge the horses through that?' a marshal asked.

'Don't be a fool,' Getherd said. 'We take no such chances.'

Two Aventan—young men in black cloaks and tunics, and one with a birthmark on his face—stood behind Heirik with swords drawn. More warriors waited behind them, at least twenty in sight, and many armed with bows. No doubt more were hiding in the trees and bushes. Razna snuck a glance at the dense thickets upstream. Perhaps even on their side of the river.

Flanking Heirik was an older man on the right, and an older woman on the left. The man watched the arrival impassively, while the woman shot Getherd a look of pure venom. The man beckoned to them and pointed to the cliff edge opposite. The High Thane sighed, climbed off his horse, and pushed through his men towards the waterfall. Razna slid off her mare and followed him over the slippery, uneven rocks.

'High Thane Getherd of Elborn!' the older man shouted over the falling water as they approached. 'I am glad to see the years have not dimmed you much!' He used Galatani.

'Nor you, Lord Sorveo Aventan!' Getherd shouted back. 'But I thought we were to meet on a field up there?' He pointed at the mountain top.

Aventan gestured at the horsemen. 'And I thought you were to come alone.'

Getherd shrugged. 'Plans can change.'

'Indeed, they can. However, Lady Razna is most welcome.' Lord Aventan bowed.

Razna nodded in response. They were only a couple of spans apart, but the gap plunged more than twenty spans into a foamy pool. She looked at Heirik.

He smiled again and gazed deep into her eyes. 'You are radiant, my she-wolf. It's been—'

An Aventan warrior jabbed Heirik with a sword pommel, and her Thane fell silent. He winked. Razna grinned.

'Are you well, nephew?' Getherd called out.

Heirik's smile tightened. 'I seem to have misplaced a finger, Uncle, but otherwise I'm in good enough health.'

The reminder filled Razna's heart with rage.

Lord Aventan gestured to the woman at Heirik's side. 'And this is my wife, the Lady Aventan.'

Getherd shook his head. 'Impossible!'

'Ha!' Lord Aventan patted Heirik's shoulder. 'Your nephew said the same.'

Lady Aventan glared at them over the abyss. Heirik scowled into the distance.

'But enough niceties,' Lord Aventan said. 'Let us commence negotiations.'

Getherd folded his arms. 'What do you want?'

'Make me Thane of Caeria in return for your nephew's life.'

'What? Don't be foolish!'

'Not *so* foolish, High Thane. Think about it. In this land, I can enforce your will far better than Heirik. You will have peace—and my loyalty. I'm sure you can find another use for the lad elsewhere. And I hear you have a daughter? Well, I have two sons, unmarried. Perhaps a union would seal our new friendship?'

Lady Aventan opened her mouth, as if to say something, but frowned at her husband instead.

'You insult me,' Getherd snarled. 'You can have silver and a pardon, and be grateful.'

The High Thane signalled to his men. The Rhenivians dragged forth three large sacks.

Lord Aventan nodded slowly. 'That's certainly a large quantity of *something*, High Thane. But I'm not sure it will be enough.'

'It will *never* be enough!' Lady Aventan cried out.

They all looked at her. Lord Aventan raised a hand as if to silence his wife. Heirik rolled his eyes.

'What are you talking about, woman?' Getherd shouted. 'I did not come to bargain with *you*.'

'How about this?' Lord Aventan called out. 'All that silver, High Thane, your pardon for myself and my family, and an official position as advisor to Thane Heirik? What do you say?'

Getherd shook his head. 'Your arrogance tries my patience.'

'How *can* you, Sorveo?' Lady Aventan shouted. 'Nothing replaces them. No silver, no title can repay the debt.'

'Debt? What debt?' Getherd waved his arms about. 'Control your wife's babbling tongue.'

Sorveo Aventan's face darkened. 'Oh, but there *is* a debt, High Thane. Three children's lives, thanks to you and your men. Our daughters and our youngest son.'

The two young men bearing swords stepped closer to Lord and Lady Aventan. They stared coldly at Getherd.

The High Thane threw his head back. '*Agh*! So, you demand silver for dead cowards. Shameful! I've had enough.' He turned away.

Almost as one, the Aventan stirred into a fury.

'Wait, High Thane!' Razna called. 'Please....'

Getherd waved her off. 'Don't you start now.' He clambered over the rocks towards the waiting Rhenivians.

'Your final chance, High Thane!' Lord Aventan shouted. 'Or I'll make another proposal.'

Getherd looked back. 'What now?'

Aventan stuck out his chin. 'I have sent some of my best warriors across the sea.'

'And?'

'They sailed on your ships, High Thane. On the return trip to Galatan. Even as we speak, they travel to your hall in Elborn, in Rhenivia, to await my instructions. If they hear you did not accept my terms, they are to take the lives of your family. Your wife, Herdi. Your son, Gethfen. And your daughter, Gethda. All of them.

Getherd strode to the cliff edge. 'You lie!'

'And if you *still* do not accept my terms, High Thane, we shall kill your dear nephew here.' The lord slapped Heirik on the arm. 'And finally, when all else is lost, we will kill you too. Thus, the debt shall be paid.'

'Utter nonsense!'

'As a kindness, we would spare Heirik—and you—for now.' Lord

Aventan grinned. 'You shall battle Zjandius and wear him down for us first.'

Getherd drew his axe. 'Is *this* your cunning plot? You won't even leave this forest alive.'

'What do you choose?'

'Enough!' Lady Aventan cried. She pulled out a dagger and plunged it into Heirik's chest.

Razna screamed, but no sound passed her lips.

The old woman stabbed Heirik again. Then a third time. It could have taken only a moment, and yet... a lifetime passed.

'The debt is paid,' Lady Aventan announced.

Heirik's grin perished on his lips. His eyes went wide, and he stared down at himself. Blood bloomed across his jerkin.

Getherd roared beside her. Lord Aventan shouted distantly. He was shouting at Lady Aventan.

Heirik looked up at Razna. He opened his mouth.

Lady Aventan shoved Heirik forward, and he toppled over the edge. His body twisted as he fell and his eyes found Razna's eyes and he held her eyes unblinking as he plunged down down with the falling water down into the foam, and was gone.

Getherd roared again. The Rhenivians screamed and charged.

The Aventan lifted their bows and swords.

Razna turned and ran.

She tripped, fell, and threw herself back to her feet and squeezed between the Rhenivians dashing around her. An arrow whistled past her ear. She stumbled onwards. She heard splashes of water, yells and screams, a clashing of metal and squealing of horses, but she did not look back. She reached the road and darted to the right, to the downhill slope.

Another arrow whizzed overhead.

Razna half-ran, half-skidded downwards, grabbing at low branches to slow herself. An arrow thudded into a tree trunk. She slipped and tumbled many spans before crashing into ferns and picking herself up to sprint onwards. She ran and ran. Her breath burned.

She found the river and pushed through the bracken to reach the bank. She sobbed and gasped as she looked upstream and downstream. There he was.

'Heirik!' she screamed.

Razna stumbled along the bank and waded into the river to reach him. Heirik floated face-down in an eddy, with his hands still tied and bandaged behind him. She flipped him over and pulled her Thane towards dry ground. Heirik faced the sky with eyes shut and the ghost of his usual smile. Blood oozed from his chest and tinted the water.

Razna stood over her Thane in the icy stream, clutching his arm, gazing upon him, her mouth twisted. She leaned down to kiss his pale lips, then looked about, sniffing and wiping her face. She grabbed smooth river stones, white as bone, and wedged them under the ropes across Heirik's chest, until he sank beneath the waters.

'Go now, Heirik son of Heiferth,' she whispered. 'Go now to your Flood Father, Corn Mother, your Wolf Lord—or wherever it is you belong. Go in peace, my love.'

Razna clambered onto the bank and gazed into the rippling stream where her Thane rested.

Footsteps thumped behind her, growing louder. The bushes rustled, and a hand gripped her shoulder.

Razna snatched her dagger from its sheath, spun about, and plunged the blade into the man.

Daga let out a gasp. The marshal blinked and gaped at her as he slid off the dagger to fall backwards to the ground, coughing blood.

Razna observed in silence as he passed. Shouts came from up the slope, then a loud blast of a horn. She flinched and ran away, into the forest.

CHAPTER FORTY-ONE

CAERIA — SUMMER'S REIGN — 437

Valcero's long march ended at a new fort, the biggest he had seen. More like a small city than a military camp. The guards herded them through the wooden gates set in an earthen dyke topped with a tall stockade. Inside was crammed with huts, tents, and thousands of Rhenivians milling about, eating, talking, sharpening axes and spears, arguing and punching each other into the mud. The noise and smell were a shock after weeks of walking. Many soldiers lay coughing and moaning in their tents. Valcero's own cough had cleared after days of fresh air and sunshine, though cuts and blisters covered his weary feet.

The guards left the Caerians in a pen beside the horses and sheep, under the full glare of the midday sun and amidst swarms of blue flies. The Caerians shook their limbs, slapped their arms, and spat the pests out of their mouths. After an hour, Valcero gave up and let the creatures crawl over him.

'You, boy!' A guard leaned over the fence.

Valcero clambered to his feet. 'Sir?' His lips cracked as he spoke.

'Go help the priest.' The guard jerked his thumb behind him and began to walk away.

'Uh…' Valcero stared after him.

The guard turned back. 'To the priest, boy!' He reached over the fence to lift Valcero out of the pen.

The boy landed on the other side, dizzy and lightheaded.

'And take a sheep.' The guard reached into the neighbouring corral and hauled out a lamb by the scruff of its neck.

The lamb bleated and kicked as the guard shoved it at Valcero. It weighed on his thin arms.

The boy looked about. 'Where's the priest, sir?'

The guard sighed and turned him around. He pointed to a wooden building, taller than the tents and huts that surrounded it. 'Over there, boy.' He squeezed Valcero's arm. 'Tell the priest you're hungry,' the man muttered.

Valcero stumbled off between the tents. Passing soldiers bumped and jostled him. The lamb cried and struggled, but the boy kept his grip on it.

When he came to the building of dark, stained wood, he stuck his head through the open door. 'Hello?' He crept inside.

The gloomy interior was lit only by a few guttering oil lamps along the walls and in the corners. Bare earth covered the floor, and the walls were undecorated. More lamps, along with sheafs of wheat and a few wrinkled apples, surrounded the base of a crude clay statue at the far end of the hall. It seemed to be of a woman, judging by its wide hips and enormous breasts, but the head was no more than an eyeless knob on the shoulders, topped by a coil of hair. But in the flickering shadows, it seemed as if the strange, squat thing could move, as if it might hop off its plinth and waddle towards him at any moment. Valcero raised his hand to flick his fingers.

'How can I help you, my boy?'

Valcero spun about. A Rhenivian man with thinning hair looked down at him with a gentle smile. He wore a long brown robe of rough wool.

'Uh, they said I must bring a lamb...'

'And I see you have, thank you.' The man reached out and stroked the lamb's curly flank. 'Could you help me? Let's put him somewhere safe for now.' He spoke perfect, though accented, Caerian. 'Follow me, please.'

Valcero went with him to a wooden post in the corner.

'Ah, let's see.' The man lifted the lamb out of Valcero's arms and set the creature on the floor. The beast tried to bolt, but he held it in place with a gentle grip. With his other hand, the Rhenivian grabbed a length of rope tied to the post and wrapped the other end around the lamb's neck. He knotted the loop in a few swift motions.

'There, that should hold him.' The man stood and caressed the lamb's head.

'Um, sir, what is that?' Valcero pointed at the statue.

'Ah, you are not familiar?' The man gently pushed Valcero's pointed finger down. 'This is our precious lady, the Corn Mother. She nourishes and protects all living things. This is Her temple, and I am Her servant, the keeper of Her house, Brother Frethi.' He bowed to the idol.

The statue's blank face somehow stared at Valcero.

The priest put his hand on the boy's shoulder. 'And what is your name, son?'

'Valcero, sir,' he replied.

'You look hungry, Valcero. Would you like some lunch?'

Valcero glanced outside. No one had called him back. 'Yes, please?'

'Right this way then, lad.' Brother Frethi shepherded him to another corner near the door. 'Take a seat, and I'll be back shortly.'

Valcero sat on the cool, packed soil and waited. Sweat trickled down his back. The lamb bleated softly and tugged on the rope.

'Ah, here we go.' Frethi returned, holding a bowl in one hand and a cup in the other.

Several priests followed him inside, all carrying bowls and cups. They all sat down to make a circle with Valcero and Frethi. The priest handed Valcero the bowl of stew and the cup of water.

The boy inhaled the rich scent. 'Thank you, sir.' His hands shook.

'Oh, don't thank me, son,' the priest replied. 'Thank the Corn Mother. She's the source of all nourishment.'

Valcero smiled and nodded.

'Go on.' Brother Frethi nudged him. 'Thank Her.' He looked to the idol at the other end of the room.

Valcero examined the priest, then the idol. He bowed his head at it. 'Thank you, Corn Mother.' Was that enough?

Frethi chuckled. 'Ah, you will have to learn the correct way.'

He held his hands over the food, and—as one—the other priests did the same. The Rhenivians bowed their heads and muttered. The prayer went on for a while, as the steam from each bowl wafted between their fingers. Finally, they raised their heads and began to eat. Valcero joined in, shovelling the warm stew into his mouth. He glanced up and found Brother Frethi watching him.

The priest grinned. 'You're certainly *very* hungry.'

Valcero shrugged and smiled. 'Yes, sir.' He scooped up more food.

When the meal was finished, the priests gathered up the dirty crockery and left, apart from a pair who remained with Frethi and Valcero.

'Now,' announced Brother Frethi, 'our most important task. Come with me, Valcero.'

They returned to the lamb and the Corn Mother. Brother Frethi untied the creature and carried it to an open patch of earth just in front of the idol, marked with a circle of white pebbles. The priest lowered the lamb into the circle.

'Could you hold him for me, Valcero?'

The boy grabbed the animal as it tried to run. Frethi drew out a knife from his robes, while the other two priests stood at his sides and began to chant. Valcero tensed. Frethi knelt and gripped the lamb by the scruff of its neck.

'Just hold his back legs like that, Valcero,' the priest said. 'Yes, like that.' Frethi joined the chanting, while gazing up at the Corn Mother.

The lamb wriggled in their grasp. The voices made Valcero dizzy. How long would it last?

And then, without warning, Frethi plunged the knife into the lamb's neck. It squealed and thrashed. The priest slowly dragged the blade along the animal's neck, sending rivulets of blood through its white wool and dripping onto the dark earth.

Valcero watched, frozen.

The lamb kicked out a leg, shivered, and collapsed.

The other priests stopped chanting and knelt beside their leader. Frethi pushed a finger into the bloody earth and raised it to daub a vertical line on his forehead. He dipped his finger again and painted dark lines on the other priests. He dipped his finger a fourth time and reached out to Valcero.

The boy shrank away. Frethi frowned, and Valcero froze again. The priest ran his finger down Valcero's forehead. The boy felt warm liquid running into his eyebrows. Then Frethi arose and took the lifeless lamb in his arms. He uttered more Rhenivian and bowed low to the idol. The priests repeated his words in a soft monotone. Frethi held the corpse out above the Corn Mother, so that blood dripped onto the statue and trickled down its empty face.

'Thank you, Valcero, you may depart.' Brother Frethi said, still facing the statue. 'I'll see you again tomorrow before noon, with a fresh lamb. We have so many more sins to wash away.'

Valcero climbed to his feet, avoiding the other priests' eyes. 'Yes, sir,' he mumbled and backed out of the temple.

He shivered outside in the bright light. He could not lose his lunch. He must not. The boy sucked in some breaths and walked between the tents. He checked that no priests were in sight, then spat on his hand and rubbed his forehead.

He noticed two Rhenivian soldiers eyeing him from inside a nearby tent. They looked vaguely familiar—perhaps soldiers from the old camp? They whispered to each other. Valcero bowed his head and hurried off.

Valcero awoke with a shout, breathing in ragged gasps.

'Shhh.' Another slave prodded him, then rolled over and fell back to sleep.

The boy stared up at the heavens awash with stars, but all he could see were knives and blood, hooves stamping him into the mud, a strange, squat woman, naked and bloodied, peering at him in the dark. His rattling heart slowed.

He lay on the dewy ground, under the rag that was his blanket, amongst the other sleeping slaves. He listened to their snores and breathing, the snickering horses and sheep, and, coming through the still air, the mutterings and sighs, coughs and whispers of thousands of soldiers crowded around him, either asleep or wishing they could be. A cricket chirped somewhere.

When Valcero awoke, it was to a chorus of horns from the tower. The slaves scrambled upright in the grey dawn light and peered over the fence. Valcero crouched amongst them. An answering fanfare came faintly over the fortress walls.

'Do you think it's Thane Heirik?' a slave woman asked.

'Probably,' another woman answered.

Valcero's blood froze.

'I don't think so,' a man said. 'I heard he was kidnapped by Torecti weeks ago.'

Valcero looked at him. 'How did it happen?'

The man shrugged. 'I don't know. Just heard it from another Caerian at my old camp.'

The gates groaned open, and a multitude of Rhenivian horsemen trotted inside, bearing black banners with a red boar.

'By the One,' a slave whispered. '*More* of them! Where are they all going to fit?'

At the front, on a dark, rust-red stallion, rode a giant of a man, with a black fur cloak draped over his broad shoulders, and two great axes strapped to his back. He sported a long, white beard and a bald head covered in intricate tattoos.

The welcoming Rhenivians bowed as he approached and swung off his horse. The newcomer paced about the dusty clearing and examined the fort with piercing blue eyes.

'Who's that?' someone whispered above Valcero.

'Don't know,' the woman replied. 'Definitely not Heirik. He's too old.' She sniggered.

Another man shushed her. 'That's High Thane Getherd. I wouldn't get on his bad side if I were you.'

'Getherd?'

'Yes, Heirik's uncle. A mean bastard from what I've heard.'

'So it's in the blood then?'

'Ha.'

Getherd began shouting in Rhenivian.

'What's he saying?' the woman whispered. 'Does anyone know?'

'I speak a little Straw-head,' one of the slave men muttered. 'It sounds like bad news.'

As Getherd continued, the Rhenivians burst out in groans and sighs. The fort echoed with hundreds of people chattering at once.

'What?' another Caerian said. 'What's going on?'

'He says Thane Heirik is dead.'

'What? Really?'

'Yes, killed by "Caerian treachery", he says.'

'Oh, by the gods, that's not good for *us*, stuck in here with these people.'

Getherd roared, and the fort fell into silence. He yelled sharp, guttural words, then raised his fist, revealing bloody rags wrapped around his arm.

The Rhenivians responded with cheers and applause.

The Caerians huddled around their compatriot who understood Rhenivian.

'He says the time for mourning Heirik comes later. For now, he is taking command. Together, they will avenge Heirik, defeat the Caerians, and make this land their own—forever.'

Within an hour of the High Thane's arrival, all Caerians were taken from their usual duties and sent to the north side of the fort. The guards ordered the slaves to dig up earth and pile it against an inner section of the dyke. A long ramp slowly took shape, leading up to the wooden stockade.

As they dug and hauled soil, other soldiers worked atop the ramp at the stockade wall. Some hacked at the bases of the poles with axes, though not quite cutting through the wood. Others climbed the inner scaffolding and lashed ropes to the fence above each side of the ramp. It was hard work under the summer sun, but better than another visit to the temple.

'What are we making here?' the slaves asked each other.

'Who knows?' was the typical whispered reply. 'Who can understand the minds of Rhenivians?'

The guards supervised and beat any Caerian who was not digging fast enough. Valcero bent low and focused on the black soil that he scooped up with his hands and dumped into a wooden bucket.

After some hours, Valcero felt thirsty, so he went to the nearest guard and bowed. 'Please, sir. May I have some water?'

'Water?' The guard looked him up and down, then shrugged. 'Yes, fine. Over there.' He pointed to a nearby well.

The well was no more than a deep hole, with a faint shimmer of water a few spans down the shaft. The boy lowered a bucket on a rope until he heard a splash and a gurgle, then hauled it back to the surface. The silty water came with a faint odour of rotten eggs.

He studied the earthworks as he slurped water out of his cupped hands. Was it another gate? What did it matter?

Two soldiers were talking to the guard, who suddenly turned and pointed at Valcero. The soldiers strode towards him with grim faces—the very same Rhenivians who watched him from the tent yesterday. Valcero turned to run, but the soldiers grabbed him by the arms.

'What did I do?' he asked.

Everyone watched.

'Help!' Valcero cried out. 'Someone? Please?'

A soldier swung his fist into the boy's face. Valcero's head spun as he fell. They dragged him away. Valcero hung limp between them. This was it. This was the end. A tear rolled down his cheek.

The guards hauled him up some steps, then dropped him on a wooden platform. Valcero lifted his aching head.

High Thane Getherd sat on a chair under the eaves of the great hall, surrounded by Rhenivian soldiers. Getherd cradled a great axe in his hands. They all stared down at the boy. Eventually, the High Thane said something to Valcero in Rhenivian—a question, perhaps. When he did not answer, Getherd repeated himself.

'I am sorry, sir,' Valcero said. 'I do not understand.'

The Rhenivian sighed. Valcero heard the name "Frethi". A soldier ran off, while several others began speaking. They pointed at the boy and nodded vigorously.

The steps creaked, and Brother Frethi appeared beside Valcero. The priest bowed to Getherd, exchanged words, then turned to the boy. 'Good day, Valcero. We missed you at the temple.'

Valcero said nothing.

'I am told you wrote a letter for Thane Heirik,' Brother Frethi said.

The boy swallowed.

'What words did you put in that letter, exactly?'

'I don't know,' Valcero replied. His eyes roamed the swirling grain in the wooden boards.

The priest said something to the High Thane, who leaned forward and slammed the butt of his axe against the floor. Valcero flinched. A damp warmth spread in his loincloth. Getherd growled more words, then soldiers hauled Valcero to his feet.

The boy trembled. 'What…what's happening?'

'They are taking you away, Valcero,' Frethi replied. 'To a place where you can think for a while.'

Getherd waved his hand irritably. The soldiers dragged the boy off the platform and through the cramped maze of tents and huts to the only stone building in the fort, the squat tower against the stockade. The soldiers hauled Valcero inside, pushed open an iron gate, and tossed him into a cell.

The bolts clanked into place. The footsteps died away. Valcero was alone in the dark.

CHAPTER FORTY-TWO

CAERIA – SUMMER'S REIGN – 437

'Do you remember this place?' Zjandius asked.

'How could I forget?' Terzjin replied.

From where they sat on their horses on the hill crest, the Emperor and Master Maltorus surveyed what had once been an empty valley. The Rhenivian stronghold, Heiriksreld, rose like an ant heap at its centre. Terzjin remembered the waves of Rhenivians pouring over the hill years ago. He shivered and let out a breath. Now, all those Rhenivians were packed inside that ring of earth and wood.

The rest of the cantaris came marching up the slope behind them.

It had taken more than a month for the Caerians to set out from Etorium. Firstly, the business of reorganising the city and surrounding villages, of the Emperor re-establishing his authority. Then they had to recruit more cantare—mostly light infantry—to fortify their numbers. Without much time for training, the generals took on veterans—many paunched and grey-bearded.

Meanwhile, they waited for Lord Octerian to return from Lastria with his own cantaris. The Octerian faced similar problems, gathering old, out-of-practice soldiers from amongst their people. In the end, they came marching up the inner-west coast with fewer than a thousand cantare to add. Riders went out to Impona in the northwest to call on Lord Eledan, but everyone agreed it would take too long for his forces to arrive.

'Besides,' Lord Octerian had muttered just before he left Etorium by ship, 'we all know Eledan has been hedging his bets. He won't move until it's clear who's winning.'

They also sent scouts to seek out the Aventan, but no one knew where they were hiding. The couriers returned empty-handed, save for welcome news that Admiral Getaelon had sunk the Rhenivian fleet off Lastria.

On top of these challenges, the omens had been poor. Strange flights of birds had crossed over the palace roof in the days following the liberation. At Emperor Zjandius' request, augurs had combed through piles of dead geese and doves in search of the right signs, only to shrug their shoulders and shake their heads. Astrologers scoured charts and almanacs for the perfect alignments of stars, moons, and wanderers—with little success.

Some generals had counselled caution, arguing it would be better to wait, train and equip more cantare—now that they had captured most of Caeria, Getherd's ships were destroyed, and time was on their side. Other generals counselled the opposite. Each day they waited only increased the chances that the Rhenivians could organise new boats and send relief. What's more, news came that Getherd was scraping the countryside bare to stock his granaries. Whatever they could not carry to Heiriksreld, the Rhenivians burnt and tore down behind them. Famine could arrive with the winter.

Emperor Zjandius favoured the second point of view, perhaps because he was impatient to end the war and bring Nanepti to Caeria before their child was born—as he confided to Terzjin one evening. And so, when a diviner found auguries that were ambiguous rather than outright doom-laden, Zjandius ordered the cantare to pack up their tents, load the wagons, and march north.

And here they were, on the eve of Summer's Fall, at an old battlefield revisited. Heiriksreld. Terzjin glowered at the fort as Master Meretan, the other generals, and lenotare joined them on the hilltop. Rhenivian horns sounded from the ramparts. The few distant figures took flight inside, and the gates swung shut. The valley fell into silence.

'They are prepared,' Lord Corilien muttered from his chariot.

Zjandius frowned. 'They had too much time.'

'It is a well-designed fort,' Colus said, 'At least, by Rhenivian standards. Wooden walls, yes, but the earthen dykes will be impervious to our siege engines.'

'The wood will burn, though, will it not?' the Emperor asked.

'Oh, of course, Your Majesty. Your cantare will just have a hard time scrambling over the slopes they have piled up. We should attack through the gate.'

Prince Astulus Vaecerion pointed. 'They built it so that the river washes along the southern edge. It would be doubly difficult to attack from that side.'

'And it seems they have only one gate,' a general remarked. 'On the eastern side.'

Zjandius nodded. 'Then we shall concentrate there.'

The cantaris descended the hill and forded the river through some boggy shallows to the east of Heiriksreld, all the while poised for an attack from the fort. Yet none came.

Colus Meretan peered through his telescope at the guards who patrolled the stockade. 'They are watching us.'

'Finish your measurements as soon as possible,' the Emperor ordered his engineer.

They set up a camp facing the gate and surrounded it with a barrier of brush and branches. The soldiers went to gather wood from a grove in a vale to the north east, but a cloud of starlings rose from the trees and dived upon the woodcutters. The birds pecked and mobbed the men until they retreated. After all the poor omens, the Caerians decided to leave the grove well alone. The cantare kept their armour as they pitched their tents so they could form ranks at a moment's notice.

Hemadir and the scouts returned from their exploration of the countryside.

'No sign of other Rhenivians nearby,' the sand prince reported. He pointed to the fortress. 'They must all be inside. But we did catch sight of another band of soldiers marching over from the west. They *look* like Caerians, though too far away to be certain.'

'So, Lord Eledan comes to our aid after all?' the Emperor wondered aloud in his tent.

Hemadir shrugged. 'They are perhaps a day's march from here, Your Majesty, so you will know soon.'

'We visited two villages over the hills,' a Caerian scout reported. 'Their granaries are bare, their fields and orchards stripped, their sheep, cows and geese taken. The villagers are grateful for their lives, and little else.'

Zjandius sat on a simple stool for his throne. 'Could they share any useful information?'

'Yes, sir. The Rhenivians have probably double our numbers—perhaps even three times as many. And at least half of their soldiers are cavalry.'

The Emperor nodded as he listened. 'They would need much hay to feed so many horses. This siege cannot endure long. We should expect an attack before they starve.'

After the meeting, the sand prince took Terzjin aside. 'My horse grows slow and fat from all this grass, Terzjin Maltorus, but I'm still a little disappointed.' He winked.

'Oh, why's that?'

'I thought the grass would be greener,' Hemadir replied. 'This looks more like the desert lands I know.'

'It turns yellow and dies as summer progresses,' Terzjin said. He gazed out of the tent towards the fortress, dark and shimmering in the afternoon heat.

That night, Terzjin dreamt of deserts and fires burning in dark holes in the sand. A swirling cloud of starlings and blackbirds rises out of the flames, and turns and swoops in the sky above. He stands in their forest, in their grove of trees between the hills. Without warning, the cloud of birds falls upon him like a wave striking a rock. A thousand wings beat against him in a twittering rush.

And, standing with him amidst the wind and feathers, is Illauri-of-the-Woods, gazing up to the heavens. She turns to him and smiles. Terzjin reaches out to her, but she steps away, just beyond his grasp, almost fading into the whirling flock.

Her whisper thunders in his ears. 'Have courage, Terzjin Maltorus. Do what you know to be right.'

He jerked awake on his mat, gasping for breath. Beyond the tent flaps, the sun peeped over the horizon, tinting the sky a rosy hue. Zjandius snored quietly in his bed at the other end of the tent.

Avenge us.

Master Maltorus stretched and yawned, then padded outside to find water. The camp was only beginning to stir.

'Nothing from the fortress?' Terzjin asked a cantarus at the barrel.

'No, sir. They sleep like the dead.'

A few hours after breakfast, a trumpet sounded from the hilltops. Not a Rhenivian horn, but something distinctly Caerian. Another cantaris crested the hill and marched down. Everyone in the camp ran to see who approached. The cantaris carried no banner, and their round shields were unmarked.

Terzjin hurried to Emperor Zjandius. 'General Divendrion is here!'

Cheers burst forth as old friends rushed to embrace. The General led his soldiers to the edge of camp, where Emperor Zjandius received him.

Divendrion bowed with his helmet tucked under his arm. 'Your Majesty, we report for duty.'

Zjandius grinned. 'A welcome sight, and a very overdue reunion, General. Come, sit with me.'

The Emperor led Divendrion towards his tent. As he passed Terzjin, the General's face clouded. He nodded in greeting and hurried after his Emperor.

Zjandius sat and ordered refreshments. 'I know a little from what Master Maltorus reported, but please, tell me everything. How did you get here?'

Divendrion took a seat opposite. 'Emperor, we have been raiding the Rhenivian camps in the west, with the Torecti's help. Whichever camps lay close to the forest, we struck—and generally with great success.' He glanced briefly at Terzjin. 'One day, we attacked a camp, but found it empty, seemingly abandoned. The next day, we tried another and found it deserted as well. We began to venture further from the Nedolian Forest, only to discover more Rhenivian strongholds without Rhenivians. The local citizens told us the invaders had marched eastwards. We congratulated ourselves, thinking we had driven off the straw-heads.' He smiled and sipped wine with the Emperor. 'A while later, word reached us that Your Majesty had returned to Caeria—no longer a king, but an Emperor.' He raised his cup and knocked it against Zjandius'. 'So, we decided it was time to join our comrades. As we marched, we gathered more volunteers, bringing our number to nearly a thousand. We also learned that you all had left Etorium and were coming here, so we decided to do the same.'

'I am glad you are here,' Zjandius said. 'And glad you are alive and well, not to mention your efforts over the years.'

Divendrion sipped more wine. 'Highness, to be honest, I was not sure this day would ever come. But I am glad to be wrong.'

'If I may be honest as well,' Zjandius replied, 'there were *many* days when I thought the same. Here is to being wrong in the best way possible.' They clinked their cups again. Zjandius swallowed and grimaced. 'But the day is not over, I am afraid. We have cornered the wolves in their lair, but there are many of them, many more of them than us—and they have teeth! I am glad to have your numbers to bolster us. We will need every measure of strength, fortitude, and cunning if we are to win.'

The Emperor dismissed Divendrion. Master Maltorus followed.

'General!' Terzjin called out. 'A word?'

Divendrion stopped outside. His shoulders slumped.

Terzjin rounded to face him. 'You didn't tell a complete tale, did you, sir? I could see it on your face.'

'Ah, Master Maltorus...' Divendrion rubbed his forehead. 'I wanted to speak privately about that.'

'Yes?'

'I... uh... have some bad news.'

Terzjin's blood turned cold. He stepped closer. 'What?'

'The boy...' The general avoided his eyes. 'He... Look, I *strictly* forbade him from joining us on raids—'

Master Maltorus shot out his hand and grabbed Divendrion by the collar of his tunic. The general yelped.

'Terzjin!' Zjandius barked out from behind.

Bystanders surrounded them, gaping in shock and confusion. The Emperor had emerged from his tent and glared with arms folded.

Terzjin released Divendrion. 'Tell me what happened,' he whispered.

'He dressed up as a cantarus,' the general replied, almost babbling. 'He snuck into our raiding party when it was dark and no one was looking. By the time we realised the boy was with us, we were right at the camp—too late to turn back. I *swear* to you, we kept him safe, away from the fighting. But then another bunch of the cursed straw-heads ambushed us, so we had to flee. And in the chaos, we lost him.'

Zjandius came to listen.

Terzjin scowled. 'What do you mean, you *lost* him?' Did you look for Valcero?'

'Yes, yes!' Divendrion swallowed. 'We went back later, when it was quiet, but there was no trace of him. The Torecti used all their woodcraft, but found nothing. Our best guess... well, we had made a funeral pyre after the battle. And it seems the Rhenivians tossed more bodies into the flames after their counterattack—all our people they struck down. I... I'm so sorry, Master Maltorus. It broke our hearts, sir, every one of us. Believe me. The Torecti sang for him. They send their condolences—Reito, Illauri, all of them.'

Terzjin's hands began to tremble.

Avenge us.

'Please, sir,' Divendrion beseeched him. 'If I could have sent him back to safety, I would have done anything...'

Master Maltorus stared at the fortress. His whole body shook.

'Terzjin...' the Emperor murmured.

Colus Meretan walked past and stopped. 'What's going on?'

'The Rhenivians killed him, Colus,' Terzjin replied, unable to look at the engineer. 'Valcero is dead.' The words tasted strange and monstrous in his mouth.

'What?' Master Meretan blinked and shook his head. He backed away. 'No. No.' He looked around. 'No.' He scratched his neck and stared at the ground. 'No.'

'Terzjin,' the Emperor murmured again.

He spun around to face Zjandius. '*I will kill every one of them*!' he shouted. He jabbed his finger at Heiriksreld. '*Every last one!*'

'Master Maltorus!' Zjandius scowled. 'With me!' He pointed at his tent and strode inside.

Terzjin stumbled after, boiling in his heart.

Zjandius flopped into his throne. 'You *cannot* speak to your Emperor that way. Not in front of everyone. Do you understand? You *cannot*, Terzjin.'

Master Maltorus breathed heavily. 'Let me go there tonight. After dark, while they sleep. Just... let me go inside, and I will deal with Thane Heirik and whoever else—'

'*Deal* with them? As they tried to *deal* with me? As you tried to *deal* with them before?'

Terzjin gazed at him, still wheezing.

Zjandius shook his head. 'We'll do things the proper way, the honourable way. We must be better.'

'Better?' Terzjin held up his hands. 'Honourable? Zjandius, these people have destroyed so much. They burn, they rape, they pillage. They *murder*. There's no honour for them.'

Avenge us.

Zjandius stood up. 'I am the Emperor, Master Maltorus!' he nearly shouted. 'You shall obey me and do your *duty*, sir. I am sorry for your loss. For your *losses*—all of them—I truly am. But these tragedies are all too commonplace. The Rhenivians must face justice for *every* crime they have committed, not only those against you. We have an entire realm to serve, an entire *people*, Terzjin. Do you understand? Our duty to them comes first. Your duty to *me* comes first.'

Terzjin buried his head in his hands. He wanted to scream.

Avenge us.

'Your Majesty?'

They both looked to the entrance. Master Meretan stood there, quite still. His face was calm and pale, like a waxen mask.

'My apologies, Majesty,' Colus said, voice quivering. 'I could not help but overhear... Well, I can adjust my calculations.'

The Emperor frowned. 'What are you talking about, Master Meretan?'

'The calculations for the siege engines, sir. Instead of hitting the walls, I can ensure we fling the pots *over* the ramparts and into the fort.' Colus breathed out and stared into the distance. 'We should have enough tecnaris to annihilate... everything inside.'

Terzjin looked to Zjandius and nodded. 'Yes! Like that, yes.'

'What?' Zjandius shook his head.' No! Absolutely not, Master Meretan.'

'Well, I...' Colus looked at the ground. 'I just thought I should suggest it, sir. The boy was, was very... important to me too.'

The Emperor rubbed his face. 'Colus, I *forbid* it. If you were eavesdropping, then everything I said to Terzjin applies to you, too. Understood?'

Master Meretan nodded.

'Please, leave us,' Zjandius said.

Colus nodded again and stumbled from the tent with his head bowed.

'Look at me, Terzjin.' Zjandius held out his hands. 'Look at me. Remember what I said before. The living? Or the dead?'

CHAPTER FORTY-THREE

CAERIA – SUMMER'S REIGN – 437

Valcero sat and tried to cry, but no tears remained. The Rhenivians brought no food, nor water. They had not come in for at least a day. His eyes had adjusted to the dim light from the barred door, revealing a windowless cell and sandy floor. The walls were built of rough stones held together by grit and mortar. He leaned against the wall. It was cool and quiet, at least.

Something crawled through the bottom of the gate and scurried over the sand. A mouse. Valcero's stomach ached. Could he eat a mouse?

He stalked towards the rodent, which stood on its haunches to sniff the air. But the creature must have caught his scent, for it shot through a hole in the opposite wall, out of sight.

Was he even *quick* enough to catch a mouse?

Footsteps scuffed over the sand, and a silhouette appeared at the doorway.

Valcero crouched in the shadows. Was this the end?

'Valcero?' the figure whispered. It was the priest, Brother Frethi. 'Are you awake, son?'

The boy did not move.

'I have brought food and water. I thought you may be hungry by now.'

Valcero's stomach gurgled loudly. He couldn't help it.

Brother Frethi chuckled. 'It is only bread and water.'

The boy arose and hobbled to the gate.

'Here you go.' The priest passed a small loaf and a cup through the bars.

'Thank you,' Valcero whispered. He threw his head back to drain the cup in a single gulp. It was muddy well water, but still, water. He devoured the bread in chunks.

The priest leaned against the bars, close enough that his eyes and mouth were just visible. 'You are *very* hungry, aren't you? The High Thane wanted you to starve before the interrogation, but I interceded. The Corn Mother can be merciful even to the most wayward, and so should we.'

Valcero chewed. The bread turned to the sweetest honey in his mouth.

'I want to be truthful with you, Valcero. The situation is not promising.' Frethi sighed. 'High Thane Getherd is angry—very angry. He wants to see you punished as much as possible.'

'I didn't do anything.'

'Please, my boy, I'm trying to help you. A confession and plea for mercy may be your best hope.'

'But—'

'Do you realise Thane Heirik *died* because of you?'

'What?'

'Yes,' the priest replied, 'Getherd lost his precious nephew, all because of you.'

'I didn't want that.' Valcero's heart beat faster. Was he a murderer?

'I know you didn't *want* it to happen, my son, but our actions have consequences.'

'If I *did* do this thing, what would happen if I confessed?'

The priest reached through the bars. 'Take my hand, Valcero. Confess now, and unburden yourself.'

The boy hesitated, then stepped closer. He rested a hand on Frethi's calloused palm. It was a little sweaty.

'Yes, actions do have consequences, Valcero, but if you confess, your heart will be clean and light before you face them. So, tell me what you did.'

'Wait, what do you mean?'

'Tell me, Valcero.'

The boy pulled his hand away. The priest tried to grab him, but the boy stepped out of reach.

'Confess, Valcero!' Frethi snapped.

'No!'

The priest sighed and slid down the bars into a crouch. His face was lost in the shadows. 'You are proud and wilful, do you know that? Punishment is what you deserve. And punishment is what you shall receive. I tried to save you, boy, but I cannot help those who cannot help themselves.'

Valcero backed away.

'They will let you starve, until you are too weak to resist,' Frethi continued. 'Then they will drag you out, and they will hurt you, my son. They will hurt you in ways you have never imagined. All the ancient punishments shall be meted out upon you. Do you know what it is to be flayed?'

Valcero bumped into the wall. He slid down onto the sand and began to sob.

'Tears will not save you now, boy.' The priest arose and strode away.

Valero sniffed and wiped his nose. He was alone. All alone.

Valcero sat against the wall, hugging his knees. Aulix and Praehenna came to mind. Would they hurt a child? Would they hurt *him*? No, it was impossible—he knew it. There must have been a mistake. But he was going to die here, and Praehenna and Aulix would never know he believed them. That he loved them. A tear rolled down his cheek.

The mouse crept out of the shadows again. It sniffed the sand and crawled towards the doorway. Pathetic little thing. Weak, cowardly thing. Valcero grabbed a fistful of grit and flung it at the creature. But the mouse was too fast and dashed back to its hole.

The boy glared and sniffed. Where was it running off to, anyway?

He crawled over to the other wall and lay on his stomach. The hole was just wide enough to push his hand through. A cool draught blew against his fingers. What about scorpions? Valcero jerked his arm back and scrambled to his feet.

Datet's face, screaming.

Another draught brushed against his cheek. He found the hole higher up in the rough brick, stones and pebbles—a hole only wide enough for a few fingers. He pressed his eye against the gap, but saw nothing but darkness. He put his ear to it, hearing only a faint sound of wind and the fortress outside.

Valcero prodded the stonework. Could he? Might he?

He picked at the shoddy, crumbling mortar. He heard a pebble fall and hit the sand. He scratched until his fingernails were chipped and bleeding. He slapped the wall. It was impossible. Hopeless. He dropped to his knees. He was useless. It was all useless. There was nothing left to do but wait for the end.

No. His heart said no. He could not. He only needed a tool. What would Master Meretan say? He needed the right tool for the task. But if the *right* tool wasn't available, then *any* tool was better than nothing.

The pebble. Of course. Valcero scrabbled in the dirt for the stone and found the hole again. He tried scraping the pebble between two bricks, but it was too big. He tried hitting it against the stonework, but that did nothing except make noise. Valcero dropped the pebble. Something else. Anything else.

The boy stood in the dark for a time. Another thing. Anything. He reached up and touched the copper band—so easily forgotten—around his neck. He pushed his fingers between the metal and his neck, and pulled. He pulled some more, but it was no use. Think for a moment.

For countless days, Valcero had seen the bands around other people's necks. A pin held the looped ends together. He found the loops at the nape of his neck. Could he push the pin out? Maybe. No, too tight. They used a hammer to knock it into place. But it was only copper. Master Meretan had taught him about copper. People use it for everything—all kinds of tools, weapons, and crafts—because it's a soft metal, easy to shape. But it's a soft metal, so... also easy to bend and break. That's why we add tin, to make it bronze.

The boy wrapped his hands around the band on each side of the loop. He pushed with one fist and pulled with the other. He tried pulling his hands apart. He twisted the band in every direction. The metal squeezed against his throat, but he would not stop. It was bending, slowly but surely, giving way. He grunted and strained. Don't stop. Keep at it.

He heard a faint pop as the pin fell out.

'Hah!' The boy grinned in the dark. He pulled on the band again and, without much effort, bent it open, releasing it from his neck. Was it really that easy?

He ran his thumbs over the loops. They were narrow and sharp enough. He dug an end into the mortar. He knocked, gouged, and chipped at the crumbling grit. The noise was loud, but no matter.

The first stone tumbled out of the wall. Then another and another. Before long, Valcero could reach inside and pull on the masonry, wiggling it, loosening it. Piece by piece, the wall broke away, until—suddenly—a huge chunk fell out and thumped on the sand. The boy sprang back to save his toes. Was the wall about to collapse? Would the tower crush him? He trembled in the dark, breathing heavily. Waiting.

But nothing more fell. Valcero lived, for a while longer. He crept forward and felt about. The hole was bigger now, enough for him crouch and squeeze through. So, he did.

The hollow between the walls was less than two cubits wide, just enough to sidle along. He looked up. A faint light shone in through another hole, maybe three or four spans above. A few wooden beams stretched between the walls, perhaps for support. Could he climb them? Perhaps he could wait for nightfall, wriggle through the outlet, and escape?

But how would he climb down on the other side? And what if someone caught him out there? He still had to escape the fort.

Enough.

Terzjin would tell him that those are tomorrow's problems, and await tomorrow's solutions. Assuming Master Maltorus would tell him anything at all. He didn't care about Valcero, did he?

The boy froze. Voices came through the hole from the passageway beyond the cell. Someone shouted and banged on the bars. The bolts slid back, and the door creaked. Shoes crunched on the sand. The men shouted in Rhenivian. One came to the hole and yelled into the hollow space.

The boy said nothing. He pressed a hand over his mouth and kept still. Don't move. Don't move. Don't move.

The footsteps hurried away. He shuffled to the hole, just as the gate slammed shut. Wait here. Keep quiet. Don't move.

It seemed only moments later when the men returned, with a flickering glow of torches. Valcero edged away from the hole, until a wooden beam blocked him.

Someone shoved a burning torch inside. The burst of light dazzled the boy as a head popped into view—a bearded Rhenivian. The man looked both ways and caught sight of Valcero. The soldier scowled at the boy, reached for him, but he was too far away. The man said something and beckoned to Valcero.

The boy's heart thumped. He shook his head.

The man shouted. Valcero trembled and wedged himself under the beam. The Rhenivian disappeared, and muttered voices came through the hole. A moment of silence. Then the torch flared back into sight, along with a speartip that poked and prodded in Valcero's direction. The boy nearly screamed, but jammed his mouth shut. No, the spear could not get him. The iron tip banged uselessly against the masonry. Another soldier looked inside and tried to aim the spear, without success. The space was simply too narrow. The soldier snarled and swore.

A giggle burst through Valcero's lips. He couldn't help it.

'Stupid boy!' the soldier yelled. 'Come out here now, stupid boy! We kill you, stupid boy!'

They flung stones at Valcero. One hit him on the thigh. Another on the cheek. Valcero yelped and threw up his arm. A pebble struck his side. He squeezed under the beam. The walls narrowed, nearly crushing his chest, but he moved out of range of their stones. The soldiers screamed and cursed some more, then retired. The gate clanged shut.

Valcero had won the first battle, it seemed.

But it was not long before the gate opened again. More low voices, then a whistle. Something padded over the sand, panting and sniffing into the hole and then dim shapes sprang at Valcero. Two snarling, barking hunting hounds. The space echoed as if an entire pack were chasing him between the walls.

Valcero panicked and grabbed a wooden beam. He pulled himself up, then reached for another. There had to be another. Oh, by the Lord of Death, please...

A soldier shoved a torch and his head into the hollow to watch. The orange light lit up his grinning, wild-eyed face. Amongst the dancing shadows, the two dogs scrabbled over each other and leapt up at Valcero, all snapping jaws, flinging spittle, snarling eyes, stiff ears and black fur.

One dog clamped its jaws on the hem of Valcero's tunic, nearly yanking the boy off the beam. He screamed and grasped for any crevice his fingers could find. The dog thrashed its head. The fabric ripped, and the boy was free. There was another beam, up there. Valcero stretched and clutched the wood. He tucked his legs against his stomach, away from the fangs and claws.

The soldier saw everything, and his grin soured to a scowl. He cursed and withdrew, leaving Valcero to the dark. The soldiers shouted at each other behind the wall, while the dogs barked and whined. Their claws scratched against the masonry below. Valcero's arms ached. He hauled himself onto the wood.

Eventually, the Rhenivians whistled for their dogs and left, not before delivering threats and parting insults.

The second battle was won.

'Valcero?' a voice came from beneath, flat and cold in the stony space. 'Valcero, my boy, why don't you come down and we can talk?'

'What do you want, Brother Frethi?' Valcero called out.

'Why, to *help* you, my son!' the priest replied. 'That's all I have ever wanted. You made some mistakes, my boy, but it's nothing that we cannot solve—together.'

The boy said nothing.

'Please, Valcero. You must be starving and thirsty after all this time. I have water, cheese, bread. Some fruit. You must rest and recover your strength.'

Cheese. Valcero's stomach ached. He licked his dry, cracked lips. Sparks of colour bloomed and wheeled before his eyes.

'Don't you want to lay down your head, my boy? Come. Come to me, and all will be well.'

'I ... I don't trust you.'

There was a sigh. 'That hurts me, Valcero. It really does. You see, I am your only hope left in this world.'

'What do you mean?'

'The Caerians were defeated, my boy. The war is over. Your ... *emperor* is dead. His army lies broken and scattered. Rhenivia reigns over this land, and it always will. Surrender, my boy. Choose *life*!'

It couldn't be. Surely? 'I don't believe you!' Valcero shouted down into the dark. 'You don't know them. You don't know how clever the Emperor and Master Meretan are. You don't know how ... how strong Terzjin is, and Admiral Getaelon, and all the others!'

'Ah, so you know them?' the priest replied. 'That is *very* interesting.'

'No! I ... I never said that.'

'Who are you really, Valcero? A spy?'

'None of your business!'

Frethi chuckled. 'Perhaps not a very skilled spy. Well, my son, you must understand you cannot escape this hole. We will winkle you out, one way or another. And when we do, the High Thane will have even more questions.'

Valcero wanted to hit himself. Stupid mouth.

'Farewell, my boy. You had so much ... promise. Believe me, I would have saved you, had you only let me.

After a moment of silence, the gate slammed shut.

The third battle ... well, the third battle was over.

There was no time to wait for what might come next. Light still shone through the hole above. Vague silhouettes of more beams lay between him and his escape. He stretched out his arm until his fingers met the next beam. He leaned forward, almost falling, then grabbed the wood and clambered onto it. Something dry, yet sticky, almost impossibly light, brushed against his arm. Cobwebs. Of course there would be spiders here.

He leapt to the next beam, jumped across the void onto a third, and then another. The space between the walls widened, just enough that he could turn about. The light floated ahead in the darkness, neither closer nor further away.

He stepped on the next beam, but it snapped apart in a puff of dry rot. The boy screamed and fell forward for a long moment, then slammed into another piece of wood. He flung his arms around it while his legs dangled beneath. The wood held. When his heart calmed, Valcero scrambled and wriggled up until he crouched atop it.

For the next step, he tapped the beam a few times with his foot. It didn't break.

'Lord of Life, hold me,' Valcero whispered and hopped over the gulf.

The wood did not break. He breathed again and repeated the process for the next beam, and then the next. He looked up. The outlet was closer.

He reached for a higher beam and pulled himself on top. Something dropped onto his face, then skittered down his chest and across his leg. Valcero screamed and slapped himself all over, until he wobbled and tipped over. The boy gasped and braced his hands against the walls. His blood thudded in his ears. His breath rasped through the gloom.

Nearly there. Nearly there.

He gingerly clambered onto the next beam, and then another. The final piece of wood stretched below the outlet, at waist height and to his left. The boy took a breath and climbed. He stood, pressing his palms against the walls, and reached up. The hole was slightly too high. He stretched, tip-toed, teetering on the beam, but it was no use. It was too high, just too high.

'No. Please,' he whispered.

A great weariness seized the boy, and he slumped to his haunches. He had to rest. Maybe if he tried later. Maybe another way would present itself. Maybe...

Valcero sat on the lower piece of wood and leaned his back against the higher beam. Just to rest for a moment. His head grew heavy. He nodded forward. And caught himself. Drowsiness wafted up to him, pulling him towards the depths with gentle hands. He could not. He fought it. He must not sleep.

The horn jolted Valcero awake. He nearly toppled off the beam. Where was he? Between the walls, still in the dark. Sunlight poured through the hole above, mocking him. And there was something else, a murkiness in the air. A smell—woodsmoke and a fume, sharp and strange, yet vaguely familiar. He coughed. The smoke was filling the space. They were smoking him out. Was this their new plan? Choke him to death in here, torture him to death out there?

Shouts came from outside, and a distant, crackling roar. Two muffled thumps shook dust and mortar from the walls, like a giant knocking at the door. The smoke stung his eyes. He was choking. Panic seized his heart.

No. No. This could not be the end.

No.

He stood and clambered onto the higher beam. Only one thing left to try. He braced his back against the inner wall and his feet against the outer. The boy shifted upwards. What if he slipped?

No, he would not slip. He would *not*.

More. Higher. Further. The stone scraped the skin off his soles. He pushed higher. The black smoke blinded him. Tears streamed from his eyes. He was nearly there. He was there, level with the outlet. But the hole, no, the hole was too small.

No.

Valcero wriggled a higher, then kicked at the masonry with his heel. He shouted and kicked, over and over, until enough bits of stone broke away. He put his feet on the bottom lip, seized the top, and pulled himself through. He dangled and kicked in the empty air. The boy wriggled about onto his belly and eased himself outside, still clutching the hole's edge with white knuckles.

Oily smoke choked the air. Flames billowed from the fort's wooden walls. A section of stockade had fallen out, where they had built the ramp. No, not fallen, but *pushed* out to make another ramp beyond the wall. A way out. Rhenivian horsemen streamed up over the earthen slope and down the other side, galloping away over the field.

He looked up. The tower's thatch roof was burning, showering ash and embers upon him. He looked down. He would break his legs if he dropped that many spans to the ground.

No. Look again.

The temple roof was close enough—a gap to jump across, but not much.

He could make it. Yes, he could.

Valcero lowered himself until he hung by his fingertips. He pushed his feet against the wall, twisted around, took a breath, and leapt.

The roof knocked the breath from him. He slid down the wood until he grasped a shingle. He groaned with pain.

There was a crack. A piece of tower roof plummeted downwards.

The boy scrambled over the edge and thudded on the ground as the temple roof caught alight.

Valcero limped past the open temple door. Inside, the priests huddled around the Corn Mother and chanted. Brother Frethi, clad in leather armour, happened to turn and caught sight of him. The priest scowled and strode towards the door. Valcero backed away and tried to run.

Noise consumed the camp—horns and horses and pounding feet. Rhenivians ran in all directions. They grabbed spears and axes and shouted. A rider galloped through the tents, and Valcero leapt aside to escape the hooves. A soldier grabbed Valcero by the arm. He glared at the boy.

'Valcero!' The bellow came from somewhere nearby.

Valcero gaped at the soldier. 'Please...'

'Valceroooo!'

The soldier studied the boy's face, then shoved him away. 'Get out of here. Go.'

'Stop, Valcero!' Brother Frethi came stalking through the camp, waving an axe.

Something crashed into the tower roof, spraying wood and fire everywhere. There was a grinding groan, and the tower leaned, sagged, then imploded in thundering smoke, flame, and rubble that buried the temple and surrounding tents. Valcero fled before the cloud of dust, as men cried out behind him.

The boy stumbled through the smoky fort. Where was the gate?

Where was the gap in the wall? The ramparts were burning and crumbling. Trumpets rang out somewhere distant. Soldiers rushed past him. A man bumped Valcero and knocked him over. The boy crawled between the tents, then clambered to his feet and found the horse pens—empty. He leaned against the fence to catch his breath. The gate had fallen, wreathed in flames. A way out.

'Valcero,' someone muttered behind him.

The priest, caked in ash and dirt, loomed over the boy.

Valcero pushed himself away from the fence and made to run, but Frethi sprang forward and gripped his arm. The boy thrashed and wriggled. The Rhenivian threw him down and pinned him against the earth.

Valcero screamed.

Frethi raised his axe.

CHAPTER FORTY-FOUR

CAERIA – SUMMER'S FALL – 437

Avenge us.

The words beat in Terzjin's skull. For two days and two nights, he had endured the words. His rage smouldered. He snapped at the lenotare, spoke curtly with his emperor and the generals, and did not speak to Master Meretan at all. In fact, he avoided Colus as best he could in the little siege camp.

Avenge us.

He lay on his back at night, staring up at nothing. Instead of dreams, old memories drifted and flashed through his heart—burning palaces, riders galloping over the rocky hillside. Crouching in the dark, damp hold of a lurching, creaking ship bound for foreign shores. All the faces of those he had lost, forsaken, and failed—his mother and father, his sisters, his brother. His aunt. Datet. Valcero. A sob wracked his body. He bit on his hand so no one would hear.

When the trumpet hailed the morning, he arose unrested. The scouts came to the Emperor's tent as Zjandius was eating a breakfast of soup and bread with his inner circle.

'My men say they heard hammering throughout the night, Majesty,' Hemadir reported. 'They are planning something.'

Zjandius nodded. 'We must be ready.' He turned to Astulus, Divendrion, Lords Corilien and Octerian, and the other generals.

'Have our troops in battle order this morning. Be prepared to fight at a moment's notice.'

The sun soared over the valley to promise another hot, windless day. It was at mid-morning when three sharp blows of a horn sounded from Heiriksreld. The gates swung open.

'Be ready!' the generals called.

The cantare gathered in their long ranks across the centre, standing at attention with tall shields and long pikes. The war elephants grumbled and groaned at the rear. Hemadir's Rugadi waited on the south flank, Astulus and the chariots on the north. Master Meretan's engineers climbed their ladders and peered through their instruments, shouting down numbers to their colleagues, who scratched calculations on wax tablets and fussed over their catapults.

Three horsemen cantered out of the gates. One carried the black banner with the red boar, while the other waved a white flag.

'So they wish to negotiate,' Emperor Zjandius murmured. 'This is good. Let them come!'

A cantarus waved a white flag in reply, and the Rhenivians rode across the field. As they approached, Zjandius took off his helmet and sent for his crown. He donned the golden wreath and sat on his horse. His breastplate flashed and gleamed in the morning light over his white tunic, and a purple cloak hung from his shoulders. Terzjin sat on his own horse at the Emperor's side, armed with spear and shield and his sword at his side, glowering under his helmet.

Along with Corilien, Octerian, and a squad of lenotare, they awaited the Rhenivians at the front of the cantaris. In the lead came an older man, tall and broad-shouldered, armed with two axes across his back and a round shield at his side. He wore a winged helmet of dark iron on his head and scales of iron across his chest. He rode a bulky, chestnut stallion. The other two riders seemed to be nothing more than escorts. The old man had blue eyes, bright and glaring. The face conjured up a memory in Terzjin, like a splinter of ice wedged in his heart.

'High Thane Getherd of Elborn,' an escort announced in Galatani. 'Favourite of King Randegar of Rhenivia and His Majesty's voice in all matters here today.

The face, the name, the red boar on the banner. All of it came crashing down upon him. This man was the one. It was *him*.

Avenge us.

'His Majesty Emperor Zjandius Vaecerion,' the herald replied, 'Lord of Caeria and the Old Kingdom.'

'*Emperor*, eh?' Getherd said in Galatani. He smiled and licked his lips. 'Well, I suppose we can award ourselves whatever titles we wish when we have some spears at our backs.'

The old man's voice cut through Terzjin, as cold and deep as the ocean. He had heard it before, on that night long ago when he hid under the bed and watched his mother on the floor.

Avenge us.

A pair of boots, smeared with mud and blood. A sneering voice. Terzjin's leg shook. His palms turned cold and sweaty. His bladder threatened to loosen.

Avenge us.

The rage surged within him, cold and hot, swirling through his limbs and driving back the fear. He released a breath.

'Where is Thane Heirik?' Zjandius asked. 'Why is he not here to treat with us?'

Getherd leaned forward and glared at the Emperor. 'You have the gall to ask that question?'

Zjandius stared back at him impassively.

The old man straightened up. 'By the gods, you don't know, do you? Ah, you Caerians and your plots...'

'What are you talking about?'

'He's dead, boy. Clearly, you're not Lord of *all* Caeria—and certainly not all-knowing.' The High Thane smiled sourly.

Zjandius frowned and glanced to his aristocrats, then back to Getherd. What are your terms, High Thane?'

'My terms?'

'Of surrender.'

Getherd burst out laughing. 'Oh no, *Emperor*, I did not come to surrender. I came to see if *you* would submit to me. You see, I could make you my thane of this land and spare your men their lives on this bright day. Do it, Zjandius, and live. You could rule this island and restore peace between Caerians and Rhenivians.'

The Emperor scowled. 'I hoped you might have something serious to propose. Your ships are sunk, High Thane. You are cut off.'

'I am deadly serious, boy. You can't win. Your army is pitiful, tiny. My horses alone could trample you all to dust. Who would stand against me when you're dead? And ships can always be rebuilt. You have no idea of the might of my people.' Getherd raised his voice. 'Do not condemn these good soldiers to die for your vanity, Zjandius Vaecerion! Why not fight me like a man? A duel in the old way?'

Zjandius sighed. 'Well, High Thane,' he said more quietly, '*my* terms for your surrender are that you and your men lay down your arms in your fortress and abandon it. None shall come to harm. We will carry the common soldiers across the sea to their homeland, but you and your marshals shall stand trial for crimes committed during the occupation.'

Terzjin seethed.

Getherd spat into the grass. 'Stand trial? *Stand trial*? Don't insult me, boy.'

His horse paced back and forth.

'I am a High Thane. I am Getherd of Elborn. I do not submit to the laws of lesser peoples.' He spat again. 'There is no law but my will. I *am* the law!' Getherd roared.

'Lesser peoples?' Zjandius folded his arms and glared at the Rhenivian.

'Listen, boy,' Getherd snapped. 'I have fought more battles than you could count, starting before you left your mother's teat. I was a boy when I vanquished heroes and kings you could only *dream* of. I have fought great champions, truly worthy warriors, men of great strength and power. You wouldn't deserve to even kiss their feet. You're *nothing*. Your people are nothing.

The lords and generals gasped. Terzjin clenched his jaw.

Getherd's voice grew louder. 'We are strong, and you are weak. And it's the natural order that the strong rule the weak.' Spittle flew from his mouth. 'You flee in the face of defeat. You fled this field before. You fled your house.'

Terzjin gripped his spear so tightly it could have shattered.

Zjandius observed the High Thane as he raved. 'Have you finished?'

Getherd gestured at the cantare as he paced on his restless steed. 'You think a bit of iron can save you? I was *born* in iron and blood. I could crush you with my very hands, you stripling. You're such a coward, you will not even dare fall on your sword when I defeat you—*again*. You'll scuttle to some dark hole and lick your wounds, you pathetic boy. Like a smacked dog. You're not worthy of the pony you sit on!'

Zjandius raised a hand. He stared at Getherd without blinking.

'Oh?' the High Thane sneered. 'Is your pride stung, boy? Do you think your *hand* could silence me? Or do you beg for a chance to speak?'

The Emperor dropped his arm.

A chorus of cracks and thuds echoed across the battle line. A flock of tiny objects whistled and hissed overhead, trailing smoke. All the while, Zjandius watched Getherd with cool contempt.

The High Thane glanced at the sky, then turned to Zjandius. 'How *dare* you! Where's your honour? We're still speak—'

Fireballs erupted along the facing fortress ramparts. A moment later, a volley of booms returned across the field. Sheets of orange flame engulfed the gatehouse roof and wooden walls. Black smoke bloomed over Heiriksreld.

Zjandius folded his arms. 'Oh, and now *you* wish to lecture on the subject of honour?'

Getherd growled at the Emperor and brandished his axe. The lenotare sprang forth, raising their shields and spears before Zjandius.

The High Thane spat and jerked on his stallion's reins to turn about. He galloped away to the fort, with his escorts trailing behind.

Avenge us.

The catapults shot off another round, a mix of stones and tecnari.

Master Maltorus looked to Zjandius. 'You would let him just run off?'

More fire blossomed on the walls. Burning wood shattered and splintered. Screams mingled with thumping explosions.

Zjandius watched the fire. 'Be calm, Master Maltorus.'

'No.' Terzjin kicked his horse's flanks.

The mare bolted forward.

'Terzjin!' the Emperor shouted.

Master Maltorus raced to catch the Rhenivians. 'Getherd!' he bellowed. 'Face me, Getherd!'

The High Thane blew his horn three times as he rode ahead. Answering horns sounded from the fort. More tecnaris exploded on the walls.

The escort with the white flag glanced back. He hefted his spear and hurled it at Master Maltorus, who leaned aside on his horse and let the shaft fly past. Terzjin came up alongside the soldier and bashed his shield against the Rhenivian, who fell off his horse.

The other escort, carrying Getherd's boar banner, wheeled about and flung his spear at Terzjin. It fell short, jabbed into the ground. Terzjin grabbed it with his left hand as he passed and threw his own spear with his right. It flew true and knocked the soldier from his mount.

'Getherd!' Terzjin roared. 'Face me, High Thane!'

Beyond the galloping hooves and the blood thumping in his ears, beyond the roaring and crackling of the burning walls, came the faint hint of a song on the wind. Only for a moment, and it was gone.

'Getherd!' Terzjin's voice strained and cracked.

The burning gatehouse groaned and shattered. The entire structure, tall doors and all, toppled and crashed to the ground in a cloud of sparks. The High Thane's stallion reared up before the flames, threw his rider to the ground, and bolted in panic.

'Hah!' Terzjin urged his horse forward.

He could see beyond the fires into the fortress. The Rhenivians milled about and retreated behind their tents to escape the flames and tumbling wood.

'Hah!' Master Maltorus charged at Getherd. He readied his spear.

The old man stood and hurled an axe at Terzjin. The weapon spun through the air. Terzjin raised his shield and pulled the horse right.

The axe blade slammed into the horse's flank, and the beast screamed and reared. Terzjin fell and crashed into the turf. He lay winded for a moment, then scrambled to his feet. More horns sounded to his right. There was a rumbling as riders galloped out from behind the north side of the fort. Hundreds—no, thousands—thundered towards the Caerian's flank. How?

The Rugadi raced across the field to meet the attack. The cantare fell into disarray, shuffling about to meet the oncoming horde. The war elephants trumpeted. Terzjin looked to Zjandius. His Emperor. He was too far away. Too far.

Boots pounded the earth. Master Maltorus leapt aside and tumbled backwards as Getherd swung another axe through the air where he had been.

The High Thane snarled and turned about. 'A battle between champions? I welcome it!'

Terzjin sprang to his feet just as Getherd strode up to him, slicing the axe from side to side. For all his years, the High Thane moved with vicious speed. Terzjin thrust the spear at him, but Getherd batted it aside and barged closer. Terzjin raised his shield and skipped backwards. Each axe blow shuddered through the shield and up his arm. He darted to the side and jabbed his spear at the Rhenivan, who retreated and used his own shield to ward off each thrust.

They paused, circling each other before the broken gates, catching their breath. The battle raged behind them, elsewhere.

Getherd nodded. 'You're a slippery bastard, but fight well for a Caerian. Who are you?'

Terzjin hesitated, then threw off his helmet.

Getherd backed away with eyes wide. 'Impossible!'

Master Maltorus raised his spear and stalked closer.

'I had you all killed years ago.'

'You *confess* it?' Terzjin screamed.

The High Thane shook his head. 'No. No, you can't be. We ended the family. Every one of them. I saw to it.'

'Did you?'

'Ah.' The Rhenivian nodded. 'But the boy who ran away... The one they *swore* they hunted down. Yes, that could be you.'

Terzjin howled and charged at Getherd with his spear. The High Thane tensed, lunged forward, grabbed the shaft under his arm, and swung his axe at Terzjin's head. Master Maltorus leaned away to evade. The spear slipped from his grasp, and he fell backwards.

Getherd snapped the spear in half and tossed the pieces aside. 'So you survived. For what? No matter. I shall end your sorry tale.' He hefted the axe above his head and slashed down.

Terzjin slithered backwards through the dirt and leapt to his feet. He raised his shield and caught a blow. Getherd struck again and again. Master Maltorus staggered backwards with each clanging thud and tugged at his sword—jammed in its sheath.

Another blow split Terzjin's shield in two. The High Thane sneered and swung his axe up in long loop, up over his head and down towards Terzjin's face.

Something snapped within Master Maltorus. His ears popped. A chime rang through his head. His breath flowed in through his nose. The battle cries, the burning fort, all sound receded. Up high in the clear sky, past the axe blade and Getherd's straining face, a swallow swooped and soared, a mere speck against the blue.

The axe descended upon his skull.

And Terzjin breathed out.

He twisted aside on the balls of his feet. The axe blade brushed past his nose, past his chest, softer than the breeze. And there, beyond the falling blade, he saw them. His family.

Avenge us.

Was that what his mother said all those years ago, as she lay upon the floor, breathing her last? Avenge us?

No, she said...

Remember us.

Of course. He saw her now, Mother with her long gown of copper rings that jingled as she walked. Father, with his dark beard that tickled Terzjin's cheek. His tall sisters, Vilna and Elatuë, with their giggles and games and long hair, black as night. His curly-haired little brother, Aril, gazing up at him, clutching his wooden bull, his favourite toy.

I remember. I remember you all. Always.

And Terzjin observed the axe head plunge into the earth before his feet, even as his own arm drew back and his sword slid from its sheath and he swung it up—the old sword from the forgotten city, bright as the day it was forged—up, up above his head, and swung it down with both hands on the hilt, down, down, down.

The sword sliced through the axe shaft. A clean cut.

Perfection.

The High Thane gaped at his broken weapon.

Terzjin grinned up at him.

Getherd scowled and jabbed at Master Maltorus with what remained of his axe. Terzjin blocked, parried and sliced the useless bit of wood with all his long-practised moves. He nicked the old man's hand with the tip of his blade. The High Thane yelped and dropped the stick. He shoved his shield at Terzjin, who dodged, then swung his sword against the shield in return. The old man stumbled away as Master Maltorus advanced upon him, as cold and relentless as the north wind.

Swing, cut, slice, jab.

The shield rang with each strike.

Swing, cut, slice.

The shield shattered. Terzjin pressed forward and slammed the pommel into Getherd's chest. The High Thane gasped. Another blow in the chest and another. The High Thane's helmet slipped off, and he tottered, almost off his feet. Terzjin punched him in the face—one, two, three times. Getherd fell backwards, then clambered to his knees to lunge forth and grapple.

But Master Maltorus held his blade high, poised above the Rhenivian's head.

Getherd gazed up at Terzjin. He wiped his face and spat blood. 'Go on then, boy. Send me to the Corn Mother. I have *no* regrets.' He grinned with red teeth.

Terzjin readied himself. The rage was gone. Only icy purpose remained.

'Terzjin!'

Who called?

From beyond the broken gate, a bunch of Rhenivians watched the duel in horror. Terzjin glanced over his shoulder. Ranks of cantare advanced in a quick march, shields locked and pikes ready.

His sword remained aloft.

'Terzjin!'

There, in the fort, behind the watchers. A soldier knelt before the tents, holding an axe in one hand. And pressing Valcero against the ground with the other.

The boy. He lived.

'Come on, you coward,' the High Thane growled. 'Get on with it.'

The soldier raised his axe.

Valcero waved and cried out. 'Terzjin! Help!'

'Come on!' Getherd rasped.

Master Maltorus sighed. He swung his blade down in an arc and struck the pommel against Getherd's head. The High Thane gasped and toppled to the side. Terzjin leapt over him and dashed through the burning gate.

CHAPTER FORTY-FIVE

CAERIA — SUMMER'S FALL — 437

'Stop squealing, you rat!' Brother Frethi shouted. He shifted his hand to grip the axe just under the blade.

'Please... ' Valcero raised his hands. 'No, please.'

The priest's bloodshot eyes bulged on his ashen face. 'You're *wicked*,' he spat. 'I'll choke you with my Mother's earth.' He shoved the boy's face into the ground, raised the axe high, and hissed in Rhenivian.

Valcero gagged and twisted his head away from the dirt.

Terzjin rushed up behind the priest, blade ready to strike. As he sprinted the final steps, he locked eyes with Valcero for a heartbeat.

Brother Frethi screamed and brought his axe down.

Terzjin swung his blade against the priest's head—and struck him with the blunt edge.

Frethi dropped the axe and collapsed to the ground, stunned.

Valcero sat on his knees and gaped at the fallen priest.

Terzjin, sword in hand, bent over and wrapped his arms around the boy. 'Enough,' he whispered. 'It's over.'

Valcero looked over Master Maltorus' shoulder. Cantare burst through the open gateway and sent the remaining Rhenivians fleeing. The flames were spreading from tent to tent across the fort. Ash rained upon him. 'Terzjin, I... I'm so sorry.'

'Never mind. Never you mind,' Terzjin replied. 'We must get out before we roast.' He straightened up and sheathed his blade. 'Come.' He helped Valcero to his feet and guided the boy towards the gateway. '*Eo*, how are you so thin, lad?'

A splintering crash came from the centre of the fort. They glanced back to see the great hall engulfed in flames, caving in.

Valcero's legs ached, his bare, blistered feet throbbed, and his head swam. 'I haven't been so well,' he murmured. He stumbled.

'Easy does it.' Terzjin put an arm around his shoulder and shepherded him to the ranks of cantare.

The cantarus captain stood before his men and shouted in Rhenivian to the soldiers lurking amongst the tents.

'Help!' 'Let us out!' 'Please!' 'Help!' Caerian slaves came running to their compatriots.

The Rhenivians made no move to stop the escape. They wavered. They dropped their axes and spears. They crept towards the cantare with hands raised.

The Caerians parted to let Valcero and Terzjin through. Valcero bumped against their shoulders, arms, and tall shields. One or two patted him on the back.

'Well done, sir,' a cantarus muttered to Master Maltorus.

They passed through the ranks, out of the fort and onto the battlefield. Valcero breathed the fresher air, even as smoke hung overhead, darkening the sky. He flinched and grimaced with each step over the thorny ground. Bodies lay strewn about like abandoned dolls, many riddled with arrows. Caerian or Rhenivian, who could tell when they lay facedown on the dusty earth. A few riderless horses roamed about, neighing and squealing.

Here and there, knots of Rhenivians stood surrounded by Caerian soldiers. Others lay or sat alone on the ground, moaning and crying. Meanwhile, a cheer arose from the Caerians on the other end of the field.

'I thought you were…gone,' Terzjin muttered as they trudged. 'I'm glad to be wrong.'

Valcero started crying. He couldn't help it. 'I'm so sorry. I should've listened. I only wanted to help.'

'No, Valcero.' Terzjin squeezed his shoulders. 'I'm sorry I spoke so badly. I shouldn't have left you like that. Never again—I promise.' He sniffed.

They passed a war elephant, collapsed and unmoving. Just ahead lay another elephant on her side. She moaned and flopped her trunk on the ground as rivers of blood ran over her flank. Her Sasiión rider crouched at her head with a mallet and spike. He raised the mallet.

Valcero looked away. They moved on.

'Terzjin.'

'Yes?'

'I... I don't think I want to be a warrior after all.'

'That's quite alright, my boy. That's perfectly fine.'

Valcero let out a sigh. 'I was scared. I've been scared for so long.'

'Me too,' Terzjin replied.

'Really?'

'Oh yes,' Terzjin said. 'I've feared the Rhenivians ever since I was a boy. Ever since they... hurt my family. But you know what? I'm not so frightened any more.'

'Why?'

'Because,' Terzjin said, 'I realised I have more important things—*and* more important people—to worry about.' He patted Valcero's back.

There was a third war elephant ahead, alive but charging back and forth, trumpeting and flapping his ears. The rider still clung to his back and cried out for help. Soldiers leapt out of the beast's path.

Valcero gasped. 'The Torecti are here!'

Terzjin glanced up. 'Huh! So they are.'

A group of maybe fifteen Torecti warriors came to surround the rampaging animal, and began a low, gentle song. Gradually, the elephant slowed to a standstill. He moaned and stamped his great feet, but the forest people kept singing the simple melody, over and over, as they formed a circle around the tall beast. Finally, the elephant grunted and knelt, and his frightened rider jumped off.

'And there's Reito.' Terzjin pointed. 'Come, let's say hello.'

Reito stood in the circle with his companions. He turned and beamed as they approached, then grabbed Valcero in a hug. 'By the Lord of Life! A miracle.' He stepped back to inspect the boy. 'What happened?'

'The Rhenivians caught me,' Valcero replied. 'I've been with them ever since. Reito, sir, I never should have—'

The warrior waved his hand. 'Do not worry, boy. You should have listened, yes, but you are here now, where you were meant to be. The village will rejoice when they hear the news.' He looked to Terzjin. 'And I believe you, too, were where you were meant to be, Terzjin Maltorus.'

Terzjin grinned. 'And you, Reito! It seems we have many thanks to give.' Master Maltorus gestured at the warriors massed on the field.

There were hundreds—no, thousands—of Torecti, armed with bows and spears. They stared about in wonder at the open valley and vast sky above. The Caerian and Sasiion soldiers gawked at them from a careful distance.

Reito smiled. 'Yes, we arrived at a good moment. As the invaders were galloping from their hole in the wall to strike your people in their sides, we gave them a little surprise from the long grass.'

'But how did you get here?' Terzjin asked. 'We had no word you were coming.'

Reito gestured to the thicket of trees between the hills. 'We came via our forest ways, with Illauri-of-the-Woods to guide us.

'Illauri?' Terzjin looked around.

'She awaits us in the grove,' Reito said. 'For our return journey. We will not keep her waiting long.'

The elephant clambered to his feet and rumbled.

Reito chuckled. 'I had no *idea* such a beast existed.'

He held out a hand, and the elephant sniffed the man's fingers with his trunk.

The Torecti smiled. 'This is a tale we will tell our children, and our children's children.'

The Caerians raised another cheer. The soldiers had gathered around Zjandius and lifted him on a shield. The Emperor grinned at his cantare soldiers and glanced over at Terzjin and Valcero.

Master Maltorus sighed. 'I'd better go.' He touched Valcero's shoulder. 'Can you wait here with Reito?'

'Could I go with you, rather?' Valcero asked. 'Please?'

'Uh, alright.' Terzjin scratched his head. 'But on your best behaviour, and it's *Emperor* Zjandius now, in case you didn't know.'

They left the Torecti to admire the elephant, and followed the Emperor and his retinue back to camp.

Terzjin looked around as they walked. 'But where's Hemadir?' he muttered.

Back in the Caerian camp, Emperor Zjandius held court on a wooden throne in an open patch in front of his tent, with the lenotare standing guard around the edges. Zjandius pulled off his helmet and put his wreath of golden leaves on his flattened, sweaty hair. He scowled as Terzjin approached, and waved them forward.

Terzjin came to the throne and bowed. 'Your Majesty, I—'

'How *dare* you desert your Emperor!' Zjandius snapped. 'I should have you whipped—or worse!'

Terzjin dropped to his knees, head bowed. 'Forgive me, Emperor.'

The Emperor leaned forward. 'How could you?' he whispered.

Terzjin looked up. 'It was necessary, Zjandius. For the living.'

'Please, your... Your Majesty, sir!' Valcero went to stand beside Terzjin. 'It was my fault.' He bowed, then rose up, slightly dizzy.

The Emperor covered his mouth with his hand.

'Uh, my lord, Your Majesty, Master Maltorus rescued me. I owe him my life, sir, especially because I... I disobeyed him.' Valcero glanced at Terzjin. 'He told me to keep out of danger and I didn't... did not listen.' He dropped to his knees and threw his hands together. 'Please, sir. If you want to punish anyone, punish me!'

The Emperor slumped in his throne and rubbed his forehead. 'Oh gods...'

'I was only trying to help, Your Majesty,' Valcero said. 'I sent a letter, to try and warn you.'

'A letter?' The Emperor sat up and frowned. He signalled to a scribe. 'What letter did—?'

'Valcero? Valcero!' Colus Meretan dashed into the court. 'By the Lords of Life and Death!' He snatched up Valcero and spun the boy around, then set him down and grinned.

The Emperor snorted and shook his head. 'I never thought I would see such a thing.' He took an unrolled parchment from the scribe and waved it in the air. 'Did you write this, Valcero?'

The boy swallowed and nodded. 'Yes, Emperor.'

Terzjin chuckled. 'You did?'

Master Meretan went to peer at the letter. 'Your Majesty, I could have told you the boy wrote this had you only shown it to me. He always writes his Ss with such big loops.'

Zjandius examined the letter and stroked his chin. 'I have many questions.'

Colus turned back to Valcero. 'I thought you were dead, boy!'

'I thought I was dead too, Master Colus. Or, about to be.'

Zjandius shook his head. 'How could I punish such a joyful reunion?' His lips twitched.

Terzjin climbed to his feet. 'Besides, Your Majesty...' He gestured to a group of approaching cantare. '...your prize is delivered.'

The captain led four soldiers who dragged High Thane Getherd up to the Emperor's throne. Lords Corilien and Octerian, as well as Prince Astulus, walked close behind.

The captain saluted. 'Your Majesty, the Rhenivians have surrendered their stronghold, with their weapons and armour left inside.'

The Emperor gestured at Getherd. 'And him?'

'He lives, sir,'

Getherd lifted his bruised face and squinted at Zjandius. Lord Octerian went to the High Thane and bent to whisper in his ear. Getherd scowled and jerked his head away from the aristocrat.

Zjandius nodded. 'Good. Chain him up somewhere out of the way. And Master Meretan?'

'Emperor?'

'As soon as everyone clears the fort, you and your engineers are to destroy it as you see fit. Whatever the fire has not yet burned, do you understand? Not a *splinter* is to remain standing.'

Colus bowed. 'Of course, Emperor.' He looked at Valcero. 'You'll have to tell me *everything* that happened to you, dear boy, especially about the Torecti. I see they are quite fascinated by elephants.'

Zjandius tapped his throne. 'Master Meretan...'

'Yes, Your Majesty. At once, sir.' Colus gave another quick bow. 'We'll talk later!' he muttered to Valcero and hurried off, along with the cantare and their captive.

Zjandius rested his chin on his fist and drummed his other hand against the armrest as he examined Terzjin. 'What helps your defence, Master Maltorus, is that people will believe your escapade was part of my winning strategy—along with the Torecti's very fortunate arrival. But had the day gone differently, people would have a darker story to tell, no?'

Terzjin sighed. 'I truly am sorry, Emperor.'

'And I accept your apology,' Zjandius replied, 'though we shall have more to discuss later. For now, I must speak to these Torecti.' He gestured to Reito and some other warriors who now entered the court. 'And perhaps the very lucky Master...Baradon—is it?—would be so good as to translate?'

Valcero coughed and nodded.

Reito, came before Zjandius with his hands behind his back.

'Valcero,' the Emperor said, 'tell this Torecti chief that I am most grateful for his aid.'

'Oh,' Reito interrupted in Caerian, 'but I am no chief, Emperor Zjandius Vaecerion. However, I am willing to accept your gratitude on behalf of the *Taurex* chiefs. They all offered warriors for this expedition.'

'Ah!' Zjandius inspected Reito with sharp eyes. 'So, you are one of these Torecti who speak our language. May I ask how you learnt it?'

Reito grinned and bobbed his head. 'Of course you may ask, Emperor, though you may find my answer evasive and unsatisfying.'

Zjandius snorted. 'Very well. But I am serious when I say thank you. Thank you for what you have done, for your efforts in the past months, *and* here today. Rhenivian horsemen were galloping into our flank like a knife in the back, but you Torecti turned the blade aside. You saved many lives today.'

'And more than a few of our people *lost* their lives today.'

Zjandius inclined his head. 'I will not forget it. Caeria will not forget it. We are in your debt.' He sighed. 'And I know my ancestors—and I—neglected our ancient vows,' he continued. 'So, I promise you—here and now—I will meet your chiefs at the next Midsummer's Day, according to the old agreements, and we shall renew our pact for the centuries to come.'

Reito held out his hands. 'I will carry your words, Emperor Zjandius Vaecerion. I know the chiefs will be glad, and happy to meet you. But now, I must depart with the warriors and carry our fallen on the long journey home.' He bowed.

Zjandius bowed in reply. 'Go in peace.'

'Reito!' Terzjin whispered.

The warrior raised his eyebrows and went to Master Maltorus.

'Can I see her?' Terzjin asked.

The Torecti warrior grinned. 'Illauri-of-the-Woods said you would ask. She also said, "Not before he knows the answer to my question." ' Reito shrugged. 'I trust that makes sense to you.'

Terzjin frowned. 'You told me we were "where we were *meant* to be", Valcero and I. And Illauri *said* I would ask for her. Did...did Illauri know...?'

Reito winked. 'Farewell, Terzjin Maltorus, and farewell, young Valcero Baradon.' He ruffled the boy's hair. 'I hope we meet again.' He bowed to the Emperor and departed.

'Well,' Zjandius clapped his hands together. 'If that's enough business for the day, I would like to wash and prepare for a hearty dinner' He stood up.

The soldiers and aristocrats laughed and cheered, but a nearby trumpet fanfare cut through the noise.

'Oh gods.' The Emperor rolled his eyes. 'What *now*?'

A cantarus hurried into the court. 'Riders approach, Your Majesty! Caerian riders. They carry the sign of the Aventan. The gryphon, sir.'

The attendees looked at each other and whispered.

'They actually survived?' Lord Octerian murmured to Lord Corilien.

The Emperor dropped back on his throne. 'Well, escort them here then.'

Terzjin took Valcero aside to wait behind the lenotare. Moments later, the cantare marched in with a group of four dressed in black travelling cloaks. They pulled back their hoods as they approached the throne, to reveal Lady Aventan, her two sons, and an older man with long, silvery hair. *Him*.

'The Lord and Lady Aventan, Your Majesty!' the cantarus announced. 'They come to pay their respects and congratulate you on your victory.'

The Aventan stepped forward and bowed.

Zjandius half-smiled and half-frowned. 'Welcome, Lady Aventan! I am glad to receive you all here. But Lord Aventan...?'

'Sorveo, you old *devil*!' Corilien strode forward and embraced the silver-haired man.

'Lord Aventan,' the Emperor continued, 'I was led to believe you had perished?' He shot a glance at Terzjin. 'Not that I am anything but glad to be wrong.' He smiled at the old aristocrat.

'Ah, Emperor Zjandius,' Lord Aventan said, 'please forgive the deception.' That same voice.

'Terzjin!' Valcero tugged his sleeve.

'Not now, lad.' Master Maltorus scrutinised Lord Aventan's face.

'Your Majesty,' Sorveo Aventan said, 'my family has lived through a very dark time.'

'I can well imagine, My Lord,' Zjandius replied. 'I lament the loss of your children.'

Aventan nodded and gave his wife and two sons a wan smile. 'Thank you, Emperor. I can only be grateful for the family I still have. It is true. A moment came when I contemplated ending my own life. But my dear Lady found me, and while I could not face the world in the darkest days, we vowed to never surrender to despair. We have endured much peril, and were not sure who to trust—if anyone—in our lonely fight. When word came that a supposed envoy of Your Majesty wished to meet with us, we elected that Lady Aventan represent our family, whilst I remain in the shadows, in case of a trap.'

'Terzjin, please,' Valcero whispered. 'I *have* to tell you something.'

'Not now!' Terzjin hissed.

'We set out for Etorium as soon as we heard of your return,' Lord Aventan continued. 'I am only sorry we were not quick enough to join this momentous battle. We arrived on the hilltop in time to see the stronghold fall, and your soldiers carry Getherd's corpse from the burning wreckage.'

Lord Corielien opened his mouth, but Zjandius raised a hand.

'I have heard something of your deeds,' the Emperor said. 'You are notorious amongst the Rhenivians.'

The lord smiled and bowed his head. 'Without wishing to boast, Majesty, we conducted more than a few raids and ambushes—enough to trouble them. Hopefully, enough for them to fear our name.'

'Do you know what became of Thane Heirik, then?' the Emperor asked. He looked around the gathering. 'So many rumours fly about.

Some say he was kidnapped, others that he died. I fear he may be skulking somewhere with more soldiers.'

Valcero nudged Master Maltorus. 'It's *important*, Terzjin. I saw that man before. In the Rhenivian camp.'

Terzjin frowned at him. 'What?'

The boy nodded. 'I saw him meet with Thane Heirik one night,' he said in a low voice. 'He told Heirik that King—Emperor Zjandius was coming back. He told Heirik to send for help from his uncle.'

Lord Aventan looked to his family and shrugged. 'I am sorry, Your Majesty. I have heard all the same stories, but we are no wiser than you. Perhaps he fell in the west, and his followers kept it a secret to preserve morale?'

Terzjin bent over and stared at the boy, deep into his eyes. 'Are you *absolutely* certain, Valcero?'

The boy nodded.

'This is a serious matter. You cannot make a mistake here.'

'Yes, it's how I knew about the High Thane coming. It's why I wrote the letter.'

Terzjin stared into the distance, then squeezed Valcero's shoulder. 'Stay here,' he muttered. Master Maltorus bowed as he approached the Emperor and went to his ear.

'Excuse me, My Lord.' Zjandius leaned aside to listen. The Emperor kept a blank face, then nodded as Master Maltorus withdrew. 'As I said, we must discover Thane Heirik's whereabouts.'

'Of course, Your Majesty.' Aventan bowed.

'So, I think we should question Getherd immediately,' Zjandius announced.

Sorveo Aventan tensed. 'The High Thane lives?'

'Oh yes.' The Emperor gestured to the cantare. 'Bring him here.'

Two soldiers saluted and left. The Aventan exchanged glances.

'May we retire and rest after our long ride, Majesty?' Lord Aventan said. 'And give you time to interrogate Getherd at your leisure?'

'No, no.' Zjandius waved a hand. 'Let us do this quickly, all together. I, too, wish to rest.'

Lady Aventan stepped forward. 'Your Highness. Of course, we should be wary of a Rhenivian's words. They are dishonourable, untrustworthy...'

'Perhaps,' Zjandius replied, with a little smile. 'But even the most untrustworthy can *accidentally* reveal much. Ah, and here he is.'

High Thane Getherd shuffled into the gathering, chained at the wrists and ankles, and escorted by four soldiers. His face was a little less bloody, and his sodden beard dripped with water. As soon as the High Thane laid eyes upon the Aventan, he snarled and shouted in Rhenivian.

As one, the Aventan backed away.

'*Aru urezjel!*' The Emperor called out. The words sounded Galatani.

Getherd fell silent and glared at Zjandius.

In a calm voice, the Emperor asked the High Thane something.

Getherd pointed at Lady Aventan and spat out a reply.

The other Lords gasped.

'Your Majesty, he lies!' Lady Aventan cried out.

'I *expressly* forbade assassination,' the Emperor said in an icy tone.

'Your Majesty,' Lord Aventan said. 'Please, you cannot trust the Rhenivian. *Every* word is a lie.'

'And *you,* Lord Aventan...' Zjandius pointed at the aristocrat. 'You met with Heirik and revealed my plans to him.'

'What? Never!'

'You encouraged him to request reinforcement from Getherd. To what end?'

'Utterly false, Your Majesty.'

Zjandius folded his arms. 'We have a witness to the meeting. A *Caerian* witness.'

Lady Aventan's eyes roamed the assembly. Valcero shrank behind a lenotarus as she spotted him.

The lady scowled and turned to the Emperor. 'They took my children!' she burst out. 'You cannot deny me justice!'

'Arrest them,' Zjandius ordered.

Lord Aventan made to run, but the lenotare sprang forward to encircle the family, spears at the ready. The Aventan boy with the red mark on his face whipped out a blade and rushed at the throne. But Master Maltorus stepped between and glared at the Aventan boy, hand ready on the pommel of his sheathed sword. Two lenotare came up behind the Aventan son, grabbed his arms, and took his weapon.

Emperor Zjandius slumped in his throne. 'Take them away. I will deal with all this later.'

After the uproar died down, Terzjin took Valcero to find Colus. As they walked through the camp, a great wailing and keening broke from a cluster of sandy brown tents.

'It's the Rugadi,' Terzjin muttered. 'Oh, gods no.'

Valcero followed him a few paces towards a crowd of the desert people singing and crying in a tight huddle.

'Wait here, please.' Terzjin went alone to the warriors.

They parted as Master Maltorus approached, to reveal Hemadir lying on his back and soaked in red. Terzjin knelt beside him. The sand prince gripped Terzjin's arm, and he put a hand on Hemadir's.

'Valcero?'

He turned to find a Sasiion boy from the palace in Elisdrium, pulling a horse along by its reins.

'Sefti! What are you doing here?'

Sefti smiled. 'I joined to help with the animals. Not to fight, though.' He shrugged. 'The pay is good.'

Valcero pointed to the Rugadi. 'What happened?'

'Ah.' Sefti's smile faded. 'The sand prince's spirit is preparing to fly away. They say he was wounded in the battle. An axe knocked him from his horse.'

Hemadir's eyes nearly closed, but his lips still moved. Terzjin bowed his head and put the Sand Prince's hand on his chest.

'What about you, Valcero?' Sefti asked. 'What are you doing here?'

The Rugadi's wailing rose to a crescendo. Terzjin stood and left them to their weeping. He wiped his eyes as he stumbled back to Valcero.

'I…' A great weariness rushed up behind the boy and wrapped itself around him. He wanted nothing more than to lie down. 'I don't know. It's a very long story.'

CHAPTER FORTY-SIX

CAERIA — AUTUMN'S REIGN — 437

Emperor Zjandius left for Etorium the very next day, after Colus and his engineers reduced Heiriksreld to ash and rubble. Only the circular dyke remained, as a scar of what had been. The Emperor sent orders ahead for ships to sail to Elisdrium and bring his beloved Nanepti to her new home.

The vessels went by the slowest and most cautious route, but within weeks, the Princess of Emzentanis arrived at the palace of Etorium, along with the rest of her household. There was much feasting and rejoicing in the city. And even more when Empress Nanepti gave birth a few days later. It was a son, an heir to the Empire. They named him Adomenus Ahencare Vaecerion, after his grandfathers.

Master Meretan and Valcero were assigned rooms in the palace walls, which Colus immediately moaned about, but there was nowhere else available. Goretonum village lay in ruins. Colus' old house would take months to rebuild, if he were so lucky.

Lord Eledan, better late than never, arrived from Impona to pay his respects and swear loyalty to the First Emperor. The aristocrat brought lavish gifts of fine furniture and silver cups inlaid with pearls from the estuary beside his city. Zjandius received the gifts and vows of fealty with good humour and magnanimity.

The Emperor invited the three surviving lords, a second member of each of their families, and Prince Astulus to form a council to help govern the Empire. Of course, it was convenient that these aristocrats would now live in Etorium under the Emperor's eye.

As for Lord Aventan and his family, they went through a public trial, with Zjandius and two magistrates presiding as tribunes. The trial lasted two weeks. High Thane Getherd testified, perhaps leniency in his own trial, perhaps out of grief and fury. Even young Valcero Baradon bravely recounted what he heard and saw that night in the camp. The tribunal pronounced the Aventan guilty of treason and murder, and sentenced the entire family to permanent exile on the isle of Deiros.

Today, Master Maltorus and the lenotari escorted Emperor Zjandius to see off the ship that would bear the traitors away.

The Emperor wore a long purple overcloak and a crisp white tunic—all hemmed with gold thread. His golden wreath atop his head gleamed and shimmered in the morning sun, while his cloak billowed and flapped in the fresh portside breeze. Prefect Suletonius, newly reelected, along with hundreds of citizens and many aristocrats, had turned out to watch the departure. Gulls wheeled and squawked overhead. The galley lay alongside the wharf, while tirentare and other sailors loaded the vessel with supplies. Admiral Getaelon, fresh from his Rhenivian expedition, was to captain this very delicate voyage.

'We burnt many, many ships,' Getaelon had told Terzjin when he returned a week ago. 'The entire coast is in chaos.' The sailor had chuckled. 'And many hundreds of Rhenivian fishers now curse our name. We sailed so far that we found the land of the Malcori northmen. A dreary coast it was—endless cliffs and deep bays drowned in fog. I was quite happy to turn the fleet back to warmer waters. No wonder they raid our shores. Probably more for the sun than anything else.'

'The ship is ready, Your Majesty,' the Admiral now declared on the stone wharf. 'The signs are good, winds are favourable, and the tide is high.'

Zjandius nodded. He turned to the four Aventan—chained, huddled, and stone-faced—before him. 'Lord and Lady Aventan,' he spoke, loud enough for the audience to hear. 'It gives no pleasure to bid you farewell.'

The son marked with red glanced at Terzjin. The boy's eyes flashed.

'Out of respect to the positions you once enjoyed,' Zjandius continued, 'I have ordered the tirentari to leave you with provisions. Apart from water and a hide tent, you shall have seed to grow crops, along with hoes, sickles, and a few other tools. You will have sheep for wool, milk and mutton, if you tend them well.' He gestured as the sailors hauled the livestock aboard. 'Have you any final words?'

'Hah!' Lady Aventan scowled at the water.

Lord Aventan stared ahead, not meeting the Emperor's eye.

'I hope you use your time on Deiros to lead honest lives and redeem your spirits,' Zjandius said. 'May the One keep you. May the Lords of Life and Death guide you.'

Nobody applauded or cheered as the soldiers led the Aventan aboard.

'Admiral,' the Emperor said, once the prisoners were below deck. 'I trust you to ensure they reach the barren island safely.'

Getaelon saluted. 'Of course, Your Majesty!'

'To be clear, Admiral,' Zjandius murmured, 'no one is to "accidentally" fall overboard and drown on the way. I want no martyrs, understood?'

'Understood!' Admiral Getaelon saluted his Emperor once more, then boarded and ordered his sailors to cast off. The oarsmen pushed away from the wharf. The ship slowly turned about and rowed out of the port and onto the river to the sea.

'Thus ends the house of Aventan,' Zjandius muttered beside Terzjin. 'Another piece of the Old Kingdom.' He sighed.

The other lords approached.

'Would you excuse me a moment, Your Majesty?' Terzjin asked. He left the Emperor and his aristocrats to their discussions and went to a familiar vessel berthed further along the port, a worn galley with flaking paint and faded eyes. The crew stood on deck, watching the prison ship depart.

Terzjin waved to the captains, one thin and short, and the other tall and heavy. 'May I come aboard?'

Jeigo Ladistrien snorted. 'Not like you to ask permission.'

'The poor devils.' Taerinus gazed at the departing ship. 'How many months do you bet before they run out of mutton and eat each other?'

'Hah!' Terzjin clambered up the gangplank. 'Not our problem, I suppose. How are you two, anyway? In good health?'

'Yes,' Jeigo looked at Taerinus and put an arm around the other man's shoulders. 'I suppose we can't complain.'

'The Prefect upheld Heirik's pardon,' Taerinus said. 'So we're going to ply our trade in a more... legitimate way.'

Jeigo shrugged. 'Or a more *boring* way, if we must be honest.'

'Well,' Terzjin said, 'I could find work for you to make it worthwhile. There's always a need for merchants with open eyes and ears.' He winked.

The Ladistrien exchanged looks.

Taerinus sighed. 'If you insist, sir.'

Master Maltorus chuckled. 'Oh, but the pay will be handsome!' His face turned serious. 'It's the least I can do.'

Taerinus shook his head. 'It is *we* who are grateful.' He pulled Jeigo closer.

'Anyway...' Terzjin reached out. 'I won't forget either of you.' He shook hands with them and strolled along the wharf to rejoin the Emperor, who was readying to leave with his bodyguards and the Prefect.

'You know,' Zjandius mused as they rode out of the Port District, ' I think I would like a detour via the Bakers' Square. I wish to lift my spirits.'

Terzjin rode with the Emperor off the main street, followed by Suletonius and lenotare, through the side alleys towards the Baker's Square. Citizens shuffled out of the way of the trotting horses. The Emperor smiled and waved at his people. Some cheered and greeted Zjandius, while others merely stared.

The Bakers' Square was still bare of market stalls and nearly deserted, save for a group of labourers at one corner, supervised by palantare armed with long staves. The workers were, in fact, all Rhenivians, mainly captured marshals. They wore rough brown tunics, with copper bands around their necks and bronze chains between their wrists and ankles. They were digging and prying up cobblestones, then hobbling barefoot to dump armfuls of stones into a cart. Terzjin fancied he saw a few stained pieces amongst the rubble.

The palantarus captain walked between the prisoners. 'Come on, you lot! Move along!' He thumped his staff on the ground for emphasis, then straightened up and saluted as Emperor Zjandius dismounted and approached. The other palantare saluted in turn.

'Good morning, sir!' Zjandius shook the captain's hand. 'How are we doing today?'

'Very good, Your Majesty,' the captain replied. 'We have nearly finished removing all the stones, and have a fresh pile, ready to replace them.' He pointed to another cart at the edge of the square. 'Then we will move on to Goretonum fort and have them dig up the courtyard there as well.'

Remember us.

Zjandius nodded. 'And what is to be done with the old stones?'

Prefect Suletonius coughed. 'Highness, we consulted the tree-keepers and undertakers. They advised we sear the cobblestones in fire, then carry them out to sea and throw them into the gulf. We will keep a portion and pound it into dust and gravel. We will bear that part to Sanadium and scatter it in their family grove.'

The Emperor listened with a sombre expression. 'Very well. I approve.' He studied the labourers. 'Have they been behaving, captain? Any trouble?'

'No, sir,' the captain replied. 'They are quite docile—now.'

'Good.' Zjandius stared grimly at the Rhenivians. 'You are dismissed, Captain.'

The palantarus saluted and returned to his duties. As the Rhenivians lumbered back and forth, Terzjin spotted an older man on his hands and knees amongst the prisoners, prying stones with a stick.

'You see, Master Maltorus?' the Emperor murmured. '*This* is how you punish a man like Getherd of Elborn.'

As if hearing Zjandius, or feeling their gaze, the High Thane paused his digging and looked up. His beard was hacked short, and his face was streaked with dirt. His bearskin cloak and armour were long gone. He glowered at Terzjin and the Emperor in silent fury.

'Thane Heirik should be here too,' the Prefect said.

Zjandius frowned. 'Yes, he should be.' He gave the old Rhenivian the slightest of nods, then turned away.

A palantarus nudged the High Thane with a staff. Getherd scowled at the guard, then hunched over and resumed his scratching.

Terzjin followed Zjandius to the horses. 'And the rest of the Rhenivians, Emperor? When do they sail home? I am sure they long to return, as we did.' He helped the Emperor climb onto his steed.

Zjandius took up his reins. 'I'm issuing an edict tomorrow. The Rhenivians shall serve twenty years of labour as punishment for their destruction.'

Terzjin mounted his own horse. 'Twenty years? Your Majesty, you abolished slavery.'

The Emperor glanced at him. 'I never *entirely* abolished slavery, Terzjin. It was always a sentence for debt. They have a debt to pay.'

'But Zjandius, you said—'

'We must be pragmatic, Master Maltorus. Practical. There is much to rebuild, and I have many plans.'

'Zjandius...'

'I am the *Emperor*, Master Maltorus, and my word is law. If you cannot accept that, I release you, and you can make your own way in the world.'

Terzjin flinched. 'No, Your Majesty, I did not mean to—'

'Good. Let us return to the palace.'

'Yes, Your Majesty.'

They rode in silence.

Zjandius sighed. 'It's only a temporary punishment, Terzjin. Twenty years and they'll go home.'

'Of course, Your Majesty.'

'And High Thane Getherd and his marshals could go home earlier, if his family ever deign to answer my letter and pay his ransom.'

Terzjin looked ahead. The city rang with hammers and saws.

'You will see, Terzjin. We are going to build great things here.'

'Yes, Emperor.'

After Zjandius returned to his rooms to work, Terzjin took his break and walked through the palace. He found Captain Wederet standing watch in the gardens.

Wederet grinned and clapped Terzjin's back. 'A good morning to you, Master Maltorus.'

Terzjin smiled in return and bowed. 'I'm here to see the Empress, about that matter...?'

'Ah, of course,' Wederet gestured behind himself. 'Her Majesty rests this morning, but she will receive visitors.'

The Empress reclined on a couch under a pergola of vine leaves curling to red and gold. She wore a cotton gown and a fine woollen shawl. Nursemaids and servants fussed around her.

Nanepti was cradling her infant son as he approached. 'Master Maltorus, you have returned. And where is my dear husband?'

Terzjin bowed. 'Highness. The Emperor meets with his scribes in the palace.'

Nanepti nodded and sighed. 'The business of the state.'

The baby Adomenus gurgled in her arms. Nanepti gazed down at him and smiled.

Her servants brought copper cups and a jug of water, as well as a platter of figs.

Terzjin sat on a stool. 'How do you find life here in Etorium, Empress?'

Nanepti looked about. 'It is quite different to the land of the Emzen. Much colder, for one thing.' She pressed her son close and pulled the shawl around her body. 'It will take time to grow accustomed. The palace is also more... austere than my own.'

'No doubt you could help the Emperor improve it,' Terzjin replied. 'Make it more fit for a great empire, or at least more like your old house?'

Nanepti shrugged. 'Perhaps. It is quite something to accept that I will probably never see my old house again.'

'I understand, Empress.'

'Do you? It is a small sacrifice on my part, but others have sacrificed far more.'

Terzjin said nothing.

'Do you know the story of how the old city of Nemeket came to be, Master Maltorus?'

'I have heard it, Empress.' He recalled the campfire tale in the desert.

'Of how the first king, name long-forgotten, found the great rock in the wilderness. How he was promised a glorious kingdom if he built a city there. And he received his prize, though it cost him his entire family.'

'I know it, Empress.'

'Master Maltorus,' Nanepti said, 'we Sasiion, we children of the Old Kingdom, do not recount this story for amusement. It is a reminder of the past, and a warning for the future. Sacrificial blood can water the roots of a tree, but it can also poison it. Do you understand?'

'I think I do, Empress.'

'Much blood has been spilt in pursuit of this great empire. Much *Sasiion* blood in particular.'

Datet appeared before Terzjin, with judging eyes that said more than his mouth ever did. Datet's wife, who wordlessly took his bag of coins, only a fraction of her husband's measure, only a fraction of what Terzjin had promised the dying man. There was Aducr, smiling Aducr, worn and bitter in the end. And Prince Hemadir of the Rugadi, gripping Terzjin's arm with the last of his strength. *Please, do not burn me with the others*, the sand prince had begged. *Let my people take me home across the sea, to sleep under the warm sand.*

'Master Maltorus?'

'Yes, of course, Empress.' Terzjin turned away to wipe his cheek.

Nanepti raised an eyebrow. 'So what will be the story of this great empire, Master Maltorus? Will it soar like the hawk in the open sky? Or turn like the wheel in a well-worn rut?'

Terzjin glanced over his shoulder at the looming palace. He drew a breath. 'I vow to you, Empress, I will do everything in my power to ensure a worthy story to tell.'

Nanepti gazed deep into his eyes. 'Very well.' She swung her legs off the couch, sat up, and passed her baby to an attendant. 'But I am sure you did not come to discuss statecraft and old stories, Master Maltorus.'

He coughed. 'No, Empress. I seek your permission to speak with your maidservant Saedelas. You know, about the...'

The Empress smiled. 'Of course. You may speak with her. But, Master Maltorus, after some thought, I have decided that Saedelas shall have the final decision. You must accept her choice, whichever it may be. Yes?'

'Absolutely, Empress.'

'You will find her in the kitchens. I sent her to fetch honey cakes.'

Terzjin returned to the palace, but found Saedelas walking down the corridor. The young girl almost dropped the silver tray when she caught sight of him.

Her eyes flared with pale fire. 'Master Maltorus?'

Terzjin smiled as warmly as he could manage. 'Saedelas, I've been looking for you.'

'Oh?'

He looked around. 'May we speak a moment?' He gestured to an alcove along the corridor.

The girl frowned. 'The Empress awaits, Master Maltorus.' She held up the tray.

'I know. She sent me this way to look for you.' Terzjin moved to the alcove and leaned against the wall.

She followed. 'I don't understand.'

'Saedelas, how do you find life in the palace?'

The girl shrugged. 'It's alright. Can't complain.'

'And what about serving the Empress? Are you happy with your position?'

Saedelas looked back the way she had come. 'It's better than the kitchen, at least.' She sniffed.

Terzjin studied the girl. She searched his face with keen eyes.

'Saedelas, have you ever thought you might want to be something... more than a maidservant?'

'What do you mean, sir?' Her eyes glowed again.

Master Maltorus swallowed. 'I would like to train you. Train you to do what I do.'

Her eyes went wide. 'Train me as a... *bodyguard*, sir? But in Elisdrium, you said fighting was not for—'

He shook his head. 'I was wrong. I believe you have a gift, Saedelas—the same as mine—and I think you know it. I would like to share with you all the skill and knowledge I have, and whatever else I may learn in the years to come. A bodyguard? Yes, perhaps. But your... ***our*** path may go further than that. I can't promise there won't be danger along the way, but I can promise you a life of purpose.' He smiled. 'So?'

Saedelas studied her tray, then the doorway to the gardens. She bit her lip and looked up at Terzjin. 'I would like that very much, Master Maltorus.'

Terzjin beamed. 'Yes! And you will be only the first. I know there are others like us. We'll find them together.'

She smiled. 'When do we begin?'

CHAPTER FORTY-SEVEN

THE FOREST

Razna sprinted until she no longer heard the fighting. Her heart thumped in her chest, and her breath came in ragged gasps. She sat on a pale rock until her spirit calmed. Now, all she heard were birds and cicadas, the whisper of the cascading river, and sighing cedars that swayed and creaked around her.

Where could she go? Back to the High Thane—assuming he had survived the battle? Could she trust Getherd? Her heart told her that fortune had abandoned the old man, drifted from him. He couldn't save his own nephew. What could—or would—he do for her?

Razna dropped her head in her hands. It had all fallen apart. Their life, her dreams, slipping away like water through her fingers. Her love, her Heirik...

No, enough of this. She wiped her eyes and stood up. The Rhenivians, all of them, were just... she was tired. That door was shut. Leave it behind. What's next?

First, Razna needed to escape this lonely, gloomy forest. Easy enough. All she had to do was follow her feet down the hill. The river would guide her down the valley, out of the mountains and into a more civilised countryside. She took a deep breath and set off.

And where would she go? There was always the farm, back in her old country. Perhaps she could make her way to Lastria, or some smaller port where her face was unknown. She could beg her way onto a ship and sail across the sea. Everything would be as it was the day she left. Mother and Father would be there, in their hovel on the hillside, surrounded by bleating sheep. Smoke would be rising from the chimney while Mother boiled a stew. Razna could learn to spin and weave again. But this time, she would listen to Mother, be more patient and willing. And Father, well, perhaps the years have mellowed him. Perhaps he would weep with joy at the sight of his lost daughter returned. And they would embrace as they never did before, and he would say that he loved...

Razna stopped dead amongst the trees. She wanted to slap herself. How *absurd* these thoughts were. Don't be *stupid*, girl.

No, she couldn't do that. She will *never* go back there. She resumed her striding, down through the grey forest.

No, Razna would find some Caerian village—actually, a city or town would be better. Too much gossiping in a village. Too many nosy, prying neighbours. Yes, she can find a city, somewhere she has never visited, and disappear in the mob. Algados is near. Or maybe Sanadium or Teredos if she walked further south. Either way, she could assume a new name, find some quiet work to do, and build a fresh life for herself. She still had her beauty, at least for a few more years. Perhaps she might meet a man, a nice, boring Caerian man. A lonely bachelor in the city who would propose marriage. And she would accept. Maybe... maybe she could even fall in love once again?

Razna burst out laughing as she walked. Let's not run ahead of ourselves.

The forest seemed larger than she remembered. Of course, they had ridden up the mountain. How many days was that? How many days would it take to descend on foot, in comparison? She had never learned mathematics beyond counting stitches and sheep. A pity.

When night fell, Razna found a hollow beneath a tree to tuck into and sleep. The night air was not so cold, at least. A warm breeze washed down the slope and over her as she dozed.

She jerked awake at some point in the night. A crack of a twig? Footsteps? Someone, or something, was nearby—there was no doubt. Razna felt around in the dark for her dagger. She clutched the blade to her chest and listened to the night noises—crickets and a distant nightjar—not daring to fall asleep again.

In the morning, she awoke, cold and stiff. She found late-season berries and scooped icy river water into her mouth before continuing downhill. Another day passed with no end to the trees. She spotted a trio of grey forest antelope that pricked up their ears and pranced away as she approached. Her belly rumbled. *It* moved inside her. Razna needed more than berries.

She found pale, cream-coloured mushrooms growing amongst the roots of a tree. She was hungry. What else could she do? Razna plucked the mushrooms and shoved them into her mouth. She chewed on the nutty, earthy things. If she died, so be it. Better than slowly starving in this godsforsaken forest. She walked and walked, ever downwards, with the river as her companion. The water splashed and gurgled over the pale stones. She heard voices in the ceaseless flow. Maybe river nymphs, murmuring secrets just out of reach? No, that was silly. She was very much alone—and lonely.

Some number of days passed. She picked more mushrooms and dangling berries as she found them. Finally, desperate and craving flesh, Razna tore bark strips from a tree until she uncovered a litter of fat, wriggling grubs. She forced the pale worms down her throat, chewing as little as possible. She gagged and retched, but somehow, she swallowed. The meal left her panting on her hands and knees, exhausted.

The forest sounds died away in an instant. No birds nor beetles sang. No trees sighed nor leaves rustled. The hairs rose on her arm. Someone was watching.

Razna scrambled to her feet. 'Hello?' she cried out. 'Hello!'

She stepped a few paces towards the river as the slope flattened out. But, where *was* the river? Thick undergrowth seemed to surround her, reaching past her head and shoulders. She craned her neck to see over the bushes.

'Hello?'

She pushed her way through the thicket. Twigs scratched her face and tore at her dress. Then, finally, Razna burst out into a small clearing amidst the tall trees.

She started.

Only three spans before her sat a girl on a pale rock. The first person she had seen in...how long? The girl was eating an apple, completely absorbed in chewing it. Each crunch echoed through the still forest. The skin of the fruit was dark and red, the flesh pale and juicy. Razna salivated. Oh, by the gods, she was coming to the forest's end. There must be a town or village nearby—or at least a farm. She could ask this girl for directions, maybe for some food. She would beg if she had to. It didn't matter.

'H...hello?' Razna called out in Caerian.

The girl glanced at Razna, but continued biting into her apple. She studied the fruit as she chewed, as if lost in it. The girl wore a long, sleeveless shift, stitched with leather strips. Not typical Caerian clothes, but who knew what the mountain peasants wore? The bare soles of her feet were blackened with soil.

Razna stepped forward. 'Please, girl, can you help me?'

The girl looked at her and smiled brightly. 'How can I help you, My Lady?' She had a soft, low voice and a lilting accent, quite unlike the city's. The girl's long black hair shone in the dappled light and spilt over her shoulders. Tiny coloured beads were woven into strands of hair on either side of her face, and each cheek had two painted black lines. Her skin was as pale as apple flesh, and her eyes were grey, like storm clouds.

'Please,' Razna said, 'I've lost my family and can't find my way. Could you lead me to a farm or village where I could find help and rest? I'm so tired and so hungry, dear girl.'

The girl glanced around the clearing. 'I certainly could help you, *Lady Razna*.'

Razna stiffened. 'Oh...w-why do you call me that, dear girl?'

'Because I know who you are, Lady Razna, and I know what you have done. *All* you have done.' The girl dropped her apple core into the bushes and wiped her hand on her lap. She regarded Razna with a tranquil expression.

Razna balled her fists and stepped closer. 'How could you possibly know me, girl?'

The girl winked. 'Marriage is sacrifice,' she intoned, 'and a marriage must be blessed in blood to endure against all trials. Those were your wedding vows, yes? For the...Lord of the Hunt?'

Razna's heart jumped. She drew out her dagger and aimed it at the girl. 'Listen, child. You'll guide me out of the forest, or I will cut your throat. And if you know me as well as you claim, then you know I can do it.' She forced her hand to be still.

The girl considered the pointed blade and nodded. The bushes beside her rustled, and a great cat sauntered into the clearing.

Razna shrieked and stumbled backwards, away from the beast.

The cat's muscles rippled under its rust-red fur, as its tall, tufted ears flicked about, and it gazed at her with bright yellow eyes on its painted face. The girl scratched the beast on its head. The cat bumped up against the girl's hand and made a noise somewhere between a purr and a growl.

The girl stood and advanced upon Razna. The cat loped alongside, tail swishing.

'Your husband may have called himself *Thane* of Caeria,' the girl said, her voice hard and sharp, 'but know this, *girl*—any place in this land where the branches meet is *my* domain, and I shall not suffer it to be corrupted or despoiled.' Her eyes burned with cold fury.

Razna backed away. 'Please, I never wanted to hurt anyone.' She swallowed. 'Heirik... he... he *forced* me.'

The girl cocked her head. 'Your heart tells otherwise, *dear girl*.' She ran her hand along the cat's arching back.

'No, please.' Razna shook, and tears pricked her eyes. She dropped the dagger and pressed her hands to her stomach. 'Please, I have—'

The girl sighed. 'An innocent life. Yes, I suppose I should be merciful. Or...' She glanced at the cat. '... at least sporting.' She fixed Razna with a grim smile. 'Here is my proposal, *Lady* Razna. I shall count to eight, and give you a moment to escape, before *her* hunt begins.' She rubbed the animal's neck.

'No, this is madness!'

'May I give counsel, *Lady* Razna? Do not show this sweet she-cat your back. She loves to chase, and you would only encourage her.'

'I... I curse you!'

'Run, *girl*.'

'No!'

'One.'

'You filthy—'

'Two.'

The bushes poked into Razna's back.

'Three.'

She turned and thrashed through the thicket, sobbing and gasping.

'Four!'

Razna fell onto a path and clambered to her feet.

'Five!'

She broke into a run.

'Six!' The voice was faint.

Razna sprinted as she had never done before. Her blood thundered in her head. '*Help!*' she screamed.

Distant sounds came from behind. A lithe body whipping through the undergrowth. Padded feet skipping over the ground. An eager growl. A song?

'*Help!*' she screamed again, but the trees swallowed her voice.

She would run for the rest of her life if she had to.

'*Help!*'

She would run forever.

CHAPTER FORTY-EIGHT

CAERIA — AUTUMN'S REIGN — 437

'Right, are you ready?'

'Yes!' Valcero tried his best to sound cheerful.

'As ready as we could be, I suppose,' Colus muttered.

They had met Terzjin in the palace courtyard, with a mule and cart containing all Master Meretan's possessions—chests, sacks, and heaps of scrolls—and what little Valcero had. After weeks of searching, the Prefect had found a new house for Colus.

The boy gazed around the busy courtyard a final time. 'Will I ever come back?'

Terzjin grinned. 'Oh, of course! I'm sure you'll run many errands for Master Meretan.' He shrugged. 'And I'll visit your house when I can.'

'Valcero!' Saedelas ran over from the palace.

The boy smiled. 'Are you ... are you coming with us?'

She grinned and shook her head. 'No, I'm staying.'

Terzjin took Colus by the arm and led him away to inspect the cart.

'Oh, I see.' Valcero looked at his sandals.

'Master Maltorus is going to train me,' Saedelas said, 'as he trained you.'

'Ah.' Valcero scratched his head. 'He didn't train me all *that* much, actually.' He sighed. 'So you'll learn to fight?'

She nodded.

'I ... uh ... I heard what happened in Elisdrium.' He bit his lip. 'I'm sorry, Saedelas. I ... I wish I could have helped you, though I don't know what I could have done. I didn't know you were having such a hard time...'

She pulled a face. 'You never asked, Valcero. Not once.'

The boy bowed his head. 'I know. I'm sorry.'

'I heard you had a difficult time, too,' she said. 'When you came back to Caeria.'

He nodded without looking up. 'I still dream about it.'

She hugged the boy. 'Let's talk more. Let's tell each other things, alright?' Her embrace was warm and safe.

He wrapped his arms around her. 'Yes, I'd like that.'

Saedelas let go and held Valcero by the shoulders. 'So, what are you going to do now?'

He shrugged. 'Something quiet, I hope. Helping Master Meretan. Things like that.'

'Oh, I must go—the Empress awaits!' Saedelas leaned close and squeezed him once again. 'I'll see you soon, Valcero Baradon.' She skipped away, half-turning for a final wave before disappearing into the palace.

Terzjin came to his side. 'I'm coming to help with the cart and unpack things. Shall we go?'

Valcero and Master Maltorus walked alongside the mule to guide the beast through the gates and across the square, while Colus sat on the cart holding the reins. The house was not far—about halfway down on the southeastern side, along a quiet road that ended at a rocky hillside outcrop.

'*Palanios Iustian*,' Terzjin read out as they passed the street tile on the corner. The Street of Rain. 'A good name.'

Colus had initially looked at a house in the Port District, but Valcero had begged him to consider elsewhere.

'I suppose you're right,' Master Meretan had replied. 'Too many noisy brothels in that neighbourhood. We shan't get any work done.'

Valcero had blushed, not knowing how to respond.

The house Colus settled on had three floors, plastered walls, and a tiled roof. Apparently, it had belonged to a merchant family that had fled Etorium during the occupation and was now settled on the coast near Enternis.

Master Meretan climbed off the cart and squinted up at the

shuttered windows. 'I suppose it will do.' He fidgeted with the key, then went unlock the front door.

Terzjin and Valcero carried the chests, tables, and chairs into the house, while Colus flung open the shutters and tramped up and down the stairs to inspect the rooms.

'Two bedrooms upstairs, and two more in the attic,' Master Meretan said to no one in particular. 'And a living room and kitchen down here. It's a lot of space. A lot of space to look after. And the ceiling is collapsing in spots.' He stood in the middle of the bare room with his hands behind his back and gazed about. 'But it's serviceable. Yes. We could set up my workshop here.'

'Well.' Terzjin dusted off his hands. 'I must leave you and return to my actual duties. Speak to Suletonius. He can send masons or carpenters—whatever you need.'

'Yes, yes. Of course,' Colus muttered, running his finger along a dusty windowsill.

Valcero looked to Terzjin. 'So, farewell, then?'

Master Maltorus chuckled. 'Don't say it as if it's the end, lad! I'll visit whenever I can—I promise.' He embraced the boy. 'I'm proud of you, Valcero,' he whispered. 'You're a hero—do you know that?'

'I am?'

'Of course! I know it, and Emperor Zjandius knows it too. He won't forget.' Terzjin ruffled the boy's hair and went to the door. 'See you soon!'

Valcero explored the ground floor while Master Meretan rummaged through his chests. The boy padded over the cool kitchen tiles and examined the bare hearth. He would need to get a fire burning soon, before Master Meretan started asking for supper. A little clay face smiled from an alcove amongst the brickwork. The house spirits would also need feeding, of course.

Valcero opened the back door and found a small courtyard behind the house. He examined the vegetable patch and snapped off a twig from the browned, brittle shrubs of rosemary and thyme. He poked his head into the outhouse and recoiled from the smell wafting up the shaft. A ragged vine clung to the garden wall, shedding red, crackling leaves. A mouse ran over the paving and into a hole in the wall.

The boy reentered the echoing house, hollow, but with the promise of life.

Colus rose from his scrolls and sighed. 'I suppose we should get to work. Zjandius still wants a port for his navy. Luckily, he now has Rhenivians to build it for him!'

'Master Meretan, do you think the Rhenivians will come back? With more soldiers, I mean. Maybe they want revenge?'

Colus shrugged. 'They may try, but now we are better prepared. Besides, if the gossip is true, they'll be too distracted to bother us.'

'Distracted, sir?'

'Apparently, their King Randegar was assassinated—while visiting the house of High Thane Getherd, of all places. The king's men blamed Getherd's family and had *them* all killed in revenge.' Colus shook his head. 'Everything you need to get a civil war going, really.' He unfurled a document and squinted at the contents. 'Hmm, no, not this one.'

Valcero sighed. 'I don't much like war, Master Meretan.'

'No, it's a terrible business, my boy, though it keeps me busy, I suppose. Keeps *us* busy, I should say.'

'Master Meretan?'

'Yes?'

'I am your assistant, sir. That is my job, of course, but...'

'What is it, boy?'

Valcero took a breath. 'Could I also be your student again, sir? Could you teach me...' He threw up his hands. '*...everything?*'

Colus looked up from his scrolls and beamed. 'Well, of course, Valcero! I assumed that was the idea.' He frowned and looked around the room. 'But how are we going to find the time? There's too much to do here, too much upkeep.'

Valcero bit his lip. 'Actually, Master Meretan, I have an idea about that.'

'Oh?'

'Would... would you consider taking on another servant—or two? For housekeeping?'

Colus pulled a face. 'Well, maybe, but I don't know how much it would—'

'Because actually, I know two people who would be perfect, sir.

They're very experienced at running a household.'

'Two, you say?' Colus wrinkled his nose. 'I don't know, Valcero. That sounds expensive.'

'They are Torecti, sir. Torecti-of-the-Trees.'

'What?' Colus stood up. 'Are you sure?'

Valcero nodded and tried to keep a straight face. 'Yes, sir. Quite sure, sir. They're the ones who taught me to speak Torecti, as it happens. So, apart from cooking and cleaning and all that, you could... probably ask them lots of questions and learn all sorts of things from them.'

'Huh.' Colus chewed on his knuckle, deep in thought.

Good day. My name is Valcero Baradon, assistant to Master Colus Meretan, Chief Imperial Engineer.

The boy walked down the street with his new pair of sandals clip-clopping against the cobblestones. His face was scrubbed, and his hair was slicked back. He wore a new, blue tunic—the finest he could afford with his saved coins—under a light-brown woollen cloak he had borrowed from Master Meretan, though it was slightly too big.

Good day. My name is Valcero Baradon, assistant to Master Colus Meretan, Chief Imperial Engineer.

He breathed in and out slowly, trying to still his thudding heart. The tall walls were so very familiar, but the sight of them only sharpened his nerves as he approached the old mansion.

Valcero came to the gate in the wall and clutched the doorknocker. 'Lord of Life, guide me,' he whispered, and banged on the gate.

There was no reply. He waited for several heartbeats, then banged the knocker again. *Good day. My name is Valcero Baradon, assistant to Master Colus Meretan, Chief Imperial Engineer. I wish to speak with...* No, no answer. This was a mistake.

The boy turned to leave, just as footsteps came faintly through the gate. The bolts squeaked.

He breathed out and wiped his sweaty palms on his tunic. He took a deep breath and straightened himself to his full height as the gate creaked open. 'Good day. My name is—'

It was Aulix.

The boy and man gaped at each other for a long moment. Then Valcero sprang forward and wrapped his arms around him.

'Oof!' Aulix gasped. 'My boy... how...?' He grasped Valcero by the shoulders.

'*Sevei*,' Valcero whispered.

'*Sevei*.' Aulix put his hand on the boy's head. 'I thought we'd never see you again.'

Valcero gulped, stepped back and looked up—no, looked *at*—the Torecti man. 'So did I.' He smiled and wiped his eyes. He took in the faint stain around Aulix's bare neck, and the circular tattoo on his forehead.

Aulix winced and covered the tattoo with his hand. 'Valcero, my boy, when we saw you last... the things the Torecti said... They never believed us.'

The boy shook his head. 'I don't care. It doesn't matter—none of it.'

'We really did not—'

Valcero took Aulix's hands in his own. 'I believe you. I *know* you.'

Aulix squeezed his hands and let out a long, shuddering sigh.

'Can I speak with you?' Valcero asked. 'And Praehenna. Is she...?'

'Yes, she's here—all well, of course. Bones a bit creaky, but anyway.' The man put his arm around the boy's shoulder. 'Come in, come in.'

Valcero stepped through the archway into the garden, as if he'd only been away an hour or two. He shivered. The Cleotan mansion was quiet. Each window was like a dark eye, watching him.

Aulix led him up the path between ragged lavender hedges. 'It's a stroke of fortune you came now, seeing as we all returned to Etorium only three days ago.'

Valcero grinned sheepishly. 'Uh, actually, there isn't much luck to it. I've come past every day for the last few weeks.'

'Good day... sir?' Another servant waited at the front door, someone unfamiliar. She looked him up and down. 'Can I help you?'

Valcero coughed. 'Good day.' He tried to deepen his voice. 'My name is Valcero Baradon, assistant to Master Colus Meretan, Chief Imperial Engineer.'

'Oh!' The servant offered a quick curtsey. 'Good day, sir, welcome. Er...Master Cleotan *is* at home. For what business shall I announce you?'

'Actually, I am here to speak with Master Aulix and Mistress Praehenna.' He glanced at the old Torecti and tried not to smile. 'Concerning a private matter.'

'I see, sir.' The servant blinked and peered into the mansion, then back at the boy. 'Please wait here.' She ducked out of sight.

Valcero breathed out slowly.

Aulix folded his arms. 'Well, you must have a story to tell.'

Before the boy could reply, Praehenna stepped out into the sunlight. She stared at him, wide-eyed, then ran down the steps and gathered him up in her arms.

'You're here. You're here,' she murmured.

Valcero trembled in her warm hug. He pressed his lips together.

'I would *never* have hurt you,' Praehenna whispered fiercely. 'Never. We have never hurt anyone.' She kissed his cheeks.

Valcero squeezed her. 'I know. I know.'

'Alright,' she let him go and wiped her eyes. 'Tell us everything. Where have you been? What happened? And by the Lord of Life, how did you end up with the *Taurex*?

The boy grinned. 'I'll give you the entire story, but not right now.'

Aulix frowned. 'Not right now?'

Valcero took both their hands. 'I said it before. And I'll say it again—*Come with me*.'

'What do you mean, boy?'

'I work for a man named Colus Meretan.'

Aulix raised an eyebrow. 'This Chief Imperial Engineer of yours?'

Valcero nodded. 'He needs two servants for his new house. It's not so big as...' He waved at the mansion. '...all this. Just the right size for a pair of housekeepers. I told him about you two. He wants to hire you.'

Praehenna put her hand on his cheek. 'Valcero, my dear, that's so sweet, but we couldn't simply leave.'

'Why not?'

'Master Cleotan would be furious, boy,' Aulix replied. 'You remember how he is.'

Valcero's cheeks flushed. 'Well, Master Meretan would treat you better. I mean, yes, he can be a little...odd sometimes, but he's never been cruel to me. Always fair. He cares for me in his own way and...and he always pays my wages.' Tears pricked his eyes. 'Please, come with me.'

'Oh, Valcero.' Praehenna squeezed his hand.

Aulix sighed. 'It's not so simple, my boy.'

'Why not?' Valcero nearly shouted.

'The Cleotan are a powerful family, lad.' Aulix's face was serious. 'They would be dangerous enemies.'

The boy sniffed and stood tall. 'Well, I have some dangerous friends.'

The man's lips twitched. 'I believe it!'

'Do you *really* want to be doing the Cleotan's bidding for the rest of your lives. Do you?'

The Torecti looked at each other.

'Can you imagine going up to Master or Mistress Cleotan,' Praehenna said, 'and telling them we are leaving? Just like that?'

Valcero shrugged. 'Why don't you talk to Graelius instead?'

'Oh, my love,' Praehenna replied, 'old Graelius passed years ago.'

'His tree stands on the country estate,' Aulix said.

'Oh. Alright.' Valcero nodded at the servant skulking at the doorway. 'So tell *her* then.'

The woman made a face and retreated inside.

Aulix and Praehenna gazed into each other's eyes.

Valcero squeezed their hands. '*Come on*. We...we could be together again. Like...a family.'

Aulix raised his eyebrows at Praehenna. She chewed her lip, then nodded.

Old Aulix blew out his breath. 'Are you serious about this, Valcero?'

'As serious as anything in my life could be.'

'Alright,' Aulix muttered to himself. 'Yes, alright.' He looked up and smiled. 'Yes, very well. Wait here a moment.' He hurried off into the mansion.

Praehenna examined the boy. 'My, how tall you've become.' She pinched his arm. 'But also very thin. Are you eating?'

Valcero grinned slyly and shrugged. 'You could help with that.'

Praehenna laughed and put her hands on her hips. She smiled at him. 'So, you went into the Nedolian Forest, where no *Caeri* is ever supposed to venture.'

'I did. Spent time with the Whispering Leaves people, actually.'

'Look at you, boy! Well, I never. We were of the Running River, as it happens.' She sighed and looked at the garden. 'I miss the forest sometimes. But only sometimes.'

A rattling sound caught their attention. Aulix strode out the door and down the steps, hauling a sack over his shoulder.

'Can I help with that?' Valcero offered.

'No, no, all fine,' the man muttered. 'And we should leave *right* now. Come along.'

Praehenna, Aulix, and Valcero trotted through the garden towards the gate. A very aristocratic shriek burst out from an upstairs window.

Praehenna giggled. 'Oh dear.' She glanced behind. 'Quickly, boys.'

Aulix fumbled with the bolts until Valcero helped to slide them free. They pulled the gate open.

'What in the *gods'* names is going on here?' a voice roared.

A red-faced Master Cleotan came storming out of the mansion, as they stepped onto the street and slammed the gate shut behind them.

'Well,' Aulix glanced around. 'Lead the way, boy.'

Valcero beamed. 'Follow me.'

They strode along the city streets, Aulix to his left and Praehenna to his right. Valcero put an arm around each as they walked, to keep them close.

And they went up the hill, together.

THE END

ABOUT THE AUTHOR

Anthony Hodge was born in Johannesburg and grew up in Cape Town, South Africa. He currently lives in Madrid, Spain. He studied film and psychology, and has worked in education for many years. He has had a lifelong fascination with myths, legends, and ancient history from around the world. This is his first novel.

www.ingramcontent.com/pod-product-compliance
Lightning Source LLC
La Vergne TN
LVHW031428170726
843492LV00010B/2899